the
etymology
of SEVEN

OMAR NOBLE

iUniverse, Inc.
New York   Bloomington

the etymology of SEVEN

iUniverse books may be ordered through booksellers or by contacting:

iUniverse
1663 Liberty Drive
Bloomington, IN 47403
www.iuniverse.com
1-800-Authors (1-800-288-4677)

ISBN: 978-1-4401-6874-1 (pbk)
ISBN: 978-1-4401-6875-8 (ebk)

Printed in the United States of America

iUniverse rev. date: 9/1/2009

It was the coldest night the island of Manhattan had seen since the blizzard of 92. Chi Chi and her two sons were dressed in expensive ski clothing and 35 below hiking boots. They were cold but not frozen stiff like anyone else crazy enough to be out in the streets in this 18 below zero weather with a wind chill factor well below a minus 35. But no one being out at this ungodly hour was exactly why her stupid ass was still out. She should have taken the kids home long ago and tucked them away but she had to get her fix before calling it a night, otherwise she would be too sick to come out in the morning. Her stomach was in knots as it was. Problem was not one dealer was out, they had sold their bundles before the sun went down and what ever was left they were keeping it for 'self. They didn't want to get caught out here like she was. Uptown was still pumping weight from apartments but her money wasn't right. The day had been really slow for vic's. The subways were like Siberia. She had managed only one Vic the entire day, and he only had two hundred and some change.

"Broke ass Jew!"

Her usual take for a day was two thousand or better, and some days she would hit a jackpot and catch a bag of diamonds or a case of Rolex's. She remembered catching the Jew Po Po had set up for her. He looked like a bum, but the tattered briefcase he carried had three hundred thou cash in it and a giant emerald that she got another twenty five for.

Of course the bastard didn't want to let go of it so she ended up having to slice his throat and cut his hand off cause he had it handcuffed to his leper wrist, but her effort got her the apartment on 1st avenue and helped furnish it.

Problem was Chi-Chi got a lot of money but she spent it just as fast. Everything she brought, or stole, was the best that money could buy. She did have a stash though. She put ten percent of everything she got away for the kids future, and she wasn't touching it under any circumstances. She had learned that much good from her father, if nothing else. She was tempted to go tap it now though, but instead she turned to Daquan and reminded him as she did each time she left them alone; "Remember, if something happens to me, you have to be a man and take care of yourself and your brother."

"Nothing gonna happen to you mommy," Daquan said, cuddling his baby brother to his chest.

"Never say never Daquan. If something happens and I don't come back, you go to the safe house. You understand? You don't go back to the apartment, and you don't go to no shelter."

"OK mommy, but ain't nothin gon happen to you."

The stairs of the old abandoned brownstone were so icy, Chi Chi had to hold on with both hands as she slipped and slid to the sidewalk below.

"Just in case Daquan... Just in case. You know where the money is?"

"Yes ma'am."

"Good. I love you."

"I love you too mommy."

Chi Chi turned, leaned into the wailing wind and fought her way slowly down the block. She hadn't gotten halfway past the next building before a blue an white patrol car passed her, then it's tires were spinning in reverse as she tried to run.

Daquan watched from the shadows as the Police car cut his mother off and a uniformed officer jumped from the passenger side of the car and tackled her, throwing her to the ground and hitting her over and over again.

"Bitch! Where's my fucking money? You thought I wouldn't fucking catch your ass?" he shouted, picking her up and hurling her against the hood of the car.

Daquan wanted to help, but he knew he was too small and his mother would want him to protect his brother, besides he had seen what his mother had done to men who tried to beat her.

As he was thinking that thought he saw the flash of light as his mother struck, her switchblade slashing across the officer's face and neck with such speed he didn't know he was cut until she was in motion to strike again and his partner pumped two bullets in her chest before she dropped.

Daquan pissed on himself but he suppressed the urge to scream and run to her aid as she flew back, the switchblade flipping through the wall of cold. She was still alive and conscious as they dragged her to the car and lifted her into the back seat.

Hiding in the doorway as the car passed Daquan caught a glimpse of his mother as she lifted her head and mouthed, "Take care of your brother. Get him into a good school." ... and he got a good look at the officer in the passenger seat as the bleeding man searched in his direction to see who his mother was mouthing to.

The car stopped and backed up again, fishtailing all over the streets. Daquan held Naquan tightly and hurried through the dark corridors of the building as footsteps rushed up the stoop and the faint illumination from a flashlight bounced off the walls behind him.

FOUR YEARS LATER

CHAPTER 1

"I WANT MY MOMMY," Naquan sniffled, backing into the corner until he could feel the vibrations in the wall from the A train passing through the tunnels.

The room, his brother called the safe house, had to be the only one of it's kind in the underground subway system. Once the heavy concrete and steel door was closed it was virtually sound proof, and it was the only hidden room he knew of that had a toilet, a sink, and a wash tub with hot and cold water. They even had heat and electricity. That's why his brother was so protective of it. If anyone living in the underworld knew two kids had a room like this they would kill them for it.

"How many times I gotta tell you?" his brother said firmly. "Mommy ain't never comin back."

"I want my daddy then," Naquan said in a voice barely above a whisper.

Daquan exploded. "Fuck that bitch ass nigga. He ain't shit to us ,"

Naquan watched Daquan dangle the last piece of bloody meat over Kilo, who waited patiently for Daquan's command before leaping up to snatch it from his hand.

"Anyway, I'm yo daddy now lil nigga," Daquan added. "Ain't that right Kilo?" Kilo looked up from his meal and seemed to nod in the affirmative.

"No!" Naquan said defiantly. Daquan was only four years older than he was, and Naquan wasn't stupid. "You the one that's stupid. How you gonna be my daddy when you a kid just like me? You gotta be more than nine years old to be somebody's daddy. I know that much." Naquan said angrily.

"Well since you know so much lil nigga, you should know that age ain't

1

nothin but a number. Anyway it don't matter how old I am if I'm the one who takes care a' yo Lil ass. You know why?"

Naquan shrugged his shoulders ...

"Because that's what a real daddy do. He take care of his family. Not like that stupid ass dope fiend you think is yo daddy. What that bum ass nigga ever do for you except try to steal all yo shit... nothin!

Daquan walked across the room and removed a cream Sean John sweat suit from the stacks of clothing he kept in see through plastic storage bags, then carefully packed it and a brand new pair of Timm's in his backpack.

"Who feed you and make sure you got someplace to sleep?" Daquan asked, zipping up the backpack and slinging it over his shoulder.

It was true. Naquan could remember Daquan taking care of him longer than he could remember his mother. Still the bond he felt for her was stronger. Even though he had no real memories of her he knew he felt more secure and loved when she was there.

Daquan walked over to the table, Naquan helped him make from an old door and cinder blocks they scavenged from the tunnels, and booted up the laptop computer.

"Who got you this computer so you could learn to read an write an do math like mommy wanted you to?" he asked without looking back.

"You," Naquan said, wiping the remaining tears from his eyes with the bottom of his throwback jersey. "An who brought you the Playstation and all the nice clothes you like?"

"It don't matter, I can't wear them anyway. You never let me go nowhere or do nothing. You the one-"

"That's right. I'm the one. I'm yo daddy lil nigga. I'm the one you listen to, otherwise it's gonna be a lot worser next time you steal sumthin. You hear me?"

Naquan didn't reply.

"I'm serious lil nigga. I catch you stealin again I'm-a fuck you up worser than Kunta Kenta." Daquan knew his little brother was scared shitless of being beaten like Kunta Kenta every since they had watched the movie Roots.

Naquan cringed. The images of his recurring nightmare playing like a movie in his mind. He was always lying in a pool of his own blood, dying, a white man standing over him twisting a shiny black boot in his chest as he choked on his own blood.

"From now on you just be the lookout like mommy taught us" Daquan said, bringing Naquan out of his vision just as his heart was beginning to race.

Daquan hesitated then turned back and gave Naquan a hard look. "Matter of fact, I ain't taking you wit me no more. Now on, you just stay here an learn so you can be a lawyer like mommy wanted you to be."

Naquan shrugged his shoulders in despair as he watched Daquan take the combination lock from the table then blurted out with an attitude, "Can I play Playstation?"

"Im-a think about it when I get back. If you know yo lessons. An don't think I ain't gon test yo lil ass.

" Every time Daquan said that about testing, Naquan had to suppress the urge to laugh.

How was Daquan gonna test him? He couldn't read. He couldn't write, and he couldn't spell. He didn't even know all his alphabets. All he knew how to do was count money.

He was the stupid one. He was the one who should stay here and learn.

"An no fuckin movies!"

"Damn! I can't do shit!" Naquan said, sinking to the floor. He knew the only reason Daquan was even leaving the movies was because they had too many DVD's to even fit in his backpack.

"Don't worry lil nigga. One day you gon be a lawyer and you gon tell me what to do, keep my ass out-a trouble. One day you gon be my daddy."

"I ain't never gon be nobody's daddy," Naquan said. "I'm gonna die before then."

"No you ain't lil nigga. We gon get this gwuap, that big house an all them nice cars you like," Daquan said, crossing the room to the only door.

Just before he closed the door behind him, Daquan issued a final warning. "An don't go sneaking out cause Kilo ain't gon let you back in if he don't hear the combination lock. Then if one of them crazy ass tunnel niggaz don't eat you, I'm-a really fuck yo ass up."

On the other side of the door he spun the combination lock and was confident that Kilo had heard it through the sound proofed walls and was scurrying across the carpet to take his guard position beside the door.

He slid the old wooden construction panels over the door to conceal it before snaking his way through the pitch-black tunnels without the need of a flashlight. He knew these tunnels like the back of his hand.

"You gotta know how to move in the dark Daquan," his mother would tell him. "You gotta learn how to move an see like a cat."

Naquan wasn't afraid of being left alone. He felt safe with Kilo. He had seen what the massive snow white pit-bull could do to an armed man, so fear was not the reason for his strong temptation to sneak out behind his brother. He was bored with all this lesson stuff. He wanted to do the things he liked to do, do the things his brother did.

The few times Daquan had taken him uptown he knew that's where he wanted to be. He liked the hustlers and the street soldiers, the way they talked, the way they dressed, the way they moved. He was only five, but he knew he wasn't made to be a lawyer. He was a hustler. Like the stories Daquan told him about his mother, he was just like her. The fast life was in his blood.

He waited for what seemed like an eternity then rose, crossed the room, and slowly turned the knob to freedom.

CHAPTER 2
CHINA

"THERE SHE GO RIGHT there lil nigga," Ra said to Daquan. "I don't know why you so thirsty for that scab bitch when you can get your first nut from any of these fine heads coming through.

Ra looked up at Big Twan shaking his head.

"Yall ain't lying .. She use to be a school teacher right," Daquan asked, looking down the block at the skeleton in a filthy mini-skirt and even nastier toes in flip-flops - the kind you find in the two for one-dollar store.

"Yea and she use to be fine too, but now I won't even serve that filthy bitch. You could catch something just standing next to her funky ass," Ra said, turning up his nose.

"What you do is your business lil man, but you better hope you live to be ten running up in that sewer," Twan warned.

Twan wasn't no get money nigga, but the crew let him hang out like he was. Daquan guessed it was because everybody in the hood knew he was probably gon get drafted to the NBA straight out of high school next year and he was gonna be making millions, so everybody was riding his dick. But that's not why Daquan liked Twan. Twan had taken a liking to him since he first started hanging around. Whenever Ratchet's soldiers kicked him off the block or tried to herb him, if Twan was around he would always take up for him. It was Twan who eventually got him put on Ratchets crew.

"Who's gonna suspect a snotty nosed six year old kid?" Twan had lobbied for him. But even though he liked Twan, Daquan didn't trust him enough to confide in him why he was really hanging around, or what he was really up too. His mother always lectured him .. "Create a goal, focus on it, and work hard at it. That's how you succeed .. an don't let anyone know anymore of your plan than they need to know, cause they will fuck it up if they know more than they're suppose to."

So Daquan kept mostly to himself and nobody really knew what Rachet had him doing, and he never told them, even when they tried to pressure him, or bribe him, or get him so fucked up off the Haze they knew he would talk. What was between him and Rachet would remain between him and Rachet.

"Snitches don't deserve to live," his mother often told him. "If you find a snitch, cut his throat first chance you get. Never befriend them, never hire them, and never trust them, even after they're dead."

"You must not know," Twan was saying to Ra. "This lil niggaz hung like a bull. He about to wear something out. Right lil nigga?" he asked, turning to look down on Daquan. Twan was so tall his head was over the doorway.

CHINA WAS FAST APPROACHING

"If you want it, you better catch it now," Twan nodded. "That bitch is like the A train, she ain't stopping till she get to Brooklyn."

"Yeah cause everybody uptown done hit it. Ain't nobody in Harlem gon serve that bitch... "Not for free," one of the street soldiers butted in.

"An not fo' no ass either. Cause the bitch ain't never got no money." Ra added.

While the street soldiers were still putting China down, Daquan spun off

CLOSE UP

Daquan could still see traces of how fine China use to be and how she got the name China. She still had pretty slanted eyes, a flat face and golden skin, and if her hair wasn't matted, and she didn't open her mouth, she was still better looking than what a lot of the soldiers on the block called dimes. If she was this pretty now Daquan couldn't imagine what she looked like before she started smoking.

"You looking?" he asked, knowing the bitch was thirsty. She slowed but didn't stop, looking past Daquan at the crew in front of Mister G's. Daquan dangled the bag of krillz in her face and she stopped dead in her tracks.

"Hell yeah I'm looking," China wanted to say. "I'm a fiend. That's what fiends do ... look!" but she wasn't about to take a loss on a kid who wasn't tall enough to pee straight. Especially since the few times she had copped on

Rachet's blocks they had served her pure garbage, shit that wouldn't burn right in her stem. Still she couldn't resist testing the kid to see if she could get a free hit. So she blurted out;

"Can I get a sample? How I'm gonna know if your shit is good?"

"Here lil nigga," one of the crew shouted, tossing a condom to Daquan. "Put a helmet on that soldier." It fell short and slid across the concrete to land directly between China's legs.

GOOD OMEN

At the same time Rachet came out of Mister G's typing some shit on his palm pilot.

BAD OMEN

China felt the tremble begin in her right leg, and by the time Rachet and his asshole entourage were walking in her direction it was shaking violently and she was fighting for control

THEY LOCKED EYES ALL THE WAY

until he was right up on her. He then turned his head and gave the kid that cocky look of affection he used to give her. "That bitch is death waiting to happen lil man," Rachet warned. "Fuck a condom. You need body armor."

China felt like she was gonna pee on herself. Now the shake was taking over her entire body. "Fuck you Rachet!" she heard herself shout with a vengeance. "You weren't saying that shit when you were eating feces out my asshole!"

It was the first time she had come face to face with Rachet in two years. He was already past her, and she didn't turn to see his reaction.

RACHET STOPPED DEAD IN HIS TRACKS

"Bitch! Don't get it fuckin twisted," he said, circling back. "Don't think I won't fuckin kill yo stink ass!"

"You already did," she almost whispered.

"Bitch! ... Shut-the-fuck-up before I…"

She found the courage to turn and face him. "Before you what Rachet?" She spit the words out. "Before you put your foot where your mouth use to stay?" Tears began to stream down her face. Her voice trembled. "I don't care what you do Rachet. You can't do shit to me you haven't already done!"

China could hardly believe what happened next. When Rachet stepped to her saying, "No, you yuck mouth bitch! I'm-a knock the rest of yo rotten teeth out," the kid pushed her behind him and said some stupid shit like, 'she was his hoe now, and he was gonna keep her away from him.

NIGGA PLEASE

"Ain't no grown ass man gon ever pimp me again and you just a baby." That's what she wanted to say .. But .. Something about the kid and the way he took control, and was stepping up for her, made her feel safe. So when the kid turned and gave her a command not to move and to shut the fuck up, she cast her eyes to the sidewalk and scanned the concrete for cracks or rocks that the dealers might have dropped.

But she didn't move -and...

She didn't open her mouth -until ...

Rachet's big BMW and Jumm's black Navigator pulled from the curb of 116th street and headed uptown, and the kid came back across the street and asked if she knew someplace they could go.

"You got money?" she asked.

The kid pulled out a knot.

China took him to the Casa Blanca on 145th street. It was a fifty-five dollar for four hours sleaze bed hotel room with a TV and mirrors around the bed. Shit! If the little bastard was paying she might as well get a little comfort out of the deal, and she probably wouldn't have to work hard at all to keep the little niggaz dick hard long enough to smoke up all his crack and rob him of that knot. What the fuck did a kid need with that much money anyway?

As soon as China came into the room and the little nigga locked the door behind her, she noticed the switchblade in his left hand. What was this mutha-fucka... some kind of midget serial killer?

China straightened right up. He might be little but a switchblade was nothing to fuck with. She had seen what it could do, and it wasn't pretty. Besides, her tiny ass was barely an inch taller than him anyway. "I got money," she said, nervously pulling the crumpled bills from her bra. "I ain't trying to steal your shit ... but I ain't fucking for free either." Daquan didn't say shit. He broke her off a piece of rock and tossed it to her, then watched as she hungrily pushed it into her stem.

A HALF HOUR LATER

The kid still hadn't spoken another word and China had smoked up her last two-dollar crack. She was still aware of the switchblade but it was beginning to look small in comparison to the big ass rock he clutched in the bag. "Break me off a little piece please! Just a little piece .. I'll suck your dick!"

The kid twirled the switchblade expertly between his fingers then flicked it open like he was about to strike. China jumped clear across the room-at least in her mind she jumped. In reality she was standing there rubbing her swollen clit through her mini-skirt the shit had her so horny. "Please!" she said.

Daquan finally spoke. "I ain't letting no crack head bitch suck my dick,"

China lifted her skirt to expose her most valuable asset, the only part of her anatomy she still made an effort to keep clean. If her head game was considered official, her pussy game was stratospheric. Her shit had so much muscle control she could hold a straw with her vagina and suck the contents out of a forty bottle then push it back out like it was piss. Or .. when she was in the need for pain, she got off stretching her pussy with the biggest shit she could find. The bigger the better, as long as she could get it past her pelvic opening.

"Damn!" she said aloud, when her theme song 'Joy and Pain' started playing in her mind, bringing back memories of the first time Rachet got both his fist in her pussy and a bottle in her ass at the same time. She had cum so hard she went into convulsions. Rachet thought he had killed her, the way her eyes rolled back and oceans of shit and cum flooded out of her body-What the fuck was she thinking about this shit and Rachet for?

"Fuck Rachet!" the words found their way out of her throat as she looked up at the kid, her face twisted in a grimace. It was too late. Just the thought of being stretched like that had her insides bubbling.

"You like grown woman pussy?" she asked as she tugged on a slab of meat that looked more like a small penis than a clitoris .

The kid stared at her pussy intensely as she played with it, opened it up, contorted her body and arched her torso towards him to offer a better view.

"You a school teacher right," he asked without looking up.

"A school teacher?" What was wrong with this kid. He was weirding her out. Making her feel all guilty that she was getting horny in front of a kid she would have been teaching in junior high a few years ago.

BUT CHINA DIDN'T STOP PLAYING WITH HER PUSSY

She couldn't ... her pussy was throbbing and right now she was feeling the need for pain. She looked around the room for something really big to push up in it.

"Nigga! As many niggaz I've shown this pussy to, not one of them ever asked if I was a school teacher." She crossed the room to an overflowing trashcan under the small desk. "Once this trick thought I was a transvestite," she said, bending to search through the trash, " ..because my clit is so fucking big-" She rose and came up with an empty fifth bottle of Johnny Walker, " ..but I know he was just pissed because my clit was longer than his little ass dic-" she caught herself, realizing she was truly playing herself. The kid probably had a little dick and was ashamed of it. That's probably why he had gotten all the way up here and chickened out. He's probably a virgin and never had his dick sucked before. This is probably the first time he's ever seen some real pussy.

"Fuck it! Better for me," she thought, picking up the bottle by the neck, rubbing it between her thighs, watching his reaction. Yep! He was a voyeur. The little mutha-fucka got off watching. Great! God was good. Now she could get her horny on and in the process still smoke up the rest of that rock. She could see in his eyes he was hooked.

"Break me off a little piece and I'll show you what I can do with this bottle," she said, putting one foot on the bed and spreading her fat lips with the bottom rim.

"I ain't trying to trick for no show," he said, looking her in her eyes. "But I'll give you all the crack you want if you fuck with my little brother."

'What the fuck did he just say? Did he just say fuck his little brother?'

"Your little brother! Nigga how old is your little brother?"

"Five."

"Five!" China dropped the bottle on the bed and looked around the room frantically. "I know ya'll got cameras around here someplace," she shouted in every direction as she headed for the door. "I just want ya'll sick bastards to know I might be a crack head bitch, and I might have done a few dog video's for Rachet's sick ass, but I don't do kiddy porn... fucking perverted bastards!" She stormed forward. "I know you're behind this shit Rachet. You dirty dick BITCH!"

Daquan raised the switchblade and stepped between her and the door.

"You just gon have to cut me up mutha-fucka 'cause I ain't doing shit with no five year old!"

*   *   *   *   *

CHAPTER 3
PITT

WHILE ALL THE STREET soldiers lounged around the stoop tight lipped, watching Pitt make a complete fool of himself, Daquan pulled his milk crate in the sun and was thinking about something his mother told him;

"Daquan. Always pay close attention to nicknames, they don't get there by accident and they can tell you a lot about a person's character. There's a history that comes before that name, and knowing a man's history can one day be the difference between you living and dying."

It still didn't make that much sense to him what his mother was trying to say, other than some nicknames you had to really figure out how somebody got em. Like Jumm. He still hadn't figured that one out. But Pitt .. Pitt fit his name perfectly. He looked just like a pit-bull, built low to the ground, stocky with a muscular forehead, neck, arms chest, thighs and legs-Pitt mixed with Roc, plus he had the vicious disposition of a fighting pit-bull.

"Don't ever forget Daquan, pit bulls can only serve one master and he will turn on you if you don't make him love and fear you at the same time."

"How am I suppose to do that?" he asked, holding the baby pit his mom had just given him in his arms.

"Don't worry," she assured him. "I'm going to teach you everything you need to know about dogs -two and four legged."

Pitt was no exception to anything his mom had taught him about real dogs. He could be the most gentle creature in the world until you got him aroused or gave him the command to attack. Once he latched on and tasted blood you couldn't beat him off.

Only problem with Pitt was he didn't fear anything and he only loved one thing, which made him a wild fighting pit without a master. They were the most dangerous because you never knew how they would react. One minute they could be licking your face then you could do one simple thing and they would be ripping your throat out. The closest thing Pitt had to a master was Leaky Leak, that Wet. When he was smoking that shit nobody in the crew felt safe around him. Not even Rachet, who was suppose to be his true master. Even Rachet steered clear of Pitt when he was smoking that shit. Which was why Pitt was out in the street with him and the rest of the street soldiers, while all the other lieutenants were in the safe house with Rachet taking care of business.

Pitt had been smoking that shit all morning. It wasn't even afternoon yet and already Pitt was so high that he was at the building trying to move it. A fucking six-story brick tenement building and this nigga was trying to move it. He grunted and shoved and got into squat positions with a scary determination. After about fifteen minutes he jumped up with a victorious shout;

"You see that shit! You see that shit? I'm a fucking beast," he shouted, flexing his biceps. "See these guns? Fucking Superman shit's son. I'm moving fucking buildings-"

One of the soldiers on the stoop snickered. Pitt spun to face him. "Fuck you laughing at BITCH! ... What you saying, I ain't did it?! You saying I ain't move the shit?" Pitt was already moving towards him.

The soldier jumped off the stoop and ran into the street, still laughing but pleading;

"Come on Pitt. I ain't laughing at you. This nigga just said some stupid shit-"

Pitt pulled a black nine from the back of his jeans and started waving it at everybody. "Who?, Who?, Who the fuck said that dumb shit?"

Everybody was running and ducking behind shit except Daquan. He stayed on the milk crate and watched. The soldier who started the shit was behind a car still pleading. "Come on Pitt. It didn't have nothing to do with you. Nigga was telling me about this bitch-"

"Yea right! First nigga I see I'm-a put some of this hot lead in they ass," Pitt shouted. That's when he turned and looked right into Daquan's eyes. "Fuck, I don't give a fuck. I shoot little niggaz too."

With the exception of taking both hands out of his pockets and holding them palms up, Daquan didn't move from the milk crate. He kept direct eye contact as Pitt approached.

Holding the gun barrel inches from Daquan's head Pitt growled "Oh you's a brave little mutha-fucka huh?"

"No," Daquan answered calmly. "I ain't brave. I ain't got nothing to run from. I ain't do nothing to you."

Pitt stood there looking down on the kid for a long time, their eyes locked, his face twisted, searching for fear, Finally Pitt started grinning; "You ain't like the rest of these BITCH ASS NIGGAZ. You got more heart than all these lame ass, frontin' ass niggaz put together." Pitt tucked the gun back in his jeans then leaned over the kid. "I heard about that shit you did to Rachet a couple of weeks ago with that bitch China. That was some wicked shit. But a word of advice lil man. Watch yo back around Rachet. Two things the nigga don't like. He don't like being embarrassed and he don't like niggaz taking his hoes, even when he don't want em no more." Pitt stood and took the keys to his rental from his pocket and beeped the alarm.

"You got gwuap?"

Daquan shrugged his shoulders. Pitt reached into his pocket, came out with a small knot and peeled off two twenty's "Tell Rachet to two-way me if he got some work. I gotta go find me some pussy. All this moving shit got my dick hard." He peeled off another twenty. "Yo! That bitch China ever show you what she can do with a forty bottle?"

Daquan nodded in the negative.

"I always wanted to see that shit .. up close an personal. Try to hook it up for a nigga... On the low. I don't want Rachet to know. He frontin, but he still hooked on that bitch."

Just before the tires of the Chrysler squealed out from the curb, Pitt shouted out;"

I'm still gonna shoot one of you bitches!"

Pitt drove up to the Drew to check out these freak strippers. He should have called first but he didn't bother. The bitches were always home this time of day. They be up all night fuckin and sucking for dough. He checked his watch. Quarter after twelve. Yea them hoes didn't need no more than four hours sleep. They were probably up right now fuckin an sucking each other. Bitches were straight nymphos and claimed they came out of the womb sucking each other's pussies. Sometimes he could get off just watching the twin bitches go at each other.

His dick was already as hard as the nine pressing against his spine as he entered their building off Eighth. Niggaz were all up in the lobby when he came through but none of them bitch asses would even give him eye contact when he entered and took the staircase to the third floor. Niggaz knew who he was. They didn't want none.

Ten minutes later, and after Pitt had 'woken half the projects by banging on the bitches door like he was the Police, he made his way back to the Chrysler, mad as a mutha-fucka. He knew them bitches were home. He saw one of the black bitches when she came to the peephole. He started to put a couple through the door before he left but changed his mind because too many of their nosey ass neighbors had peeped out and seen him.

In the car he screened through the numbers in his 2-way, "Fuck that bitch, her pussy stink ... Nope! You's a fuckin gold digger an yo shit ain't all that .. I know you ain't home. You got a J.O.B." Finally he came to a number that made his eyes light up. A Dominican mommi he met at Rucker. She was official, and at the game she had been on his dick hard body, but Pitt hadn't bothered to call because she lived smack in the middle of Diablo territory, and Rachet told him to stay the fuck off The Hill.

She answered. Her voice sounded like sex. "Ahlo. Ahlo!"

"Yo! This is Pitt. I met you at the Rucker…"

"Yes I remember you very well Pitt. I've been waiting by the phone for two weeks for you to call…"

Damn her voice was sexy. "You bullshittin'?"

"Basically… But…" Sounded like the bitch was having an orgasm… And..

Basically she was… And…

Basically he didn't even have to lay his pimp game down.

Mommi told him at the moment he called she was laying there playing with herself, thinking about him, and hearing his voice had just made her climax. No shit! Then she asked how fast he could get there.

HOW FAST?

Faster than a speeding bullet. He put fire to another stick of wet then hit the gas.

Pitt parked in the hospital parking lot, like mommi told him, then walked down 167th to Broadway. He was feeling extra crispy as he stopped to adjust his Yankee fitted in a storefront window. Everything he had on was matching and official. Blue, Red Monkey jeans with matching Remix Uptowns, a button up pinstripe Purple Label long sleeve, a red gold bicycle link, 5 carat light bulbs in both ears. He checked his red gold, iced out Techno Marina. Damn! He had made it all the way up The Hill, parked, and was half way to the bitches' house and it had only taken him thirty seconds. Yea he was on some real Superman shit today.

As soon as he hit the block and the Oyay's saw his Harlem swagger, they started coming at him like roaches, on some real annoying shit, flashing saran wrapped bags of powder.

"Yo Poppie I got that fisskale… I'm the only one down here… Just me Poppie. They got the bullshit .. I got that real shit .. "

Every last one of them mutha-fuckaz had the same exact line, they shit was the real shit an the next niggaz shit was the bullshit. Pitt tried to ignore them but by the third or forth building the wet had him so paranoid he swore they were scheming on his shit, trying to get at him.

"That's word to my dead mother," he said aloud, the sun glittering off two rows of diamond-capped teeth. "The next one-a you clowns run up on me I'm puttin' fire in they ass." His hand instinctively moved to the back of his shirt.

He had barely gotten the words out of his mouth before an Oyay was practically in his chest like he wanted it.

"Yo Poppie-"

So Pitt gave it to him. Two in his chest. He hit him so close that the niggaz shirt caught on fire.

"The hospital ain't but four blocks up," Pitt grinned, before shooting at anything that moved as he made his way off the block.

*   *   *   *   *

CHAPTER 4
RACHET

RACHET WAS SO FURIOUS veins were popping out of his forehead. "Nigga are you crazy? Every Oyay on The Hill know you shot that fuckin kid."

"Them Oyay mutha-fuckaz was trying to jux me. I'm s'pose to just let it happen?"

"You suppose to stay the fuck off The Hill!"

"Yea right! If you seen this mommi I went to check, yo ass would a been on the hill yo goddamn self. Bitch is crazy. She took it up the ass, everything. Matter fact, remember that Biggie shit?" Pitt went straight into an animated imitation of Biggie Smalls.

"I comes up in the spot or whatever, the bitch got the candles lit or whatever, so she telling me whatever, she wanna get her freak on or whatever. So I'm like what's up? What you wanna do? So I'm ready to wear it out or whatever, the bitch told me she wanted me to shit on her, straight up shit on her. So I'm like, what you mean? I might shit on you after I hit it. I might not call you no more, shit on you like that. She talkin bout, No! She want me to cock over her an SHIT on her stomach. I say Bitch, what da... what da fuck I'm spose to do after I shit on you? I'm spose to hit that after that? Bitch is wilding out... So after I shits on the bitch right... You should-a known I shit on her."

Rachet could no longer constrain his laughter, though it was more like chuckles that he allowed to escape. Pitt gave him his silly smile and continued in his own voice. "That's my word cous', this Dominican bitch re-enacted that whole Biggie shit, candles and all. An you know what I did right? Yea you know it. I cocked over the bitch and sprayed her fine ass with some real diarrhea shit. Some foul ass smelling nasty gooey shit."

Rachet clenched the bridge of his nose to suppress his laughter and try to regain his angry face, but he couldn't look Pitt in the eye when he said "You know you gonna have to pay for this shit right. Cause of you chasing pussy we got a dead mutha-fucka on The Hill and that means we ain't gon be getting no paper on the streets-"

The smile wiped right off Pitts face. "Don't start that bullshit Rachet," Pitt told him. "I'm yo fuckin cousin. I ain't one of these herb ass niggaz that's gonna let you do what you wanna do."

Rachet looked up. Pitt was right. He was the only one who he allowed in the safe room with street clothes. Everybody else had to be stripped at the first check point to make sure they weren't wired or carried concealed weapons. He knew right now Pitt had his hand on his nine and the safety was off.

Rachet looked down on the two massive Rottweilers standing on either side of Pitt. "If I give them the signal they'd be eatin' you alive before you could get that nine from under your shirt."

"I ain't scared of dying cous, you know that," Pitt said smirking, glancing down at the Rottweilers at his heels. "It's like going to sleep, 'cept you never wake Up."

"Yeah, well don't think it can't happen because we first cousins. That blood relationship shit is highly overrated. Next time you fuck up I'm going to do what I have to do." Rachet then quoted a line from Biggie. "Seven, this rule is so underrated, keep yo family an bizness completely separated, money an blood don't mix, like two dicks an no chick, find yo'self in serious shit."

Pitt looked at Rachet like he wanted to kill him right then and there... Until... His head started bobbing to a beat only he could hear. Then he started spitting the beginning of the rhyme, staring at Rachet with a grill face. "Number two, never let em know yo next move, don't you know bad boys move in silence, and violence, take it from yo highness-"

Rachet joined in. "I dun squeezed mad clips at these cats fo they bricks an chips, number three, never trust nobody, yo mom will set that ass up, properly gassed up, leave the mask up, fo that fast buck, she be laying in da bushes to light that ass Up."

Rachet opened his arms and a big smile warmed his face. "I still got love for you nigga. We family. Come over here and show your cousin some love, then we gon figure out how to make this shit work for us." Pitt hugged him loosely, making sure no body parts touched below the shoulders.

Turns out Pitt shooting the kid on The Hill was a good thing, and Rachet was just mad because he disobeyed a direct order, which wasn't shit new, and

Rachet as usual was trying to push his buttons, make him feel guilty and see how far he could be pushed. They had always gone at each other since kids.

Turns out the kid Pitt shot was trying to blackmail the Columbian distributor, Petey Rodriquez.

"You know how long I been waiting to snatch that mutha-fucka?" Rachet asked, a gleam replacing the anger in his eyes. "But the mutha-fuckaz security is tighter than a fat Jews fist."

"Wait a minute. Back up. How you know the Oyay I shot was trying to blackmail Petey Rodriquez?"

Rachet puffed up with pride. "That's what I do cous, I find shit out. There ain't nothing I ain't gonna eventually find out about."

Pitt gave him a look that read, "Yea right!"

"Actually it was lil man," Rachet confessed. "Nobody knows he's been mule-ing for me for the last two years, not even the Oyay's. Only Old man Diablo himself-"

OK. So that answered what the kid was doing for Rachet. Pitt was beginning to have his suspicions.

"You know that's a smart lil mutha-fucka. He joined old man Diablo's little league team so he'd have a reason to be up there all the time, especially carrying a knapsack filled with that much product and money-"

"Yea! Yea! I know the lil niggaz smart," Pitt cut him off. "But what's that got to do with Petey?" If he let Rachet go on and on, he'd be here all day, and Pitt had shit to do. He had to meet Mommi cross-town and get his freak on.

"Turns out one of the kids on the team freaked out when he heard about the kid you killed, thought it was a hit by Petey and he was gonna be next."

"So this kid was in on the blackmail too?" Pitt gave him a quizzed look.

"Shut up and listen!" Rachet said. "Petey likes to suck little boy dicks. He had been molesting the kid you shot since he was a little nigga and he's been molesting the kid who told lil man. He said Petey had threatened to murder his entire family if he told, but the kid was so terrified he had to tell somebody, so he spilled his brains out to lil man and lil man confided in me." He gave Pitt a look. "I hate to admit it but if you hadn't murked that kid I would have never been able to get at this mutha-fucka." Pitt returned the look, his face all scrunched up, and if looks could kill.

"Every man has his weakness." Rachet said, looking away and snapping his fingers to summon his fighters. "Yours is smoking that shit and tricking bitches."

"When I get my hands on that pet'a'file mutha-fucka..."

"You ain't gon do shit, you hear me? You ain't gonna touch that mutha-fucka till we get this gwuap. This nigga's just a stepping stone. His little six hundred g ain't shit to what it's gonna get us. I'm talking 15, 30 mil easy. Now listen nigga. This how we gon do this shit."

Pitt was listening but his mind was drifting. He was already digging Melisa's back out, and at the same time he wanted to kill something - REAL BAD.

*　　*　　*　　*　　*

CHAPTER 5

NAQUAN WOKE UP EXTRA early, washed, put on clean underwear and packed a nice outfit in his knapsack. He took a seat at the computer and looked over at Daquan sound asleep on the inflatable mattress he had stolen from the warehouse of a sporting goods store on Broadway in the Village. He wanted to wake him up, but he knew Daquan had only gotten home a few hours earlier and would be real mad if he woke him. But Naquan was anxious to see China again. Since he had been going to see her he wasn't having nightmares anymore. Now he only had dreams about her. He booted up the laptop and studied until Daquan woke up.

*   *   *   *   *

China rolled from the bed, picked up the stem from the nightstand and lit the Egyptian musk in the brass incense burner before heading for the bath. Daquan would be bringing the kid at seven and she needed at least a couple hours to prepare herself. She never knew a five year old could be so exhausting.

There was some commotion going on in the garbage below her window. She stopped, pressed her forehead against the coolness of the windowpane, and looked down to the streets below. A homeless man was ripping the bags open in search of cans. She stood there watching and pushing back last nights residue in her stem as dawn begin to break, and suddenly tears came from no place. She didn't want to go back to that life, but she knew that as long as she held on to the stem nothing was ever going to really change. In two months, after she had finished the contract with the kid, as sure as she was watching the sun rise through her tears, she would be back in the life, fucked up with no where to go and no one who cared.

SHE DIDN'T PUT THE STEM DOWN

in fact she pushed and scraped every particle she could burn until the stem was clear then went to take a long luxurious bath while she waited for Daquan to deliver his baby brother with her morning hit.

As she lay there in water so hot it nearly burned her skin, she thought back, as she had every morning since, to the day that had turned her life around. The day she thought Rachet had set her up to make another one of his perverted films.

It had taken Daquan over an hour and most of the rock he had in the bag to convince her there were no cameras and Rachet didn't have anything to do with him being there, and that the very last thing in the world he wanted was for him or his brother to have sex with her. Lil nigga had some good shit too. Her jaws were locked and her pussy was on fire as she listened to him tell her how he had raised his little brother since Naquan was one, and how smart his brother was, and how the only thing Daquan wanted in the world was to get Naquan in a good private school so that he could become a lawyer one day. As he talked and talked, she sat on the bed in front of him working the bottom half of the Johnny Walker bottle in her pussy. He was talking but he was looking too. She couldn't tell if he was excited or whether he thought she had lost her damn mind, but she was beyond caring what he thought at that point. He was a kid and she was a two-dollar crack head whore.

"I'm a crack head," she told him. "I ain't no teacher. Not anymore." That part of her life was gone. Even her proper English grammar had disappeared with that life. She no longer heard what he was saying, only the squishy sounds from her insides, and her own crying moans, as she pumped the Johnny Walker bottle. She didn't want to hear what he was saying. She didn't want to be reminded of who she used to be.

"You wanna see how much I can put inside me?" she said. "Wanna see how much I can take?" Shit! fuck teaching! It would be much easier to masturbate for the lil nigga to keep her stem filled .. and before she knew it, most of the bottle was lost inside her, and she was squirting cum all over the place, having one of the most intense orgasms she had ever had in her life.

Nearly two months had gone by since that day Daquan gave her all that money to go down to the lobby and pay for a full weeks rent, even after she told him there was no way in hell she was going to teach his little brother. Her first impulse was to take the money and run, and that's just what she did. But two blocks away, as she passed the abortion clinic, she caught a vision of the son Rachet had beaten out of her, and turned back in a daze.

Now Naquan was beginning to feel like the son she lost. She was already growing attached to him. He was smart, well mannered, handsome, and he loved to learn as much as she loved teaching him. And Daquan! Damn! She didn't know what to think of him, other than if he were a little older she would ask him to marry her. He was mature far beyond his age, and he treated her like Rachet did when he first started pampering her, except Daquan had a sexiness that Rachet, nor any man she met would ever have. The kid was sort of like amazing, and she was still living in a dream, because shit like this didn't happen in real life.

'Quan', as she began calling him, only kept her in the Casa Blanca for two weeks before he found her the room she was in now, a real nice place off Convent over looking the park. He had her hair and nails done before she moved in, brought her new clothes, and kept her stem packed with shit so good it made her cum on herself. Her hands went between her thighs as she lay there soaking. As bad as she tried not to think about Quan that way, her fingers still danced between her thighs. He told her everything he knew about women he had learned from his mother. She must have been a hell of a lady because he definitely knew how to treat her. He knew when she was lying and he knew when she was playing her little girl games, and he never let her get away with shit. But most of all he never lied to her, and he had a sixth sense of when to be diplomatic with the truth.

China climaxed almost as soon as she touched herself and went for another one while wondering what happened to Quan's parents, and why God had given a nine year old the ability to have a plan and take control of his destiny while she was in her twenties and she didn't know what the fuck she was doing.

She fell asleep in the tub after her fifth orgasm and dreamed she was back in China, the land she was born in, with her biological mother and she was happy again.

She woke up when the water got cool then turned on the hot water to reheat it. She liked her water hot, it took out the toxins and already her skin was getting that glow again.

China drifted back into the dream with the water still running. She was awakened by banging on the floor, which was immediately followed by a hard knock on the front door. As soon as she opened her eyes she realized that the hot water had been running so long it was ice cold and the tub was flooding over. "Fuck! Now the old bitch was going to kick her out for sure. This was the third time in a week China had flooded the rooms below. The last time the bitch had given her a final warning. "Fuck!!!" she turned the water off and jumped out of the tub all in one motion. "Fuck!"

China was rushing so fast to drain the tub and throw towels and dirty clothes on the floor to stop the flood, that she forgot to cover herself before rushing to open the door. The landlady was furious for the first few seconds, then she took a long hard look at China from head to toe. Her gaze settled on the fat lips and long ass clitoris hanging between China's soaked thighs and the old bitch's entire expression changed.

"You don't worry bout a ting," the old bitch told her, trying to hide her Jamaican accent. "I've got plenty rags. You just stay ear till I get back."

China wasn't stupid. She recognized that look and when the old landlord bitch returned with a bag of rags, China was on her hands and knees, her back to the bathroom door, soaking up water, still butt ass naked.

"I'm gonna ave to do something to fix this tub," the old bitch said as she got on her knees behind China and passed her some rags. China grinned to herself and spread her legs a little wider.

* * * * *

"Why can't I stay with China?" Naquan asked Daquan as they got off the # 9 train on 138th. "She could be my mommy." Daquan ignored him as they weaved their way through the early morning crowd and through the turnstile. "Her room is nice, she's got windows and you can see the park. We can't see nothing in our room."

"If you can see out you can see in, lil nigga," Daquan said as they came out on Broadway.

"Yea, what that mean?"

"It mean that where we at now is safe."

At the top of the stairs Daquan stopped, wet his fingertip with spit then bent to wipe a spot off of Naquan's brand new Uptowns. "An it mean instead of you worrying bout having a mommy, you need to be worrying bout getting in that school." He rose and adjusted Naquan's fitted.

"I know all my work," Naquan stated with a twinge of arrogance. "China says I'm the smartest kid she ever taught."

"Don't let yo head get bigger than yo fitted lil nigga. Everybody say that test is mad hard."

Naquan pursed his lips and started sucking in air like he often saw China doing.

"Stop doing that!"

"What?"

"That shit wit yo lips. Niggaz gon think you's a fiend or sump-in."

"Fuck!"

"What I tell you bout cursing?"

"You curse!"

"So what? I ain't the one who's going to school."

The rest of the walk to 145th and Convent was in silence. Daquan on super alert for any of Rachet's crew, and Naquan already dreading that by the evening rush hour he would be heading back into the filth of darkness. They came in through the back and ran smack into the landlady, Ms. Perno, coming down the stairs in a hurry.

"Why you boys always enter pan da back like servants when ya look so fresh an clean? The alleyway is filled with filth an stray dog an ting." She blocked their way. "Come Naquan. give Ms. Perno er kiss." She bent and hugged him then kissed him on both cheeks. "OK, where's mine?" she grinned, turning her cheek to him. Naquan scrunched up his face and kissed the air twice.

China's room was on the top floor. It was the biggest and nicest, and Daquan said it was perfect because you could see all the way down 145th through her windows, which was where a lot of Rachet's crew came through. But Daquan said none of them niggaz ventured up the hill, that was Diablo territory, and the back way led directly to The Hill so they could always make a quick getaway.

The entire climb to China's apartment Naquan kept wiping his face over and over with his sleeves.

"You alright, lil nigga," Daquan asked before knocking on her door.

"No! Her face was sticky .. an it smelled funny."

China came to the door in a short towel and rushed back into the bathroom. She stuck her head back out the door. "Quan .. Can you do me a favor and zip me up?"

While Daquan went to the bathroom Naquan took the laptop from his knapsack and put it on the bed, then ran to the window and looked out. "We can go to the park later?" he called out to China.

"Maybe," she answered through the closed door. "And it's may we go to the park later."

"May we," he asked happily.

"I don't know. You'll have to ask your brother."

"Can we Daquan?"

China dropped the towel and got dressed right in front of Quan as he broke her off a nice piece of rock and left her a few dollars on the counter. She didn't think twice about being naked around him.

"You need to get yo teeth fixed," was the last thing he said before leaving, right after he reminded her to make sure she went out the back way and circled round if she took Naquan to the park.

*   *   *   *   *

Daquan's coach was a tall slender good looking man, with silver hair, named Ray Ray Carrero. He was a really rich investment lawyer who didn't really fit in the Diablo circle. He always looked out of place around the thugs and murderers surrounding Old Man Diablo. Ray Ray, as he insisted on Daquan calling him, was Old Man Diablo's only daughter's boyfriend.

"That's the only way you could have ever gotten me into this crazy family," Ray Ray had laughed, while having one of his mano a' mano talks with Daquan. "If I didn't love Amillia so much I would be out like a bat out of hell." Daquan knew that everyone in Amillia's family loved Ray Ray, her brothers, her uncles, her cousins, her father, everybody. But that didn't stop the jokes about him being a square peg in a round hole.

Ray Ray taught Daquan a lot about money management, investment banking, and how to play the game of baseball. Most of all, he was the one who introduced Daquan to his neighbor, Senior Encarnacion and the twins. Senior Encarnacion had become almost like a father to him.

"There's my star short stop," Ray Ray called out from the field, as Daquan entered the park. "On time as always." He popped a fly ball out to center field and little Pablo reeled it in as Ray Ray looked over his shoulder. "Put your bag down and grab a glove."

Daquan dropped his beat up knapsack in the same corner he always dropped it and grabbed a glove from the team bag. His knapsack was empty now but he knew that after the practice it would be filled with keys of uncut cocaine. He didn't know who would put it there, and he had no interest in finding out. "What you don't know you can't tell nobody."

Daquan forgot about the bag and got lost in the game, only a dead man would steal something from this park. Ray Ray often told him that he was a natural, and that if he really pursued it he could probably play in the Majors one day. That's how much potential Ray Ray said he saw in him. It was an option, but like his mother use to tell him, "Don't put all your eggs in one basket."

Ray Ray started hitting choppers to his position. Daquan missed everyone. After a couple of dozen or so, Ray Ray stopped and called out

"What's wrong with you today?"

Daquan's body language told it all.

Ray Ray walked across the field to him. "Wanna talk about it?"

"No! Ain't nothing to talk about. I'm just messing up, that's all." As much as he loved and trusted Ray Ray, he could never tell him what was bothering him was the sick shit Rachet wanted him to do with Petey Rodriquez.

"Come on, hit. I ain't gon miss no more." And he didn't. He managed to put the Petey thing in the back of his mind until he was totally into playing his position, in the zone, as Ray Ray would say. After practice Ray Ray pulled him to the side.

"You're going to be ready for the playoff Saturday?"

"Yea, I'll be ready," he said, picking up his knapsack and slinging it over his shoulder. He could tell from the weight there were three keys in the bag.

"You're my star player," Ray Ray reminded him. "I want you to get plenty of sleep the night before the game."

"A-ight," Daquan turned to walk away. Ray Ray put a hand on his shoulder.

"Oh! I almost forgot. The E twins wanted me to ask you if you wanted to come over this evening for dinner?"

"Is Mister E gonna be there?"

"I suppose so. He doesn't usually stray too far from the roost."

"Which twin? Amilio?"

"Both actually. They said to arrive early so you'd have time to hang out before dinner .. Oh! Carlo did say to bring your rhyme book."

"A-ight!" Daquan said happily. "Yea! I'll be there."

He was happy he was going to Mister E's, but all the way uptown all Daquan could think about was what Rachet wanted him to do with Petey Rodriquez. When he dropped the work off to Rachet, Rachet reminded him again

"You ain't got nothin to worry about lil man. Once Petey sees that monster dick you got, he's gonna be waving chunks of dough at you to take you to a motel. You ain't even got to let him touch you. Just get him to the motel room and we'll do the rest."

Daquan didn't acknowledge Rachet's persistence one way or the other, but on the #9 train back uptown to pick up his little brother, he woke the man up beside him when he blurted out, "I ain't letting no man suck my dick!" The man looked around to see if any of the passengers thought Daquan was making a reference to him, then went back to sleep.

Daquan wished he had the luxury of sleeping on the train, he was fuckin exhausted the way Rachet had him running all over the place, plus all the other shit he still had to do. After he picked up Naquan he still had to hit Micky D's for Naquan an China, then slide all the way cross town for some Eukanuba for Kilo, then that long ass journey in the tunnels to tuck Naquan away, then he still had to go back uptown to China's to drop off her fuckin hit an food, an still take a shower an get dressed to go to Mister E's for dinner.

Daquan was really tempted to sleep on the ride to Brooklyn, but he didn't and he wouldn't let Naquan sleep either. His mother had shown him too many things that happen to people that sleep on the trains, most of it he watched her do herself. "If you don't want to be a Vic," she constantly reminded him, "you gotta learn what to watch out for." Yea, his mother number one. Nobody was safe on the trains when she was riding. She even robbed bums. He remembered once a bum got on the subway car they were in and sat across from them.

"What's wrong with that picture?" she leaned over and whispered, holding the baby Naquan in her arms. Daquan studied the bum. His clothes were filthy, like he had never taken them off or washed them in a year. His hair was all matted and nasty and so was a beard that covered three quarters of his face. He wasn't wearing shoes and his feet were filthy, swollen an crusty, like the baked earth he had seen in pictures of the dessert.

"I 'ont know. What," he had asked her, still studying the bum.

"Think and observe, and use all your senses."

He thought, and he observed, and he used all his senses, but he still couldn't figure out what was wrong.

"I ont know!" he finally said, shrugging his shoulders.

"Smell anything?" she whispered?" He sniffed the air.

"Nope. I ont smell nuthin." And then he realized it. Before she even told him he knew. A smile broke across his face. "I know .. I know!"

"What?" she asked.

He rose from the seat to his knees and whispered in her ear.

"He ain't no bum, he don't smell. If he was a bum he'd be smelling like shit .. He a cop." "That's my lil man ," she smiled, and the very next stop they got off.

"They ain't never gon catch us, right mommy. We too smart."

*   *   *   *   *

When he and Naquan finally arrived at the room in the tunnel, Daquan barely had enough energy to feed Kilo, but he did. Then he gave Naquan his favorite games to play, packed some fresh gear and underwear then headed back uptown. By the time he reached China's room to bathe and dress, he was so exhausted he fell asleep in the tub. China had to wake him or he might have drowned. He wrapped a towel around himself and stumbled to her bed, where he fell asleep again before he could pull his underwear above his knees, and in that exhausted state he dreamed for the first time, in his close to ten years, that he was getting his dick sucked, deep throated like he had seen some of the heads do for krillz back on the block. The shit got so good that his body started arching and he was busting his very first nut down her throat. She started gagging and he opened his eyes to see who she was, except it wasn't a she... It was fuckin Petey Rodriquez! Daquan jerked out of his sleep, desperately searching for his switchblade, the shit was so real.

It took him a minute or two to realize it wasn't Petey. He exhaled a sigh of relief as China lifted her head and smiled, slowly letting his dick slide from her throat. Still he was pissed off.

"Get off me! Get the fuck off me!" He practically kicked her off and rushed to the bathroom where he started washing his dick like crazy.

China rose and followed, butt ass naked, looking like a little girl in a grown woman's body, she was so short. She came up behind him and reached around for his still stiff dick. "Damn Quan! This is the first dick I ever choked on. I didn't know your shit was this big. I've never even seen a dick this big before. I didn't even think they exist."

Daquan spun around, "Get the fuck away from me you crack head bitch! Word to my dead mother. If you ever even touch me again I'm-a split yo fuckin throat." He started examining the head of his dick, opening it up and looking inside. "I 'ont know what the fuck you got," he said, washing his dick again. "You probably got Aids."

China burst out in tears and ran back to the bedroom, threw herself on the bed, and started sobbing like she was having convulsions.

"Now I 'ont even trust you round my little brother," Daquan told her, pulling on his pants, gathering his clothes and heading for the door. "Fuckin crack head bitch!" He slammed the door behind him.

As soon as he turned Ms. Perno popped up from the staircase like she was hiding. "Is everyting OK Daquan?" she asked, reaching out for him.

"Get away from me you nosey bitch," he said, brushing past her and pulling the rest of his clothes on as he scurried down the steps. Ms. Perno watched him, wide mouth, until he was no longer an image, just footsteps pounding on creaky stairs, then pushed the door to China's room.

"I don't know what's wrong with me," China sobbed into the pillow as Ms. Perno sat on the edge of the bed stroking her back. "I don't want to be like this .. I'm sick .. I need help."

"Not to worry, Mamma Perno is ear China Doll," Ms. Perno consoled, her knobby hand now stroking all the way down to the velvety white skin of China's ass cheeks. "Don't worry, Mamma will make er China doll feel better." She laid her face on China's back and started kissing it, her rough hand now rubbing between China's soft thighs. "Mamma wiil take away all-l-l da pain."

*   *   *   *   *

CHAPTER 6
MISTER 'E'

VERNICIA ENCARNACION WATCHED HER husband from the kitchen as she removed the roast chicken from the oven and placed it in the serving dish. Abel Encarnacion sat on the fire escape drinking a cold Corona and watching their sons, Amilio and Carlo with the kid Daquan below. Abel was a good man, a family man, and he was so handsome, and though some years had past since they were wed, in her heart of hearts, she was still that love sick thirteen year old virgin who fell in love with him the first minute he came to visit in her small village of Saba De La Marina. Abel was twenty-one then and she had only three days before they met, began her very first blood cycle, yet before the summer months were over he had proposed and she had enthusiastically accepted.

Why her family had so vehemently opposed the marriage was to this day a mystery to her. Of course they had used the argument her Nana had expressed to her, smelling of Marlboro's, cooking oil and double mint gum, "It's bad enough he is related, but he is the son of your mother's oldest sister."

Saba De La Marina was an incestuous little town where everyone was related in some way or another, so that theory of first cousins didn't hold. In fact the man Nana married, as Vernicia candidly pointed out to her, was her first cousin. So Nana, not to be out done, switched gears.

"He is nothing but a male whore. Look how the women flock to him. If you marry him you will be stuck in this poor village for the rest of your life and he will have babies from here to Santa Cruz."

She didn't believe he would be unfaithful, but she would have never held it against him either. It was evident to a fool that every unmarried girl in her village had the hots for Abel Encarnacion, even the married women often gave him sly, lustful glances. That much was true, but what her Nana didn't understand, or perhaps she did, was that Vernicia didn't care if he slept with the entire village. She would have still married him. That's how strong her love was for him.

"He is no Good!" had been her final argument. "He will never amount to anything. You are the most beautiful girl in Santo Domingo. You could easily find a rich husband."

"I will live in a one room hut without a roof and eat mush each day as long as Abel will have me for a wife, and if he has a thousand illegitimate children, I will embrace them as if they came from my own womb." Vernicia responded. And that was that! Nana finally relented and gave them her blessings.

Now that Abel had become rich beyond anyone's expectations, and built Nana a mansion in Saba De La Marina, complete with servants, a driver and bodyguards, Abel had become her son. Now she often bragged that she always knew he would make something of himself, and that she had persuaded Vernicia to marry him.

A lingering smile blessed Vernicia's face as she checked the remaining pots, remembering how Abel had sworn his love and devotion to her, and only her, less than an hour after he first laid eyes on her. The memory was one of her fondest and still as vivid in her mind as the day it happened...

Of him crossing the room full of guest and family to her circle of girlfriends, while they all held their breaths wondering who he was coming to see.

Of him coming directly to her while her heart nearly stopped.

Of him bowing before her then extending his hand while her friends blushed and giggled and her heart truly stopped.

"I am Abel Encarnacion," he said, smiling perfect white teeth, "and I have found my completion." She didn't breath again until much later in the day, after he had gone and her friends joked that it was such a corny line. But she didn't mind their jokes, they were only jealous, besides, as soon as her hand had touched Abel's, all the longing and emptiness she had known before in her life was replaced with a certainty .. he also completed her.

Her Nana had also been very wrong about his being unfaithful. In all the years past, and as rich as he had become, he had never once slept outside of his marriage. This Vernicia was as certain of as the air she breathed. She had long since given Abel permission to sleep with other women. She had gone so far on their fifth anniversary as to dress one of her friend's, she was certain he was attracted to, in nothing but her birthday suit and a red bow and placed her on their bed as a present.

It was a near disaster, the closest she had ever seen Abel show anger towards her in the thirteen years of their marriage.

"You have disgraced not only me," he told her, turning away in disgust after she took the blindfold off, " ..but you have now lost a dear friend. Never will she be allowed in this house again, and you are forbidden to ever speak to her for as long as you are my wife and the mother of my sons." After the woman got dressed, he had gone on to give her a large sum of money to live anyplace but New York. He then went on to explain to her that if she were truly Vernicia's friend she would have never allowed herself 'to disrespect his wife, or his family, or her own womanhood.

Immediately after she left, Abel ushered Vernicia and the two boys out, with only the clothing on their backs, to a hotel where they lived for a month until he moved them into this place. He kept nothing from the old apartment. Everything in it had been tainted. They would start anew. There would be no reminders of that day.

It was only then that Vernicia truly understood how devoted her husband was to the tenets of marriage, respect, and family.

Vernicia called out to him. "Would you like another beer, Mio."

"No my love," he said, giving her a look that told of what he really desired. She blushed a smile. She was always willing when he was ready, and if he wasn't working he was always ready.

"If you do not wish the food to become cold," she blushed again, "you will call the children and I will set the table .. Unless you prefer to wait awhile. It can always be reheated," she said, giving him that look.

Vernicia was as beautiful now as she was the first minute he laid eyes on her, since that moment he saw her across the room where she stood out like a bright lamp in a dark cave. He looked back to the boys rhyming in the park below, then again to his wife. The boy Daquan would have to be leaving soon, otherwise ..

"Amilio, Carlo. Dinner in five minutes," he shouted down, then pushed himself through the window, back into the apartment. He crept up behind Vernicia, who was leaning over placing the roast chicken on the table, and slid his hand under her dress.

"Mio," she said playfully. "You are going to make me drop the tray."

He whispered in her ear, "You still drive me so wild I can't keep my hands off you."

"You should not have called the children if you are still so filled with passion. You must wash your hands quickly, for now you have the scent of my passion all over them and the children will be rushing through the door any minute." She turned to face him, he pressed against her, and she could feel he was ready. "Go.. Go .." she urged him, pressing him gently on his chest. "Go before I forget we have children."

Abel kissed her passionately until she was pressing back against him-until there was a knock on the door. Only then did he hurry to the bathroom. Vernicia waited until he closed the door then straightened her dress and let the boys in.

The twins were identical but Amilio was the oldest by only a few minutes, and first in line for his father's fortune. But the way his father seemingly praised Daquan had Amilio seething. Just in the space of time since they sat down at the dinner table his father had complemented or compared him and Carlo to Daquan exactly eighteen times. Amilio had counted every single one of them. Daquan this, Daquan that. You should take examples from Daquan. You should be more like Daquan. Amilio was sick of Daquan. One more Daquan and Amilio swore he would throw up all over the dinner table. It seemed like his father was setting Daquan up to be next in line.

Daquan didn't belong at their dinner table, gorging himself on their food. In fact he didn't belong in their building, or in their neighborhood. There were no Blacks in a twenty-block radius of their apartment. They couldn't even come to their section of the public park without being turned away by Complex Security. Even worse, Daquan was an idiot. He couldn't even read or write. Carlo had to write all his poems in his rhyme book for him then read them back to him.

It was definitely a twin thing, because as soon as he thought rhymes, Carlo blurted out

"Daquan is the best rapper ever. My friends say he's better than Eminem and Jay-Z, and he doesn't even curse in his rhymes."

That was the straw that broke the camels back. Amilio found it impossible to hold back his anger any longer and blurted out, "Porque tu tanto 'olguyo? Con este negro mieldoso. El es una pile de mielda y tu saves, y abuelo dise que todos los negros son cabrones."

Every jaw at the table dropped except Daquan's, who didn't look up from devouring a leg of chicken.

"I think it is time you left the table and go to your room." Abel said calmly, folding his napkin and placing it on the table.

Amilio shoved his chair back and stomped angrily from the dinning area and disappeared down the long hallway. Daquan never looked up from his plate, but Abel had a strong suspicion the kid understood every word.

After dinner, Carlo helped Vernicia with the dishes while Abel and Daquan talked in the study, Vernicia understood Amilio's concerns. She had similar concerns when Abel first invited the kid to the apartment, with the exception of Ray Ray and a few close friend's, Abel never invited anyone to his home, and absolutely never a stranger. But when Abel explained to her the boys circumstances, how he was raising himself and his younger brother since his mother passed away nearly five years ago, her heart went out to him.

"Why don't you find him someplace. Someone who will love and take care of them?" she had asked.

"The boy is proud. He will not take handouts."

"How does he survive," she asked, seeing how well dressed, neat and clean he was whenever he visited.

"The same as I did when I was his age. I worked hard and I never gave up on my dream. I was also fortunate enough to have a mentor."

So Abel had become the boy's mentor, and truth was Vernicia had grown very fond of the boy herself over the past year. She especially loved watching him eat, and felt proud that he liked her cooking so much that he never left anything for seconds. That's why she always put food away for his little brother before it reached the dinner table.

"Carlo, do you like Daquan?" she asked.

"Yes. He's very nice Mom. I don't know why Amilio doesn't like him. All my friends like him, even my Jewish friends."

"Perhaps he's just afraid."

"Of what Mom?"

"That your father might love Daquan more than he loves him."

"No Mom. Amilio knows father would never love a stranger more than he loves his own family."

"I know. I'm just not so sure Amilio knows."

"I'll talk to him mom. Sometimes he listens to me."

Vernicia hoped that Carlo could get through to Amilio. If not she would have to talk to Abel. As fond as she was of Daquan, she did not wish to see the harmony of their family broken up.

Abel Encarnacion was not surprised when the President of the Tenant board rang his doorbell minutes after they got up from the dinner table. He had felt a squeeze coming for a long time now. In the past months lesser Board Members had approached him, on numerous occasions, with 'concerns'. Though their concerns were covert questions and comments he heard the underlying warnings, "Get rid of the black kid. We don't want him hanging around the complex."

Abel bought into the complex for strategic reasons. His entire floor on the top of one of the newly renovated, secured tenement buildings offered a spectacular panoramic view, from the Jersey Shores, looking across the Hudson River, to the Brooklyn Bridge all lit up like a postcard at night, but the best view was looking over to Dominican Harlem on the opposite side of Broadway, The real barrio, where the Devil lived.

Like the Jews and Columbia University owned most of the property on the West side of Broadway, Abel, through a network of secret holdings, owned a large chunk of Dominican Harlem, known as The Hill. His business and The Hill was a match made in heaven. A boulevard where college students intermingled with drug dealers in it's many restaurants, theatres and clubs once the sun set and the Jinn's were let loose. Where money and drugs flowed like water from kids cramming for exams or just splurging on recreational drugs, and dealers flocked from every corner of the States to purchase weight from his complex of tenements.

Now he was being asked to give up this magnificent perch by the stout Jew standing outside his door. Of course Bernstein didn't have the guts to come right out and tell him why he was twisting the clamp. 'The Committee had come up with some serious violations concerning his references. The board had reviewed his application, done over six years ago, and found serious flaws in his banking records, also that he had once been investigated by the Feds for money laundering.' He was reminded that The Board had the authority to force a tenant to sell his or her unit at the slightest hint of misconduct. Abel reminded him, that six years prior, his banking records, credit ratings, references and life history had been scrutinized more thoroughly than a foreign translator seeking a job at the Pentagon, and they had found no fault. He also pointed out that he and the gentleman Ray Ray Carero were the only two ethnic's left in the complex and perhaps they were trying to cleanse the apartments. Of course Bernstein understood Abel's inference and promptly departed.

Vernicia gave Abel a look of concern when he came back in the apartment. He gestured a smile then headed down the hallway to the study where Daquan was waiting. Something was going on. Bernstein lived several buildings away and he never visited a tenant unless he was bearing bad news. Whatever it was, Abel would tell her soon enough. Still she felt it was about the boy.

* * * * *

Daquan stood at the window watching the sunset over the Jersey Shore.

"Nice view," Abel said softly, crossing the room and joining him. Daquan did not look up and the sadness he felt from the boy since he had arrived was still in his voice.

"Yea, but I like the bridge better. Specially at night."

"Yes, so do I, but this room is much more secure."

"Yea I know," Daquan said solemnly.

Abel liked the kid, he reminded him of himself when he was his age, loyal, tenacious, reliable, and most of all he had common sense, an attribute he had been hoping would rub off on Amilio. In many ways Abel and the boys life were parallel. Both had lost all family at a young age, both chose to take on adult responsibilities rather than take on handouts, both had dedicated their lives and efforts to another. He looked down on the kid then placed an arm over his shoulder. He knew what was bothering the kid. Abel had eyes and ears every place, there were few things he didn't know about those who worked for him. He even had things on Bernstein that he would use in the future.

"You want to talk about it?" he asked, as the orange in the sky began to dissolve into a dark blue.

"Yea, it's a goldmine Mister E-"

"Not that. We'll get to that later. I want to know what has you so down."

"Nothin."

"It has something to do with China doesn't it?" He waited for an answer, but Daquan stood there looking down on himself. Abel gave him a few minutes as the sky became completely dark and the sprinkling lights from the Shore lit up like stars in the night. "I've seen that look before, in fact when I wasn't much older than you I lost my virginity to a woman nearly twice my age."

Daquan looked up at him and there was a mixture of fire and sadness in his eyes, "How did you know Mister E?"

"Just a guess. You're a man and you treat China better than any man has ever treated her, there's bound to be an attraction. Besides she's a woman alone, she has urges, you're available-"

"She did it while I was sleep," he said angrily. "I ain't want my first time to be wit no crack head."

"Stop referring to her as a crack head," Abel said softly. "If you want to pull this off you have to begin thinking of her as the mother of your brother... Let me tell you something about people, women in particular. You get out of them what you put in. If you continue to live in her past then she will carry the past with her into the future. You have to let go of her past, visualize and treat her like the woman you want her to be in the future. Give her confidence in herself," he paused for a long second to give his words time to sink in, then continued. "As long as you refer to her as nothing more than a crack head she will always think of herself as nothing more than a crack head and she will never have the confidence to change."

"I know Mister E, but crack heads don't never change anyway."

"Well if you want to get your little brother in this school, you have better be trying everything you can to change this one. I've done what I can with the paperwork and references, but I don't care if your brother scores the highest in the nation he won't get past admissions without a convincing parent. He'll end up in a foster home at best."

"Yea I know," Daquan said dejectedly.

"OK, now tell me about this goldmine in the Bronx China told you about."

"She say that all the heads got to go through there to get to Hunts Point an ain't nobody claimed it yet."

"Have you checked it out for yourself?"

"Yea. Heads be coming through all day from all over."

Abel thought about it then turned his back to the window.

"I'm going to give you two shooters and some work," he told Daquan softly, holding him by both shoulders and looking him in the eye before continuing. "I'm going to leave you with a supplier, but you'll be on your own after that."

Thank you Mister E." Daquan suddenly felt a heaviness taking over his body.

Abel straightened and looked back to the Shores. "I'm just paying back a debt," he said to himself. "And I pray I won't be sending the boy to hell."

At the door of the study, he paused and gave Daquan the envelope containing the thousand dollars he paid the boy a week. It was the going rate for a local mule, and although it was Rachet who officially employed the boy, and whom the boy did the vast majority of carries for, Rachet only threw the boy fifty or a hundred dollars a week. That was another reason Abel had taken the boy under his wings. Abel despised people who took advantage of the weak or the needy.

No one knew of the secret relationship between Abel and the boy, and the boy was the only one, besides his partner, who knew Abel was still involved in the drug game, He hoped it wouldn't come back to haunt him.

"I won't be seeing you anymore," he told Daquan, as the boy stuffed the money in his backpack. He saw the boy almost go limp, and there were tears in his eyes when he looked up.

"Why Mister E? I did sum thin wrong?"

"You don't need me anymore. You're sharp enough to handle yourself from here on out." Abel reached down and hugged the boy and patted him on the back. "You take care... Son."

There were tears in Abel's eyes as he escorted the boy to the front door. He knew this day would eventually come, he just didn't think it would be this soon.

Abel was at his laptop computer making travel arrangements when Vernicia entered the master bedroom disrobing and heading directly to the bathroom, giving him a look before disappearing inside. Abel quickly closed the laptop and followed. Vernicia always made him forget about the bad things in life.

*   *   *   *   *

CHAPTER 7

THE SHOOTERS MISTER E gave him were barely older than he was but they had a reputation in the BX for puttin' that work in. In fact Daquan had heard of them as far as Brooklyn.

Scarecrow and Speedy. The best little shooters on the East coast. Plus they had their own little crew and all them niggaz was deadly and Daquan was certain that if Mister E had sent them they were loyal and could be trusted. The three of them stood in the short cut the head's took to get to the Point. Speedy, who was clearly the leader was surveying the area.

"This is perfect. We can see everybody coming from here. We can put Bear over there and Lite in that cut. We get the perfect cross fire."

"Yea. Niggaz gon' get a big surprise, they come through here on some ra ra shit," Scarecrow added.

"Yea and you know they will be coming. Soon as they find out this spot is bubbling." He turned to Daquan. "You got niggaz to cook an' sling?"

"I was gon' do it till I found some niggaz I could trust." Daquan told him.

"Naw. We got a crew for you. All you gotta do is supply the raw and pick up the gwuap," Scarecrow said.

"That's if it's O.K. with you Lil' Man. You the boss. We're just soldiers," Speedy said, quickly. "You call the shots."

"Yea that's good but I gotta know who they are first. I 'ont want 'em if I think I can't trust 'em."

"Don't worry," Scarecrow assured him. "Niggaz know what time it is."

"Look Lil' Man. We independents, we don't usually join no crews. It ain't safe and it ain't profitable. We just take on hits and keep it moving," Speedy told him, his eyes still darting around the area.

"Yea," Scarecrow talked right on top of him. "But you came 'highly' recommended. They say you might look like a lil nigga but you making moves from the top down."

"Bottom line is, the set that linked us use to work with my uncle... an' they the truth. They say fuck wit' you and treat you right, that's what we do. We follow orders."

"Yea. We independents in the street. But in the order we follow a chain of command." Speedy turned and gave Scarecrow a look that read; 'shut the fuck up! "Sometimes this nigga talks too fucking much," Speedy said, turning to Daquan.

Daquan hardly heard two words in the last sentence. He was so tired he nearly fell asleep standing up. "Snap out of it..." Daquan remembered his mother saying. "I know you tired and you don't wanna get up Daquan. But if you don't we won't have anything to eat tomorrow and you definitely won't have new clothes." Even as a kid Daquan liked the smell and texture of new clothing and his mother kept him and Naquan in something new and fresh everyday. So even if it was ten below and he had finally gotten comfortable under a ton of blankets, he would struggle awake and join his mother as a decoy on one of her deadly crusades.

* * * * *

Over the next few days Speedy selected a crew and instructed them to put little cut on the product and to distribute lots of free samples, so it wasn't long before he had heads coming from as far away as Manhattan to get A Chunk Of Heaven.

As for Daquan, he had learned well from Mister E. He was still hand's on, but even the crew working for Speedy didn't realize Daquan was the real boss. They thought he was just some kid Speedy had put on as a runner. So did everybody else, including the few times five-O stopped and hassled him they had no idea that underneath the dirty clothing in his knapsack was well over ten to twenty thousand dollars he left 'The Cut' with each day. They wouldn't know how to find a cheese in a paper bag unless they had a rat to tell them, and Daquan's mother had taught him how to keep rats at bay. You kept them happy and dependent, and his crew was happy. He gave them fifty cents on the dollar and every week he would give Speedy five thousand to take them shopping for sneakers and new gear so they could learn how to stack their own dough.

It wasn't long before word got back to Rachet though, about some lil' niggaz bubbling in the BX near the Point. He sent some heads up to see what it looked like. Sounded like easy money to him. They had seen Lil' Man up there running too. Which explained why he hadn't seen the lil' mutha-fucka in three weeks. Rachet was tempted to torture the lil' mutha-fucka, when he caught him, for nearly fucking up his plans for Petey Rodriquez. Luckily he had found another kid that Petey liked, cause right now Petey was in one of Rachet's safe houses while he waited for his wife to put together the ransom money. Lucky again because Petey drilled the boy a new asshole and Rachet had to feed the kid to the dogs to keep him from talking.

*   *   *   *   *

China rolled from the bed and nearly crawled to the bathroom after Mrs. Perno left. Her pussy was on fire but it wasn't from the krillz the old bitch brought her. It was from all the huge shit the bitch had been pushing up in her for the last three hours. Her pussy was burning so bad she couldn't even piss it stung so much. She ran hot water over a towel, wrapped it around her swollen lips, then sat on the edge of the toilet and cried.

She missed little 'Na and 'Quan so much that it hurt more than her battered pussy. She wanted to tell Quan how sorry she was and how she was trying her hardest to quit smoking crack. And how much she needed them in her life in order to change. Every time she got the urge to smoke, if the old bitch wasn't trying to get up in her coochie, she would sneak out the back way to the park and watch the kids play while remembering Naquan and how much he liked to play with his new friends. In fact one of the kids had asked about him the last time she was there.

"Where is Naquan Miss China. Is he sick?"

"No. He went on a trip with his father. He'll be back soon," she half lied and hoped in the same breath. It had been three weeks since Daquan stormed out of her room and she doubted she would ever see him again. "God please. I'll do anything," she sobbed.

China fell asleep on the edge of the toilet, with her head in her lap, and dreamed she was Naquan's biological mother and she was 'clean' and they lived with Daquan in a mansion with many rooms and a big shimmering blue pool in the shape of a seven surrounded by palm trees.

She woke up to the voice of Naquan calling her name and thought she was still in the dream. Until she heard his footsteps across the bedroom floor and then he was banging on the door.

"China China, It's me. Naquan. Daquan says I can live with you if you let me."

China couldn't get her robe on fast enough. She opened the door and dropped to her knees and hugged him so tight she almost took the air out of him.

"Please! May I live with you China? Please!"

She looked up at the shadow standing over her as if to ask his approval and hardly recognized Daquan. He had grown at least a foot in the few weeks since she had seen him and he looked much older, more like he was in his late teens.

"It's up to you," he said. "He ain't stopped crying for you since he left."

"Yes! Yes! Yes!" China said, smothering Naquan's face with kisses.

"You gonna be my mommy then?"

"Yes," China said, new tears streaming down her face-and I'm going to be a good mommy too," she looked up at Daquan. "I'm not going to do the things I use to do. I promise."

Twenty minutes later, two kids she had never seen around before were still carting bags and boxes up the staircase to her room, more clothes and shoes and sneakers than she had ever seen in her life and they were all designer stuff, top of the line. Makeup, Victoria Secrets, the latest perfumes, everything.

"Where did you get all this stuff Daquan? This had to cost a fortune."

"Yea it did," Daquan shrugged his shoulders. "But ain't nothing too good for my brother's mother. Besides. You gotta look rich if you gon' play rich."

"Wait until you see the TV. he got you," Naquan held up his forefinger and his thumb. " It's only this thick."

Daquan followed her into the bathroom as she took an outfit to try on. "I'm sorry I called you a crack head," he told her.

"I am a crack head," she responded. "I don't want to be but I am." She started to drop her robe but thought twice and pulled the dress on under it.

"You ain't gotta be You can be anything you believe you can be. If you keep believing you a crack head you gon' always be a crack head." He paused and helped her zip up the dress after she removed the robe. "I use to believe you was a crack head but I 'ont believe that no more." He stepped back to admire her in the dress. "You beautiful. I 'ont know nobody more beautiful than you, except my mom, an she's dead."

China didn't know how to react so she pulled her hair in a bun and examined herself in the mirror. She was still beautiful. Even after all the abuse of the last three years, That was if she didn't open her mouth.

"I found you a dentist up in the Bronx," he informed her, reading her thoughts and stopping them at the same time. "I ' ma have somebody come get you. It's next Thursday."

China looked back at him and for a split second all she could see was him standing there with that big hard beautiful dick rising to the ceiling and she was riding it. She shook it off. She had to stop thinking this sick shit.

"Damn Daquan. You making me feel like a queen."

"You are a queen," he said, giving her that sexy smile. "You just ain't caught up wit' yo'self yet."

Daquan leaned back on the counter and watched her as she pulled the Monolo's over her pretty toes. Damn she was sexy.

"Come here." It was a soft command but a command nevertheless. She walked to him and stood a foot away. "No. Closer." She took a step and he reached out and pulled her closer. Until she could feel him growing against her. "Damn! You so fuckin' sexy," he whispered in her ear. She felt safe in his arms and the nearness had her coochie burning and her sticky dripping.

He had grown so much. Even with her heels on she was now looking up into his eyes. Then he kissed her. First softly then with a hunger. And before she could get her dress up he had her on the counter and she could feel him all up in her stomach, thumping against her kidneys. And then the waves hit her, one after another. Each building in intensity, until she was coming in floods. And he didn't stop. He turned her around and hit it from the back-long and hard, until she was flooding again. Then he picked her up, her legs on his shoulders, her face in his chest and he found her G-spot until she was crying and wailing like a newborn. And she wanted more. She didn't ever want it to end. And while she was screaming for more at the top of her lungs, Naquan was calling her from the bedroom. Softly at first, then it got louder and louder.

"China! China! China!! You alright China?" And then he was rapping desperately on the door. She wanted to stop her orgasms, push Daquan off, but she couldn't. It was too late. Her floodgates were open and there was no shutting them down.

It wasn't until Mrs. Perno started banging on the door that China realized she was dreaming. When she stood the rag was soaked with icky.

"I'm O. K. Mama," China called out, gathering herself. She was still having after shocks and there was no way she was going to open the door for this black bitch to start digging in her pussy again. Even though she knew the door had to be locked, she checked it again.

"I'm O.K.. I'm O.K. I'll be out later."

"There's someone here to see you," Mrs. Perno called through the door.

"I said later!" China shouted back. She wasn't falling for that dumb shit.

"It's me China. Naquan," a tiny voice called out.

China had to throw cold water on her face and look at herself in the mirror to make sure she wasn't still dreaming. There were bags under her eyes and her hair was a mess.

"I'll be right out," she called back, busy trying to pull herself together. She didn't want either of them to see her like this, especially Daquan.

"I ran away. I'm never going back," Naquan explained to her as soon as she exited the bathroom. "I hate Daquan. I'm going to live here with you."

China began looking around for Daquan. Mrs. Perno gave China an expression while rocking her head in the negative.

"You can't live here with me Naquan. Where's your brother?"

"I don't know and I don't care. And I'm not going back," he said.

"You can't Naquan. Not without your brothers permission."

"I don't need him to tell me what to do. You could take care of me. You could be my mother," he said.

"Naquan I can't baby. I can't even take care of myself."

China let Naquan spend the night but she made him promise to let her take him home the next day. And she gave him her word that she would talk to Daquan about him staying with her. However she expressed her strong doubts about it.

*   *   *   *   *

CHAPTER 8

CHINA HAD SUNK TO her lowest of lows before Daquan stopped her on the street that day. But even at her lowest she never imagined that any human could live in conditions like this. In certain spots it smelled so bad she actually had to hold back her mornings breakfast.

"You actually live down here," she asked, astonished.

"Yes," Naquan answered in a sorrowful voice. "That's why I want to come live with you.

Despite the squalid conditions, China was impressed with Naquan's improved English. Each time he opened his mouth she felt a sense of accomplishment.

"So where do you sleep?"

"You'll see. As soon as Daquan gets here."

"And how long do you think that will be?

" China didn't have a watch but she estimated they had been in the tunnel system for well over an hour and at least twenty minutes of it had been spent sitting here in the dark, waiting. She lit her lighter again and held it up. "I can't believe Daquan would actually make you live down here."

"Daquan says it's safer than in the real world." China could hardly believe that, remembering how frightened she was when Naquan pushed her into a crawl space when he heard voices coming in their direction.

"Be real quiet and don't move," he instructed her. If she was scared, he seemed terrified. She held her breath as three homeless men passed inches from their hiding place.

"They eat people," Naquan whispered after their voices faded into the darkness.

"What do you mean, they eat people?" China asked.

"They eat people while they're still alive-"

"I'm sure they are bad men, Naquan. But people don't eat people," she assured him. "Not in the civilized world they don't."

"Yes they do," he insisted. "Daquan told me, then I saw them myself one time."

"You saw.. those.. those three.. men eat a person?"

"Yes! Two men were holding her down and another man was between her legs and he was eating her. It must have hurt real bad because she started cursing and screaming. That's when I ran. Daquan told me they eat kids too."

China chuckled.

"Why are you laughing? You don't believe me?"

"Yes I believe you Naquan." How could she begin to explain what really happened to a five year old. Still it was evident from his story that the men had more than likely forced the woman and she made up her mind right then and there, that no matter what Daquan, or that old freaky bitch Mrs. Perno said, Naquan was coming back with her. Even if Mrs. Perno kicked her out, living in abandoned buildings would be better than this.

"I love you China," Naquan said, cuddling up to her.

"I love you too, Naquan."

As they waited, China drifted off into another one of her crazy dreams.

Daquan's anger woke her so suddenly she couldn't even remember fragments of her dream. She just knew it wasn't sexual thank God.

"What I tell you? Huh, huh?" Daquan's voice rang out from the darkness. "You don't bring nobody down here. Nobody! You don't let nobody know where you live!"

It was pitch black and his voice echoed off the tunnel walls. She lit her lighter and held it up, still she couldn't see where they were. Until .. Daquan stepped out of the darkness like a ghost and stood there staring at her.

"I ain't living here no more." Naquan cried out from the void. "I'm going to live with China. I don't care what you say. You still ain't my real daddy."

"Take off yo' shoes when you go in," Daquan instructed her as he spun the dial on a combination lock. "An' don't touch nuthin' till you wash up."

"Oh he is so adorable," China commented on the snow white pit-bull as she removed her sneakers. There was only a dim red light over the doorway and except for the dog, China could hardly see anything in the pitch black.

Naquan darted into the darkness and seconds later a light flicked on across from her. China could hardly believe what she was seeing. It was nothing like what she envisioned. In fact she was no longer in the subway tunnels, She was in some loft in lower Manhattan, Some futuristic room straight out of an apartment magazine.

"Come on China," Naquan called out. "We have to wash up and change clothes."

She crossed to him with her head turning in every direction. The dozens of oriental carpets covering the floor brought back memories of her childhood in China. They felt luxuriant beneath her feet and she knew they were the real things. Everything else was white and ultra modern.

The bathroom was the only thing that reminded her she was in a room in the subway tunnels. Not that he hadn't attempted to decorate it, but it was the size of a broom closet with only a toilet, a hand sink, and a slop tub converted into a make shift shower. It had the same layout as all the other subway bathrooms she sometimes snuck into. There were plenty of towels though, a stack as tall as her of nice fluffy ones. And there was a really nice mirror over the sink. Naquan gave her a washcloth and soap and Daquan brought her a brand new burgundy sweat suit that still had the tags on it.

China took her time washing the soot from the tunnels away. She was actually afraid to be left alone with Daquan, knowing that once she left the bathroom, Naquan would enter and it would just be her and Ouan in the room. She would have to face him sooner or later. She brushed her hair back in a bun and twisted it into one long braid that fell down her back while watching herself in the mirror. She was a little frightened girl trapped in a grown woman's body and Quan was a grown ass man trapped it the body of a kid. Life was not fair.

On her way out she whispered to Naquan as they passed, "Make it quick!"

"I can't," he said with a frown. "I have to wash my clothes, brush my teeth and take a bath." He closed the door behind him and the room she had re-entered suddenly got real small.

Daquan stood across the room with his arms folded, staring at her. He had grown and in the subdued lighting he looked much older. She couldn't believe how tall he had gotten, a half a head taller than her. Which, when she thought about it, wasn't all that tall. Her midget ass only stood four foot ten in her New Balance, an inch shorter than Lil Kim. But there was something else different about him, something that both frightened and excited her at the same time. Something she felt guilty about feeling herself, a reflection of her own emotions. She adverted his glare. It was just wishful thinking she told herself, A sick thought she had to suppress.

While he stared, she looked nervously around the room, this time taking in all the details.

Futuristic lamps were everywhere, filling the room with a soft romantic glow. One spilled down a pristine white wall, from which two twin beds jutted out, another illuminated a bookcase of Plexiglas cubes displaying an exquisite collection of model exotic cars rising from behind the far bed. It was framed by a wall of posters of the same hundred thousand dollar cars from car shows. An incandescent blue halo glowed behind a small flat screen television rising from the carpets on sleek aluminum pedestals.

On the farthest wall, from corner to corner, zip up plastic storage bags filled with neatly folded clothing were stacked like a clothing store display on long wooden boards resting on gray cinder blocks. The only thing remotely out of place was the makeshift desk where Naquan had flopped his laptop computer down.

China was the first to break the silence. Covering her mouth as she turned to look at him she asked, "You did all this yourself?"

"No my Mom." There was pride in his voice. "Why, you like it?"

"It's very nice but why would-"

"We ain't really live here," Daquan cut her off. "You shoulda seen our real apartment. We just came here to hide."

"To hide?" She looked around again, puzzled. "From what?"

"It ain't important," Daquan said pointedly as if catching himself before revealing a secret. She didn't press.

He crossed to the bed and sat near the wall then motioned for her, issuing a command she had heard repeatedly in her dream.

"Come over here."

She was stuck on stupid. She couldn't believe the overwhelming attraction she had for this little nigga but she knew it wasn't right. She looked away and didn't move.

"Come here. I don't want Naquan to hear."

She hesitated then sat on the far edge like a shy schoolgirl. He patted a spot right next to him until she slid over, her hand still covering her ragged teeth, until she could feel the warmth of his skin and the smell of his body chemistry. Her own chemistry rose. She closed her eyes and took a deep breath, pulling him into her emptiness.

He gently removed her hand from her mouth and turned her face towards him, his touch sending shivers through her body.

"Open your eyes," he whispered. "You don't have to be afraid."

When She opened them, she tried to look back at the bathroom door where she could hear Naquan splashing water around. He held her face firmly, looking deep into her eyes, his lips just inches from hers.

Oh God. Please don't, she silently pleaded. If he does you know I can't resist. Her body was aching for him. He didn't kiss her. He just stared through her slant eyes, deep into her soul until he finally whispered;

"I want Naquan to go live with you. Mister E was right. You and him was meant for each other."

Just like I was meant for you, she thought, and she could no longer hold back what had been building inside her since she sat down.

China buried her face in the nape of Daquan's neck and let her tears flow silently down the front of his shirt. He put his arms around her and held her firmly. This was where she belonged. Even before she left China and came to America to live with her father, this was the family she had been dreaming of.

"You want him to come live wit' you," he asked once her sobbing had subsided.

"No," she lied into his chest. "I'm a crack head Daquan. I can't take care of Naquan. He doesn't need to be around a crack head like me. He's too smart. He has a future. I don't."

"You ain't no crack head China," he comforted her.

"Yes I am," she sobbed. "I'm a crack head. I'm a nymphomaniac, and I'm sick."

Daquan raised her head and forced her to look at him. "Look at me China. I ain't old but I know a crack head when I see one, and you ain't no crack head. Rachet got you thinking that stupid shit. You ain't no crack head. You just smoke crack."

"There is no difference Daquan. If you smoke crack you're a crack head. It's just that simple."

"No it ain't. Look at that laptop computer over there. Yo know how much that shit cost? You think if you was a real crack head you or that computer would still be down here. Hell no! A crack head would-a been sold that shit and right now you would be smackin' yo lips and seeing what else you could sell outta his backpack."

"Why all of a sudden I'm not a crack head Daquan? I was a crack head when you left me."

"I use to think you was a crack head until Mister E explained it to me..."

"Who's Mister E?"

"That ain't important. He says you beautiful an' you smart an' you ain't gotta be no crack head. You can be anything you wanna be..."

"I bet he's a crack head."

No," Daquan said calmly. "He's a billionaire and he don't even smoke cigarettes. He's a family man. He says family is everything. If he had to choose between his family an his money he would give every dollar away."

"I wouldn't," China said. "Fuck Family! Family is highly overrated. They never did shit for me."

Daquan held her by the chin and looked her firmly in the eye. "You ain't never had the right family then."

He was right. Every family she ever had had sooner or later disowned her, and she had always given them her all. She wasn't willing to take that chance ever again.

"I gotta go Daquan," she said, rising and wiping the tears away. "I'm not who ever it is you think I am. I'm just a fucking crack head. Nothing more, nothing less."

Daquan pulled her back, "No. You ain't gon' never be more than who 'you' think you are. What I think ain't important."

"Whatever! I gotta go," she said, pulling away.

* * * * *

On the train ride back Uptown, China kept thinking about this mysterious Mister E and how he was obviously orchestrating not only Quan and Naquan's lives but also her own as well.

Before Naquan finished bathing Quan had explained to her that his original plan was only for her to teach Naquan and get his academics to test level. He had another woman who would act as his mother for enrollment. Evidently he had gone back and told this Mister E every little single detail about her. Everything! Quan told her that when Mister E learned how much Naquan loved her and how much they looked like mother and son when they were together, Mister E began trying to persuade Quan that she was the better choice. "If they love each other, who wouldn't believe that bond?" Quan quoted him as saying. But Quan was not convinced that she loved his brother equally or that she would be able to pull it off, or if she even wanted to play his mother. It was then that she broke down and confessed about the son she lost who would have been exactly Naquan's age if he had lived. And how often she thought that God had sent Naquan into her life to replace him, and how these last three weeks without him were more painful than her attempts at withdrawing from her addiction.

Then Quan confessed that he had stood in the darkness watching and listening to her and his little brother for over an hour and she reminded him so much of how his mother use to be with him. He knew then that neither of them would ever be happy without the other.

"You can still smoke crack," he told her, "but you ain't never gon' be no crack head. I swear on my dead mother. I'll make sure you live real good an' you ain't gon' never have to work or do nuthin long as you be Naquan's mother."

Real convincing coming from a nine year old, but then when she thought about it, he had been taking care of all her needs for the past few months. And she hadn't needed for anything, except him and Naquan, after he left. Even though he was pissed at her he still left money for food and rent on the counter before he stormed out, and enough krillz for her to smoke herself to death, which she nearly did before she flushed the rest of it down the toilet and went cold turkey.

China was so deep in her thoughts that if it weren't for Quan she would have missed the 138th and Broadway stop for sure. She was still in them as they climbed the stairs to sunlight.

"I'm ten now," Quan told her, finally breaking her trance as he took her from store to store on the boulevard buying her everything she would need, from toothpaste to underwear she would probably never put on. "My mom told me I was a man when I was five. But I ain't never feel like it 'til now." He was definitely more of a man than most men she had known. In fact every man she had ever known. Her father included… Especially her father.

"Sometimes I feel like you're my man," she took the chance of saying. He just looked at her, then handed her the bag with the sundresses, and asked her if she could carry all the bags by herself. He had someplace to go and he was already late. Then he reminded her once more that Naquan couldn't stay with her until the new apartment was finished and all the paper work came through.

Daquan was just about to hand her some money when a brand new Chrysler 300M, all rimmed out, pulled to the curb with a screeching halt. Daquan's hands went instinctively to his pockets. China looked up and kept walking, rolling her eyes and pursing her lips. The car pulled right up on the sidewalk and cut her off.

"Where you going China Doll?" the man in the passenger seat asked. Daquan was about to answer for her when China cut him off.

"Aren't you a little out of your territory Sergeant Denareo. Shouldn't you be downtown fleecing some hookers?"

"Still with the jokes huh? Where you been. I ain't seen you around in a couple of months. Look like you cleaned up your act though. In fact you looking kinda delicious."

"Yeah? You wanna eat me?"

"I ain't say all that. Aren't you a little bit out of your environment though? This is weight capital. You want krillz you gotta go down the Hill."

"I don't smoke crack anymore, I'm clean."

Denareo looked past China to see the kid staring at him with fire in his eyes. He gave him a quick once over. Crispy cut, neatly dressed-some real fly expensive shit- no jewelry and a backpack, about fourteen or fifteen. Probably a little hooky for some nooky. Kid looked like he came from money

"Who's the kid?"

"He's my cousin," China said defensively.

Denareo ran his hand unconsciously across the thick keloid scar running from his ear, across his throat and into his open neck shirt. "I thought you didn't have family."

"I lied. Now can I go? I have things to do."

The kid was making Denareo uncomfortable the way he kept staring at his scar then back into his eyes with a hatred. Like he had done something to the kid before.

"You look familiar." Usually Denareo threw that line out to read the reaction. This kids eyes didn't move up or down or side to side. There was nothing to read in them besides hatred. There was definitely no fear registered in them. "Where you from?"

The kid didn't answer, just continued his piercing stare.

"You heard me you little mutha-fucka. I asked you where you're from!" Still the kid didn't answer, so Denareo flipped out his gold badge and held it out the window. "You wanna go to jail?"

Daquan finally spoke. "For what?"

"Boosting for starters," he said, looking at all the bags China was holding. "Looks like the two of you got an early start."

"I didn't steal shit! I paid for everything in these bags and I can prove it." China reached in her purse and pulled out all the receipts and showed them to him. He took them from her hand, looked at them then stuck them down the front of his pants.

"I didn't see any receipts. You saw some receipts?" he turned and asked his partner. His partner nodded and shrugged like he had seen nothing. "Oh did I forget to tell you I made lead detective, but nothing's changed. Now get in the car bitch. You know how this goes. Whenever I see you I want half… And I told my partner how pretty that pussy is. But he doesn't believe me. He wants to see for himself."

Daquan stepped forward. China grabbed him and pulled him back. "It's O.K. Daquan. I got this. You just tell uncle Fred I couldn't come, I had a job interview or something." She opened the back door, threw the bags inside and got in. She didn't look back at Daquan.

The kid was staring hard at Denareo's scar. Like he knew something about it.

"You like this shit huh?" Denareo asked, tilting his head to display the scar proudly. "The bitch that gave me this they found her in so many strips she looked like a barrel of Beef Jerky."

The car backed off the sidewalk. And as they sped away, Denareo was thinking he knew that kid. He just couldn't remember from where. It would come to him sooner or later though. It always did.

CHAPTER 9
EL DIABLO

OLD MAN DIABLO TOOK a three hundred dollar cigar from the humidor and went through the careful ritual of preparing it, looking up from time to time at the black kid seated opposite him.

"So who are you loyal to," he asked, lighting the cigar with a bejeweled lighter personally given to him by a famous icon in the music world for a few rocks of cocaine. It was shameful what drugs could do to a person's life if a person fell on the wrong side of them. Fortunately for Diablo he had fallen on the right side, and as far as he could see so had the kid. Diablo had gotten word from over seas that what ever the kid wanted, the kid got.

"I'm loyal to my word," the kid said. "That's all I got that's worth keeping. Everything else gon' come an' go."

It wasn't a practiced response. Old man Diablo knew the kid felt every word. Still he pressed him, the odor of the cigar like the scent of heaven to his struggling soul.

"If you were forced to take sides between Rachet and his Murder One crew and EI Diablo, which side would you fall on?"

"I ain't no snitch if that's what you asking," Daquan said easily. "I 'ont like a lot of what Rachet do but I 'ont run 'round talking 'bout it."

Diablo didn't like what Rachet was doing either. Rachet and his Murder One Crew were bringing too much heat and making a bad name for the game. The black bastard had no morals, no principles, and no respect for family or rules. In fact he was intimidating all the Families, extortion's, kidnappings, tortures, murder. You name it Rachet and his lowlifes were involved in it. The problem was, the Rachet family was so large they had the entire Harlem on lock. From 145th to 110th, everyone feared their ruthlessness. He knew that Rachet was behind the latest kidnapping of Petey Rodriquez and he also knew that it wouldn't be long before Rachet was trying to snatch him up. If Petey was worth 100 thousand, Old Man Diablo's family would be willing to pay millions to get him back. But Rachet had to understand that would mean war and that hundred's of lives would be lost in the aftermath. He might have Harlem on lock but Diablo was globally strong. The only thing saving him now was that overseas couldn't see a drug war as being anything but counter productive. He had to do something about Rachet though. Some way he had to be contained. Somehow. Diablo's instincts told him the kid was key to his solution. He pushed an envelope towards the boy,

"A hundred thousand cash."

*   *   *   *   *

Detective Denareo was surprised as hell to see the kid he had seen with China a day earlier coming out of Old man Diablo's office. The black kid noticed him right away and gave him a look of pure evil. 'Who the hell is this kid ?' He was thinking as one of Diablo's bodyguards patted the boy affectionately on the shoulder and escorted him to a side door.

Denareo was deep in thought when a lovely Dominican girl with nice legs and a pretty smile crossed over.

"Senior Diablo will see you now," she said, her eyes and smile lingering a bit too long. She had to be no older than nineteen and Denareo would bet a months pay check the fat mutha-fucka Diablo was eating her pussy every chance he got. At the office door he winked at her and resisted the temptation to grab her firm ass. She clicked away, her hips sending him a message that he could hit it if he wanted.

It wasn't the office girl on his mind as he entered the dark paneled office smelling of sweet Cubana cigars, it was the black kid with the spooky eyes. Where did he know him from? The kid had become like an irritating word on the tip of your tongue that you knew but couldn't quite remember.

"Como estas?" The old man greeted him warmly in their native tongue, extending his hand.

"Vien y tu?"

They shook hands like old friends but there had never been any love lost between them. He thought the old man was a fool and the old man thought he was crass. However they both respected the boundaries that had been drawn and were also bonded by the somewhat weak adhesiveness of the Dominican flag.

"Please. Please." Diablo motioned him to a leather lounge chair in front of a large ornate desk. It was Denareo's first visit to this office and it looked remarkably like the Presidents White House suite. Instead of the Presidential Seals and the view of the Washington Memorial, the Dominican flags stood on flagstaffs and the windows overlooked Washington Heights. The fat fuck even had the Dominican Seal on the floor.

Diablo was at a small bar in the far corner of the room preparing to pour drinks. "How is your father?" Diablo asked, then not waiting for an answer, continued, "If I remember correctly you like your drinks dark."

Denareo didn't bother to respond to either question. The old man crossed and handed him a full glass of rum with ice cubes in the shape of naked women then sat on the corner of the antique desk facing him. "It's been a while," Diablo said, raising his glass to the ceiling. "And by the way congratulations." He swirled the drink and sniffed instead of drinking. "Welcome back to the neighborhood."

"It's just a stepping stone," Denareo answered without feeling. "Politics is where the real money is." He took another swig and looked around the room.

"So what can I do for you," Diablo asked, thinking God protect the President if Denareo got anywhere near the White House.

Something across the room caught Denareo's eye. He rose and crossed to a bookcase filled with memorabilia and studied the photograph in a silver frame of a little league baseball team.

"That's Don Silva's boy Tony. Ralph's kids, Jeminez and Julio from 158th-" He walked back still studying the photograph. "That's funny. All these kids are from the Hill except one. This black kid number seven."

"Oh! Daquan. He's our star short stop-"

"Where's he from?" Denareo asked abruptly.

"Around," Diablo said, his beady eyes turning into slits. "He comes from a very respectful family," he added defensively. The piece of shit hadn't been in his office more than two minutes and already he was annoying the shit out of him.

"And who would that be," Denareo asked, staring him in the eye.

Diablo blinked nervously and shuffled some papers on his desk. "Is that why you're here, to ask me about some damn kid who's a model to this community?"

Denareo grinned. He had touched a nerve. The kid wasn't ordinary. He was important. But to who? And why?

"The kid must be important to be such a model citizen."

"A lot more important than you are at the moment." Diablo grinned back. "And for the record he's hands off."

Diablo paused, gave Denareo a hard look, swirled the lady's around in his glass and sniffed. What was this bastard here for? Didn't he realize he was stepping on his father's turf.

Denareo traced his scar affectionately with slender manicured fingers down his neck to his crispy white shirt and adjusted his tie. He half grinned half smirked at Diablo. "Since when did you become a nigga lover Senior Diablo," he asked, standing and practically breathing down Diablo's neck. Diablo straightened, rose from the edge of the desk and circled around to his chair to put some space between them. The idiot had no tact. No sense of respect. He was a loose cannon. Always had been.

Denareo chuckled. The vice was tightening.

"Is this official police business?" Diablo asked, puffing his cigar now to curb his anger as he slid into the luxurious leather. "Or did you come here to stick your hands in my pockets."

"A little of both." Denareo said, doubling back for the drink and gulping it down before continuing."You have some thing I need and vice versa." He paused and looked around the office. "Something that might help me afford a place like this."

Whatever Denareo had, he was building and it was big. "Get to the point," Diablo demanded, his left thumb paused over the panic button under the desk

"You know word on the street is Petey Rodriquez got snatched a couple days ago by some Harlem cats and- "

Diablo cut him off. "And you think I had something to do with it?"

"Maybe!" Denareo gave him a long penetrating stare. "You did know Petey had gone into film making before the niggers snatched his dumb ass?"

Diablo's bushy gray eyebrows went ·up. "Oh really? Don't tell me its porno's. And he's suppose to be such a family man."

Denareo thought for a long, hard exaggerated minute. "I think I remember a few scenes with strippers, but what I mostly remember are the drug transactions, the murder contracts and money transactions.

Diablo gave Denareo a blank quizzed look, like he didn't know what the fuck he was talking about, but the old man didn't have a lead veneer like the black kid. He was as transparent as the glass he was holding.

"So why would I be interested in this.. this film," Diablo asked swirling the ladies around again, still without taking a sip.

" It's a basic plot but I thought you might be interested. The principles characters are these two figurehead mob bosses who cook the cartel books and kill anyone who might be able to turn that information over to the real bosses. It's got lots of dates and times and names in it, lots of actual documentary footage, all the elements a great picture needs-greed, deception, murder, more greed, large shipments of drugs that disappear, more greed. You get the picture."

Old Man Diablo's forehead had already begun to bead with sweat.

"So you're telling me that Petey Rodriquez made a film." Diablo asked, finally taking a long swig from his glass. "And?"

"Just thought you might be interested in owning it."

"Depends."

"On?"

"How complete it is and the price of admission." Diablo knew Denareo was holding a heavy hammer when he walked through the door. Fucking Petey Rodriquez, a goddamn snitch.

"It's complete. Not a frame missing." Denareo assured him. Probably the only good thing about Denareo was that he didn't bluff and he didn't lie when it came to shaking you down.

Diablo rose and walked to the window, turning his back on the detective, looking out past Broadway to Riverside, silently reprimanding himself for letting his greed consume his better judgment about jumping in bed with the likes of Petey Rodriquez.

"Who's the executive director?"

"God himself."

Godilla didn't touch a case himself unless it was absolutely airtight. That meant Petey had to be working with the DA's office for a while. "So you have a preview?"

Denareo reached into his back pocket, retrieved a flash drive and slid it across the desk. The files on the flash drive said it all. Petey Rodriquez had turned out to be a real fucking rat bastard.

"How much?" Diablo asked dejectedly.

"A hundred thou to start the bidding That's just for the flash drive."

Diablo clipped his cigar carefully. "There's nothing left for an indictment? You're absolutely positive?"

"Absolutely. Guaranteed irretrievable. Even God couldn't bring this shit back."

"For every thing?"

"Ten-to Fifty mill somewhere in that range. I'm just brokering." Denareo watched the fat man's reaction. It was like someone had just shot him in the heart with a fifty cal. Denareo raised one eyebrow and resisted a grin.

"Ten mil! I don't have that kind of money." Diablo protested.

"Who are you kidding," Denareo said, looking around the office as Old Man "Diablo rose and made his way back to the window. "This office alone must have set you back a mill. I bet everything in it is bomb and bullet proof."

This was true, but all the bullet proofing in the world wouldn't save him from the cartel if this shit went to court. They would strip his flesh off and hire special medical staff to keep him alive so that they could torture him forever if they found out how much money he and Petey had been skimming from them. Fifty million was like candy money compared to what they had stolen .

"Not personal. I couldn't even come up with that kind of cash if I sold everything."

"Stop the bullshit Diablo," Denareo said. "I don't have time for it. And since you feel the necessity to lie to me, the price of admission just went up to the high end."

Diablo winched. "I really don't have that kinda of cash of my own. I might be able to piece together ten, but fifty is out of the question."

"Denareo walked back to the desk and picked up the photo of the black kid. "I'll give you six hours and since we're family I'll meet you halfway, but after that it's a bidders market. And remember Fat Man, God don't like ugly." He turned to leave, the photo in his hand, then stopped. "You don't mind if I borrow this do you? I'm kinda taking an interest in this nigreto."

*   *   *   *   *

CHAPTER 10

GLORIA RODRIQUEZ HAD BARELY replaced the phone in its cradle before it was ringing again. Her heart raced, as it had done every time the phone rang for the past five days. He never gave her a time that he would call just a computerized voice giving her instructions and warning her to remain by the phone.

She hesitated, looking over her shoulder at the bright red carrying bag on the bed, then at the wedding band she clasped tightly in her sweaty palm, and burst into tears. She crossed her heart and mumbled a quick verse to the Virgin Mary, then grabbed for the receiver.

"Yes," she said anxiously. It wasn't him. It was Mami

"Where is Petey?" Mami demanded without as much as a hello, a 'how are you Gloria?'. "He's on his way to see you Mami," she reminded her.

"Don't give me that bullshit," she practically shouted, switching over to rapid fire Spanish. "He would have called me himself if he were coming. I might be old but I know a lie when I hear one." She was clearly angry. "It doesn't take five days to drive from New York to Miami-"

"I swear to Saint Mary," Gloria lied again, crossing her heart and reciting a silent pardoner.

"Bullshit Gloria. You have never been a good liar."

"1 swear."'

"Don't swear," she cut her off. "You already have one foot in the hellfire, you don't want to put the other one in." There was a long silence with neither woman speaking then Mami came back, softer.

"Do you need money? I could mortgage the house and I've already scraped together seventy five thousand in cash..."

"Mami!! Nothing has happened to Petey..."

"Did I say something has happened to Petey? Are you..."

"No but I know how much you worry about Pete Mami."

"..afraid to tell me something Gloria, because I've been hearing things," Mami talked over what Gloria was saying.

On CNN, footage of the storm that was still ravaging North and South Carolina with severe flooding and power outages caught Gloria's attention.

"Mami, Pete didn't want you to worry," she said, watching the news piece intently. "He got caught up in that storm in North Carolina, but he's OK. I just talked to him an hour ago when he finally got to a phone that worked but it went out again. I'm sure he'll call you as soon as the phones are back on."

"I don't believe a word you're saying. My baby's in trouble, I can feel it. Mothers can always feel when their babies are in trouble." The other line buzzed, just as Mami was saying; "Don't think that I don't have ears in New York Gloria. Do you hear me? People are talking and they are concerned. He didn't tell anyone about this so-called trip you're telling me about, and that's not like Petey at all. Petey would never take a trip without calling to let me know he was coming"

"Mami I have to go. This might be Pete on the other line. I'll call you back." She hung up without waiting for a response.

It was The Voice. The words were choppy, like they came from a computer. "Stay by the door and follow all the instructions to the letter." She listened for more but after a long beep she got nothing but a dial tone. Was someone coming to whisper instructions to her through the door? That would be stupid. Well at least the door wouldn't be as busy as the phone, she thought. Everyone, including Pete's Mom had been calling nonstop for the past few days about Pete's whereabouts. But no one dared to come to their door. They all knew it was forbidden to visit Pete's wife when Pete wasn't at home. And if they did come they knew she would never answer.

One thing she was thankful for, she had the foresight to send the boys to Columbia to live with her parents six months ago. There was no way she was able to lie to them the way she lied to Pete's mother. She took the chance of taking the phone off the receiver before pulling a chair up by the front door. She knew her caller well enough now to know that if he wanted her to remain by the phone he would have reminded her. No! Whatever the next step was, it would be coming through her front door.

She had been sitting there for thirty-five minutes when she got a thought and her heart started pounding. She jumped up and raced to the bedroom, grabbed the bag with the six hundred thousand dollars and put it back in its original hiding place. Not a minute too soon!

The doorbell rang and her heart started pumping like it was going to jump out of her skin. She did her best to pull herself together and crept silently to the door. The Security camera showed a White man in a brown uniform carrying a small box and a clip pad. UPS. But she wasn't expecting any packages and Pete never had anything delivered to the apartment. She was about to turn him away when she realized, this was the messenger. She hurriedly buzzed him in and signed the electronic pad.

Gloria hadn't taken half dozen steps away from the door after locking it behind the UPS man, before a musical chime began emitting from the package. She nearly dropped it in shock before realizing it was not a bomb but a cellular phone. She ripped the box open to find the phone and two silver disks labeled ONE and XXX. She flipped the phone open while studying the disk. "Yes?" she answered.

"At seven forty five," the voice instructed. "You will get on the Long Island Expressway and head towards exit twenty six. If we see any police activity in a miles distance or in the sky, you can keep the money and the next box you receive will have your husband's head in it. Oh! I thought you might enjoy the DVD's. They're encrypted so you won't be able to play them until after the exchange, we'll give you the codes then, but I assure you he's alive and that he will stay that way as long as you don't fuck up. Keep the phone. I'll be talking to you later on."

* * * * *

Rachet slid the mobile phone out of the voice modulator, opened it, removed the chip and tossed it into a bucket of water.

"Take Petey and move him to the Island," he turned and told Jumm as he placed another chip in the phone. It lit up and his fingers flew over the keypad. "Take this number and call me if you have any problems." He held up the phone for Jumm to memorize it off the information screen. "Got it?"

"Yea! What about Pitt," Jumm asked, knowing that Rachet knew what he was asking.

"What about him?" Rachet gave him a look. "He made the snatch, he's in. You just make sure there' no problems. Understand!"

What problems could Jumm possibly have. Having Pitt around Petey was like leaving a magnifying glass in a dry California forest in the middle of a Santa Anna.

* * * * *

Detective Denareo and his partner sat in an unmarked sedan outside the Everwood apartment complex watching the gold Cadillac convertible parked in the space marked C-347.

The space and the car belonged to Gloria Rodriquez and he was certain that she would soon get in that car with a bag filled with money to make the exchange for her husband. It was going to happen today. He could feel it in his gut. And his gut never lied. He looked over at his partner who was deep in thought. Denareo was in deep contemplation also. He was weighing the difference between just flat out robbing Petey's wife against the promotions and publicity that would come from busting a drug kingpin for kidnapping and extortion. He also took into consideration that he had had a very good week. Petey had already netted him a considerable sum and his other enterprises were equally lucrative, but Denareo had bigger plans and he needed as much money as he could get his hands on. Your pockets had to be really deep to run a political campaign against the established machine.

'Still thinking about how good that pussy was, huh?" Denareo broke the silence with a crooked smile that women always told him was 'sexy'.

Ralph looked up as if he were coming out of a trance. ""Not really, But now that you mention it."

Denareo chuckled. "I told you she was good."

"Good? I need to take her home and let her train my wife. I didn't know a vagina could get so big and still have so much muscle control. Her pussy was so good I was tempted to take my condom off and go raw."

Denareo looked down at his partners lap and grinned to himself. His partner was getting a hard-on just thinking about the first half Black and Chinese pussy he had ever gotten.

"First time I ever got a blow job with some pussy lips," the big man in the drivers seat continued. "Damn!" He instinctively reached down and touched himself.

"Why don't you try a threesome. I could arrange it."

"What are you crazy? Serafina would never go for that. I'd be out on my ass as soon as the words came off my lips."

"You'd be surprised at what you get when you just ask."

"No way! I know my wife."

Secretly Denareo knew his wife also and he knew that after three kids he couldn't even feel the walls of her vagina when he hit it, but her asshole was as tight as China's pussy and she came so much when he pounded it out that she dripped puddles of cum on Ralphs kitchen floor.

"You'd be surprised at what women will do with a little nudging."

"My wife is straight laced, Church, PTA, and home. I can't even get her to watch a porn movie. Straight missionary and that's it. We married young and I'm the only man she's ever been with," His partner said, straightening up and adjusting the rear view mirror.

"Maybe she wants to make a porno, not watch one," Denareo said straight faced, remembering how he punished her by punch fisting her pussy violently after he discovered the small video camera she had hidden between a stack of towels and her contorted confessions as her head banged against the bathroom mirror. "You trying to blackmail me bitch?" he had shouted, wrapping his hand around her long black hair and beating the inside of her pussy like he was beating a man.

"No! No! Oh Yes! No! I just.. always.. wanted.. to see myself on video. I'm sorry.. I should have asked. Oh Jesus… Oh Jesus.. Oh Jesus!"

"Damn right you should have asked, and leave Jesus out of it. I'm your God now bitch!"

Denareo flipped out his cell phone and leaned against the window to dial a number. As it rang he reached over and turned on the radio to a 'Lite' station. "How many women do you have?" his partner asked, turning the music down a little.

"You can never have too many," Denareo smiled, then clutched the phone tightly to his ear. "Damn! I cant' stop thinking about that fat ass and that wet pussy," he whispered seductively into the phone. He grinned and looked at his partner. "Who did you think it was? Your nerdy husband?" Ralph started to say something but Denareo put a finger up to his lips. "Yea! So? What if he is?" Denareo was looking his partner in the eye as he spoke. "Husbands are so stupid. They never know when their wives are cheating. Anyway set up the camera. I'll be over tonight." He clicked the phone shut. "If more criminals were like married bitches, we'd be out of a job."

An hour later Gloria Rodriquez stepped out of her condo carrying a bright red bag and threw it in the front seat of her convertible before pulling out of the parking lot. They waited a beat then trailed at a comfortable distance.

* * * * *

Jumm could feel it as soon as he got through the first security check in the safe house off Park. It was the smell in the air, shit and blood. His step quickened and… Sure enough…There was Petey Rodriquez tied to a kitchen chair in the middle of the interrogation room, slumped over and lifeless, bullet holes in his head and half his back blown out.

Great met him as soon as he stepped through the door. "I couldn't stop him," he said, almost as a plea. "I told Rachet not to leave Pitt up here-"

"He left you in charge," Jumm said. "You were suppose to…"

"I couldn't do shit!" Great protested in his own defense. "Pitt just kept staring at the mutha-fucka, just like he's staring at the wall now, and then he got up like he was coming over to grab another forty and just started slugging the nigga. Shit happened so fast I didn't even see him pullout."

"Fuck!! You couldn't stop him?" He looked over at Pitt sitting on a milk crate facing the wall like a kid being punished by his teacher. 'Sit in the corner and don't you dare move a muscle! '

"Even if I would-a shot Pitt it wouldn't have saved this mutha-fucka. First shot pushed his wig back."

Pitt came to life and rose from the crate, his glock still clutched tightly in his hand. He turned his head slowly and blinked his eyes into focus. "You lying on me bitch?"

Jumm looked at him like he was the dumbest nigga on earth. Great automatically put his hand on his nine and slid the safety off then crossed his arms. resting the weapon on the side of his ribcage. Just that quick Pitt had his weapon raised and had crossed the room in what seemed like lighting speed, at least to himself it did, pointing the gun directly at Greats head. He glanced down at Petey and with a look and expression of sheer surprise asked;

"What the fuck happened to this mutha-fucka?"

"You murked the mutha-fucka. That's what happened," he said feeling the cold muzzle of Pitts steel pressing against his forehead.

"Go ahead. Try it! You lying bitch ass nigga!" Pitt grilled him with ice cold eyes. "I hate liars almost as much as I hate pedophiles, and I ain't never liked yo' stupid ass. Yo smell like Po Po to me."

"You ain't shooting shit Pitt. You already emptied your clip in that dead mutha-fucka."

Pitt looked at his weapon then back at Great with the motion of a pit bull about to strike, and pulled the trigger;

CLICK!

CLICK!

CLICK!

CLICK!

CLICK!

Great jumped back and raised his weapon on Pitt with two hands.

Jumm was on the phone to Rachet.

"I don't want this crazy mutha-fucka around me no more," Great said to Jumm, sweat pouring down his angular face.

Pitt just stared at him like he was about to strike.

Jumm was on his cell phone; "Remember that problem you didn't want? … Yea well you got it… No I can't take care of it," he looked over at Pitt, scrunched his face and shook his head. "Naw! Shit is getting heated. It's family business. You need to take care of this yourself... Ar'ight, one!" He hung up and said to Pitt, "Rachet says don't move 'til he gets here."

Rachet stood in the middle of the room for a long time just staring at Petey Rodriquez. No one dared utter a word. Rachet was so angry they didn't even want to breath. Finally Rachet turned, walked slowly over to Pitt and whispered in his ear with Pitt occasionally nodding in the affirmative.

Pitt spun over to Petey and started carefully unbuttoning his shirt as Rachet crossed over to Great and Jumm.

"Ar'ight. One of you bitches owe me six hundred g' and you gon' pay every single G dub outta your asshole." He glanced back and forth from each man. "I'm a let Yall decide which one."

"I wasn't here," Jumm said, throwing up his hands. "I don't know shit about it."

"I told you not to leave that crazy mutha-fucka around Petey. Especially when he's smoking that shit," Great said, pursing his lips with a grill face in Pitts direction.

"Yea. But I left you in charge so you owe me," Rachet said, pulling some huge weapon from his coat that Great had only seen in action movies.

"I don't owe you shit," Great said, looking at the big gun. "Fuckin' Pitt shot the mutha-fucka, not me." "Yea. Well take it up with your attorney. Right now you about to give me my first installment."

"I ain't giving you shit," Great said, backing away.

"Oh you gon give it to me one way or another," Rachet told him, reaching over and pulling Greats gun from his shoulder harness. "We can do this the hard way or the easy way. It's your choice. But you're gonna give me mine!"

Pitt laughed.

"Fuck you laughing at?" Great spit the words out.

"I'm laughing at yo bitch ass," Pitt said, amused as Rachet nudged Great towards the stairs. After Rachet and Great disappeared up the stairs Pitt turned to Jumm, "Help me get this fat mutha-fucka's clothes off and lift him to the tub.

Fucked up on wet or not, Pitt was an expert with the boning knives. A coroner couldn't have dissected Petey's body any better than Pitt was doing. Jumm watched as Pitt traced a thin cut down the back of Petey's scalp, around his neck and carefully separated his face from his skull until it looked like an expensive Halloween mask. He placed it in a solution to keep it soft then began his precision and meticulous cuts to dissect and de-bone the rest of Petey's body.

They had cut him into sections of feet, legs, shoulders, hands and midsections with the small Coroner's saw and bagged his intestines in a heavy duty plastic bag, and were just about to crack his ribcage open to remove his heart and liver and shit, when Great rushed into the bathroom and headed straight for the toilet.

"Yall got to get the fuck out. 1 gotta take a shit!" Great said hurriedly.

"Nigga you smell this dead mutha-fucka in this tub?" Jumm asked without looking up, "And you worried about a nigga smelling your shit?"

"1 can't shit with nobody watching me."

Jumm and Pitt looked up from what they were doing.

"I'm serious. Get the fuck out before I shit on myself."

"Well get to shitting Barbie, cause we ain't going a mutha-fuckin place," Pitt said then went back to cutting, leaving Great with a dumb expression on his face.

Within seconds, Jumm watched Pitt cut Petey's shriveled up dick off and stuff it in the top pocket of the army jacket he always wore to dissect bodies. He could no longer restrain himself from Pitt's strange habit.

"You got a dick fetish or something," he blurted out. "What the fuck you be doing with all them nigga's dicks?" Pitt hesitated long enough to give him a blank look then picked up a hand and began to dissect it as he explained the complexities and ignored the question.

"First we make a transverse incision across the front of the wrist, then a second across the heads of the metacarpal bones. Then we connect the two with a vertical incision in the tre of the middle finger-"

"Where do you learn all this stuff from," Jumm asked. He never could understand half the words Pitt used when he started cutting up bodies. "You sound like a doctor or something."

"I read a lot," Pitt said. "If you wanna know something all you gotta do is read. They got books that'll tell you how to do anything."

"Well did the books tell you that if the Feds ever catch you with all that DNA you lugging around, you and everybody around you is gonna be doing football numbers."

"Yea! And… If cows had square asses they'd shit bricks?"

Great called out almost in a panic, "Oh shit! Mutha-fucka!!"

Jumm looked up in time to catch a glimpse of Greats blood soaked underwear as he sat down on the toilet. He nudged Pitt and whispered;

"This niggaz bleeding out-a his asshole."

Pitt didn't bother to look up.

"What? This nigga on his period? He bleeding like a bitch," Jumm attempted to joke. Pitt didn't laugh. He stopped and gave Jumm a look.

"Where the fuck you been at?" He asked, handing Jumm some finger bones from Petey's hand. Jumm placed them in the bag of bones without taking his eyes off Great. "Rachet just drilled that mutha-fucka a new asshole."

"What?" Jumm asked, looking at Great strangely now.

"Shut the fuck up!" Great strained, as his bowels exploded into the bowl.

"Goddamn!!!" Jumm's face contorted and curled up. "Smell like you the dead mutha-fucka and this nigga in here just need a bath."

"Fuck you!" Great strained as his bowel exploded again. This time blood splattered up from the bowl. Jumm's eyes widened.

"Might as well get use to it," Pitt mused. "For six hundred thousand Rachet gon' be fuckin' you in your bitch ass till you get pregnant..."

"Fuck you bitch!" Great strained again, placed his elbows on his knees, his head in his hands and grunted. Jumm gave Great a long hard stare then looked back at Pitt.

"You ain't know?" Pitt smirked.

Jumm gave him a look of disbelief.

"You mean to tell me all this time you been with Rachet you didn't know he be fuckin' niggaz in they ass when they fuck up?"

"Hell no!" Jumm said, amazed. "You mean that niggaz a homo?"

"Don't' tell him that. Not if you wanna live. But I know that bitch ass nigga sittin' on that bowl is an official homo as of now. And you know what they say. Let a nigga fuck you in the ass pretty soon you'll be suckin' his dick!"

"Suck my dick!" Great squeezed the words out.

"See this," Pitt said calmly, taking Petey's dick from his pocket and dangling it in the air. "I cut 'em off bitch! I don't suck 'em off. You lucky you Rachet's bitch now otherwise I'd cut your shit off for pulling out on me. But one more suck my dick outta your mouth and I might just forget all about Rachet and yo' punk ass might end up beside Petey here."

He tossed Jumm another bone and threw Petey's dick to Great. "Here.. Get some practice suckin nigga. You gon' need it."

Great didn't say shit after that and Jumm just continued to stare at him in disbelief until Rachet appeared at the door and then Great couldn't look Rachet in the eye. Rachet was staring his ass down though, looking at him like a nigga would look at a new bitch he had just bagged..

"Pitt, I need to holla at you outside for a minute," Rachet called out, not taking his eyes off Great.

As Pitt left the room he turned to Great and said:

"I don't give a fuck who a nigga is, I'd have to be dead before I let another man stick his dick up my ass. I bodied this bitch once because she tried to stick her finger up my shit. Bitch ass nigga!"

Rachet closed the door behind Pitt, but before he did he threw Great a sarcastic kiss.

Jumm and Great could hear Pitt and Rachet outside in a heated dispute but their voices were so muted neither could follow the conversation.

Five minutes later, Pitt returned looking real aggravated and told Great,

"Rachet wants you to wash Petey's clothes and have them pressed before six o-clock. So that means you don't have much time. And he gave me orders to kill your bitch ass if you fuck up. Seems like you liked getting fucked in yo ass too much, and Rachet don't like it unless the nigga he fucking don't like it. "

Great didn't respond.

Another five minutes expired and Great asked, "Ain't no toilet paper in here?"

"Wipe it with your hand," Pitt called back. To Jumm he then issued a command. "Grab the other side of this niggaz ribcage." They cracked it and began removing Petey's vital organs as Great's eyes wandered the room in search of something to wipe his bloody ass.

CHAPTER 11

IN THE SIX WEEKS since Speedy and Scarecrow entered Daquan's life, he had grown six inches and already he could see results in his physique from the strenuous daily workouts they put him through.

"Come on, get that money," Speedy urged on Scarecrow who was on the pull up bar finishing his next to last set out of ten. "Forty seven, forty eight, forty nine, fifty, Good money," Speedy said as Scarecrow dropped down from the bar.

Scarecrow was fifteen, tall and lanky. With the baggy jerseys he liked to wear, he looked mad skinny, exactly what he wanted people to think, and there were few signs to warn you of the powerful, trained and chiseled body underneath. He might have been small but he was cut up and he had a six pack like stone, in fact his entire body felt like stone. That was one reason he didn't allow people to touch him, no friendly hugs or brotherly embraces. Scarecrow had that innocent look, like a little kid that had grown over night into a tall body. He didn't look his age. In fact Daquan looked more like fifteen than he did.

Daquan was last in the rotation. He watched Scarecrow fall to the ground to do push ups then stepped up to the bar. They had him doing only ten reps to a set and he had had to work himself up to that, so he was surprised when Speedy shouted out;

"OK give me twenty five for your last two."

"Twenty five?" Daquan responded, his eyes widening.

"Twenty five. You can do it." Speedy encouraged. And too his surprise, and although he had to gut the last five out and Speedy had to give him a little support under his wings, he completed the twenty five.

"You're going to be a beast," Speedy offered in a way of congratulation.

"Damn right he is," Scarecrow added, popping up from his fifty on the ground.

It was really a compliment coming from Speedy who was truly a beast. He was seventeen and had a body that looked like it came out of a muscle magazine. In many ways he resembled Pitt, only better looking with more cuts.

After the workout they all retired to Speedy's Grandmothers basement which was filled with Army stuff, books, manuals, all sorts of ropes and gadgets, all once belonging to his uncle, who was a Special Forces Assassin, as Speedy referred to him. He was the one responsible for much of what Speedy knew.

Speedy and Scarecrow were very secretive and Daquan was the very first person they had ever brought to their secret hideaway and opened up to in the slightest. Speedy lived with his grandmother but no one in the neighborhood knew him as Speedy. To them he was Recardo the quiet, respectful, somewhat nerdy kid who was an A student and who could often be seen sitting on the stoop of his grandmothers house reading books and studying with his friend, a skinny kid from another neighborhood that often visited him.

Scarecrow was from Puerto Rico originally, and had moved to New York when his mother packed a few of their belongings in a tattered bag and fled an abusive father in the middle of the night while he lay in a drunken stupor. She arrived in the city with her seven year old son, dressed in summer clothes, in the middle of winter, with no money, no family, and no where to go. So the moment she stepped off the plane she began using the three gifts that the Lord had given her. Her extraordinary good looks, her ability to think quick on her feet, and the warmth between her thighs.

That night they slept in a warm hotel room with a businessman who had been eyeing her since she boarded the plane, and they had not been homeless since. But Scarecrow never forgot his father or how he used to savagely beat them both. So when he was eight and saw Speedy beat up three boys much bigger and older than he was, he practically begged Speedy to teach him how to fight. His only intention was to one day return to Puerto Rico and beat the living shit out of his father. That was then. Now Scarecrow was a trained warrior, as deadly as any soldier who graduated the Rangers and according to neighborhood myths, had more kills.

"Don't believe everything you hear," Speedy warned him. 'Rumors are like playing the word game. It starts out a single phrase and by the time it's whispered around the room it's a whole book."

"What's a phrase?' Daquan asked.

"It's a sequence of words meant to have a meaning," Speedy answered.

"So what's a sequence?"

"It's like when one thing follows after another, in an order. Like when we work out. First we warm up, then we stretch, then we do sit ups, bar, pushups, then weights, one after another, It' a sequence. Every thing relating to the thing before it.'

"Oh. So Life and death would be a phrase?'

"Yep and a deep one too.'

Aduela knocked lightly on the door, and though it was not locked, waited until Speedy invited her in before entering. In many ways she was just as disciplined in the ways of the military as Speedy and Scarecrow were.

She entered carrying tall glasses of protein mix on a serving tray, sat it down on the only empty table space in the entire room, announced that dinner would be ready in an hour, smiled at Daquan and departed. She had absolute respect for their privacy.

They discussed The Pass at Hunts Point. How much money was coming out of it, who could be trusted, and who they needed to get rid of. What kind of trouble they were having and what kind of trouble they were expecting to have. Daquan suggested that they include two of the crews in Hunts Point, who were growing edgy over their territory, to form a coalition, a new word he had learned, that way they would all be stronger, instead of fighting each other over peanuts.

"Zebra might go for it but I know the Zulu crew ain't. They already sent two shooters at us," Scarecrow said.

"Yea and we sent 'em back," Speedy snapped.

"We need to get somebody older," Daquan said, a distant look in his eyes. Ain't nobody taking us serious because we so young."

"They take this serious," Scarecrow said with a sardonic smile, pulling an automatic weapon from beneath his seat.

"Yeah but what we gon do? Keep shooting up everybody? Then the spot gon get hot. Ain't nobody gon make no money and everybody is going to jail."

"Daquan's right," Speedy said. We don't need to be up front anyway. Let somebody else take the heat."

"Yeah he gotta be smart but not too smart. He gotta be at least twenty four twenty five and he can't be no snitch," Daquan said, looking over at Speedy. "I know you know somebody."

"Maybe. But I don't know if I can trust him like that."

"Don't tell him he's working for you. Tell him you just hooking him up wit some mob guys who don't want to be known."

*   *   *   *   *

Denareo tailed Gloria Rodriquez all the way to Saint Albans Queens, to a modest two story brick faced house on a quiet tree lined street. They then watched as a young woman came out of the house as soon as the convertible pulled to the curb and jumped in the front seat.

They followed her to Green Acres Mall where the women brought two sun dresses from Small and Petite, two dozen thong underwear and a pair of beet red pointed toe stiletto's. From there they took the mall elevator back downstairs and window shopped their way to a sporting goods outlet, took the store escalator downstairs, walked to the back, to the hunting department, where Gloria Rodriquez purchased a box of bullets for a thirty-eight revolver.

That meant she was armed! That changed everything. She was messing with some very dangerous men who wouldn't hesitate to blow her and Petey's brains out. She wouldn't stand a chance trying to take the situation in her own hands .. And.. To compound that, Denareo was way out of his jurisdiction without calling it in.

He had underestimated Rachet, had assumed he would keep the exchange local, downtown or in the Heights. But if the wife was all the way in Queens and the sun was due to set in less than two hours, he doubted if she was going to drive all the way back to Harlem. No she was just wasting time and the drop was somewhere in this area. And he was beginning to expect he had underestimated Gloria Rodriquez. Petey more than likely trained her well and by now she probably knew she was being trailed.

They had followed her back from the Mall where she and the girl took the bags into the house while he and his partner parked three houses down, waiting, and standing out like two white men in a Black Muslim rally.

"You think she might have slipped out the back," his partner asked, concern written on his face.

"I doubt it," Denareo said, that dangerous look in his eyes. "But you know what we gotta do?"

"I don't know. I'm not feeling right about this one," There was a momentary silence as his partner turned away then returned his gaze to the front door. "I think we need to turn this one over. You could still get some political mileage out of it," he faked a smile.

"Not enough to make a difference," Denareo mumbled then looked over at his partner and shook his head. "How much money have you made since you partnered with me?"

"I don't know." Ralph paused as if in serious thought.

"Since you're having problems let me count it for you. Let's see, there's the condo in South Florida, the boat, the minks and diamonds for your wife, the new addition to your house, all the money you keep blowing on horses and the tables. Should I continue?"

"I get your point."

"I don't think you do. Because right now that gambling habit has got you so broke you're about to lose all that and probably your wife and kids in the process. The way I see it, you need this few hundred thousand a lot more than I do,"

"I don't know-" Ralph said, casting his eyes down at the steering wheel. "She's armed. We might have too…"

"Well you had better make up your mind quick," Denareo said, sitting up, feeling the rush and excitement coursing through his body. "She's on the move."

When Ralph looked up, Gloria Rodriquez was walking down the walkway in her brand new red stilettos and the big red bag over her shoulder, headed for the gold convertible.

* * * * *

The gold convertible headed in the direction of the Mall through the streets making a series of rights and lefts to see if she was being tailed. Detective Ralph Santiago threw all caution to the wind and made it obvious that he was on her backside. Every block she moved through there were people on the street. They needed a stretch where they or their vehicle could not be identified by on lookers, just in case they had to body the bitch. He didn't want to do it but he would have no choice if she pulled out on him or his partner.

She hit the service road to the Belt Parkway headed back into the city, crossed Merrick Blvd. and ran straight into a deserted park on a one way street that stretched into a dark overpass. Perfect. It was a deserted area and she had to make a right.

Just before she hit the underpass Denareo threw the light on the dashboard and hit the siren as Santiago sped up and cut her off. Both men approached the car with their weapons drawn. Gloria Rodriquez had her drivers license and registration ready.

"I wasn't speeding," she said. "And I know I didn't run any lights."

"No you weren't," Detective Denareo smiled, taking her identification. "Just a routine check. Do you have a cell phone?"

"Yes but why are you asking for my cell phone?" She asked reaching into her purse.

Both Detectives raised their weapons and braced themselves.

"Step out of the car please and keep your hands where I can see them," Denareo said.

"Why? What did I do officer?" Her hand remained inside her purse.

Denareo's finger was already wrapped around his trigger. "Mamn. Remove your hand slowly from the hand bag and step out of the car."

Santiago looked around nervously as Gloria Rodriquez slowly removed her hand from the purse and slid out of the car. Santiago took her to the back, forced her down on the trunk and handcuffed her with plastic restraints while Denareo went through her purse, took out her cell phone and did a quick search of the car for the gun. He couldn't find it but took the red bag, unzipped it just enough to see stacks of crisp hundreds, took the keys from the ignition and signaled his partner.

"Don't lift your head up until we check this out," Santiago commanded.

Two minutes later they were on the Van Wyke Expressway headed back to Manhattan. Denareo threw the cell phone and the car keys out the side window the first chance he got then reached into the back seat for the bag to see what the take was. From the weight it felt like at least four or five hundred thou.

*   *   *   *   *

CHAPTER 12

Jumm hit the Southern State Parkway at six forty five. If traffic was backed up at any point they were fucked.

Mutha-fuckin' Great took all day getting the clothes washed and pressed. He then had to rush Pitt all the way to Canal Street to get some fucking art supplies and shit. Now he had to drive all the way out to fuckin' Huntington. He wanted to smoke a blunt bad. He was tempted to spark one but that would probably wake up Pitt, and the only time this nigga was tranquil was when he was sleep plus it would probably make him wanna spark some wet, which he was not willing to gamble with. He slid Mary J Blige into the CD player and turned the system down low. Another hour and it would be all over.

*   *   *   *   *

The cell phone lying on the front seat of the black 2001 Honda Accord rang twice before the driver picked it up. She didn't answer. She just listened. Six miles down the road she pulled off the Southern State Parkway into a small rest stop with phones. There she waited for ten minutes until the cell phone rang again.

*   *   *   *   *

Detectives Denareo and Santiago got exactly two thousand dollars cash out of the red bag. The rest was funny money, crisp cotton laid tinted paper cut into bundles with bank wrappings and a hundred spot on top. Denareo was mad as hell and wanted to go back and smash the bitch, but traffic was backed up from the 59th street Bridge and besides, Santiago refused to turn the car around. 'Cut your losses and move on.' was his motto, at least when he wasn't gambling.

Ralph Santiago was pretty relieved that they hadn't had to shoot the Rodriquez woman, besides he was a family man and he could imagine how Serafina would feel if he were kidnapped and two crooked cops stole the ransom money. Sure he could have used the money to pay off some gambling debts, but at what price? Ralph felt a strange sense of tranquility, almost like a drug. Like a heavy moral weight had been lifted. Denareo on the other hand was so pissed he turned red and you could see the tension in his body. He was on the phone now with one of his sleaze balls telling her how he was gonna drill her a new ass hole tonight, cum all in her mouth so her husband could taste him and put it all on film so she could get her self off when the fat bastard wasn't at home. He was the real scumbag, Ralph was thinking. He wished he knew the poor slob husband of the wife Denareo was talking to. The way he was feeling right now he would call the poor bastard and let him know Denareo was fucking his wife. Santiago was thankful that his wife wasn't the cheating kind. And he was also thankful that he had an extra thousand bucks to play with at the tables tonight. The way he was feeling, his luck was about to change. All he needed was one good winning streak to get from under then, he had promised himself, he would quit forever.

"You're in the produce department? " Denareo barked into the phone. "Now get the biggest cucumber you can find.. OK now push it up inside you... Look Mami, I really don't give a fuck how cold it is or how many people are around. Just do it!.. Oh you're not?. How 'bout I invite my partner over and let him watch some tapes.. In a heartbeat.. Yea that's it.. Put the phone down there and send me some photos."

When the photos showed up on Denareo's phone screen Ralph got a glimpse of them, Nasty bitch actually had her skirt up in the supermarket diddling herself with the biggest cucumber Ralph had ever seen. Denareo started rubbing himself.

"Do you mind," Santiago asked. "This is not a porn shop."

"Look and learn big fellow," Denareo said holding the camera up to his face. "One day you might get Serafina to do some shit like this for you."

*   *   *   *   *

What Denareo nor Ralph Santiago knew was Gloria Rodriquez had an exact twin sister and while they waited outside the Rodriquez residence Gloria and her sister Jean switched clothing, ID and car keys, matched Jeans hairdo and makeup with her own and sent her out as a decoy.

They were also so consumed with following her sister that they failed to notice the black Honda that kept popping up a few blocks behind them from time to time. She and Jean stayed in contact via their cell phones with Jean relaying her location every block, street and boulevard she turned on. Gloria always kept an extra set of keys to the Caddy in a magnetic case under the wheel casing so after she saw the unmarked car peel off she simply waited a few minutes then went and rescued her sister. After that she pulled her baseball cap over her bun, slid on her sunglasses and jumped on the Belt to the Southern State. Pete was right. Cops had to be the dumbest creatures on earth, even the smart ones.

The phone rang again and Gloria was told to take the Huntington exit on to 110. When she got to 110 she would receive another phone call. She was to travel at the speed limit at all times and not break it.

Gloria took out the box of bullets and loaded the thirty-eight on her lap before pulling the Honda back on the Parkway.

*   *   *   *   *

Shit! If Petey was as smart as his wife he might be alive right now, Rachet was thinking. She was smart enough not to keep the money on her. Once she saw Petey alive she would tell him where to pick up the money. It would be in Harlem, somewhere on 125th street. She would stay with Petey and whoever was guarding him until they received the money at which point she and Petey would be free to go and the person protecting him would disappear. Only problem was there was no Petey, unless what he had planned would work. It was all up to crazy ass Pitt now.

*   *   *   *   *

Jumm pulled into the driveway of the abandoned house on the door and climbed out. They went in through the back door and took the first door on the right to the basement where two hispanic men dressed in all black met them.

"He's in there," one of them said.

Jumm peeled them off five hundred a piece and told them they didn't see nothing, and to keep the area clear of stray fiends.

"You got it."

Pitt was already in the next room where a Spanish dude Petey Rodriquez's size was duct taped to a metal chair. Only a bare blue bulb hanging from a wire in the corner illuminated the room.

*   *   *   *   *

It was eight fifteen when the black Honda Accord turned into New York Avenue. It continued pass the train station, then Maria Pizza Chicken and Ribs then made a left on Church and a right on Academy and slowly pulled into the driveway of the first house on the right.

Night had fallen, the house was dark and there were few streetlights in the residential area of Huntington. In fact Gloria had trouble reading the street signs, as most were unlit or partially hidden behind forage . She drove all the way to the back and cut the headlights, the only illumination coming from the cockpit like dials of her dashboard. The smell of grass mixed with cool night air filled her nostrils as soon as she opened the door. Crickets chirped back and forth serenading each other. An occasional dog barked in the distance as she took time to evaluate her new environment. The house was isolated on two sides by thickets of motionless trees. A chorus of frogs joined in the melee, and coming from the other side of the trees, bottles broke on concrete and tires screeched off into the night. A woman screamed profanities and a door slammed. Gloria closed the door to the Honda and took the thirty-eight from her hand purse.

The backyard was a muddle of discarded materials, everything from old rusting bicycle parts to broken glass, used condoms, crack pipes and loose tobacco from Duchess, crushed or squished beneath her Reeboks as she made her way through the tall uncut grass to the back door of the house.

The three steps going up creaked and the wooden porch, weather worn and rotting, threatened to give way under her with each step. At the door she was immediately assaulted by the acid stench of urine and feces, mixed with a sweet foul odor she could almost taste. The darkness was complete. So much so that she had to feel her way to follow his instructions.

' A right at the entrance, down a short hallway, the first door leads to the basement. She was tempted to go back to the car for the flashlight when a man's voice rang out from the darkness causing her heart to skip and she turned right into a punch in the face. At least she thought she had been punched. The light now shining in her face revealed she had actually walked into an opened door.

"I'm gonna have to search you before you go down."

She couldn't see the man behind the flashlight but his voice sounded tall and almost apologetic, but she knew chances were he had a gun pointed at her.

"All I have is my cell phone," she told him, slowly raising both hands high above her. "And I'm going to need it if you want your money."

"I still have to search you," he insisted.

The basement was dimly lit. The bare blue bulb, hanging directly above Pete's head, gave him an eerie look. He seemed like he didn't recognize her, as if she were a stranger. There was no spark in his eyes like she expected once he realized she had come to his rescue.

"Are you alright Pete?" she called across the room.

He nodded vigorously. She attempted to cross to him but the tall man with the dreds pulled her back. "After the call," he reminded her."

Pete attempted to say something through the duct tape covering his mouth, but she couldn't understand his mumbles.

"You sure you're alright," she asked again as the Dred nudged her back towards the staircase. "I'll be right back for you honey. I promise."

She made the call from the front seat of the Honda as the Dred looked on.

"Go to the One Fish Two Fish and ask for a waitress named Maria. Tell her this exactly. 'Gloria needs you at home. Call me as soon as you get the money... Please!" She passed the phone to the Dred who nodded as he listened then hung up.

"What do we do now," she asked.

"We wait," he said, walking around to the passenger side and sliding in. "Nice ride," he smiled, running his gloved hand over the interior. "How's the system?"

Gloria pushed the keys in the ignition and as he scanned through the channels, slid her hand under the cushion she sat on and gripped the thirty-eight she had the foresight to leave in the car. Men were such assholes she thought.

* * * * *

CHAPTER 13

CHINA GUESSED THE BLACK girl doing her nails was around eighteen but no older than twenty, possibly as young as seventeen. She was cute, some kind of European mixed with Black, bright round eyes, clean teeth and breath, a good thing because she hadn't stopped talking in the last hour, nor had she stopped stealing glances at Daquan sitting in the waiting area watching the streets through the plate glass window.

"You like?" China smirked, the next time the girl stole a glance.

"What?" the girl asked, looking up at her. China looked over at Daquan.

"My cousin. You've been looking at him since he came in."

She blushed. "He's cute…"

"Girl. He ain't cute. He's fine " China leaned forward and whispered. "And he's sexy. If he wasn't my cousin…"

The girl grinned. "You'd be robbing the cradle."

"Girl, age ain't nothing but a number."

"Yeah I heard that one before. How old is he anyway?"

"How old are you?"

"Too old for him if that's what you're getting at."

"Sometimes looks can fool you," China said, as the girl glued the last gold tip on her last toe.

"Does he have any older brothers?"

"You didn't answer my question," China said, admiring the foot that was done. She had real sexy feet. Men always told her that.

"What?" miss all in 'her' business five minutes ago asked.

80

"How old are you?"

"Nineteen,"

"See. You don't look your age either."

"How old do I look?" She stopped and gave her a stern face.

"I would have guessed around the same age as Daquan." She frowned up her face. "Which is?" "No older than seventeen."

The girl sat up and examined Daquan like he was under a microscope. "He doesn't look seventeen to me," she turned back to what she was doing. "More like fourteen, fifteen at the most."

"Hey. What I just said. Looks can be deceiving. It runs in the family. I don't look like I'm twenty six either. Do I?'

"No you look my age."

China dug in her purse and pulled out her Board of Education photo from three years ago and handed it to her. "You do the math."

"Wow!" the girl said and looked back at Daquan.

China leaned over and whispered when the girl handed her the ID back. "This is between me and you. The nigga is hung like a bull. I'm talking Terminator."

The girl looked at Daquan again, this time hard. China knew she had her. The girl was a size queen. Just like her, she liked them big. The bigger the better. She wasn't worried about Daquan's age. Nobody had to know. She was worried about what he was holding. China was having fun with her new teeth.

"How you know?" the girl asked, turning back to her.

"He's my cousin," China lied. "I get to see him when he wakes up. Besides, This is between you and me again, a couple of late nights I watched him doing his thing. And I can't lie. I wish I had something like that beating my pussy up."

China sat back and for the next half hour miss motor mouth didn't say another word, and she barely managed to finish painting her toes. But when she was done and Daquan came over and peeled off a big tip from the knot he pulled out, China saw the girl press a slip of paper in his hand and whisper in his ear,

"Call me. I'll be home by ten."

China smiled as they left the beauty saloon. Not because of her hair and her nails being done or the new designer clothes she wore or the dentures in her mouth that she had been fitted for before she had fucked up by sucking Daquan's dick. Yes, she had her swagger back, but that's not why she was smiling when they headed into the night. Her man was about to get his first real piece of pussy and it would be a secret gift from her.

*   *   *   *   *

Gloria Rodriquez re-entered the house carrying a flashlight in one hand and the thirty-eight revolver in the other. She hurried to the basement to where Pete was duct taped to the chair and stood before him. He squirmed and shook and began mumbling frantically when she raised the weapon and aimed it at his head.

"You slimy fucking bastard," Gloria Rodriquez hissed angrily. "You thought you could fuck my little nephews and get away with it? You degenerate fuck! I knew that sooner or later you would slip up and I would get my chance."

She lowered the gun to his privates and held it with two hands.

"You want to fuck little kids?"

He trembled in his seat and tried to rock it away from her mumbling desperately.

"You want to see how a little kid feels when you rape them? Stick your dick in their assholes "You fucking piece of shit!"

She fired a single shot into his privates and watched the pain and fear in his eyes as the screams muffled through his silver gag and what ever they had stuffed in his mouth.

"Huh! You like that Pete? You like getting your dick wet?"

She fired another shot.

"Let's get it wet some more."

She fired two more shots in the same location and the blood soaked his pants, spilling down his legs to the concrete floor like she had opened a fire hydrant.

"That was for the kids," she said, gritting her teeth and raising the gun to his forehead. this is for shoving your nasty pedophile dick in me for all these years."

She pulled the trigger and watched his head jerk back and explode all over the back wall.

"And this is for security" She put the final bullet through his heart then made her way back to the Honda and headed back to the Southern State Parkway. It was time to bring the children home. She dialed her sister when she reached The Belt.

"You don't have to worry about that bastard again."

"Why? What happened?" her sister asked.

"They killed him anyway," Gloria said, and burst into tears.

As soon as she hung up she tossed the phone onto the highway and she heard it bounce and shatter, just like Pete had bounced and shattered the lives of her and her family for the last ten years.

* * * * *

While Ralph was on his way to Jersey to gamble his thousand dollars away, Denareo was coming out of the Treasure Chest on Broadway with The Bullet-a small clitoris vibrator with a remote control, some nipple clamps, a flesh colored dildo the size of his leg, a black leather mask and a red ball mouth restraint, because Ralph's wife, Serafina Santiago, had a fetish for being the submissive slave and she was into pain, hard body.

The night was still young and Denareo was still very much pissed at being out foxed by Petey's wife. Serafina Santiago was in for a world of pain.

* * * * *

Serafina Santiago was a beautiful dark haired woman with large breasts, an hourglass shape, wide hips and shapely legs. She played down her sexuality by dressing modestly, three quarter length skirts, jackets instead of clinging tops, very little make up if any, glasses and her hair pulled back or in a bun. She could have easily passed for a librarian. She was just that subdued in appearance and demeanor. She had always been this way, although she had always had her fantasies. But all her life they had been just that fantasy's. That was until Romereo Denareo came into her life.

She had been attracted to him from the first time Ralph had him over for dinner. And that first day, while they were sitting there eating she was having one of her fantasies. And it would have remained that way had he not come up behind her while she was washing dishes and Ralph was less than ten feet away settling down to watch the game, and slid his hand down the front of her skirt. She was so shocked she couldn't find the voice to scream but she was so excited she got wet instantly. He slid his fingers between her and grabbed a handful of her juices then forced all four of his fingers in her mouth and she sucked every bit of herself from them trembling from the excitement and fear of being discovered.

"I knew you didn't wear underwear," he whispered in her ear before going back to watch the game with Ralph. Every time Denareo raised one of his fingers to his mouth and sucked it while watching her she felt him inside. Before that night was over, she had positioned herself so that only he could see between her legs. Now she was addicted. And the more her guilt grew for cheating on Ralph the stronger her addiction for Denareo.

She dropped the kids off at her mothers and gave her the excuse of Ralphs gambling giving her migraines and the kids driving her crazy. She then rushed back and put on the thigh high stilettos she had hidden in the bottom of the closet and waited spread eagle on the bed wearing only the shoes, a blindfold and nothing else, exactly as her master had instructed her to do.

* * * * *

Twenty minutes later Denareo came in through the back door using the key Serafina had given him and turned off the alarm before climbing the stairs to his partners master bedroom.

* * * * *

CHAPTER 14

THE SUMMER MONTHS HAD come and gone like fast money on a shopping spree. School had let out and today would resume. China was so proud of Naquan. She adjusted his striped tie and slid her manicured fingers down the lapels of his school blazer.

"You look so handsome," she smiled. "I'm so proud of you." And she was proud for good reason. Naquan had scored tenth out of fifteen hundred applicants applying for Saint Mary's Academy, the most prestigious private school in New York, rated number five nation wide and he had been accepted with open arms.

"You look good too Mommy," Naquan said proudly. "You look rich."

China felt rich. Gone were the ghetto nails, clothes and hairdos. Now she was Chanel and Prada and Henri Bendel and fancy Midtown salons that only the truly rich could afford consistently.

"Why thank you kind Sir," she smiled, bending her knees to a curtsy.

"I wish Daquan was here."

"So do I. But this is your day." She checked the de Grisogono Daquan had just added to her watch collection.

7:10

The car would be here any minute.

China ran back into the master bedroom. She had almost forgotten the most important part of her illusion. She dashed down the hallway, past the study, past Naquan's bedroom and another she was trying to persuade Daquan to move into, and almost slid into the dresser by the window overlooking the George Washington Bridge.

It was resting in its velvet coffin, sparkling light like a thousand twinkling stars. She lifted it reverently and pressed it to her bosom and made a wish before slipping it on her ring finger. While she was there she exchanged her Chanel bag for a smaller Dior and checked herself in the mirror once more. She wore make-up but she had the 'no make-up look', which had been really difficult to achieve until she got the hang of it. Her bleached hair, as her stylist Fredrico exclaimed, was a perfect fit for her face and life style, "A mix of Drew Barrymore on a windy day and a world class gymnast on a balance beam." She couldn't understand his analogy but it worked for her. Her once straight hair, a product of her Chinese genetics, was now wavy from perms, pulled back with little wisp of strands falling gently across the sides of her face. Her entire look was 'meticulously natural' and according to Fredrico, very difficult to achieve. But she had not only pulled off the look but parenthood as well. No one suspected that she was not Naquan's biological mother. In fact there was a remarkable resemblance between them, if not physical at least in spirit.

She found Naquan in the study, looking down at the Hudson River Drive watching all the cars fly by.

"You afraid," she asked after joining him.

"Yes." he said, not looking up. "And it is are you Afraid, Mom" he corrected her.

She smiled. "Now look who's teaching who." Her cell phone vibrated. "Oops! That's us," she said before digging it out of her handbag and answering. "Yes. We'll be right down."

She flipped the phone shut and turned to Naquan. "Nervous?"

"Yes."

"Me too," she said, and took his tiny hand in hers.

* * * * *

Thomas King, AKA Big Kountry, had also had a dramatic change of fortune in the past three months. Originally from Atlanta, where he had done a five-year bid, he had resettled in New York trying to put his feet back on the ground after doing another three joints in the Feds. He had been home for a while and he was doing a little something on 169 and Sheridan, but he wasn't exactly stackin'. Niggaz was copping the bullshit Hard White he was slinging only because they respected his handle. Niggaz knew he would lay something down with the quickness. It was just that he didn't have no real connects for the good shit and even if he did, he didn't have enough gwuap to git his weight up. He was about to give up and take his ass back to Atlanta when out of the blue, some spaghetti heads saw how he was moving and put him on, gave him a team and a spot and the best shit in the Bronx. In three months he had gone from a hoopty to a big Benz and two trucks, all of them kitted out with crazy systems. And his team had the whole Hunts Point on lock. Now Thomas King AKA Big Kountry was AKA That Nigga!

Trina met Kountry every Thursday, like clockwork, all the way on the other side of the Bronx in an Italian Diner on Arthur Avenue and Fordham road, Little Italy of the Bronx where they would have breakfast, eggs over easy, toast and a tall glass of orange juice for him, two greasy burgers with sliced onions, tomato's, ketchup and mayo and a hot pitcher of coffee for her. From there they would drive to the Days Motel near the highway and spend an hour like lovers on the sneak.

Kountry watched her woof the burgers down.

"What," Trina asked, looking up, juice, ketchup, and mayo dripping down her chin.

"You eat like a fucking man."

Still chewing she mumbled, "I'm half Sicilian remember," He refilled her coffee cup.

"Where does all that shit go?" Trina was barely five feet, a hundred pounds weighted down with burgers and a gallon of coffee. "Where do you put all that shit?"

"In the ba-du-ka-dunnk. Right where you like it baby," she flirted, wiping her chin with a napkin and starting on the other burger.

He had to admit, she had the crazy fat ass. Only problem was she wouldn't let him get in it. "So when you gon' let me back that thang up?"

"As soon as you get me to a telly."

"Yea right! Anyway you gon' be eating all day," he scowled.

"No I'm not." She rushed another bite, took a gulp of coffee, grabbed the overnight bag on the seat beside her and slid from the table. "Pay the tab, I'll meet you in the car."

Kountry watched her disappear through the corridor leading to the bathrooms and office in the back then called for the tab. He left a ten spot for the waitress, paid the bill at the counter and waited five minutes for Trina in the car.

"How you get mixed up in this shit?" he asked as she got in the front seat.

"You ask too many fucking questions," she snapped, all the while smiling as she leaned over and gave him a big kiss. "Now can we get to the telly. I wanna get back and see my man." Just that quickly she had turned to ice, and he was back to the realization that her public affection for him was only an act.

*   *   *   *   *

It was 10:15 when Trina punched her monthly ticket and pulled into the Fordham University parking lot. She turned the silver Eclipse into the nearest vacancy, snatched the canvas bag from the back seat and flipped open her cell phone.

"I'll be there in ten minutes," she said opening the door and exiting the car. "I miss you baby," she added sweetly before hanging up.

Trina stepped back and admired the car before beeping the alarm. She loved the way the black rag top made it stand out from all the other cars in the lot yet it was simple enough that it didn't make her stand out or be easily profiled. It was her first car and she loved it almost as much as she loved her man. She could thank China for that. China had been right. Every girl needed a Daquan to beat her pussy up.

Trina loved Daquan's body, it was like warm steel, chiseled and cut, smooth to her touch. Watching him reminded her of the nude bronze Adonis she often snuck away to admire during school outings to the Met, except no leaf would ever be able to cover Daquan, not unless it was a rubber plant leaf or some giant Everglade.

If he would let her she would just lay there and play with it for hours, watching it grow and jump and twitch beneath her touch and kisses before she tried to take more of it in her womb than she had the last time. But Daquan was always in a rush. Not that he didn't satisfy her, he always left her pussy with a soreness that she enjoyed for hours after he departed. It was just that:

He wouldn't sleep over.. and..

He went ballistic if she touched him while he was asleep.

Right now he was sound asleep, and who ever he was dreaming about had him growing until his big shiny head was arched a few inches beyond his belly button trying to jump to the ceiling.

Trina sat Indian style, playing with her nipples as she willed him awake until she couldn't take it any more and headed for the bathroom where she washed and dressed for classes she had intended to skip for the day. She was sitting on the edge of the bed tying up her sneakers when Daquan asked: "Where you goin' Tree?"

"I was going to class," she turned to him and said" He was propped on both elbows giving her that sexy look and the Terminator was growing to massive proportions. "But I'd rather stay and play."

"Go to class," he said, falling back and pulling the pillow over his head.

"No!" she said, untying her sneakers. "And leave you here dreaming about your cousin?"

"You my cousin, remember?" he said through the pillow.

"That's just so my friends don't think I'm robbing the cradle. I'm talking about your real cousin." Trina was already coming out of her sweat suit.

"You jealous of my cousin?" Daquan asked, a big smile on his face when he removed the pillow.

"Yes!" Trina said honestly. "She gets more of this in your dreams than I get in real life."

Daquan laughed.

"Oh you think it's funny," Trina said, coming out of her panties and tossing them across the room. She practically jumped on his chest and guided his big muscle into her. "You think it's funny huh? I know you wanna fuck your cousin Daquan but her pussy will never be as good as this. You love stretching this tight pussy don't you Daquan. Huh? You love the way it sounds.. Yea fuck it.. Fuck this tight pussy.. Oh shit!. Damn Daquan.. You so fucking big…"

"I ain't that big. You just small. My cousin could take all of it easy."

"Whatever." Trina moaned as her eyes rolled back and she worked him deeper inside her. "Oh shit Daquan... Fuck!! I'm cummin' already."

*   *   *   *   *

Besides his teachers, Naquan didn't like school at all. He was the only Black kid in the entire school and none of the other kids would talk to him. They all whispered and stared when he walked the corridors, and at lunch they had scattered from the table he sat at like rats in the tunnel when Daquan would shine the bright light on them.

Naquan was in the lobby waiting for China to pick him up when the only girl who had remained at the table approached him, clutching her book bag to her chest.

"Waiting for your parents," she asked. She was a little taller than him and she had a thousand pink spots on her white face, plus she had red hair and metal teeth.

He didn't answer. He looked through her like she wasn't standing there.

"I'm waiting for my dad," she said, ignoring the fact that he was ignoring her. "He's usually a little late because of the traffic." She scanned the street outside the gate where rows of cars, chauffeurs and nannies waited with the flux of students being released on the first day.

Naquan searched through the crowd and cars but he didn't see either China or the Limousine that brought them.

"What's your name?" she asked, rocking side to side. He didn't answer.

"I'm Amanda."

Go away Amanda, he thought. Where was China.

"It's O.K. to be different," she said. "My father says that when people don't like you when you're different they're the one's who lose."

"Naquan," he said, still searching for China.

"What?" she asked as if she were hard of hearing.

"Naquan. My name is Naquan."

"That's a nice name."

"Thank you," he answered, remembering what China told him about being polite. "Amanda is a nice name too."

"I don't think so," she frowned. "My father wanted to name me Katrina after my grandmother but my mom said it was too..." she hesitated. "Well I like it. My father calls me that sometimes when my mom is not around. You can call me that too if you like it better."

He nodded.

"How old are you?"

"Six," he said proudly.

"I'm nine but that's O.K. My mom is older than my father."

Naquan looked around the lobby. A group of older boys were staring at him and Ama-Katrina. He wasn't intimidated. Daquan could whip all of them by himself. He stared back.

"Hey! There's your mom," Katrina said in an excited voice.

"You don't know what my mom looks like," Naquan said, turning back to her.

"Yes I do. She looks exactly like you. She's real pretty."

"Where," Naquan asked, looking around. "I don't see her."

"Over there," she pointed to a second gate entrance near the end of the street. "You must be really rich," she added.

"Why?" Naquan asked, picking up his book bag from the floor and trying not to look as hurried as he was.

"You have a chauffeur and your mom is wearing Narcisco Rodriquez."

Naquan examined China, crossing the courtyard. What was a Narciso Rodriquez? "How do you know," he asked, deciding to let his mother come to the lobby so all the boys staring at him could see how pretty she was and how rich she looked.

"They're shoes and they cost twenty five hundred dollars a pair."

"How do you know," he asked as China climbed the stairs to Saint Mary's.

"I know everything about clothes. I'm going to be a fashion designer one day."

Naquan stole a glance at the boys who were staring at him as he and China left the lobby and he was filled with satisfaction from the way all their jaws dropped open. All the way to the car everyone looked at his mother that way.

"Who was that," China asked as the chauffeur opened the back door for them.

"Who Mommy?"

"That pretty girl."

"Oh that was my friend Katrina. She's going to be a fashion designer."

"Mommy'," Naquan said, once they were inside the limousine. "You could marry Naquan and then I would have a mother and a father."

"I can't marry Daquan Nay Nay."

"Why not. You love him."

"Not like that. Besides he's too young and he's your brother. He could never be your father."

"He is my father. He takes care of me and he takes care of you too. That's what a father and a husband does. He takes care of his family."

"He's too young," China said absently.

"Katrina says a wife can be older than her husband. Her mother is older than her Dad." "Naquan. I can't marry Daquan. It's a bad idea to even consider."

*   *   *   *   *

"When you're in me," Trina said, tracing her fingers across Daquan's nipple and down to the Terminator, her head nestled in his chest as she gently bit and licked his other nipple between words. "It's almost like getting my pussy eaten and getting fucked at the same time."

"I never ate no pussy before," Daquan said, turning up his nose." It wasn't the first time they broached this subject.

"You keep saying you never did, but does that mean you Never Ever did it.?"

"NEVER! And I ain't never gonna do it neither. That shit is nasty."

"Oh! I can suck your dick, but eating my pussy is nasty," Trina said, kissing her way down his rock hard abs to a dormant Terminator that was longer and fatter soft than the hard dick of any other man she had ever slept with.

"I ain't never asked you to suck it."

"Oh but you like it though."

"I ain't never said that neither."

She kissed the length of it then back to the tip and took him in her mouth until he started to grow. "So you wouldn't eat my pussy if I begged you," She asked, straddling his chest so that her vagina was inches away from his face. He liked to look at it and play with it while she sucked him off, but he wouldn't eat it.

"Tree. You know I ain't gon' eat yo' pussy so why you keep playing head games," he asked, opening her pussy up wide with both hands.

The Terminator rose in front of her like a majestic phallic god.

"It doesn't matter anyway," she said, her breathing shallow, grasping the Terminator firmly with both hands and sucking only a third of it's length down her throat before she was choking and about to throw up.

"Why," he asked, doubling the pillow under his head while manipulating her clitoris with his thumb.

She stopped long enough to tell him, "You don't ever have to eat my pussy as long as you fucking me with this, but it would be nice if you were eating me while I suck your dick." then went back to choking on the Terminator again.

The sun was setting over the Bronx skyline and for the first time since his mother left this earth Daquan spent the entire night in an apartment on the surface world, in the arms of some one who loved him and he felt safe.

"Quan. "

"What?"

"You love me?"

He stared at the ceiling for a beat and then said, "Yeah"

* * * * *

Bernstein watched the new occupants of Senior Encarnacion's penthouse apartment as they entered the back of the limousine. A Black woman and a Black kid, it was unthinkable and the board was livid. "If you let one family in the next thing you know they'll be swarming the complex like roaches."

Bernstein felt the same way. He didn't consider himself prejudiced. He was from the old culture where Jews lived with Jews so that their culture would not be tainted or threatened by outsiders. Proof that he was not prejudiced were the millions of dollars his charities over the years to Black organizations to aid the development of Black people. But this complex was developed as a Jewish Community and the Board was determined to keep it as such.

Bernstein was caught in a crossfire. On one hand, as president of the Board it was his obligation to carry out its decisions and mandates. On the other, Able Encarnacion had him over a barrel. If anyone found out about the things Abel held over his head, not only would it cause him great discomfort but possibly a stretch in a Federal prison. At the very least it would result in years of litigation and tons of negative publicity. His company stocks would plummet.

The half-breeds limousine pulled away and Bernstein walked back to the cluttered desk in his study and picked up the office phone. The girl and her son would be out within the next six months he had promised the Board and himself. After all they were Jews, he was Jewish and if the Jews could push the Palestinian's from their homeland certainly it couldn't be too difficult to circumvent a Dominican blackmailer, no matter how rich he thought he was, or a half breed Black and Chinese woman.

"Yeah Fred, this is Bernstein, I need you to find out what you can about a Yuet Ying Jackson and her son Naquan Jackson.. Yes of course I have all that. I need you to get me some dirt.. Whatever you can dig up… friends, relatives, drugs, sexual activities, something I can use as leverage."

He hung up. Now he would put the ball in motion for Abel. Never would a Dominican beat a Jew at a game the Jews invented. He dialed another number. He still had friends in the IDF who had friends who had friends.

* * * * *

Gloria Rodriquez slammed down the phone on Rosa Rodriquez. Pete's mother had never liked her from the day she met her, and had done her best to persuade Pete not to marry her. Now the old Bruja Vieja was telling anybody that would listen to her that she had killed Petey. Even the kids had called to ask if it were true, if she had indeed murdered their father. Now there were talks and whispers everywhere. It wouldn't be long before she convinced the authorities and they began to investigate. And God forbid they put her sister under pressure. She wasn't as strong as Gloria. She was sure to break and reveal the ransom and what she knew about the exchange and what Gloria had told her about them killing Pete.

What had happened to Pete any way? The kidnappers had to have come back and removed his body. It was never found. She had checked every news source for months for news of his discovery but still to this very day there was nothing. Pete had disappeared without a trace. Gloria's biggest fear, until Pete's mother started her campaign, was that they would find Pete's body and someone in Huntington would remember her sisters black Honda and the petite woman with the baseball cap and glasses driving that night. That she had stepped in his pool of blood and left footprints that could be linked to her. She had watched the O.J. trial. One thing was for certain. Something had to be done about Rosa. She was determined to link her to Pete's murder and that was not an option.

* * * * *

CHAPTER 15

NAQUAN WAS A GENIUS and China was proud of him, An IQ of 185, Skipped six grades in the last two year's. The Deans list two years running-A ton of awards and certificates for Outstanding Academic achievements, Even a cover article in the Times comparing him with Dougie Howser, the twelve year old surgeon Hollywood had made a movie and popular sitcom about. China had been approached by agents interested in developing Naquan's story but she nor Naquan were excited by the offers, especially since Daquan was furious over the Times article. He was so protective.

Naquan seemed to be interested in only three things other than excelling. One was Katrina. The two had become inseparable, which sort of explained the other two. He and Katrina were both desperate to complete their family and so had decided to consolidate and hook China up with Katrina's father who was recently divorced contributing to Katrina officially adopting her nickname and losing the braces and conservative clothing.

Katrina hated her mother and adored her father and he deserved someone better, which of course was China. Katrina adored China also, she often told her she was the mother she always wanted,

The third thing was really disturbing and she really needed to talk to Daquan about it but she was seeing less and less of him, besides she didn't know how to put it to him anyway. "I think Nay Nay is stealing, not only from me but from other people as well."

China first began noticing a few dollars missing from her purse here and there, but two weeks ago she took thirty seven hundred dollars from her checking account to pay for a package tour for the two of them to Mexico and when she arrived at the travel agency to pay, discovered six of the crisp bank notes were missing.

Also Naquan had too many expensive toys and gadgets' in his room that his friends had 'given' him. Only yesterday a neighbor showed up at her door with his son accusing Naquan of stealing two of his video games. Of course she had defended him and afterwards he told her that he had not stolen from the boy. But China knew he was lying. The night before she came into his room when he was playing a game she had never seen before. It was really intriguing so she sat and watched for a while before asking, "When did Daquan give you this game?"

"He didn't," Nay Nay told her without looking up. "My friend gave it to me."

"What's the Name of it?"

It was the same game the neighbor said was stolen.

She would deal with that later, right now she had amassed a pile of clothing on her bed trying to figure out what outfit would be appropriate for a day in the park and dinner at a fancy restaurant.

"I thought we would have dinner at the Tavern On The Green and afterwards a short stroll through the park to the Shakespearean theatre. That's if it sounds OK to you," Larry Karolyi told her over the phone.

A fancy restaurant and Shakespeare in the park seemed to go together as much as her and a White man. But the kids had spent months persuading them both and China suspected Larry Karolyi felt just as pressured and uncomfortable about this date as she did.

She finally decided on an Adam Jones silk tank dress and Gucci open toe three-inch pumps and viewed herself in the full-length mirror. The almost primitive geometric patterns of the dress clung to her every curve and her only under garment, a pair of sheer panties, showed revealing lines across her Black girl hump. According to Fredrico 'A distraction to the fluidity of line.' She stepped out of them and tossed them into her almost empty underwear drawer. She hated wearing any type of undergarments anyway.

Naquan peeped in, "You'd better hurry Mom. He's going to be here any minute."

"How do I look," she asked, pulling her golden hair into a bun.

"Great."

"You always say that," she teased.

"Because you always look great Mom. You're perfect."

"I wouldn't say that." She pulled a wooden ball and cube choker around her neck and fastened it. "How's this?"

"Almost perfect," he said, going to her jewelry box and taking a wooden ankle bracelet and fastening it around her left ankle. "Now you're perfect," he smiled gleefully.

The doorbell rang. "That's him Mom."

"Go let him in. I'll only be a minute."

"No Mom. The first thing he should see when the door opens is the most beautiful woman in the world."

She blushed, shook her head and grabbed an embroidered Chloe bag, emptied her previous bag into it, kissed Naquan and gave him a warning to stay out of trouble before heading nervously to the door.

*   *   *   *   *

It was the first date China had been on since Rachet invited her out six years ago and the shake in her leg was beginning to become noticeable. She had been with at least a hundred men while she was lost in her crack world and had pretty much learned how to twist any one of them around her pretty little finger, but the minute she opened the door she sensed that Larry Karolyi was different from most men. Something about him strangely reminded her of a Daquan mixed with a pinch of Rachet. She didn't know whether to embrace him or run away from him as fast she could.

"Katrina tells me you were once a teacher," he said, turning the big Chrysler 300 onto Broadway and heading downtown. She smiled and placed both hands on her knee to sturdy it.

"Did you like it?"

"I was never really a very good teacher."

"Is that why you gave it up?"

"No. After I had Naquan my husband thought it best I remain home and raise our son. He was successful, we didn't need the money." She stared out the window trying to catch a glimpse of Ms. Perno's building as they passed 145th Street.

The afternoon traffic was heavy but moving. She took notice that Larry Karolyi had timed the lights perfectly so that he could catch each light on green. He was a good driver.

" And you didn't mind?"

"Why should I?"

"I don't know… Twentieth century… Women's Lib."

"I'm lazy, and I like nice things. My husband spoiled me rotten."

She crossed the sturdy leg over the one that was shaking and adjusted the hem of her dress back over her thighs as he glanced over at her.

"I can see why he would spoil you rotten."

China took the bait. "Why because you think I'm beautiful?"

"You are not just beautiful. You are the most beautiful woman I have seen on this earth."

"Oh here we go with the bullshit!" China said, looking up at him as he devoted his attention back to the road.

"No I'm serious," he said, the iridescence of his blue eyes competing with the brightness of the summer day. "I'm not just complimenting you. I have never seen anyone as beautiful as you."

China followed his eyes to her lap. The silk had conformed to the shape of her thighs and girl lump, on top of that, the dress matched her skin color perfectly. If it weren't for the bold prints-

"If you have the slightest fantasy of getting into my panties," she warned him. "You should know up front I don't wear any, and I definitely have not and will not, in this lifetime or the hereafter, have sex with a White man."

He laughed. And his laughter turned into one of those chuckles that would not go away. He laughed so long it was pissing her off, however she didn't bother to comment. She endured it until his face turned into the most gorgeous smile. It reminded her so much of Daquan's.

"Forgive me," he apologized. "It's just the way your face looked when you said that."

"Oh! You think I'm funny?" She covered her lap with her bag and crossed her arms. "I don't think this is going to work."

"Probably not," he smiled, still amused.

They didn't speak until they passed Central Park and the Chrysler was on Fifth Avenue headed downtown.

I thought we were going to Tavern On The Green," she said, sitting up straight and unbuckling her seatbelt.

"There's someone I want you to meet first."

*   *   *   *   *

All his brothers and sisters looked like him, blue eyes, and dark hair. But his biological mother, Mama Karolyi was as dark as African coffee and she was small, smaller than China.

"Don't ask me what happened," Mama Karolyi said, taking the photo album from China's hands and replacing it with a glass of cola and ice. "For the life of me I tried to make a black baby but they all kept coming out like this." She reached over and pinched her son's cheeks.

"Must be my strong African genes. I came from a long line of royalty dating all the way back to Queen Nefertiti. " She smiled and China could see exactly where Larry's smile derived from. Daquan could probably trace his linage right back to this woman, she was thinking. She saw so much of him in her also.

"Tell her what you told father Ma when he first pursued you."

"My life that was one persistent man who would not take no for an answer."

"Tell her what you told him the first time he told you, you were the most beautiful woman in the world."

Her took on one of the funniest expressions China had ever seen. "Lord, I told that man. if you think you going to get in my panties you have to be stone cold crazy. The last thing I need in my drawers is a White man. I told him I'd have to be dead and buried before I'd have sex with a White man. Back then I liked my meat black. The blacker the berry-"

"And then what happened," China asked, intrigued.

"Then he proceeded to show the part of him that was beyond any color and I fell in love. I'm glad I did, otherwise I would have never had this rascal or the best thirty three years of my life.
"

* * * * *

Their reservation at the Tavern had been canceled and there was an indefinite wait and a long line ahead of them to be seated. It was either the bar for the wait or a picnic in the park Larry suggested.

"I don't drink, China told him.

Neither did he.

They walked to 1st Avenue where Larry found a D'Agestinos where he purchased a picnic basket and filled it with cheeses, bread loaves, crackers, garlic spreads and two magnum bottles of a nonalcoholic apple wine.

The walk was long from 1st and 56th to the Shakespearean Arena. They chose to walk along Fifth Avenue on the park side where vendors sold art prints, and t-shlrts and souvenirs of the city. With the sun behind her, everyone stared as she approached.

They sat on the steps of the Metropolitan Museum when they reached 82nd street and watched a comedian, where China attracted a larger crowd than the comedian did until she realized she was sitting with her legs wide opened. Worst was when she caught her reflection in the slanted glass panels on the side of the museum as they climbed the short hill leading to the park and the baseball fields. It wasn't until then that China realized she might as well be naked the way the sun turned her dress transparent. She had been walking around the city all this time with a silk halo around her naked body. No wonder every one kept staring as she passed.

"May I borrow your jacket?" she stopped and asked Larry Karoyli.

"I was hoping you would ask," he smiled, taking it off and handing it to her.

She tied it around her waist angrily. "You mean all this time you knew I was walking around the city naked. I mean you can see right through this thing, and you didn't bother to tell me?"

"Well you're not completely naked. There are a couple of nice African prints around your body," he grinned.

"Uggggh! Men you're all freaking perverts." She scrunched her face.

"And you are so damn sexy."

The remainder of the day was completely enjoyable. China was beginning to warm up to Larry as they sat on the grass eating cheese and crackers and watching one of the baseball games played by corporate teams, however she was not attracted to him physically. The urge was there for something though. She hadn't had sex for over two years and right now with all the ambiance the gushy was bubbling inside her and she was tempted to either flash him her growing assets or take the apple cider bottle with her to the ladies room, the latter of which she would have attempted an hour ago if the line to the ladies room hadn't been so long. She was stroking the width of the bottle now, an unconscious act until she realized she was feeling each stroke deep in her vulva. Her assets were demanding attention. She looked at Larry and resisted opening up wide for him for the forth time in the last half hour.

"How much longer?" she asked. "

He checked his watch. "They usually give the tickets out around six thirty or so."

China had been checking out this old mansion on a hill opposite the lake. It looked abandoned. She was thinking about either taking the wine bottle up there and fucking her own brains out, or taking Larry Karolyi up there and fucking his brains out.

She grabbed the wine bottle by the neck and stood. "I need to stretch my legs," she told him. "I think I'm going for a short walk. I'll be back before the play begins."

"Want some company?" he asked.

She looked at him for a while before answering. "Wanna play a game?"

"I'm all for games. What do you have in mind?"

"Damsel in distress, you have to recue me from that castle."

"OK, I'll go for that."

"I go first, you give me twenty minutes to hide and then you come find where my horrible captors are keeping me.

"And what does Sir Lancelot get for saving the beautiful Princess?"

"Why do men always have to have something in return… And why is it just the beautiful women they are inclined to rescue. Pretend that I'm an ugly duckling and the only motive you have to rescue me is the fact that I'm in a state of distress, not that you expect some reward at the end. Other wise don't play my game."

Larry looked at his watch. "OK lets synchronize. I've got Five Forty Seven and fifteen seconds, sixteen, seventeen…"

China set her watch to match his. "We on the same page now?"

"Sure, twenty minutes to rescue the ugly Princess, and even if she turns out to be as beautiful as you, I promise I won't expect a thing, not even a peck on the cheek."

*   *   *   *   *

CHAPTER 16

"WHERE YOU RUSHING TO Demi Moore?" One of her classmates called out to Trina as she rushed across campus to the parking lot. The girls accompanying her giggled. "To find your cous-innn?" the fat bitch added.

"No! I'm trying to catch your mother before she leaves so she can eat my pussy," Trina called back. "Not unless you wanna eat it for her." That stopped all that giggling shit.

Bitches stayed trying to get on her because Daquan was so young. They stayed trying to get her to openly admit she was fucking the lil nigga. So fucking what if she was?

Trina no longer cared what the bitches thought about her and Daquan. Besides anyone around them for more than twenty seconds could see that she was completely in love with the lil nigga, if only for how jealous she got if one of her 'ho' friends or any other bitch looked at him the wrong way, actually if any bitch looked at him in any way she was ready to put her fist in their mouths. It didn't take a rocket scientist to figure out she and her cous-innn were a lot more than kissing cousins, that they were fucking, sucking, I can't get enough of that monster dick cousins.

In the two years she and Daquan had been fucking around she still hadn't been able to take all of that big shit inside of her.

"Girl if he's that big," her best friend Kisha exclaimed wide eyed the day Trina showed her how far up in her gut Daquan would be when they made love. "You need to let me get some. At least let me see it… How big is it anyway?" Trina held up both hands a foot apart."

"No way! You're exaggerating."

"I swear…"

"That's like over… like twelve inches!"

Trina's eyebrow went up along with the corner of her lip. "Why you think I can't leave that lil nigga. He's got me whipped girl. I ain't lying, he be beating this pussy up."

"Girl if what you saying is true he'd have my black ass whipped too. Maybe I should start fuckin' lil niggaz. Fuckin' Omar's six foot seven ass ain't really doing shit with this pussy."

"I thought you told me Omar was holding."

"Girl I thought he was holding too until you told me this shit.."

"Omar still getting drafted into the NBA," Trina asked.

"Girl who cares what Omar is doing right now, you're getting off the subject. How thick is it?"

"Heineken bottle thick, like this." She made an opening with two hands. "Swear to God."

Kisha cocked her head and gave Trina a look. "You my girl an' all Trina, but honestly I don't believe a word you're saying. Ain't no grown ass man holding like that, I know that little nigga ain't."

* * * * *

It was just as well Kisha didn't believe her Trina was thinking as she turned the key to the apartment. She shouldn't have slipped up and confided in her in the first place. She was her best friend and all but she knew the ho would be sneaking behind her back trying to get some if she really believed her.

Daquan was home, BET was blasting from the surround sound in the living room and the aroma of fast foods welcomed her from the kitchen.

"Hey baby," she said, bending from behind the sofa to kiss him in the mouth.

"What happened with Kountry today," he asked, looking up from the Flat screen. Trina had almost forgotten about the voice mail she had left Daquan.

"That niggaz tripping. He actually tried to rape me this morning."

"Was his money right?"

"Four hundred and twenty thousand. I counted it twice." Trina said, her mood changing. She slung the big bag on her shoulder over the sofa onto the seat beside him.

"You want to count it again?"

"Naw I trust you."

"You don't care if the stupid mutha-fucka tried to rape me," she asked, throwing the rest of her belongings on the leather sofa.

"He didn't right?"

"Not this time. Only because I stuck this three eighty down his throat."

Trina flopped down on the sofa beside the bag, Daquan on the other side. "Daquan what happens the next time he tries to rape me. He almost took the gun away from me this time."

"Don't worry. Ain't gon be no next time Tree. Dudes you work for say Country's head don' got too big for his fitted."

"And?"

"And don't worry 'bout it. They gon take care of it." He handed her an envelope with the three thousand dollars she earned every Thursday for her drop and delivery. "Ain't gon' be no next time., an ain't gon be no more pick up an deliverys."

"But Daquan I need this money. I got my car note, rent, school-"

"Don't worry bout it I got you Tree," he assured her. "Now come over here an' let me see how that shit look." She got up and stood in front of him then unbuttoned her low-rise jeans and slowly rolled her thong down past her thighs. "Damn!" he reached out and touched her. "This shit is mad smooth. Let me see all of it." She stepped out of her jeans and panties and opened up for him to examine her wax job. She felt real clean down there. "Damn," Daquan said, it ain't no monkey no more" And that night, for the first time ever, Daquan ate her pussy while she sucked his dick and he ate it like he had been eating pussy all his life.

*   *   *   *   *

Pitt stood in the lobby of the Empire State building reading an article in the Times about Daquan's little brother while waiting for the elevator to the observation deck.

He stood on the far wall, away from the group of tourist gathered at the elevators, thinking that this little dude was about to become a major player in the world. Shit! His face on the cover of Times, he had seen him in Newsweek, in People Magazine. The little nigga was doing big things, in a big way.

Pitt kept one eye on the ass of a woman in the front of the gathering who wore an ankle length skirt with a slit up the back nearly to her ass.

"Yeah Im-a get some of that," he said to himself.

When the elevator doors opened and passengers spilled in and out, he waited to be the very last man before squeezing in. The woman he had his eye on was all the way in the back against the hand railing. He pushed his way through the crowd and forced his way behind her until his dick was pressed right in the crack of her ass cheeks. He was hard as rock.

She didn't turn to look at him, and she didn't try to move away. In fact she had given a slight arch to her butt and was grinding into him ever so slightly.

"Yeah you freaky White bitch. You want this Black dick," he said to himself. He rolled the magazine up and slid it between the slits in her dress to test the waters. She didn't say anything as he massaged her pussy with it. He dropped the magazine to the floor and replaced it with his hand. Her panties were moist. Still she didn't move. He could swear a moan escaped her throat.

It was only a hundred and something floors to the observation deck and it only took minutes for the elevators to climb, they were so quick. Already he could feel the weightlessness in his stomach. If he was going to do something, he had better do it fast. The lady touching elbows beside him glanced down and gasped when he whipped out his dick and slid it between the slits in his victims' skirt. He gave the other woman a threatening look, pulled his victims panties to the side, bent his knees and slid in.

Everybody on the elevator had to know what was going on, because although she tried to keep a straight face like nothing was happening, her breathing and the involuntary sounds from her chest and him beating it, gave it away. But no one dared look back or to the side. They kept their focus to the front of the car like they were suppose to. They knew where they were. This was fuckin New York, where you could get your fuckin' head blown off for not minding your fuckin business, or for trying to play the fuckin hero.

He did have to bark on one man who dared to look around.

"Fuck you looking at BITCH?"

The man turned back and Pitt could actually see him trembling. He wasn't the only one trembling, just as the elevator was peaking, and the big elevator knot was forming in his stomach, the woman started trembling and bust all over his nuts.

Pitt couldn't stop his own nut from exploding. He pulled out and skeeted globs on the backside of a woman sandwiched next to his victim. She had no idea what he had just done. He wished he could stick around and see her expression when she found out.

When the elevator doors opened, the woman he had just got through boning made a conscious effort not to look back or even glance at him, she straightened her skirt and followed the crowd to the observation deck like nothing had happened, while he quickly crossed over to an elevator taking him back to the lobby.

It wasn't the first time Pitt had fucked a stranger in a public place. He had fucked a stranger in just about every public place in New York, with the exception of the Twin Tower buildings. They were off limits, too close to home base Melisa told him. Too many clients who might recognize her.

This was Melisa's game not Pitts. It was her favorite fantasy game. She was heavy into role-playing and had a bunch of identities, the tourist, the catholic schoolgirl, the public librarian, one of his favorites. He had fucked Melisa as a librarian in every isles of the New York Public library on 42nd street, where he rolled her around on a stocking cart they had stolen, and fucked her from behind while she actually stocked books on the shelves. They had almost gone to jail on that one.

The best though was one rush hour on the 6 train when Melisa played a Wall Street Broker, and some real Wall Street Broker chick, jammed next to them by the rush hour crowd, reached down out of the clear blue, grabbed his dick and jerked the cum out of it when he pulled out from under Melisa's short business skirt. The real Broker chick caught most of his nut in her hand then tasted it before getting off at the very next stop. Shit was bugged the fuck out. Bitch was young and fine and looked like she was swimming in old money.

Right now he knew Melisa would spend the next ten or fifteen minutes on the observation deck before taking the elevator back down and making her way back to work at the World Trade Center. They would both live off today's fantasy for the rest of the day, and when night came it was bound to get real freaky up on the Hill.

Pitt made his way to the parking garage in midtown. There were mad bad bitches parading the streets of Manhattan giving him the eye, but they couldn't attract him to sway. He had the baddest bitch in the world, and on any given day she could convincingly become any bad bitch she wanted to be, any nationality, any status, any age, and even her pussy would change identities to match.

*   *   *   *   *

Rachet drove all the way out to St. Albans Queens to meet Jeidar at her boyfriends house. Neither he nor she wanted to run the risk of any of the Diablo team seeing them together in the city, and no one knew about Jeidar's Queens hideaway. Even he didn't know until a few hours ago.

He had been waiting for nearly two years for the information she had for him today. For two long years he had been sitting on Petey's 600 thousand ransom, waiting for her to come through with the final key to their fortune, the combination to the bank vault inside El Diablo's stronghold. He and Jumm and three shooters arrived in two Ford rentals, shits that Rachet would never be caught in uptown. But Jeidar told him to be real low key so they played everything down, but they couldn't play down that uptown swagger.

Two houses away on the opposite side of the street, a black 2006 Honda Accord was about to back out of the driveway when the two Fords stopped in front of Jeidar's boyfriends house and it's occupants spilled from the cars. The driver of the Honda gasped and ducked down when she saw the driver of the lead car. The tall dark skinned dreadlock exited and surveyed the area before signaling for his passenger to get out.

The Dred was the man from Huntington. Gloria peeped again to make sure. It was him, she would never forget that face. She remained hidden until she was certain they had gone into the house on the other side of the street then eased the car back into the driveway and snuck around the side of the house to use the back entrance.

She searched for her sisters binoculars and found them fifteen minutes later in of all places the china cabinet, all the while checking every other minute through the living room blinds on the house and cars across from her. At the angle she was situated she could barely make out the numbers on the plates. Rentals She jotted down the numbers.

Fate was the strangest thing, Gloria thought. This wasn't accidental. They had crossed paths again for a reason. Most likely so that she could resolve the issue of what happened to Pete's body. But did she really want to know that badly? These were dangerous men, kidnappers and murderers. And how was she supposed to find out anyway? Follow them? And then what?

What if they were there for her? What if they had found out about her twin. What if they really worked for the cops that tailed her out here and tried to steal the ransom money? What was she suppose to do now?

*   *   *   *   *

Jeidar was El Diablo's secretary and mistress, dick sucker and gopher. She was Dominican fine, smart and extremely ambitious. The kind of woman no man in his right mind would trust. But mami deep throated and she swallowed and she knew what to say and when to say it, so men she dealt with were rarely in their right minds, not after she put that mojo on them,

and Jeidar was spreading that mojo around.

Besides Bamm, who she truly adored and who had worked a more powerful mojo on her, and Senior Diablo, who she despised, she was getting her back blown out once a week by Detective Denareo, just for the thrill of fucking a cop and she was fucking a famous rapper when ever he came into town. She had also let Rachet fuck her in her ass a few times. But all that was just fun or business, she was truly in love with Bamm, who lived with his grandmother and really wasn't about shit, couldn't fuck and didn't know any of her spots, but there was something about him that attracted her from day one and she had been hooked every since. So much so that she fully intended to take her share of the millions and turn it over to him so he could buy that house in Florida he wanted and get his independent music label up and popping.

As soon as Rachet and his crew left, Jeidar rushed back to the basement and flung herself on a reclining Bamm and smothered him with kisses.

"Wait a minute," she said, when he started returning her affection. She sat upright and took ten crisp one thousand dollar bills from her bra and handed them to him. "For you baby, there's a lot more where this came from."

*　*　*　*　*

CHAPTER 17

Gui Song Li was born in Guahgzhou China to a very wealthy and prestigious family who still held on to the old traditions of women backing out of rooms, Mao Zedong's Little Red Book of Communist laws and values, high collared jackets, bounded feet and drab fu' trousers, while most of the nations young people were motivated to the elimination of old constraints. Effects of the youth movement could be seen in Chinese girls wearing mini-skirts barely below the panty line, in public places, Karaoke bars and American rap music slowly cropping up, especially in Guahgzhou which was geographically joined at the hip with Hong Kong and a less submissive attitude among the women. There was also an ever-growing movement for the spread of literacy, organization and the doctrines of equality and opportunity.

Gui Song's parents however were not so liberated. They hated this movement. To them it represented everything American, whom they considered a disease among cultured people. They were extremely strict on Gui Song Li so when they announced she would be going to Hong Kong to visit cousins for the summer, she was in shock. She did not know what to think. According to her parents, every foul and disgusting thing exiled from China festered and flourished in Hong Kong.

Was she being exiled? Had she shamed her family's honor in some way she had not realized? Gui Song was a very devoted daughter. Instead of protesting or even questioning their motives she simply stayed in her room and cried for a week until they shipped her off.

When she reached Hong Kong she was met at the port by cousin's who were very much Americanized, and it was evident before they reached home their goal was to Americanize her as quickly as they could. They had exclusive tickets to a dope concert with backstage tickets. They had one for her also. She was coming whether she wanted to or not.

The very first thing they did when they reached home was strip her of the traditional clothing she wore and marvel at her overly ripe and developed body as they bombarded her with hip-hugger jeans, micro mini-skirts and tight tops to try on, refusing to acknowledge her extreme modesty and self consciousness. They fussed with her hair, painted her face and nails and finally decided on low cut jeans, low cut jeans they said accented her black girl bumm, a short top with something written in English she couldn't understand-B I T C H., open toe sandals with tiny heels that she found very uncomfortable and difficult to walk in, and... A pack of American filtered cigarettes just so she could look cool.

The concert was for a Reggae group called Steel something and though she didn't understand more than two words of the rapid Jamaican they spoke, she quickly fell in love with not only the music but everything about reggae, the lights, the bass vibrating her entire body, the sweet smell of marijuana, the fervor of the crowd, the chants and screams of hundreds of Japanese girls as they danced and gyrated to the music. It was the first time she had ever seen Japanese girls with dreadlocks, the first time she had seen anyone with dreadlocks. In fact it was the first time she had been close enough to a Black man that she could touch him.

Needless to say, she was feeling pretty ostracized until Ming dragged her back stage and introduced her to the mellowness of marijuana and a gorgeous Black Naval Officer named Robert Johnson who everybody called Red. Between the marijuana and Robert Johnson's outrageous good looks, her innocence didn't stand a chance at survival.

It didn't take long before, there, in the wings of that arena, she received her first passionate kiss and felt the first glorious hardness of a male organ pressed against her stomach. She liked them both so much, she kept Red there until it was time to leave and her panties were drenched and soggy from her excitement.

From that daybreak, Gui Song spent every available and clandestine moment she could with the handsome sailor, learning American slang, smoking weed, dry humping as much as she could and eventually performing her very first blow job, an act she initiated because he wanted more but she wasn't ready to give up her virginity, finding she was much better at it than either of then suspected for a premiere performance.

Seven days after learning how to swallow without choking and a few inches away from deep throating, Gui Song, with the help of Ming and one of her friends, rented a room in the Marriot hotel and invited her red haired lover to a candlelight dinner. She met him at the door in a baby doll so sheer it left nothing to the imagination.

It was her fifteenth birthday and she was celebrating by losing her virginity to the man she loved, a man nearly twice her age. A Black man with natural red hair who spoke perfect Mandarin and bits of the 13 sub languages of her native China. He was the most unusual, fascinating, mesmerizing, erotic creature on the planet, and he was all she wanted in this world.

That night, as she released herself from all inhibitions, she discovered she was sexually insatiable and ended up keeping Robert there for three extra days, until he had to leave her or otherwise be listed as AOL. After that, that's all they did-fuck ...like rabbits!

By the time Robert Jackson's ship departed from its six month tour of duty, Gui Song was already pregnant and hiding it from everyone but him, and despite all the logical reasons he gave her for not having it, Gui-Sung refused to abort the child. Eventually Robert professed his undying love for her then made a vow upon his mother's life to return and arrange for their marriage and her American citizenship. Gui Song believed him, but once his ship left shore, she grew so depressed she ended up confiding in her cousin Ming.

"You should abort the child," Ming advised her. "Red will never return for you. He is an American sailor, they never do. Maybe if he were an American businessman, yes, but a sailor, no!"

"He will," she said stubbornly. "and so what if he does not, I will still have my child.. our child."

"Don't be foolish Gui-Sung," Ming warned her, "You will lose all your family if you have this child, besides you are not much more than a child yourself. Who will take care of him? You must arrange for an abortion."

" Robert will return, I believe him even if you don't."

"And if he doesn't Gui-Sung, how will you support yourself and a child? You know your parents will disown you and cut your allowance."

"I will find a way." Gui-Sung said stubbornly, rubbing her stomach. "I will never abandon my child. "

"Abortions are not bad Gui Sung. I've had three myself. Actually four if you count the miscarriage. "

Four? Ming was only half a year older than she was.

"I'm not having an abortion," she said growing more frustrated with Ming's pessimism with each additional negative out of her mouth. She had known it was a bad idea to confide in Ming in the first place, " Robert will be back before the new year and me and our child will be here waiting for him."

"When your parents find out..."

"Who cares? I'm not going back to China. I'm going to America."

The New Year had come and gone and her red-headed lover still had not returned-not even a letter. Gui Sung was nearing the end of her second trimester and Ming had not stopped acting stupid, and now because Gui-Sung's pregnancy had become so obvious, Ming's family had become involved. They too were trying to persuade her to have a third trimester abortion, but they had sworn they would not tell her parents. Ming on the other hand was threatening to contact Gui-Sungs mother and tell her of the pregnancy, she didn't want to be caught up as a co-conspirator-it could ruin not only her life but the life of her family as well. Gui Sung's parents were very powerful and extremely wealthy, their influence could easily consume Ming's family's moderate wealth, Ming complained.

Gui Song could no longer trust her cousin, so on a cold January night, she gathered a few clothing, the money she had saved from the generous allowances her parents sent monthly, and moved to another section of town, a small room in Hong Kong's triad district arranged by a stranger who had befriended her and whom she had confided in on one of her many excursions into Hong Kong's back streets to get away from Ming's prying eyes.

She had hardly become familiar with her new environment when, alone, on a freezing night, her water broke and Gui Song delivered her own child, a small dark fragile baby girl with bright red hair. The child was so small in fact that Gui-Sung could cradle her in one hand.

When it showed no signs of life she wrapped the miniature infant in a table napkin and, was filled with the temptation to throw her in the dumpster down the street behind the restaurant. Her heart was heavy with sadness but she couldn't do it. Instead she clutched the lifeless child against her chest and began to weep. Soon her weeping turned to a sick wrenching wail. A wail that could have easily raised the dead or caused some retched soul to join them. Gui_Sung cried herself into a deep sleep where she dreamed her baby was alive and searching for a nipple to feed from.

*　*　*　*　*

Jon John bowed in respect to the shrine behind the curtain door dedicated to Ts'oi Pak Shing Kawn -the god of wealth, before stepping through the main entrance of the Triad owned girlie bar.

It was his favorite haunt because all the girls were Chinese and wore cheong sams, the traditional dress with slits up to mid-thigh and which were often extended even higher with a zip. Here he could get anything from a blowjob to an all night session simply by choosing and paying the barman to walk out with her. Of course he had still had to pay the girl the negotiated price, which was pretty steep compared to other bars, but it was well worth every Yen. The women were the most beautiful, pampered and diseased free in all of Hong Kong and there were always new faces to chose from. John John Wi was on his second drink and was in the process of negotiating an agreement with an exotic bar girl when he saw Gui Song Li step into the club. Even though he had seen her only briefly on two separate occasions, and both had been over a year ago, her beauty was overwhelmingly unmistakable. He recognized her instantly. John John excused himself and gave the girl a twenty for her time. Her disappointment didn't even register in the wide smile she offered.

Gui Song crossed over to a Triad soldier who had to be her pimp, Yip Kai-Foon, a dangerous thug with a reputation for murder and robbery. Yip Kai-Foon pointed Gui Song to a table where a stout Japanese businessman sat eyeing her. She made her way to his table and John John followed. She had hardly taken a seat before John John was at the table introducing himself, a rudeness that would never had been tolerated in Japan, but this was Hong Kong and this was his district.

"She's taken," the Japanese gentleman said in a menacing tone.

John John flashed his Hong Kong Police credentials. "She would be if this weren't official business," he shrugged as if he really didn't want to interrupt but it was a necessity then motioned for him to leave the booth.

The Japanese man immediately looked to Yip Kai-Foon who nodded him away with a frown. John John had no intention of spooking the girl but the Japanese client looked like an all nighter and John John did not have that kind of patience. He needed to get the girl away from Yip Kai-Foon to talk her, find out if she was here of her own free will or if she had been forced. Slavery was still a much-practiced occupation in Hong Kong.

John John studied her face. She was spooked although she was doing an excellent job at hiding it. "I'm really not on official business," he offered as a way to calm her fear. "It's just that he didn't look like your type."

She forced a smile, "And you do?"

He slid into the cubicle and she began looking around for Yip Kai-Foon. John John had seen him slip out a side door after nodding at the Japanese. She caught the eye of a waitress who was at their table in a flash, then exchanged glances, Gui Song's eye shifting quickly to John John and back.

The waitress bent to give John John a kiss on his cheek. "He's harmless," she offered. "And he can't keep it up for more than two minutes, especially with you." She winked then turned back to him. "She is very special John John. Very Special."

Very special in her jargon translated into, the new hot twat on the block, worth her weight in gold. To John John it meant a family that was distraught over her disappearance and a huge finders fee.

He smiled and told her to bring him a double and a double for the girl. Her drinks would cost him twice as much and there would be nothing in them stronger than Coca Cola, ice tea or colored mineral water. His drinks would be extra strong. The drunker he got the more money he was likely to spend, while she would remain sober enough to work all night.

"So what do you want?" she asked after the waitress departed.

"An all nighter."

She looked him in the eye without flinching, "Two thousand American."

"Five hundred HK is tops."

"The gentleman you just ran away has already made a bid of two thousand American. If you wish to take his place you pay what he is willing to pay, otherwise I thank you for the drinks. Mister more my type."

He looked over at the Japanese gentleman staring across at them from the bar. He was obviously rich. He could afford two thousand American for the night. Two thousand was a month's splurge for Detective John John Wi. He looked back at the girl. She was beyond exotic and he wanted her more than he wanted the money returning her to her family would bring.

"Two thousand? That's a little over my budget."

"I like you Mister Detective," she said, lifting a drink and guzzling it down in one swoop. "But you are definitely not my type." She gulped down the second drink and slid around the horseshoe table, stood and straightened her cheong sam's. "My type can afford me."

Bernstein repeated a portion of the last sentence he read, "She gulped down the second drink and slid around the horse shoe table, stood and straightened her cheong sam's -my type can afford me?" He slapped the manuscript on the glass top angrily. "What the fuck is this shit? I wait two years for a goddamn report and this is what I get!" He snatched up the phone and hit a speed dial number. "Goddamn it Fred, What in the Gods hell is this crap you sent me?"

"You have to admit it's an interesting story Bernie, my daughter saw the report and she just went with it. Thought you might want to get a first peek. Could be your next best seller."

Bernstein picked the manuscript from the table and stared at it. "Fuck a goddamn script Fred. I don't give a shit if your cute little girl wrote it. Where's the goddamn dirt I asked you for. You remember the report? The one you've already billed me a few hundred thousand for."

"You want the goddamn report Bernie? All you had to do was turn to the back. There's a complete summary. All the dirt you'll need."

Bernstein hurriedly turned to the back. "Well if you had placed it in the front where it damn well should have gone, maybe I would have read the goddamn manuscript afterwards,"

"It's your loss Bernie. I'll have my cute little grown up girl shop it to Gotham. They've already expressed some interest in it.

"Do that. And have them send the check you're expecting from me along with that interest." He hung the phone up abruptly, and scanned through the summarization. It was a detailed history that even included a DVD labeled; 'Sex with a Great Dame'. As he continued to scroll a name jumped off the page at him. A name he was all too familiar with. Anthony'Madd Dogg' Rachet.

Bernstein leaned back in his chair and studied the DVD before slipping it into the player. "This could turn out to be something very interesting," he said softly to himself.

CHAPTER 18

Melisa was usually the first one in and the last one out of the offices of Schumeyer and Fisch. She had never been late and had missed only one day of work in the three years she had been with the firm. She knew all the partners on a first name basis, not because of her sexuality but because they all respected her professionalism, her hard work and dedication to any assignment she was given.

She designed herself after the senior partner Simon Schumeyer, who had never missed a day's work in the twenty-seven years since he founded the firm and was still the first to turn a key into any of the suites and always put on the first pot of freshly brewed.

Schumeyer and Fisch occupied the top three floors of two Plaza in the World Trade Center. They were the largest law firm in the Tower's. Melisa was rising to the top and she hadn't even passed the bar yet.

Today, for the first time, she was running a little late, twenty minutes to be exact, and she was being very hard on herself as she stepped off the elevator into the mahogany paneled lobby smelling of old money.

Mrs. Larson was sitting at the receptionist desk and her switchboard was lit up like a Christmas tree. She was juggling calls expertly but Melisa could tell she was being overwhelmed.

"Did Simon ask about me?" Melisa bent and asked.

Mrs. Larson covered her headset and answered. "He's not here, None of the partners came to work today and only a handful of attorneys."

As Melisa made her way through the hub of cubicles to her work station she couldn't help but notice two things, one was the absence of the strong scent of fresh brewed coffee that Simon kept going all morning long, and the second, the largest portion of the work force that did show up was Black and Latino, there were very few White faces on the floor.

"What's going on?" she asked Gary, one of the young Black lawyers recently assigned to her section. "Where is everyone?"

"It's still early," he said, glancing through a folder. "Probably got a late start."

"Everybody," she asked. "This place is like a ghost town."

"It'll be hectic before you know it," he assured her.

"Well I don't know about you but I need a cup of strong coffee to start my day, what about you?"

"You know how to work that thing?"

"No. I think the only person in the world that can operate that coffee maker is Simon. I was thinking about going down for a cup."

Gary dug in his wallet and came out with a five.

"My treat," she said. "Anything else, a croissant, a hot biscuit?"

"No. Just a strong cup. Black no cream, two sugars."

At the lobby Melisa took an order for the gray haired receptionist.

As the elevator dropped, she couldn't shake the feeling that something was strangely out of place.

* * * * *

At 8:45 AM Rachet stood outside Saint Mary's and watched as an extraordinarily beautiful woman and a preppy Black kid emerged from the back of a Lincoln Town car. She looked like a movie star. Bernstein told him she would be the most attractive woman there but he had no idea China had transformed into this. If Bernstein hadn't told him, and he had passed her on the streets, he would have never recognized her in a million years, she was just that far removed from the ordinary.

Old feelings began to stir but he checked them. This was about money. Who ever was keeping her was rich beyond comparison Bernstein had assured him. The apartment she lived in alone was worth ten million and according to Bernstein her benefactor was worth billions, he also assured him he would be willing to pay millions to get her back. Bernstein had even thrown in the deed to another abandoned building in Harlem to sweeten the deal.

Rachet watched her driver, the man was alert, highly trained, ten years in the FBI as a Protector for foreign dignitaries, now retired and in the employ of a private security firm, which also supplied Contractors to governments around the world. Bernstein had given him a complete rundown, everything except the name of her benefactor. He wasn't about to let him become an independent.

"Goddamn China," he said to himself as rays of light danced from a diamond bracelet she wore. "I knew your pussy was good but I didn't know it was this good!"

Rachet was glad he had taken Bernstein's advice and worn a suit and tie, otherwise he would be standing out like a sore thumb. The place was crawling with security and the filthy rich. Right now he blended in like he was Secret Service or a Protector he thought, giving, the school another once over. He would never be able to snatch her here and the complex she lived in was high security with cameras everywhere. Besides Bernstein didn't want her snatched there, it would bring too much attention to his gated community. She rarely went out and when she did she was always accompanied. She wasn't smoking crack any more, that was evident. But she was seeing someone, a White earthmover salesman named Larry Karolyi. He was most likely the weakest link.

But Rachet would get to that part later. He wasn't really concerned with snatching China right now. He was here this early morning more out of curiosity than anything else. Right now it was thirty million sitting in El Diablo's safe that dominated his thoughts. The 'Team' would only go in when the timing was absolutely right. When the fuck was that going to be? Jeidar had seen the fucking money, it was ready to be boxed and shipped.

"Just be ready to go." he was told. "It's going to happen any day now."

Fuck it. If it didn't happen at least he now had something to fall back on. China could still make him a multi-millionaire. He watched China kiss the kid, who hurried off with the little redhead, then slide back in the car like she was royalty.

As the Lincoln pulled into traffic, Rachet was thinking a few things, he couldn't believe how good she looked, or how well she had done for herself, or what the fat Jew bastard wanted her snatched for. It wasn't like Bernstein was a slouch in the money department himself, he owned half of Manhattan and a large chunk of the money market. He wasn't hurting, so it had to be about more than money. Bernstein was a beast. Rachet had seen it first hand. So China meant more to him than a pretty penny. What ever it was Rachet could smell mo' money, mo' money mo money.

*   *   *   *   *

Ray Ray Carrero received an encoded I-Mail at 9 AM sharp, instructing him to find China a modest apartment in another section of town and to liquidate the Washington Heights property. It was a secured transmission, written in code as were all the I-Mails he received from or transmitted overseas. There was also an inquiry about the boy Daquan.

"All plans effective, " he typed in encrypted code. "Boy is maturing quite well. Still our star player."

He received another set of instructions, committed them to memory before signing off and flipping through a portfolio of No Ho properties while following the Wall Street Report on CNN. His instructions were clear, someone was digging hard into China's background and the reason for the digging had to be severed, i.e., Washington Heights and all connections with China and the boy.

Whatever property he secured the boy would have to be able to afford after the initial payment, which would come out of a trust fund set up for China by her 'late husband.' But that money was quickly diminishing with all the expenses of a lavish life style. Ray Ray had created a portfolio for her but it would take time to mature and there was a penalty for early withdrawal.

Daquan would be OK though. He had a few million stashed and he was doing quite well for himself, having made a few wise investments. His ties with Diablo weren't being severed. He was still being considered a player. Still Ray Ray wished Daquan would do something with the rest of his earnings besides hiding them in a hole where they collected no interest and made no profits.

*   *   *   *   *

Pitt was still smoking wet, although he hadn't smoked in the last forty-eight hours. He thought maybe he was having flashbacks from what he was seeing on television. He had to get right up on the screen to make sure he wasn't hallucinating. A fuckin' plane had just flown into the World Trade building. No fuckin' way! He turned up the volume then instinctively dialed Melisa's cellular. It just kept ringing.

"Come on boo. Answer the fuckin' phone!" he shouted over the comments of the Newscaster. "Fuck! I don't believe this shit." And then before he knew it the building was coming down. Floor after, floor after, floor. Like some demolition shit. Pitt grabbed the keys to the rental and dialed Melisa again as he dashed from the apartment. Damn! That was his baby's building, and her floor the plane crashed into. He knew she was in it. She never missed a day's work. Never!

He had just revved up the engine and was figuring out the quickest way to get downtown when his cell phone rang. It wasn't Melisa. It was Rachet. He started not to answer as he pulled off. He didn't want to waste his batteries in case he had to help Melisa.

"You see what just fuckin' happened?" he shouted into the phone, swerving to barely miss another car. "Get the fuck off the road you stupid mutha-fucka, " he screamed. "Fuckin ' terrorist just blew up the World Trade Center!"

"It's on," Rachet said over the phone.

"Damn right it's on," Pitt said. "Fuckin' Ben Laden's attacking the United States-"

"No the heist. The team called. They say it's a perfect time to go."

"Fuck a mutha-fuckin' heist. My baby's in that building."

"Nigga fuck that bitch. It's time to get this gwaup."

*   *   *   *   *

At Saint Mary's all the classes were herded into the auditorium while an awed and confused administration and teaching staff tried to come to grips with what was going on in lower Manhattan.

In the mist of all the chaos, Naquan slipped quietly and undetected, through a side door and snuck his way back to his homeroom. In all the confusion, Mrs. Muller had left her purse unlocked in the second drawer where she kept it. Naquan knew she didn't have it when she ushered them out of homeroom so it had to still be there. He had noticed a crisp stack of bank notes just before one of the teachers from A2 rushed in and Mrs. Muller was searching her bag for her favorite mints.

*   *   *   *   *

Rosa Rodriguez was recovering from her third heart bypass and the specialist had warned her over and over to control her emotions. Her heart was fragile and couldn't withstand undue strain. She had to come to terms with her son's disappearance in no uncertain terms. She had to let go of her hatred for Gloria.

It wasn't going to happen. As long as there was a breath in her lungs and a beat in her heart, she would do everything in her power to get to the bottom of Pete's death.

The detective she hired had found out Gloria purchased a 38 revolver six months before Pete's demise and a box of bullets from a mall sporting goods store during the same week of his disappearance. She had used her driver's license to purchase both. To the detective it didn't prove anything other than the possibility Gloria might have had the intention of foul play, but without a body it was at most theory. But to Rosa it was conclusive. Gloria had murdered Petey and done away with the body. There was a latest development though. Huntington Police had run the plates of a 2001 Honda Accord as a suspected stolen vehicle. The car belonged to Gloria's twin sister, and it was the same night Gloria told her Pete was caught in a storm•

The case was taking a turn for the better, clues were beginning to come together. Rosa was certain Gloria would be in the electric chair before her own heart failed. She would live to see the heartless bitch executed. After all what was Gloria doing in Huntington eight o-clock at night? She had no family in Long Island, no friends and the neighborhood she had been spotted in was drug infested and a crime hotspot. Someone had to have seen her. Gloria came from money. She certainly would have had to stand out in a neighborhood like that. Someone would have had to have seen her. Rosa instructed the detective to offer a fifty thousand dollar reward to anyone who could remember Gloria and offer a substantial clue as to what happened on that night.

She hung up and pressed the button for her care attendant. Jamillah arrived within moments, dressed in a crispy white nurses uniform.

"How are you feeling Mrs. Rodriquez?" she asked cheerfully.

"Fine Jamillah. Fine. Could you turn it on Regis for me and fix me a cup of coffee?" The remote was inches away from Rosa Rodriquez and she knew that she was not to have coffee under any circumstances.

Jamillah picked up the remote and flicked on the television. "There is no coffee Mrs. Rodriquez," Jamillah said calmly.

Rosa responded angrily. "Why is there no coffee. I specifically ordered you to purchase coffee on your last trip to the store-"

"They were out," Jamillah lied.

"You're not a very good liar Jamillah," Rosa told her, struggling to pull herself upright against the headboard. "Perhaps I should call the agency and have you replaced.

Jamillah helped her. "And then who would help you play detective?"

"Oh my God!" Rosa shouted, grabbing her heart, her eyes wide in astonishment.

Jamillah sprang into action. The woman was having a heart attack. As she reached for the syringe and medication by the bedside she caught a glimpse of what had brought on the attack. Jamillah's own heart fluttered and she almost dropped the syringe.

"Oh my God! It's the end of the world."

*   *   *   *   *

Gloria watched the black Navigator parked across Lenox Avenue from the corner window of a small West Indian restaurant. She wore jeans, New Balance, and a Nike tee. She had also dyed her hair black and rented a Ford Eclipse.

She had no idea what she was doing or what she was going to do when this led to whatever it led too. She had been following the Dred since the day he showed up in St. Albans, hoping to find some clue as to what happened to Petey's body after she left him that night. The more she thought about it the dumber this whole spying thing was becoming, not that it wasn't dumb when she had reacted just off her instincts. Now it was becoming dangerously dumb. If they caught her she might find out what happened to Petey by ending up buried next to him. Anyway the problem wasn't really these guys. The problem was Rosa snooping around with her private detectives, just two days ago one had posed as an insurance agent and questioned her twin about the Honda.

The Dred came out of the bodega with three other men. The medium complexion one with the hazel eyes was Rachet, the leader of the drug crew. She had watched him, he was always giving money out to the kids, kind and courteous to people in the neighborhood, even crack heads he treated with respect. But the waitress who served her each morning, assured her he was completely homicidal.

"That's a nigga you don't ever wanna get on his bad side," she told her one morning. "You ain't a cop are you?"

"Naw!" Gloria assured her. "Just thought I knew him from someplace."

"Honey if you did know him, don't renew the relationship . Every girl he's ever messed with he either turned them out.. Or chopped them up and fed em to his dogs."

Maybe that's what happened to Pete, Gloria was thinking. Maybe they chopped him up and fed him to the dogs. If they had it would solve all her problems.

"He's fine though," the waitress said to her as she gathered dishes from surrounding tables. "I'm talking 'bout Jumm, not Rachet. He's always in here flirting, a nice rap too, but I don't mess with thugs. There's no future. They either gonna end up in the morgue or worse, up North." The waitress could have been a juggler the way she was balancing dishes on one arm. "You really don't want a man doing time, you'd be better off if he was dead," she continued. "Niggaz want you to work your ass off so they can have fifty-five dollar buys every two weeks. Then they want you to come and see they ass on the regular, send 'em food packages an' shit..." The waitress was becoming emotional as she added more dishes to the pile. "Meanwhile you be the one that's struggling with the rent, the light bills, trying to keep food on your own table and clothes on your kids back, lunch money, transportation! Then on top of that shit, niggaz wanna run up your phone bill 'til they cut that shit off."

"Gloria was sorry she got the woman started. Evidently she had a man in prison, or did have one.

121

"Then these mutha-fuckaz so stupid," she put her free hand on her hip and almost spit the words out. "They want you to stuff drugs in your ass so you can run the risk of ending up the same place they are. Then... "

Looked like the woman was about to shed a tear so Gloria averted her eyes and looked back at the crew. Just in time too, they were headed-in the direction of Jumm's Navigator.

"The mutha-fucka don't even come back to yo' ass. He gets out of prison and runs straight to a three hundred pound pink toe," the waitress concluded.

Gloria hurriedly fished money from her purse, left the tab and a generous tip then slid from the cubicle. Today would be the last time she followed them she promised herself as she left the diner speed walking to her rental around the corner. This was becoming too much like a drug. Her adrenalin was pumping.. and what was even more dangerous was she was beginning to find Jumm very attractive and she was wondering if this whole obsession was about Pete.. Or about the handsome Dred she couldn't stop thinking about.

Honey's got a problem with the bends/she likes to bend over then she spreads the skins/a hoe is just a hoe and that's without no controversy/she can make the bedsprings sing a song of mercy-

Brand Nubian

Grand Puba

CHAPTER 19
SLOW DOWN

THE LITTLE NIGGA DAQUAN had been beating Trina's pussy since 1 o'clock last night, eight non-stop hours, while Kisha was left wide-awake staring at the cable clock. Now the bitch was screaming like she was in labor, having 'another ' fucking orgasm. How many this made Kisha had no idea, having lost count at around eighteen.

Trina was a horny beast and the little nigga was putting that serious work in. The apartment's walls were paper thin and Kisha could hear every nuance of sound effects coming from their love making -if you could call it that -he was working that pussy, making it fart and slurp and cry until Trina's screaming demons took over, like they were taking over now.

"Oh God Daquan...Oh God... Oh God..Oh God! Fuck this pussy.. put it all in me.. Un huh.. Oh Shit!-Oh God... OOOOOOOHHHH Fuck me... Fuck me... Fuck me... Fuck me!"

Kisha promised herself she would never-never-ever-in her life masturbate but her pussy was so wet from listening to this shit all night that she slid her hands between her thighs and worked her clit with one hand while trying to get as much of the other in as she could.

Kisha came a minute after Trina, but instead of Trina rolling over and calling it quits, she was on a dick revival mission, slurping the little niggaz knob until she was choking on it and they were going at it again. Drained, but far from satisfied, Kisha fell back and looked at the clock

8:15

Didn't this hoe know she had exams this morning? Fuck! They were on some serious marathon shit. The way they were going at it looked like she was gonna be spending the day here for nothing.

"Get the fuck out bitch!" Kisha whispered under her breath. "Go to class. Do something!" She could tell Trina was riding him again, especially when Daquan yelled out

"Damn Tree. What the fuck you trying to do, break my shit?" Trina was grunting and moaning like she was trying to get a major turd out her ass. "You ain't never gon' get it all in.. You might as well stop trying."

"I can feel it opening up some more Quan," she said, her voice so strained Kisha could hardly make out the words. She let out a long animal grunt. "Un huh.. A little bit more. It's opening up. Ah shit... I'm-a get all this shit in me..."

"The only thing you gon' do Tree is end up breaking my dick."

"No!" Trina said between grunts and moans. "I'm-a get all this in me or I'm gonna die trying."

"Yeah, you gon' be dead an' I'm gon' be at yo funeral with a big ass cast on my dick."

"Why does everything have to be a joke Daquan?" Trina smirked, then followed the question with a couple of "ah shits! and long, agonizing, guttural moans.

"Fuck!" Daquan shouted.

He must have pushed her off because she was suddenly breathing like she was having an asthma attack and her tone was almost pleading

"Why you do that Quan? I was almost there."

"Ain't you got test or something," he asked. Kisha could sense the irritation in his voice.

"Oh I get it," Trina's voice went up an octave. "You trying to get rid of me so you can fuck Kisha."

"Get da fuck outta here Tree. You crazy."

"I'm crazy.. I saw the way you were looking at the bitch last night..."

"Ahhh shit! Here we go with that jealous shit again!"

"Jealous? I can tell when you're looking at the next pussy Daquan. I ain't stupid!"

"Tree, you's a fuckin' nymphomaniac. My dick stay sore. How you think I'm trying to get up in some other bitch? I'm just saying you need to take care of yo' obligations. School is more important than gettin' yo' freak on."

"Oh now I'm a fucking freak?"

"Ah fuck. Here we go," Daquan mumbled.

"Damn right you're a freak, bitch," Kisha wanted to yell out. "If you fuck the whole football squad then go to a club and fuck some nasty ass Jamaican on the dance floor the same night, I think that damn well qualifies you as a freak. Matter-fact, that makes you a Super Freak.. And a Super Ho." Kisha rolled over to her side. Her head was throbbing from the alcohol. She pulled the covers over her hangover to block out the word war Trina and Daquan were having.

How the hell you fuck all night and start fighting like strangers in the morning?

Basically it was her fault, Kisha was thinking. They were arguing over her ass. She rolled over, sat up and started searching for her underwear in the pile of clothes she had torn off in the middle of the night. "OK I'm up... I'm out."

"Fuck that! You know I don't leave anybody in my apartment when I'm not here," Trina was saying intentionally loud. "Not even my Mamma."

"All I'm sayin' Tree, is if you don't trust me then I'll leave with you. But you need to let your friend sleep that shit off."

"That bitch ain't drunk. She just hanging around till I leave so she can get some of 'my' dick," Trina said loudly. Then she shouted. "But it ain't gonna fuckin' happen!.. Bitch better be up and ready by the time I get dressed or I'm-a drag her in the hallway and leave her naked ass out there."

"Na Na!" Kisha dropped her underwear back in the pile. "You gon' drag me in the hallway and leave me butt-ass? I gotta see this shit," she whispered to herself, pulling the covers back over her. "No you are absolutely right. It's not gonna happen. I'm not going a mutha-fuckin place. . An' now I'm-a really fuck your man.. BITCH! She said the last word out loud .

While everyone in the Diablo hub was crowded around the flat screen watching the World Trade Center Buildings come down, Jeidar found a corner in the outer office and secretly dialed a number on her cell phone.

"It's crazy in here," she whispered into the headpiece. "Everybody's in front of the TV and the fucking safe room is wide open. Yall coming or what?"

*   *   *   *   *

Jumm flicked his cell phone and glanced into the side view mirror as he made the right off Lenox into 127th street. He wondered for the hundredth time if he should let Rachet know they were being followed. He had known for over three weeks but it wasn't the Federalizes or the Roc squad, it was Petey Rodriquez's wife.. in living color..

What the hell was he thinking that night in Huntington he slid into her car and had a conversation with her? What did he possibly think would happen, that she would forget his face?

He knew what he was thinking, that Petey's wife was the finest female he ever laid eyes on and that Jah Almighty had finally sent him his angel.

Now his Angel was stalking him and he was trying to figure out what that was all about before he had to body her pretty ass. The last thing he wanted was for Rachet to know Petey Rodriquez's wife was following them. In fact Jumm had been doing everything in his power to keep Rachet from finding out. Rachet would body her for sure. Something Jumm should have done himself two years ago.

"Your girl Jeidar is going to be a problem. She doesn't understand the code of silence," Jumm said, slowing the big truck and turning into the underground parking lot next to the State Building. He glanced over his shoulder at the white Eclipse just turning into the block. "I don't trust her. It might not be wise to keep her around after it's over."

Jumm gave a half nod to the girl in the attendant booth and swiped his monthly. The arm went up and he zipped through.

It was his intention to body the Rodriquez chick after she could pick him out of a line-up. In fact he had doubled back to do just that. He was a few steps away from putting one in her head before she started unloading the thirty-eight in Petey's double. He slipped in the darkness and watched as she broke him down. From that moment on he couldn't get her off his mind.

Rachet snapped to life, reaching his hand across the cab. "Gimme the phone." He dialed a number "Rover One at home base," he said, then listened. A static voice responded, "Second level, thirty-eight, reserved." Rachet clicked the phone shut and motioned to Jumm. "Second level." Jumm eased the Navigator down the curving ramp hoping the Rodriquez broad had enough sense not to follow him down here. "See that reserved space? Pull in there." Jumm checked his rearview before turning the big SUV expertly into the narrow space. No sign of the Rodriquez chick.

"What now?" he asked, popping a full clip in his nine millimeter and locking one in the head, looking over both shoulders, giving the entire garage a visual sweep.

"We wait until we get the signal to move," Rachet said, handing him back the phone.

*   *   *   *   *

Gloria got lucky and found an open meter on Martin Luther King a half block away. She dropped quarters for the full two-hour limit, her adrenaline pumping through her like she had taken an overdose of Prozac, which in fact she just might have.

"What a dangerous game we play," she said aloud, feeling the lump in the shoulder bag she carried. She had made up her mind. She was going to purposely bump into the Dred and see where it led. She took a deep breath and ran full speed back to the garage.

* * * * *

Rachet was nervous. He didn't know anything about the team doing the hit other than they were mercenaries for hire and Preacher had assured him they would get the job done. That part he wasn't worried about. It was the 'once they got it' part that had him on edge. Their fee was four hundred thousand up front, the balance just before they went in. He was sitting on the last two hundred right now plus the two hundred needed to bait EI Diablo. They didn't want a dollar over the agreed amount, Preacher assured him. If the hit was for a hundred million they would deliver it to the last dollar. Their reputation in the mercenary community was worth a lot more than any amount over their agreed contract.

'Fuck that!' Rachet was thinking. 'Give me thirty million of the next niggaz money and he don't know my face or who I am, see if he ever sees me or his thirty mil in this life time.'

Rachet couldn't see how anyone could be that honest with that amount of money.

A Manhattan Cable Van pulled into the reserved space next to him. 'Fuck it! If they juxed him, Rachet would find a way to murder Preacher, his entire stable of whores and every family member even remotely related to him. It was too late to pull out now.

Jumm's cell phone rang. He answered and immediately passed it over to Rachet who listened for a few then hung up and dialed a number. "Senior Diablo?" he said in the phone, studying the cable van curiously. "Yeah this is Rachet. You said call when I wanted to talk.. right now..." He turned and stared at Jumm as he listened. "It's now or never. Plus I got two thousand Franklin's in case we can't come to an agreement... Yeah, give me fifteen." He hung up and smiled at Jumm. "We on."

* * * * *

Gloria reached the second level just in time to see Rachet open the passenger side door and drop a paper bag by the running board while the Navigator was backing out of the space. She ducked between two cars as the big truck swooped past and waited until she could hear its tires on the upper level before rising. She was about to make a mad dash for her rental when the door to the cable van opened and a white man in dark glasses and blond hair stepped out, picked up the bag and got back in. The way he was holding it, it looked like a stack of money instead of the trash she originally thought it was. Her curiosity mixed with the Prozac and a minute later she found herself rapping on the driver's side window.

"Excuse me, do you do house calls?" she asked, standing on her toes to see into the cab. "My cable went out and I was wondering if you had one of those zapper things."

He shook his head and gave her a generous smile. "You'll have to call the office," he said politely.

"The office? Why do you think I want it zapped?"

He smiled again. "Sorry. I don't zap,"

"Just thought I'd give it a try," she offered in a way of explanation. "You know Puerto Rican's ain't trying to pay for no cable bill." She turned and headed for the nearest exit. The cable man hadn't even tried to conceal the stack of hundreds he was counting. She knew it wasn't money he collected for cable bills and he damn sure didn't look like a drug dealer, so something was going on and now her curiosity was really peaking. Gloria never knew she could get such a rush from playing detective. The game was becoming more and more dangerous and the greater the danger the more she craved the fear.

*   *   *   *   *

Rachet and his crew of misfits might be ruthless killers and thugs but they would have never been able to pull this heist off. Diablo's security would have murdered every last one of them before they got anywhere close to the money. Even for Triple-K, the best that ever did it, it was nearly impossible. They had a 60 second window of opportunity before Diablo was whisked into the second safe room and the entire operation shut down. Once he was in, there was no getting him out, and the money would be locked in with him, sealed in an atomic proofed chamber. Triple-K had to give credit to the girl Jeidar though. She had provided all the details of the interior and personnel he hadn't been able to obtain. Still, Diablo was as protected as a foreign dignitary in a hostile environment.

He recognized two Protectors he fought with in Afghanistan. If they were here that meant a few good men were about to die. It was the only way to accomplish the mission.

Triple-K raised the FAL sniper variant high velocity rifle, pressed the wood stock to his shoulder, rested the side of his face against it's coolness, took a couple of deep breaths and relaxed as he peered through the sniper scope.

"One shot-one kill.'

*   *   *   *   *

With the exception of the World Trade buildings coming down and the excitement it was causing among his comrades, today was just like every other day in the last two years for Junior Speresman, boring. But even so he stayed alert, more so to keep his skills highly tuned than for the paycheck, although Diablo paid more than when he worked as a contractor, nearly three times as much for doing practically nothing. One shot in two years.

Junior took another sweep of the block through his binoculars, then leaned back against the sloping edge of the roof, laid the special equipped 30-30 across his lap and took the luxury of smoking a cigarette. What the hell were his comrades so upset about? If the Arabs did blow up the World Trade buildings it was nothing in comparison to what the U.S. had done in their countries. They were there just like he was, shooting babies and family members of Terrorist who the U.S. couldn't get to, just to send a message.

Junior was deep in thought and in the motion of extinguishing the cigarette flame when the high velocity 50cal round pierced the 2-inch horizontal between the bottom of his nose and his upper lip. The back of his cranium opened and all connections to his nervous system and this world were instantly severed. He didn't even twitch-the shot was so clean. He just sat there, eyes wide open like he was still deep in thought. He had never really believed in the Angel of Death but now he was face to face and he was one ugly mutha-fucka.

*   *   *   *   *

Traffic was so backed up from the Midtown tunnel that Pitt left the rental and jogged through the blaring of horns and constant shouts of frustrations. He didn't stop until he was on the other side of the tunnel.

On Thirty-fifth and Second Avenue it looked like the world was coming to an end. The great cloud he had watched rising from the Queens side now seemed to envelope him. He could smell it, taste the grit, grime and chemicals heavy in his mouth and lungs.

The sirens of ambulances, fire trucks and Police cars were coming from every direction, many racing past as he took a short rest and again went into an even paced jog. Police were cordoning off all cars and pedestrians but no one made an attempt at stopping him. He didn't realize until he was on Wall street, approaching a line of barricades and police in full riot gear, that it had gotten so hot in the car, he had taken his shirt off and in all the confusion forgotten to put it back on. Now the brown shoulder harness holstering the big black plastic glock was the only thing covering his upper body.

"Fuck it," he said aloud. He wasn't stopping. They would just have to stop him.

They didn't. They opened the barrier and waved him through.

"One cop did ask him, "What precinct are you from?"

"Three-two," he shouted back.

"You're a long way from home-"

"My girl is in there!"

"Oh!" the officer' shouted, sympathetically. "Good luck, and you'd better clip your shield' on. Those NSA boys are taking no prisoners."

*　*　*　*　*

Rachet checked his Jacob's, nine-thirty, he was right on time as the Navigator glided into EI-Diablo's fortified block. He handed Jumm his nine before climbing out.

Seconds later Jumm watched Rachet, carrying the two hundred thousand, being escorted up the stairs before disappearing into the gray brownstone in the middle of the block. He waited a beat then punched a number into his cell phone.

"You in position?" he asked, pausing to look up and down the block without being too conspicuous. He knew all the shooters by heart. He had been watching them for months, waiting for Rachet to put this shit together. Now it was here and his heart was skipping like a mutha-fucka. "I got two shooters on the south, one wearing a black and white print shirt, the other is right across from him on the other side of the street playing with some kids. He's got on a yellow skully and white and yellow New Balance."

Triple-K followed the shooters through his sniper scope as Jumm gave him descriptions and locations. Jumm was an amateur, and Triple-K hated working with amateurs. He was a professional, one of the most decorated snipers to come out of the Frogs and be elected to a team so secret even the Pentagon didn't know it exist. In that elite group he sometimes had to work with civilians who didn't know what the fuck they were doing. Though he had learned how to adjust to their ineptness it still didn't sit too well in his palate. He had had too many close calls in the past including the untrained in his missions. He would have never taken this mission if it weren't for Preacher, who he owed his life to. Preacher had given him a big window and allowed for his overseas tours and all the variants, which had boiled down to two years and this perfect day. Company policy was that a contractor, especially protectors, couldn't work over eighteen months continuously without taking at least two months off for R&R, so he took on side jobs when he wasn't protecting some Dignitary in Iraq or Afgan doing what he loved to do. it gave him the opportunity to train new recruits and make a little extra cash. He had a large family and they all needed to be fed.

He listened through the earplug as his amateur spotter rambled on and was thankful for the foresight to give him a cell phone that scrambled, otherwise who knew what agency could be listening in on the dumb shit he was saying?

After Jumm gave him the last spotter, Triple-K turned to glance at the lookout who's throat he had split minutes earlier, crossed his gloved hand across his heart and allowed himself a few seconds to say a silent prayer for the merc. After all he had killed a professional and the man deserved the respect he was due. He died in the line of duty, protecting the interest of his client.

"Position secured," he whispered into his clip on headset. "P2?"

"Secured," came the reply.

"P3?"

"We're in, waiting for flyby."

"That's a copy," Triple-K responded, going back to check the order he would take down the shooters. "Team set, we go in three."

*   *   *   *   *

The man they called EI Diablo sat across from Rachet smoking an expensive cigar while on a table across the room a money counter spit out the contents of the bag Rachet delivered. The old man didn't say anything. He sat and watched Rachet with a silly smile on his face, blowing small puffs of smoke out until one of the men at the table came over and whispered in his ear.

"There's an extra fifty thousand," the old man said to Rachet, a twinkle of greed in his eye. Rachet leaned over and spoke softly. "That's for you personally, Senior Diablo. For taking the time to hear my side of the story."

"Thank you," the greedy mutha-fucka said, confirming to Rachet that the fat bastard couldn't possibly be the real EI Diablo, a man as shrewd as the real boss running EI Diablo would have never accepted the extra fifty. He would have known something fucked up was attached to it.

"No! Thank you, Senior Diablo," Rachet said, rising to leave. "For seeing me personally on such a short notice, and for allowing us to buy product from you again." The old man stood and shook hands before patting him on the back and signaling two men to deliver the uncut cocaine and escort him back to the Navigator.

They hadn't taken two steps before all the lights went out in the room.

Rachet ducked to the floor as he had been instructed to do as small burst of automatic gunfire could be heard in the hallways outside the room.

Two Protector's immediately surrounded Senior Diablo, weapons drawn they pushed him towards the safe room. He resisted, turning back and looking down on Rachet. "I know this is not the leader of the notorious Murder One Crew squirming on the floor like a frightened old woman," he chuckled. "There is no need for worry," he added with the utmost confidence. "There is so much steel in these windows and doors-"

Before he could finish the sentence there was a deafening explosion and a brilliant flash of light as a portion of the outer wall came crashing in. Instantly the room was lit with burst of gunfire from automatic weapons. The invasion was so lightning fast, the old man's Protectors never had a chance.

The old man backed himself under the counting table, trying to hide as four heavily armed Swat team members secured the room.

"Get on the floor ! Get on the fucking floor!"

"Hands behind your heads. Finger's interlocked!"

"Don't you fucking move!"

Old man Diablo saw two Swat team agents assembling a dolly system from their backpacks before disappearing into the adjoining safe room. It was the fucking money they were after. He had been set up. Fucking Denareo. Slime ball. He would die for this. They were cuffing everyone on the floor with plastic zip ties. Then Old man Diablo was being dragged from his hiding place. He felt sick to his stomach and he had the feeling that Rachet was involved with the setup. That was before the swat dragged Rachet over so close his shoulder rested on Old man Diablo's arm then pumped three bullets in his chest. It was at that point that Diablo began begging for his life.

Triple-K's team was in and out in less than four minutes. He didn't have to look up to know his men were repelling from the back of the building at this very moment. Triple-K counted down from ten... the back door of the van opened and the remaining bags of money and his trusted team flew in. Just as he expected-a piece of cake.

Sirens and flashing lights converged on the mayhem they had just caused as Triple-K eased the Manhattan Cable Van into the busy Broadway traffic. One of his men started pulling off the prosthetic nose to reveal his real complexion.

"How did I do?" he asked.

"You would make your uncle proud," Triple-K said.

"Damn this is a lot of fuckin' money," a second teammate said. "We could keep half of it and they would never know it was missing."

"But you would know." Triple-K reminded him. "And that would compromise your integrity. Without integrity in this game you won't last long."

"Yea. Just day dreaming•."

"Well don't day dream too long. Your drop off is twenty blocks away." The team members busied themselves removing the swat uniforms and their painstaking disquises. Everyone but Triple-K-no one would ever know who he was.

*   *   *   *   *

The biggest thing to happen in the Heights in the last hundred years, probably ever, and Detective Romereo Denareo was not going to profit one iota of lime light from it. If it had happened on any other day the case would have gone nation wide and NYPD would be fighting news crews away. Now there was only one news van on the scene and a scattering of reporters, all local. Channel 36 was a college cable station which no one of importance watched and the papers being represented had circulations of fewer than 30 thousand. What a fucking bummer, this shit would have to happen the day the Twin Towers came down. As if that wasn't bad enough, three black Yukons had arrived on the crime scene filled with suits trying to take over 'his' crime scene. What else would they be here for?

He met them with an extended hand. "Denareo. I'm lead detective on this case. What brings you Fed boys in. This is local," he greeted them with an edge of sarcasm he meant for them to pick up on.

"I'm Agent Green from the National Security Agency. This is Agent Foster, he's with the State Department."

Damn! This was larger than Denareo thought it was. State Department? NSA? "Aren't you boys a little out of your jurisdiction? This is just a local gang war. I could see the Feds sticking their noses in but National Security. That's a little far fetched don't you think?"

Agent Green smiled, the other agent kept a stone face.

"Just curious," Agent Green answered.

Denareo sized him up quickly. Late thirty's, criminal law graduate, came into the agency young and moved up quickly due to family affiliations. Denareo would bet two paychecks he had family in some real high places.

"So am I," Denareo nodded towards the convoy of Yukons and agents holding his investigation teams at bay. "The last I heard this was an NYPD crime scene and until I'm officially removed, I am the lead detective. If you have any problems with that, take it up with my superiors. But right now you suits are impeding my investigation and disturbing my crime scene . " He was getting heated, plus the weariness of his marathon bouts with his partners wife was beginning to take its toll. He hadn't slept in forty-eight hours.

"Look. We just need to run some Haz-mat teams through, collect some forensics' then we'll be out of your hair."

"Maybe you didn't understand me Agent," he purposely didn't say his name though he remembered it. "It's not my hair I'm concerned with. It's you guys trampling through my crime scene."

"Perhaps you didn't understand me Detective Denareo," Agent Green said politely. "We are not trying to steal the air from your balloon. We have information that leads us to believe this was a terrorist act. We only need to take a look, see if our Intel has any teeth to it. Whatever we find we turn over to you. We dig the bones, you take the glory. I assure you we're a lot better at this terrorist thing than you are."

"I'll give you guys half an hour while we canvas the neighborhood," Denareo said, already seeing the possibilities. "My team works alongside."

"No problem. As long as the Haz-mats go in first to make sure nothings contaminated." "You've got half an hour,"

*　　*　　*　　*　　*

Kisha kept her ears tuned to the bathroom. Right now Trina was brushing all the babies off her teeth but Kisha knew she was staring at her. Trina had left the bathroom door open so she could see if Kisha was as drunk and unconscious as she was pretending to be. Seconds later Trina was duck walking and pussy farting her way over to the sofa Kisha was sprawled out on. The little nigga had pumped a lot of air into that cavity.

"Come on bitch! you got to get your funky ass up. It's time to go!" Trina said, tugging at her arm. Kisha went limp, mumbled something then rolled to her side, giving Trina her back. "Bitch! I don't know who the fuck you think you're playing with," Trina said, rolling her back over. "But I'm not the one!"

Kisha felt the nausea rise to her throat and forced it out.

Trina's voice went up three octaves as she jumped back. "You fucking bitch," she shouted. "Nasty ass bitch. That shit is fucking disgusting. I should rub your fucking face in this shit."

"Yea! Picture that." Kisha said in her head, rolling back over. "You remember what happen the last time you tried me bitch."

Trina did remember, and even now that they were best friends again she still harbored the seed of revenge. "This ain't high school bitch!" she hissed, picking up on Kisha's thoughts. But Trina didn't fuck with her after that, she must have also picked up on the fact that Kisha was one more tug away from wiping up her own throw-up with Trina's ass.

Trina stomped and pussy farted her way back to the bathroom, returned with towels to clean up the vomit then took another shower before changing clothes and taking her ass to school like she should have done two hours ago. She didn't leave though. Not before a final warning so Kisha could hear. "That bitch better be up and out of here by the time I come back. And if I find out she even tried to come on to you I'm-a shoot her stupid ass. That's word to my dead mother."

It had to have been a good fifteen minutes after Kisha heard Trina's keys lock the front door from the outside that the bedroom door finally opened.

Kisha pushed the covers off quickly, and as she threw one sexy leg over the edge of the sofa and spread the other on the hardwood floor to give the little nigga a wide-open view of her own wax job, her pussy lips smacked loudly in anticipation.

Kisha stole a squinted peek. The nigga was in the bathroom, standing at the bowl butt ass naked and Kisha almost choked on her own saliva when she saw the size of what he was trying to hold down.

*   *   *   *   *

Trina was feeling just a tiny bit guilty of the rage she unleashed on her best friend before leaving. Kisha never came on to any of her boyfriends behind her back since she had known her. She on the other hand had fucked and sucked every boyfriend Kisha ever had that she found or even suspected of having a big dick. In fact Trina had started their friendship off her sophomore year in high school by disrespecting her.

Trina pulled into a campus parking space, killed the ignition and sat back, thinking about the time they had fought like cats. It was all over some 6'-6" dude who's name she couldn't even remember right now. But back then the rumors were spreading through the corridors that he had the biggest dick in the school and since Trina could remember she always went after the biggest dicks she could find. Only problem was this one belonged to her best friend and her best friend was madly in love with him.

That didn't stop Trina though. One afternoon she waited for him on the back stairs leading to the showers after practice and pulled him to the side when the team came out. She told him Kisha had sent her to show him something. When he asked her what it was she told him she didn't want anyone else to see it so they waited until the last man left the shower and she pulled up her cheerleader skirt to show him she wasn't wearing any panties. He didn't waste any time boning her.

He had cum twice in her pussy, once down her throat and was cumming again as he punished her pussy more, when Kisha came barreling down the stairs like a complete maniac and tackled her, throwing a barrage of punches that not only nearly knocked her out but forced her into an intense multiple orgasm. Actually they hadn't fought at all. The few attempts Trina made at fighting back were futile and pathetic. Kisha beat the living daylights out of her, dragged her limp, half naked' ass into the gym and further disrobed her in front of everybody. She had to stumble out butt-ass with globs of cum dripping down her thighs and half the school population laughing. That's probably why to this day she was still fucking Kisha's men. She had just recently fucked Omar and Kisha was right, he was big but nowhere near the super dick league.

She would make it up to her friend she decided, swinging out of the car. She would take her to dinner or something. Right now she had to fabricate a story of why she had missed the first half of the test.

She was two thirds of the way cross campus when she ran into a group of girls coming in her direction.

"Girl, where you going," one of the sista's asked. "there aren't any test today."

"There aren't? What happen," Trina asked, suddenly relieved.

"Girl you don't know?"

"Not really!" Trina answered, giving her a 'like I'm suppose to know' look.

"This might be the end of the world," another girl called back. "Terrorist just blew up the World Trade Center."

"What?"

*   *   *   *   *

"Nigga come and get this pussy," Kisha was saying in her mind. Her eyes were closed but she could hear Daquan in the bathroom brushing his teeth. Her pussy was wet and her clitoris was throbbing. "You know you wanna tear this tight pink pussy up."

When he left the bathroom she was sure he was headed in her direction but seconds later the bedroom door opened and closed and when she stole another peek he was gone.

Damn! She didn't want to make a move herself and the little nigga rejected her. Then not only would she feel like shit, but if he went back and told Trina the shit would really get ugly. Best thing for her to do she decided, after laying there looking at the ceiling for a while, was get her ass up and back to her room where she could take a nice long cold shower. Besides, honestly, the dick was scaring her. She couldn't even imagine how Trina was taking it.

She was in the motion of swinging her leg off the sofa when the bedroom door opened again. "Don't move," Daquan called out, still butt ass naked. "I'm-a take a shower then I'm coming back to git some of that." He had caught her with her eyes and her legs wide open. He paused at the bathroom door and added, "Unless you wanna take one wit me."

*   *   *   *   *

It was 11:45 when the Manhattan Cable Van pulled into the RESERVED space in the underground parking next to the state Building. Triple-K exited the vehicle empty handed and took the staircase to the street level. From there he crossed the courtyard to 125th street, walked up to the multiplex theatre, brought a matinee ticket to an action movie, and took a seat in the darkness. There were only half a dozen people in the movie he chose. He would have preferred to have more but it didn't matter. When he emerged he would no longer be a White man in his late thirty's with a bad complexion and a hooknose, but he wouldn't be himself either. Triple-K was a master at disguise. In another six hours he would be in another state meeting the Haz-mat team. Rachet's money was in the van, the key in a magnetic box. Mission accomplished. Michael Thomas had a plane to catch. He had delivered what the client expected so there was no dishonor in taking the leftovers of the spoils, even if he had postponed the mission for nearly two years after he learned the old man Diablo was skimming' a good ten million a month from the shipments and stashing it in a secret compartment in the saferoom.

*   *   *   *   *

Trina walked up Fordham to the shopping strip, brought a family sized bucket of Kentucky extra crispy, Kisha's favorite, a giant tube of Super Lube from the corner drug store, not for Daquan but for Kountry, and then stopped and bought Kisha a nice outfit and a pair of Pumas she saw in the window of Dr. J's. She walked back to the campus parking lot and had just beeped the alarm to her car when the Mrs. Packman ring tone chimed from her phone. She checked the caller I.D. It was Kountry. What the fuck was he calling for, more important-

She flicked the phone open and snapped into the receiver,

"Nigga what the fuck you doing calling me?"

"I can't wait till Thursday, I need to see you today," Kountry whispered into the phone like someone was listening to his conversation.

"Fuck Thursday! How you get my number."

"I got my ways. So what's up? I can't stop thinking bout that fat ass-"

"I don't know how you got my number Kountry," she said, opening the car door and sliding in. "But lose it. If my man sees this number on my phone he will go ballistic."

"Fuck that buster. I know he ain't hitting it like I did."

"You wish. Your shit wasn't all that, believe me."

"That's why you came like fifty times?" Kountry stated with pride.

"Well call me again Kountry and it won't be fifty-one. I'm-a get a three hundred pound brolic nigga named Debo to meet you Thursday, see how many times you cum when he fucks you in your ass like a savage."

Kountry was laughing on the other end.

"You think it's funny? Call me again mutha-fucka!" Trina slapped the phone shut and started the ignition angrily then reached over and searched the shopping bag for the Super Lube. She was throwing that shit out the window. She knew it was a mistake to let Kountry fuck her in her ass. It was just the nigga was always begging and constantly trying to rape her and there was no way she was going to let him in her coochie so last Thursday she just up and offered to let him fuck her in her ass, and he fucked the shit out of it, literally. Fuck! Daquan wouldn't do it and she always wondered about it anyway. The shit was so good that in truth she couldn't wait until next Thursday came around herself. She didn't know there were that many nerve endings in an asshole.

Trina studied the Super Lube for a minute, she was getting excited already just thinking about using it. Maybe she could meet Kountry. Daquan wouldn't miss her. He thought she was taking tests all day. She replaced the Super Lube then took it out again. "Make up your mind bitch!" She put the Super Lube back in her bag and backed out of the parking space. At the campus exit she said to herself, "A right to my honey, a left to get my back blown out."

*   *   *   *   *

CHAPTER 20

PEOPLE RUSHED TOWARDS HIM covered in gray ash from head to toe. Others wandered aimlessly, disoriented, while still others searched as Pitt did, calling out names of loved ones or co-workers. For him it was like a scene out of the movie, Night Of The Living Dead.

Pitt's checked his cell phone again. The battery was still good, but it wouldn't give him a connection. It wasn't just his phone. Every single person he approached who were trying to make the same desperate calls he was, were having the identical problem, their service providers refused to give them a connection. It was like someone didn't want the victims to be found. After all it would be so much easier to locate them if you could hear their cell phone when you called.

He thought he had found her at least a dozen times, running up to embrace or turn around some woman he was sure was his heart. Now he was checking all the EMS stations, refusing to even consider digging in the rubble like many people were doing. His boo was alive. She might be hurt but she was alive. He could feel it.

Pitt was holding up two ambulance workers to check the woman in the stretcher they were sliding into an ambulance when a seductive female voice behind him asked. "Excuse me. Mister Policeman. Could you help me find my poodle?"

Minutes later the woman was dragging him through the rubble in a frantic search for her missing dog, finally pulling him into an alleyway and kissing him passionately. He slid his hand down her skirt.

"Uhh! What are you doing officer?" she asked, pulling away.

"Ma'am, I think I might have just located your poodle," Pitt grinned, pulling her back.

"Uhhh! Poor baby, she's drooling. I think she needs mouth to mouth," she cooed, pushing Pitts head down. The woman closed her eyes and moaned, "Your woman is so lucky to have a man like you."

*   *   *   *   *

Detective Denareo came out of the corner bodega tapping a pack of Marlboro's when Poochie approached him.

"Excuse me. Could you spare one of those?" he asked, with a flamboyant motion of his hand.

"Sure, I might be willing to spare even more if you have something to offer," Denareo said, popping a filter from the pack.

"I have a lot to offer," Poochie said, pushing up his implants then smoothing his hips in the skintight pants he wore. "Question is are you man enough to handle it?"

Denareo glanced down the block at his partner who was questioning a couple of women from the building directly behind the Diablo complex on the next block. "Depends on what you have."

"A white cable van that's been parked around here for the last couple of days."

"And…"

"And…" Poochie held out his palm, one hand on his hip. "You know how this goes." Denareo smiled and slipped two twenties in the Marlboro hard pack.

After hearing what Poochie had to tell him Denareo forgot all about the NSA guys and signaled for his partner. Two minutes after that the lights were flashing on the unmarked car and the siren was screaming as they raced downtown with Ralph putting out an APB for any Manhattan Cable vans or any blue and whites that might have sighted one in the last half hour.

"Seems like a wild goose chase to me," Ralph said as the dispatcher garbled over the radio.

"But if we find that van," Denareo smiled. "You'll never have to work another day in your life."

*   *   *   *   *

Trina was feeling really good about herself when she stepped off the elevator. She had decided that Kountry or the sweet pleasures of getting fucked in her ass was not worth the chance of losing her man and that monster dick. From now on, she had made up her mind, she would not sleep with another man no matter how intriguing it might be. She had finally found someone she wanted to settle down with, someone she was sure that from this moment on she could be faithful too. Besides.. According to Daquan, Kountry wasn't long for this world anyway.

"If I ever get fucked in my ass again," she said as she turned the key to her apartment. "My man will be doing the fucking." She picked the bags up and stepped in.

* * * * *

Maybe the reason Daquan was so fascinated with Kisha was that she reminded him so much of China. He had a thing for her since the first time Trina introduced them. Not so much her physical beauty as the vibes he got from her and the easy way she moved. Plus Kisha had some really sexy toes and Daquan was crazy about sexy toes. Most of all Kisha had that 'you wanna see what I can do with this pussy?' look that China had when she use to masturbate for him. Kisha had that look permanently plastered on her face. Whenever he looked at her he found himself getting turned on. Daquan knew the sex was gonna be this good.

Kisha was biting her upper lip and staring him in the eyes as he moved deeper and deeper inside her. Her muscles caressed him, massaged him deeper into her, their resistance consistently yielding as she moved beneath him, meeting him thrust for thrust with a steady determination to drive him deeper. Unlike Trina it didn't hurt at all. Her muscles fit snugly around him but it wasn't like he was banging into a brick wall. Their bodies fit like a perfect cast in a perfect mold.

A low throaty moan began vibrating from her chest as she pulled his face into her neck and held him firmly. It almost seemed as if she were crying when she whispered in his ear,

"Fuck me Daquan. Fuck me like you wanna hurt me."

Kisha always knew she was deep. Born with a white liver. It was the curse of the Patterson women. They were all born with their uterus in their chest. She clenched her teeth and closed her eyes as Daquan slipped so deep inside her she swore she could feel him in her chest. Wherever he was, he was hitting that spot that no man had ever come remotely close to being able to reach before, and Kisha was going into explosive convulsions, like she was having an epileptic fit.

It was the very first vaginal orgasm she ever had and little was she aware that Trina had chosen this timing to burst happily through the bedroom door.

* * * * *

Trina dropped her bags to the carpet, her mouth open in shock. Their backs were to her and her man was fucking her best friend the way he was fucking her only hours before. Only her best friend was taking the entire dick, every single inch of it. Shit she had been trying to do for the past two years. Daquan was so deep in her pussy his balls were slapping against her ass. Trina didn't know whether to cry, play with herself or shoot them both. She stood there transfixed for a good while. Daquan was fucking Kisha so hard they didn't even realize she was in the room.

Trina clenched her bag tightly to the knot forming in her stomach. She felt detached from her own body and everything was moving in slow motion as her hand slid inside to caress the cold steel of the 380 …'Fucking bitch!'

* * * * *

The wave started in Kisha's inner thighs and gripped her entire midsection as Daquan nursed on her left nipple, spiraling electrical activity to every nerve fiber in her body. She was having wave on top of wave of orgasms and then it seemed as if Daquan was sucking on both nipples at the same time as the Terminator continued to ravage her insides. She exploded with such force, cum shot out of her womb. She was so delirious with pleasure when an elongated nipple found it's way to her lips, Kisha sucked on it hungrily without thinking.

* * * * *

A hungry mouth on her nipple was feeling a lot better than what Trina imagined blood on her hands would feel like. If this was going to be her first lesbian experience it might as well be with her best friend and the man she loved.

* * * * *

Kisha felt the cold metallic object pressed against her temple and opened her eyes to her butt ass naked friends titty in her mouth staring up at her with a sheepish grin.

"Bitch! You lost your fucking mind," Kisha whispered in total disbelief.

"No. You lost your fucking mind.. bitch!" Trina said in a menacing tone.

143

"Fucking 'my' man, in 'my' apartment in 'my' bed..." she stood erect and shoved the gun in Kisha's face.

Daquan, without missing a stroke, looked up and asked, "Tree, why you ain't in school taking yo' fuckin' test?" Trina and Kisha both looked at Daquan, back at each other, then burst out laughing.

* * * * *

The three of them spent the rest of the day fucking and sucking each other.

Trina finally took all of Daquan, even though it was in her ass. He had fucked her so violently in it that she couldn't move her legs and she knew that for the next few days walking would not be an option. She fell asleep for the first time ever fully satisfied.

Kisha was equally elated. She had finally found someone who could massage her white liver, although she had vowed that it would be a one-night affair no matter how good it turned out to be, and God was it good, and that afterwards she would marry Omar and raise the family they talked about. Her fantasy had finally been fulfilled. She could live off the memory of it for the rest of her life.

Daquan had slept with two drop dead gorgeous women, but he was truly only interested in one.

The world would never be the same after this day. The day the Twin Towers came down.

CHAPTER 21

ABEL LISTENED AS RAY Ray explained what happened on 156th street.

"The old man is dead, executed, on his knees, a bullet in the back of his cranium took his entire face off. He'll have to have a closed casket, there's nothing left to reconstruct." Ray Ray looked out over the grove of palm trees surrounding the lush landscape and knew that beyond them, this property was secured better than a Federal prison. Nothing like that would ever happen to Abel.

"So who's taking over now?" Abel asked.

"Well, there's no one left in the immediate family. Jose was killed, so was Enrique and Jorge is on life support. Even if he survives, doctors say there's a ninety-nine percent chance he'll be brain dead. There's a slew of cousins and nephews but frankly I don't see any underlings that are competent, but it's your call on that. I've never been adept at this mob thing."

"What about Amillia?"

"Amillia? .. My girl Amillia?" Ray Ray looked at him. He couldn't believe he would even suggest Amillia.

"Why not?" Abel asked, "She was the closest to the old man, she knows the business and you yourself said that she would make a better capon than the old man or her brothers could ever make."

"I was joking," Ray Ray said.

"Were you?" Abel gave him a look.

Ray Ray didn't have to think long about it. Actually Amillia could probably run the business better than he or Abel could. It was just-

"It's your call," Abel injected.

"She's a woman Abel. And she's a woman I was planning on marrying."

"Like I said. It's your call. But she has my vote."

"I'll think about it," Ray Ray said. "Meanwhile what do I do about the two hundred million we lost. You know we also lost three times that in product?"

"It was taken by professionals. Someone in the community has to know something about it. Don't worry we'll find the culprit."

Ray Ray understood the 'community' was a network of elite mercenary agencies and government sources. If they were professionals they couldn't hide for long.

"We lost twelve good men. What about their families?"

"Find out how much each were sending home to their families and double it," he instructed. "For the families left in the states, a hundred thousand each and assure them we will always be there whenever they are in need."

"The Harlem cats claim they lost five million cash and Rachet suffered broken ribs and a punctured lung," Ray Ray chuckled before adding, "He claims he needs to be compensated for that also."

"Tell them to hire a lawyer," Abel smiled, "Then call the EI Salvadorian's."

Ray Ray forced back a smile. He had long been advising Abel that they needed to send the EI Salvadorian's in to get rid of the Rachet crew. The whole bunch of them were like roaches infesting everything they touched.

"Now," Abel continued, "On to more important things. We have a traitor in our camp. When you find him I want him sent back to the old country and kept alive. He will suffer for many years. And you will bring him the head of each of his family members one by one until his family name lives no more in this world.

They both understood that the traitor would reveal himself in a short time. His share had to be large and no one would be able to sit on that much money long without spending it.

* * * * *

"You should stay another week, enjoy the sun," Abel told Ray Ray as he handed his bags to the driver. "You need a tan. Look at how pale you are."

Ray Ray did need a tan. This much was true. But there was much that had to be attended too back in the states and already he was considering the three days he had been away an extended vacation.

"Stay a few more days," Abel urged. "Business can wait."

"Actually it can't," Ray Ray turned and took in the ocean, the white sand and the palm trees surrounding Abel's modest home. He wanted to stay. He truly missed the island life, and Abel since he had moved away. "I really can't, dear cousin. As much as I would like too, more pressing issues call."

*   *   *   *   *

As the car pulled away Ray Ray was thinking how much the boy Daquan reminded him of the man waving good-bye to him. The boy and Abel were definitely cut from the same cloth and had indeed come from the same circumstances. When Abel was no longer in sight Ray Ray leaned back in the car and lightly dozed off as a re-occurring dream of Abel's past came back to visit.

*   *   *   *   *

"Quickly, quickly, take the children," Tusimo Encarnacion whispered urgently to his wife. She began grabbing bags that were already packed. "No. "No! There is no time for that. Just take the children and go. Out the back way-" Tusimo pushed a banana clip in an AK-47 as he talked and snatched a couple of grenades from a crate. He was arming himself to the teeth.

Miriam ran through the house, grabbed the newborn from her cradle, then woke all seven of her remaining kids up and urgently instructed them to go out the back door and run as fast as they could.

"What are you doing Abel," Miriam asked her seven year old son who had sank in the corner of his room refusing to move.

"Haven't you and father always told me, never to bite the hand that feeds you," Abel asked.

"There is no time for this Abel. We have to go," she said, turning to leave.

"You go," he said. "But you won't get far. You and father have already signed all our death warrants. Our family name will be wiped from the face of the earth-"

She stopped and turned back quickly. "You are of your grandfathers blood. That's why he died a nothing," she spit the word out with contempt. "He had nothing and he left nothing. And you will be just like him."

"No I won't," Abel said. "When I go to heaven I will be able to tell God I did nothing wrong just like my grandfather. You will have to tell him that you stole and you have the blood of all your family on your hands."

Miriam crossed over to him and attempted to snatch him up. "One day I'm going to wash that little nasty mouth yours out but right now we have to go."

Abel kicked at her wildly. "Get off me, get off me, get off me!" he screamed, tears now streaming down his face. When he almost kicked the baby, Miriam hauled off and smacked him. "You want to stay here you stay," she said turning to leave again. "When you meet your grandfather tell him to suck the womb you dropped from."

Miriam didn't reach the door before a loud explosion outside shook the house and Tusimo was screaming for her to leave. Then there was an exchange of gunfire and his mother was gone.

Abel took the beads his grandfather had left him and began to pray the way he had taught him. He didn't pray that he would live to see his eighth birthday but that the Lord would forgive him and his brothers and sisters for the sins of their parents. The gunfire grew closer and Abel waited for the death he was sure would come.

"Mister Carero.. Mister Carero."

The driver woke Ray Ray from his dream just as Acosta's men were blasting their way into the house. "Mister Carero," the driver shook him gently. Ray Ray opened his eyes to the small airport, they were watery from the dream.

* * * * *

The plane hadn't left the ground before Ray Ray was fast asleep in first class and the dream continued with Acosta's men blasting their way into the house.

"On the floor. Get on the fucking floor, you piece of shit!" one of Acosta's men commanded while other soldiers stormed the house, searching each room. Tusimo was already shot up pretty badly. He dropped to his knees.

"Please," he immediately began to beg. "Don't harm my children."

The soldier kicked him again, sending more teeth and blood flying. Another soldier shoved Abel into the room at gunpoint. "What do I do with the kid," he asked the soldier apparently in charge.

"Cuff him. We wait for the others and Senior Ascosta." Abel's hands and feet were tied and he was forced to lie down on his stomach. The blood flowing from his pleading father was forming a puddle around him but Abel remained calm, never taking his eyes off his father.

"Here's the money," one soldier called out. Abel didn't have to look up to know he was talking about the suitcases on the sofa filled with stacks of American dollars.

"Think it's all there?"

"I don't know but we're about to find out."

Abel could hear the crisp bills as they separated rapidly, stack after stack while they waited. It wasn't long before Able heard his brothers and sisters approaching from the courtyard accompanied by heavy footsteps and loud shouts of commands from soldiers.

His sisters and brothers were separated, boys on one-side girls on the other. They were all born within a year of each other and the oldest was Loreen who was twelve, looked exactly like her mother, and was already sprouting little ta-ta's.

The soldiers kept her standing and forced everyone else to lie down on the floor. They didn't even cuff her.

Kitchen chairs were brought in and his mother and father were tied to them, feet to the legs, hands to seat. They waited with Loreen standing in the middle of the room and time slowed down until it seemed to stand still.. Until Senior Ramon Acosta entered and the room came alive again.

General Ramon Acosta stood there for a long time just looking from Abel's mother to his father. He then said softly,

"Because of your marriage to my sister I treated you like a son, like you were my own flesh and blood. I gave you everything," He looked around the room. "And still you want more?"

By any standards in Santo Domingo they were rich, very rich.

"You rape and steal from the hand that feeds you from this virgin enterprise that means so much to our country. You don't give it a chance to mature gracefully before you corrupt and pollute it with your greed. If you had been patient and waited I would have wed you to her and you could have enjoyed all her fruits rightfully and it would have been so much more after it matured." He nodded to one of the soldiers to bring the girl over, placed an arm around her and pulled her close.

"How are you Loreen," he asked, looking down on her tiny frame.

"Fine uncle Ramon," she said, her voice quivering, her body shaking like a leaf in a hurricane.

"Let me ask you Loreen. Are you still a virgin?"

"Yes."

"You mean to tell me your father hasn't molested you. He seems to have an affinity for virgins."

"No uncle Ramon. Father would never..."

"He would never what?" he asked gently, pulling her tightly into his side. "Never molest you? Never rape you? Never steal what is precious to you? Never violate your trust?"

Loreen remained silent. She was shaking to hard to speak.

"How do you think your father would feel Loreen if someone were to rape his precious virgin. I know how much you mean to him. Do you think he would want to kill or do you think he would be willing to forgive?"

Abel could feel the despair of his sister even before the two men crossed the room and held her by her arms as a third began to strip her of her clothing. Loreen began squirming between them and sobbing uncontrollably as she strained to look past the man undressing her to her stoic uncle.

"Uncle Ramon please!" Loreen pleaded. "Please.. Please uncle Ramon. Please."

Abel's father had already lost consciousness as the soldier pulled her panties down her legs and forced her feet from the openings, but his mother finally spoke up.

"Not her Ramon, I beg you. Not Loreen…"

"Then who would you prefer Miriam, you? That would be redundant. I don't think there's a soldier here that hasn't already been between your thighs."

"Please Ramon," she begged. "Anything…"

"You have nothing left to bargain with," he said as a matter of fact. "But Loreen still has the world." He turned to the soldier guarding the door. "Get me twenty men who don't have women to sleep with."

"Uncle Ramon please. Don't let them do this to me. Please!"

The man was halfway out the door when Acosta stopped him. "Also bring back a medic. I want Tusimo to witness every second of this."

"Ramon," Miriam called out, "I'll show you where the rest of the money and the jewels are. Just let her go_"

"I don't care about the money Miriam. If I recover it I'm going to burn it anyway, and the jewels, I would feed them to hogs and let some poor person discover them. This is not about money, it's about loyalty and family. The two most important things in life. Much more important than money or material things."

He walked across the room and held Miriam's face in his hand, forcing her to look up to him. "Because you were family I overlooked all your faults both major and minor. I was always there for you and your family. Even if you had stolen from me I might have overlooked it but you stole from the hand that feeds all the families. The hand that keeps our very country alive."

Senior Acosta walked over to Abel and lifted him from the floor. He embraced him tightly and Abel could swear he could feel the man sobbing inside. Then Senior Acosta passed him to a soldier and left the room without a word. Miriam's voice screeched after him;

"Please uncle Ramon. Please don't let them do this to me.. Oh God.. Please!-"

*   *   *   *   *

Ray Ray had been awakened from his dream by an apologetic flight attendant instructing him the flight had been diverted to Puerto Rico and all passengers were required to leave the plane. She had no further explanation for the inconvenience. Ray Ray assumed, like most of the other passengers, that it had to do with terrorist. Probably a bomb threat so no one complained. In fact they hurried from the plane to the terminal.

He brought a coffee and burrito and stood eating it at a food counter as he waited, the dream still lingering. It was Abel's experience, but Ray Ray had been having these vivid dreams of it since Abel first relayed his memories to him of how it all happened. Now they had become Ray Ray's vivid dreams, as if he were Abel, as if he had lived through the horrible experience himself .

Ray Ray's own memories were of desperately wanting to attend Miriam's funeral but being told by his parents that it was much too dangerous to show support by attending. Miriam was his age and they often played together whenever his family was invited for some celebration or another, which was quite a lot when she was alive. Her parents were very wealthy and enjoyed showing off their wealth as often as they had an excuse to do so. Actually he attended their every function because he was very much in love with Miriam and had hopes of making enough money to eventually ask for her hand in marriage one day. He was so pissed at his parents for not letting him pay his last respects that he was tempted to run away and never return. Eventually he came to realize his parents were right. If he had gone he would have been the only one. Not a single soul showed for the burials except the gravediggers and it was rumored they had disappeared afterwards, or had been buried in the same graves.

Everyone in Abel's family was executed, including the cats and dogs. Another rumor was that the house had been fumigated so that not even an insect lived to tell of what they witnessed.

The only survivor, he learned, was his little cousin Abel who had been shot in the back of the head twice and lay in a coma. No one expected him to survive and no one visited him as he lay in the hospital with all sorts of tubes and machines keeping him alive. No one except Ray Ray, who would sneak away every chance he got to hold his tiny cousin's hand and tell him stories of how when he came out of it he was going to take care of him, and how they were going to live in America and become rich and famous.

Ray Ray's parents eventually found out he was sneaking to see his cousin and grounded him. He was playing not only with his own life, they warned him, but the life of all those dear to him. It didn't stop Ray Ray. He still found ways. And one day, Six months after having half his head blown off, Abel opened his eyes and forced a smile at his cousin who was standing there telling him he would never leave his side. He tried to talk but found it extremely difficult. What Ray Ray finally understood him to say was that he had just had the craziest dream.

Who Abel's benefactor was, absolutely no one knew. But without him Abel would not have survived a day, much less the nine months he stayed in the hospital. In Santo Domingo if you were seriously ill and you didn't have money you died. It was as simple as that. Hospitals were not paying for life support or aftercare out of their pockets. They were just as impoverished as the average man.

* * * * *

When Abel was finally released from the hospital he was nine years old with no place to go. None of his surviving relatives were willing to risk the fate of his parents and siblings by offering him shelter. They shunned him as if he had the plague. When he came around they locked their doors and pretended he didn't exist. But Abel never came around with his hand out. He always offered to work for a plate of food or the opportunity to wash himself and his clothing or a corner to rest for the night. He never wanted something for nothing.

Ray Ray secretly cursed his family for not doing more than the little handouts they permitted him to deliver to Abel from time to time. They were poor but they could have done a lot more. Abel however was never depressed over his situation. Always optimistic, he had an inner strength that Ray Ray would always envy.

By the time Ray Ray graduated high school, it was rumored that Abel was working as a courier for the same drug cartel his parents had stolen from. He had already been to America twice to visit his grandmother on his mother's side, or such was the story he gave.

Ray Ray also had dreams of going to America. In fact he had been accepted to Columbia University with a limited scholarship. All he had to do was get there and have someplace to live, which effectively destroyed all his hopes. His family was too poor for the plane ticket let alone a place to live. America was very expensive. What they spent on a place to live for one month you could live on for years in Santo Domingo. He was feeling extra depressed when Abel showed up for his graduation in shabby clothing and shoes with flapping soles. Still he embraced him while the rest of his family, like everyone else in the town, shunned him.

Abel urged him away from the crowd after ceremonies were over, he seemed unusually anxious. Under a palm tree he pulled a small gift wrapped box from his back and presented it to him proudly.

"What is this," Ray Ray asked, not willing to accept it. Whatever it was Abel needed it much more than he did.

"You are my only family," Abel said. "And family takes care of family."

Ray Ray examined the box. The only things he could imagine it containing was a watch or a wallet, something too expensive for Ray Ray, purchased with money best spent on himself.

"Abel I can't take this," he said. "Whatever it is I really appreciate it but you should return it. You need the money more than I need this." He could see the hurt from rejection in Abel's eyes.

"It's money for you to go to school. If you don't want it give it to someone who does," Abel said, backing away. "It's bad luck to take things back once you have given them."

"Abel," Ray Ray said, stepping towards him. " I can't take this, especially if it's money."

"Then burn it, throw it away, do whatever you want with it. It's yours now," Abel said close to tears. He turned and sprinted across the schoolyard. Ray Ray didn't bother to chase him. Abel had always been faster than he was.

Ray Ray stared at the box for a long time before opening it, then his eyes widened, a stack of American 100 dollar bills. He pulled them out and counted two hundred. That was twenty thousand dollars. Remaining in the box was an envelope with a one-way ticket to Kennedy Airport in New York, and a note printed in a childish handwriting that read;

When I was in a coma I heard everything you said. We are family Ray and family takes care of family. If Ray Ray could have returned the money he would have. He knew Abel had gotten it through his involvement with the cartel and he didn't want anything to do with it. But he wasn't going to throw it away. Abel would never take it back and if he gave it to someone else it would still be drug money. There was only one thing to do he decided.

*   *   *   *   *

It was three years before he saw Abel again but every month, like clockwork, UPS or Fed EX or some postal service delivered a package of money. Soon the packages became boxes and by the time Abel showed up Ray Ray was so paranoid he almost didn't make the Dean's List thinking that either the police were going to raid his apartment or worse, the cartel would burst in and butcher him like they had done Abel's family.

It was graduation again and Ray Ray was valedictorian, top of his class, with job offers coming out the kazoo. He hardly recognized Abel when he approached him, he had grown so and was so elegantly dressed. But his girlfriends surely noticed him.

"Who is this Ray," Cicily asked, tugging on Tiffany's arm.

"Cute." Tiffany said. "I like them young anyway."

"I know you do," Cicily smiled, "Friend or foe," she asked Abel .

Abel and Ray must have looked like homosexuals the way they so passionately embraced and smothered each other with kisses. Because Cicily was saying, "Did I miss something this year?"

"Damn Abel. Look at you. I would have never recognized you-God-I missed you cousin. Look at you…"

Abel smiled and started to say something but Ray Ray cut him off. "This is my cousin," he said proudly. "Abel this is Cicily,"

"Pleased to meet you," she said, making a slight curtsy. "

Tiffany … "

"Charmed," she said, giving him a seductive once over.

"And my ace rival, and love of my life, Casey."

"So this is the infamous Abel?" Casey asked, cocking her head to the side to 'survey' him rather than observe' him. "There's no way you're going to convince me he's only fifteen,"

For some reason Ray Ray felt an instant embarrassment for Abel. Abel however smiled,

"Not only am I fifteen," he said "But I am a virgin as well." He spoke with a strong accent from the old country but his English was really good.

"No way!" Tiffany twisted her face to say.

"Yes way," he assured with the arch of an eyebrow and a nod of the head. "I intend to stay that way until I marry."

"Oh my God!" Tiffany faked astonishment. "There might not be another man like you in America…"

"In the world." Cicily chimed in. "You know seventeen is legal in New York," she added. "Mind if I wait for you. I'll even buy the ring."

The girls spent the rest of the ceremony pampering Abel like he was a favorite little brother, taking him everywhere and introducing him to every available girl. They tried to kidnap him for the evening but Abel explained that he only had a few more hours in the states and he wanted to spend them with his cousin who he hadn't seen in three years.

"I am so impressed with your cousin," Casey pulled Ray Ray aside and whispered before leaving. Casey was never impressed with anything or anyone unless it was Casey. "Bring him to dinner when he returns, I'll arrange it. I want father to meet him." Casey's father was the most influential investment broker in the Western hemisphere. Ray Ray hadn't even been invited to meet him yet.

*   *   *   *   *

"I don't know what it is you're doing," Ray Ray finally said to Abel after the waitress left the tab. "I don't want any part of it."

They were sitting in a Cuban restaurant on Broadway less than three blocks away from where Ray Ray lived and this was the first time he had noticed it. All the help seemed to recognize Abel though.

"What is it you're doing?" Ray Ray whispered across the table. "It can't possibly lead to anything good."

"It got you through school," Abel reminded him. "It's given you a nice place to live, good food in your belly, nice clothes. You don't think Casey would even notice you if she thought you were dirt poor do you?."

"These are the same people that murdered your family," Ray Ray whispered. "How can you work for them?"

"You are my family," Abel leaned and said in earnest. "You are the only family I have left. You are the only person in this entire world I trust."

Everything about Abel was worldly, the way he spoke, the way he moved, the way he interacted with people. If Ray Ray didn't know his age for a certainty there was no way he would have believed Abel was a fifteen year old either.

"Family or not Abel. I can't have that kind of money around."

Abel slid a piece of paper across the table. "A friend of mine said these were good investments."

"What am I suppose to do..?"

"What you went to school to do. Invest money. I make it you invest it. We take care of each other."

"You're asking me to launder dirty money. I can't do it. I didn't go to school to become a pawn for some drug cartel. Whatever personal money you've given me I'll pay it back Abel, I swear. But I can't do this."

"It's my money," Abel said, rising to leave. "I worked hard for it, but it doesn't mean anything to me without you."

"So take it with you," Ray Ray said.

"And what am I suppose to do with it? I don't need that kind of money. Without you the only family I have is me. I don't need very much to survive."

"Abel," Ray Ray stopped him, clutching the sleeve of his jacket. "There is over five hundred thousand dollars in my apartment right now, five hundred and eighty seven thousand to be exact. What am I suppose to do with that kind of money lying around?

"If we are family you will invest it, If we are not-" he shrugged his shoulders. "I don't care what you do with it. I'm not taking it back."

*　*　*　*　*

Ray Ray placed a call from the airport to a restaurant in Hackensack New Jersey. He left a short coded message with the manager. It would reach the El-Salvadorians before he re-boarded the plane. A coded response would be bounced around the globe through several satellites and onto his laptop computer. The ball was in motion. When the dust settled, Daquan would be running the whole of Harlem.

*   *   *   *   *

Three weeks had passed since Trina caught Kisha with her man and since then Kisha had practically moved into her apartment. She said to take care of her, help her out, but all the bitch did since she insisted on being available 24/7, was fuck her man every chance she got. Right now Trina could hear them in the living room going at it.

She eased her legs from the bed and attempted to stand. It was much too painful but she forced herself, then forced herself to take a first step, then another and another, until she finally reached the bedroom door. She stood there for a while, the pain too intense to continue, bracing herself against the doorknob and the hardwood panels. This was basically where it started three weeks ago, except she was coming in, instead of going out.

She should have shot the bitch three weeks ago when she first caught her fucking her man, but instead she had found herself playing with her own nipples and coming out of her sweat suit before she even fully realized what she was doing, she was caught up in such a trance. When she came to her senses she was already sucking on her best friends nipple helping her to have the kind of super orgasms she herself had always dreamed of. By that time it was too late. Kisha was having the kind of orgasms that made her eyeballs roll to the back of her head and Trina just got caught up in her ecstasy.

Again she should have shot the bitch when she had the gun pointed at her head. She probably would have if Daquan hadn't said that stupid shit and Kisha hadn't pulled her torso to her and started eating Mrs. Packman, the nickname Daquan had given her pussy after she waxed it and the reason she changed the ring tone on her cell phone.

Trina gathered a little more strength and cracked the door. Kisha was on top, riding him, and they were tongue kissing, slobbering spit. She closed the door and leaned her back against it. Now she was really pissed. The nigga never tongue kissed her when they were having sex.

"That shit is nasty Tree," she mocked Daquan out loud. "You just got through swallowing cum and you want me to kiss you? I love you Tree but it ain't gonna happen. Be like sucking my own dick."

Trina's emotional pain was taking over her physical pain. Fucking Kisha had just got through sucking his dick, now he was kissing her like they were in love or some shit, while she was bedridden from the shit that he did to her and now he was acting like she didn't exist.

Trina remembered being awakened by Kisha in the middle of the night in a pool of blood, so much blood she was sinking in it. When she jerked out of her sleep, a sharp piercing pain shot through her stomach and rectum, she couldn't move after that. She had lost so much blood by the time the paramedics arrived, she was unconscious and barely clinging to life. When she woke up she was coming out of anesthesia, in a hospital room with her ass and legs in a sling, tubes coming out of every part of her body and in so much pain, she wanted to die, especially when the doctors told her her colon was shredded and she would possibly be wearing a shit bag for the rest of her life because of some rare blood type she had and it not healing right. Daquan had also severely damaged several of her vertebrae. Still she loved the little nigga. She was willing to give up everything and change her life for his little ass, only now he was treating her like shit. Disrespecting her in her own apartment with her best friend. He didn't give a fuck about her! Neither one of them did. All they cared about right now was each other.

Trina tried to fight back the tears welling in her eyes but it was useless. She hadn't been able to stop crying since she returned from the hospital, the sobbing producing red bolts of unbearable pain with each contraction of her stomach they caused. Still she found the strength to straighten and force her legs to carry her to the Gucci bag hanging inside her closet door.

"God give me strength," she murmured when she reached it, sliding a trembling hand inside to clutch the familiar coolness of the 380. She didn't care about living anymore. What was the sense of living when everything she loved was gone?

*   *   *   *   *

The first time Trina came into the room and caught him fucking Kisha, Daquan knew she was coming in the apartment as soon as she opened the front door. Speedy had given him a tiny transmitter to install over the top of the door frame that sent a beep to another transmitter Speedy installed in his cell phone.

He had kept boning partly because he wanted to see how she would react but mostly because Kisha's pussy was so tantalizing he had to get to the bottom of it. He couldn't have stopped if he wanted too.

He was so lost in her pussy right now that for the long minutes of excruciating pain it took Trina to cross from the bedroom to the sofa, he hadn't heard so much as a foot shuffle or a floorboard creak. He should have been on point but he didn't have a clue she was even in the room until he felt the hard metal tap the side of his head. He looked up to see Trina jerk back, hatred taunt in her face, the 380 braced in two hands the way he taught her. Before he could react the gun was exploding and blood was spilling from his ears, his eyes and his nose.

Daquan's head was on fire.

As he faded into oblivion he could hear Kisha screaming as more shots went off, then an unearthly silence overtook him and he could swear in the moments that followed his mother was standing over him shaking his body,

"Wake up Daquan. Come on, get up. We can't get no money sleeping. Sleep is the cousin to death. If I let you, you would sleep your life away," she tugged at him gently. "Come on.. Time to go Little Man."

Daquan knew he was never waking up. His mothers voice was traveling an eon away. Already he was in the center of the universe being sucked into a peace so inviting he had no desire to return. Kisha clutched him tightly while their spirits meshed. "I'm coming with you Daquan," she whispered. "We're one now. Where ever you go I go ...

*   *   *   *   *

"Get off him bitch.. Get off him!" Trina screamed as she struggled to separate Kisha from Daquan. Look at what you made me do, You fucking bitch! It's all your fault." Trina managed to roll Kisha to the edge of the sofa, where she tethered before falling solidly to the hardwood floor at Trina's feet.

Kisha was still conscious though she couldn't move and her head felt like it was still exploding. There was no sound but she could read Trina's lips as she stepped over her limp body.

"You fucking bitch. If you hadn't fucked my man none of this shit would have ever happened."

Blood flowed from Daquan's ear, slithering down his limp arm, down an extended finger, to drip with the consistency of a second hand on a clock on Kisha's arm to remind her she was still alive.

Trina was so hysterical, trying to get Daquan to wake up, she didn't realize her stitches had ruptured and blood was now flowing from between her own legs.

*   *   *   *   *

It was twenty one-thirty hours military time when the distress signal came into a LSS computer terminal station. The operator bypassed the emergency notifications -Police, EMS, Fire, etc. -and instead notified the priority number as the screen instructed her to do.

*   *   *   *   *

Speedy received the call just when he and Scarecrow were about to make a move on Kountry to send him to an early grave. If it hadn't been the emergency vibration he would have never aborted the mission but distress signals took precedence over everything. It meant they had a soldier down and in this case it was the boss. Kountry was one lucky bitch-he had just been granted another twenty-four hours to live.

"Abort. Abort." he said into his headpiece.

The dispatcher had given him the address in the Bronx and within minutes he and Scarecrow were in a private cab, driven by one of their trusted soldiers, who figured out the quickest route with the same reckless abandon of every other cabbie in the Bronx.

In the back of the cab they quickly changed to some really nerdy catholic schoolboy appearance, broke down their weapons and placed them in the false bottom of their knapsacks.

Speedy knew it had something to do with that crazy bitch 'Quan was living with. The very last thing any man needed in his life was an overly jealous woman. He often tried to tell him but it was the one thing Quan refused to listen to him about.

*   *   *   *   *

The lock to the apartment was an over the counter job. Scarecrow located the master key from his ring and they were in before anybody could notice. As soon as they entered Speedy knew exactly what had happened and exactly what needed to be done. He didn't have to tell Scarecrow, who was already leaving to break in through the bathroom window.

While Scarecrow was climbing the fire escape Speedy checked Daquan and the two girls for vitals, then located and cleaned the gun of prints. One girl was still conscious. He told her what to say to Police when they arrived, then grabbed a sheet from the bedroom and began tossing valuables from the apartment into it.

As he and Scarecrow were leaving, he reminded her what to say then dialed 911 on her cell phone and passed it to her.

Scarecrow did another quick scan of the apartment and found 85 thousand dollars in small bills and a half-key of cocaine sitting in plain view on the kitchen counter in a brown paper bag. It wasn't something Daquan would do and if the cops had discovered it, it would have changed the whole dynamics of the investigation.

"It's clean," Scarecrow announced, coming out of the kitchen. "Which way out?"

* * * * *

"Who is this?" China asked, her leg shaking so badly she had to sit on the edge of the bed. "How did you get this number?" It was unlisted. There were only three people that had it, Larry, Katrina and Daquan. "Is Daquan all right?" She started to ask, but stopped before she got the 'Quan' out. Her instincts told her something terrible had happened to Daquan. Why else would she be receiving a call in the middle of the night from a complete stranger who knew her maiden name?

"Actually he's not," Speedy said cautiously.

"Oh my God!.. Oh my God… Oh my God!" was all China could manage to say as Speedy explained what had happened. She didn't bother to wake Naquan. She threw a coat over her nightclothes, slipped on the first pair of shoes she grabbed and dialed the limo service.

The dispatcher informed her that her driver was off for the night and the first available car would be forty-five minutes. She couldn't wait forty-five minutes. She dialed Larry then hung up on the second ring. She really didn't want him in her personal business. Her only other alternatives were the two things Daquan had drilled in her head never to do;

Never, ever, ever go out alone and never take public transportation. She grabbed her bag and threw caution to the wind.

After coming off the elevator, China took off her heels and ran from the complex up to Broadway to hail a cab. The boulevard was alive with restaurant goers, bar hoppers and weekend clubbers. There was no shortage of cabs except they were all occupied.

She was so anxious to find a cab that she didn't notice the black BMW and the two black Navigators on the opposite side of the street make a sharp turn at the next corner and speed in her direction.

* * * * *

There was no long procession of luxury cars following the late model hearse, no priest in all his finery reciting Latin verses to a horseshoe crowd of mourners, no screeching, wailing outburst from family or love ones of the deceased. On this unusually warm September day there was only an elegantly dressed woman in all black with a heavy veil over her face, a tall gentleman with super dark shades, and a young boy in suit and tie sobbing heavily, clutching at the woman's jacket as she shoveled a spade of dirt into the open grave. There had not even been an audible sermon recited, each had silently paid their final homage in their own way, their own language, their own degree of religious devoutness.

There were others watching their ceremony however and the woman was more conscious of them than she cared to be. They were paparazzi and government agents pretending to be mourners at another gravesite, secretly taking photo's of her beloved's burial. That was the reason she had requested of all his friends and associates not to attend either his wake or his funeral. It would have been a who's who of Dominican and Columbian mafia and Amillia didn't want her brother's name smeared any further.

She handed the spade back to the gravedigger, crossed her heart and headed back to the waiting limousine.

Ray Ray turned to her after they were settled in the back of the limousine. "We need to talk."

"If it's about Father's estate," Amillia said, wiping at her tears. "Leave it to the boy. I've told you. I don't want any of it."

"There is no estate," Ray Ray said solemnly. " The Old Man owed more than you think he's worth. In fact the very apartment you live in is being threatened by the banks."

"That's impossible. Father had millions…"

"Keyword, Had. He misappropriated millions would be more accurate. I warned him against it but he cashed out all his investments months ago. I don't know where he put the money but I assume it was in that vault."

"What about the boy?" she said, looking over at her late brother's son who was now fast asleep across from them. "Jorge left a little inheritance but not enough to ensure the boy's future. Now without that I'm going to be forced to take a more serious job."

"That's what I want to talk to you about."

"You want me to come work for you," she asked, skeptical.

"Well sort of," he answered, taking both her hands in his and looking her sternly in the eyes. "There's a lot I need to confess about what I actually do."

She gave him another incredulous look and he went immediately into explaining his secret relationship with her father and the EI-Diablo organization. He told her everything, stopping short of revealing Abel's identity.

"So why are you telling me this Ray," she asked after listening patiently to his long confession.

"Because EI-Diablo needs someone to head it if it is going to survive and you are the only capable person responsible or trustworthy enough to take it over." He waited for a response. Amillia stared at him for a long while as though he had just asked her to cut her own throat. She then turned her head and stared out the tinted window as city life passed in a blur. She didn't utter another word. When the limousine let her off at her apartment she wouldn't even look at him as she removed the boy from the back seat.

As the car pulled from the curb Ray Ray's heart sank. He knew it was a mistake to ask her. By doing so he had risked everything. He knew Amillia too well. For her it had always been all or nothing at all. She was mulling over two extremes. Distance herself from all her father represented, which now, since his confession, would include him. Or-Embrace it with enthusiasm, after all the cartel was in her blood and she was exceptionally good at it. While Diablo was alive he often went to her for council when he had to make a hard decision. All he could do now was give her time and hope for the best, though he really was not prepared to lose the only woman he truly loved. Ray Ray flipped open his Blackberry and typed in a coded message. Everything was going to be shut down for a while until it worked itself out.

*   *   *   *   *

Everything was shut down. From Detroit to Cali there was a drought since El-Diablo got hit. Not to mention Rachet had not seen a dollar of the millions stolen from the heist and mutha-fucking Preacher had died before he got a chance to question him or exact his revenge. He was told he died of natural causes but suspected the mutha-fuckaz who stole the money bumped him off so Rachet would never learn their identities.

Now the mutha-fucking Dominican's were hitting not just his spots but also all his cousin's shits. They weren't just robbing them either. They were executing his workers and soldiers and doing some gruesome shit to anyone they found to be a Rachet or related to him. They were leaving his cousins with their eyeballs cut out, tongues sliced off and stuffed up their ass holes.

The latest, a cousin on his mother's side who had a numbers spot uptown, was dumped on Seventh Avenue with his dick in his throat and his little sister's legs crudely sewn on at the hips to replace the one's they had cut from his body. These mutha-fuckaz were taking it to a whole new level. They were making Rachet and Pitt look like choirboys.

Rachet could play just as dirty as they were except there was no one to strike out against. The Dominicans had shut The Hill down so effectively you couldn't even buy a bag of weed. College students were coming all the way downtown trying to find shit. There was absolutely nothing and no money coming out of the streets and Rachet was down on chips. He couldn't kidnap shit, every drug dealer he knew of was in the same fucked up situation he was. He had tried extorting shit but it seemed like every time he sent a team in, niggaz got plucked off by some roof top sniper they hadn't been able to locate yet. It was like he was in some third world country and shit, fighting a fucking guerrilla war against an enemy he couldn't see or locate.

But a week ago his luck had turned around. He was in the process of scouting The Hill to make his own statement when he spotted China all alone, trying to hail a cab on Broadway. He snatched her ass up immediately. At least she could solve one problem. Bernstein had assured him she would bring a hefty sum. Only problem was, now that he had the bitch he didn't know who the fuck her benefactor was. She honestly didn't seem to know either. Only that fat fuck Bernstein knew and he was thousands of miles away according to his secretary, on some extended business trip.

He had to beat the shit out of the bitch but she did finally tell him that Daquan had mentioned her benefactor's name once but she couldn't remember it, and she insisted the lil' nigga was the only one she knew footing the bills.

"I'm going to give you one last chance to tell me," Rachet said calmly, reaching out to fondle her nipples. "You like that don't you?" he smiled.

China had both hands behind her cuffed to a radiator pole, her nightgown was open and as hard as she fought against it her nipples were elongating and getting as hard as stone.

"Fuck you Rachet!" she spit out at him.

"I bet you 'would' like that," he mused. "But I ain't got time right now. Maybe when I come back. Right now I need to know where that lil nigga Daquan is resting his head so I can get Mister Billionaire to come to the rescue of his damsel in distress."

"I told you. I don't know where he lives Rachet. He just shows up when he feels like it to see Naquan and then he leaves. He never tells me anything about his business or where he lives, and I don't ask..."

"Let me get this straight," Rachet said, pinching a nipple between finger and thumb and resting the razor sharp edge of a knife on the point of her breast where the nipple protruded. "Mister Big ain't fucking you, the little nigga ain't getting none, they just taking care of you so you can play mommy to the little brother?"

"Rachet. You gon' cut my nipple off go on and cut it off. I told you everything I know I don't have anything else to tell you except, I have to shit badly. Why don't you put your mouth down there and catch it for me like you use to do, Mister Shitty Man. You can eat my pussy while you're at it. I gotta piss too!" she taunted in as sarcastic a tone as she could muster.

Rachet suppressed the urge to knee the bitch in her stomach and instead gave her a big grin as he released the nipple and dug in his jacket pocket.

"Oh, I almost forgot." Evidently it wasn't in the pocket he went to. He started patting all his pockets till he located what he was searching for. "I think this belongs to your son," he said, shoving the pinky finger of a young boy in her face.

China gasped then turned her face away. Rachet snatched her face back to look at him, the knife returning to rest on her nipple.

"I don't know Rachet, I swear I don't know..."

Rachet turned to Pitt, standing behind him. "Go get me another piece of the lil' nigga. I don't think this bitch remembers how shit works around here."

Pitt was at the door when China said meekly, "Montefiore."

"What?" Rachet asked, turning his good ear to her.

"Montefiore hospital in the Bronx. Room 319 in the trauma unit."

"Trauma unit? What the fuck happened to his ass?"

"He got shot."

"He ain't gon' die is he?"

"I don't know Rachet," the tears were already falling. "You had me here for at least a week. He might be dead already.

"Rachet dropped the finger between her feet and turned to Pitt who was still standing at the door posed to open it. "Get this bitch some food, let her take a shit then clean her ass up." Rachet turned back to China, still talking to Pitt. "If you wanna fuck the bitch, fuck her. But don't get crazy and kill the bitch Pitt. Right now she's like an insurance policy. I got a feeling the same mutha-fucka insuring her is the same mutha-fucka trying to bury my ass!"

After Rachet hurriedly left, Pitt walked over to China and stood before her, admiring her body.

"Damn China. I always liked your little pretty little ass," he said through sparkling teeth, shaking his head with that sick grin of his cocked across his face. "Mutha-fucking Rachet don't know how to treat a pretty bitch like you."

* * * * *

"A woman who's dismembered body parts were found stuffed in a bag on a Harlem street yesterday has been identified as the sister of the notorious drug kingpin and alleged extortion king, Anthony-Madd Dogg-Rachet. The discovery was the latest in a series of horrific and sadistic murders plaguing the Harlem community in the past few weeks. A spokesman for the Police Department declined to give a specific number of deaths related to what they call 'an internal drug war', but a source close to the investigation who wishes to remain anonymous, claims the murders to be the most gruesome he has witnessed in his twenty two years on the force, and adds the official statements being spoon fed to the media are completely misleading.

"It's more like a vigilante force than a drug war," he added. "To my knowledge, there have been several massacres and a couple individual murders connected to this spree but the city is withholding this information so as not to alarm the developing Harlem tourist trade."

Our source went on to add, completely off the record: "We've arrested Madd Dogg Rachet in past years for everything from rape to murder to racketeering and he's beaten every single case. As a Police department we are legally prohibited from doing what is necessary to rid our communities of these vermin, so I applaud 'who ever and what ever' force is taking him down."

When asked if he thought rumors that the 'vigilante force' could actually be a group of renegade Law Enforcement Officers, he responded;

"I sincerely doubt it. But hey! This is New York. Anything is possible."

"Yeah! Anything except getting my fucking bail posted," Jumm muttered to himself, folding the newspaper and tossing it on his locker. Seemed like outside of the niggaz in C-74 who respected his handle, the whole world had forgotten about him. Shit. If he wasn't locked up in this mutha-fucka he could be out there in the war. Somebody was tearing their asses up and it wasn't the Dominicans. Half the fucking Hill was in the four building with him and they were just as much in the blind as anybody else. His boy Teardrop whispered something about the El-Salvadorian's, but somebody had told him that shit and the story was still loose. Jumm was waiting to hear from Teardrop now so he could try to get word to Rachet. J.B. was going home in two days and he told him how to get in touch with the nigga on the street and what to say to keep from getting his ass blasted. He also told him where his stash was so he could bail him out. He didn't really trust the nigga like that but everybody knew Jumm's reputation, so he doubted he would violate him and expect to live long. Anyway what could he lose. Didn't seem like Rachet had any intention of bailing him out, nigga probably thought he stole all the fucking money. He didn't but he had a strong suspicion of who did.

Big D came over and asked if he needed slot time. "Naw! Give it to the new kid." Jumm told him, motioning towards 26 bed. There was no one left for him to call. The bitches he was fucking with wouldn't accept his calls.

"I love the shit out of you baby," his favorite girl Twanna told him, "But just knowing one of ya'll niggaz right now is like signing a death warrant. Don't take it personal baby but as soon as you hang up I'm changing my number." That pretty much summed up everybody else's reason for distancing themselves from his life, Every number he called after that was disconnected, unlisted or had a block on it.

"When C.O. Allen called him to the bubble he thought she wanted to flirt and he wasn't in the mood. He took his time, lying there for a while until she called him again.

"What took you so long?" she asked, giving him a creepy look.

"I'm not feeling too well today Miss A."

"Maybe you'll feel better after you pack it up," she said, giving him that 'you've been punished' look.

"Ah! Come on Miss A. I'm not trying to go to another house. You know you my baby-"

"Yeah sure," she cut him off, looking up from her desk with her lips pursed. "Twenty minutes from now you won't remember my name."

"I'll remember that fat ass of yours though," he leaned over the desk. "And how sweet you always smell."

She blushed. "Nigga you ain't gon' remember shit."

"You can't pull no strings for me Miss A? You know I run this house."

"I don't know why you wanna stay here when you could be on the other side of the bridge before the next shift."

Jumm straightened. "You bullshittin'?"

"Somebody bailed your pretty ass out."

"'Bout fucking time," Jumm said, holding back from jumping up and shouting. "I'm not gonna forget you Miss A."

"I hope not," she smiled as she slid a folded slip of paper across the desk. "Put this in your Bible. I want to see if you just talk a good one."

"You're not ready for me Miss A."

"We'll see."

*   *   *   *   *

What Jumm didn't know but would have surely found out before J.B. left for home was in the wall behind J.B.'s bed there was an official hunting knife as sharp as a barber's razor that he intended to cut Jumm's throat with. He had gotten the contract from Rachet by way of a visit from one of his girls a few days earlier. He could have had that money plus Jumm's stash if he hadn't waited. Now the nigga was out. Rachet could hit him his self now. J.B. got up, went to the phone and dialed the number Rachet's mule had given him, thinking he should have cut the niggaz throat in his sleep last night like he started too.

*   *   *   *   *

Processing went real slow. Fucking asshole C.O.'s were playing around with his paper work but Jumm remained patient. He'd see one of these bitches on the street one day and then it would be a different story. Right now it was their world but whatever game they were playing he knew they couldn't hold him up for too much longer.

A guard appeared at the cell door. "Jerome Wilson?" he called out. "Twelve, twenty-seven, eighty-four." He held the pad up to the gate to compare photos then put the keys in the lock.

Processing went real quick after that. Ten minutes before the next shift Jumm was on the big bus headed across the bridge trying to figure out the best way to handle Rachet's rage before he got his hand on a gun. He knew the nigga was gonna be on some supreme bullshit. Jumm was supposed to follow the van and pick up the money. Instead he had gotten pulled over for running a red light and busted on a gun possession charge and the D.A. was trying to give him natural life because it was armed with silicone-coated armor piercing bullets.

Jumm got off at the parking lot when he caught a glimpse of his Navigator sparkling in the sun. Not only was he surprised to see the big truck, but also after seeing it, he was definitely expecting to see either Rachet or Pitt behind the wheel. Not so. As it pulled to the exit he couldn't believe who was driving. It swerved and stopped beside him.

"Don't stand there with your mouth wide open," Petey's wife called down to him. "Get in." He slid in beside her and she was looking even better than what he remembered.

"How the fuck…"

"Did I get your wheels?" she completed his sentence, pulling off as soon as he closed the door. "It's a long story. I'll tell you all about it once we reach the hotel and you take a nice shower, put on some new clothes and get some real food in your stomach." She made a left at the light. "You may want to kill me afterwards but it's a chance I'm willing to take."

"Wait a minute. You bailed me out?"

"Yours truly."

"Why. You don't even know me. You've been following me around but you don't know me. Why?"

"You ever met someone and you knew it wasn't by accident. That you were destined to be together?"

"Oh yeah?"

"I was half way to Florida when I realized I was never going to get you out of my thoughts so first chance I got to turn around… Well here I am. It took a lot to find you, though. I remembered your plates. I have a few friends in the DMV. They gave me a name. I did some checking, found out you were in here, decided to be brave and well, like I said, here I am. Out on a limb but I would have never been able to go on until I found out."

"Found out what?" Jumm turned to her. He was truly intrigued by this brazen woman.

"If you feel the same about me."

"Look lady. I appreciate you bailing me and getting my truck out of the pound but me and you are from two different worlds."

"They say that opposites attract."

She was right. All Jumm wanted right now was to jump her bones but he wasn't about to let her know that.

"Yeah that's what they say," he leaned back and crossed his arms over his forehead. "You wouldn't happen to know anything about the money?" He threw the question out there, setting her up.

"What money," she asked, a quizzed look on her face.

He looked over and studied her face for a reaction, "The money you stole from the cable van."

"Huh?" From the look on her face she didn't know what the fuck he was talking about. The hotel they checked into was a five-minute ride from Rikers. An upscale hotel with a circular drive, an elaborate lobby with bellhops in fancy blue and white uniforms, desk clerks in five hundred dollar suits or immaculate dresses. It definitely was not the tele's he was accustomed too. They didn't bother to check in. Jumm followed the Rodriquez chick across an expanse of geometric carpet to a row of stark white elevators. They didn't speak on the ride up or during the walk down the long corridor to a door with a 'Do Not Disturb' sign hanging on its latch. She slid a magnetic card key through the lock and smiled back at him. They hardly managed to close the door behind them before they were tearing at each other's clothing.

Two hours and a shower later (where they went at each other again) Gloria was sitting crossed legged in the center of the bed, looking like an angel in a crisp white men's button down, going through piles of travel brochures. Jumm was propped against the headboard, shirtless, muscles rippling, dreds pulled to the back, looking divinely sexy eating sushi for the first time.

"How long you been planning this shit?" he asked, his face contorted from just the smell of the mustard sauce he dipped the raw fish in. It had the kind of hot that grabbed the roof of your nostrils and shot straight to your brain. But he liked it. He liked it a lot. And he liked her.

"Actually it's spur of the moment," she said, concentrating on arranging the brochures in some semblance of order.

Damn she was sexy. Jumm's head was getting a little hazy from the saki (another first) and maybe it was the combination of that, the raw fish and three weeks without seeing any pussy that had him rising again.

"I was thinking," she said, looking up. (He had the urge to toss the tray to the floor and pull her to him, suck those delicious lips, feel her tongue in his mouth. "We could go to Brazil first, rent this villa," she held a picture up to him. "Isn't this a great place? It's practically isolated. No one around for miles."

"Wait a minute, wait a minute. You're moving too fast. I'm from the hood baby. I don't know shit about no foreign country. The farthest I ever been is Cancun. Besides you need a passport and all kinds of shit."

"I can get you a passport," she said. "I know people."

"I just can't leave my friends and family..."

"What friends? Rachet? He would just as soon cut your throat. You're no more worth to him. He didn't bail you out of jail did he. I bet he didn't even pay you a visit or send you a commissary buy-"

This much was true. Rachet had turned his back on him and now that he thought about it, he probably had a hit out on him too. He knew how Rachet's mind worked. Right now he was blaming him for whoever stole the money.

"Haven't you ever just wanted to just get up and go, do what you feel without worrying about this or that or whatever? We could just go. Live like gypsies."

"That's pretty much what I've been doing since I was like-like nine,"

"Not me," Gloria said. "Since I can remember I've been told what to do, where to go, how to dress, what to say. Little girls don't do this. Little girls don't do that. You can't climb trees Gloria, that's for boys. But I liked climbing trees, getting dirty and running around half naked. If boys could do it why couldn't I?" She was stacking the brochures in bad piles, good piles and this is where we're gonna go piles. "Do you know how old I was when I married Pete?" She didn't wait for an answer. "Seventeen. And Pete was thirty-seven."

_.

"Oh. So he always liked them young," Jumm dipped the sushi and took another bite while Gloria stopped what she was doing giving him a look. "I'm just sayin'" he coughed as the mustard rose to fry his brain.

"I took birth control for ten years without Pete ever knowing it. There was no way I was going to have children and have them go through what I went through."

"So why you marry him in the first place. You must have loved him."

"This is the first time I've ever come close to love," she said, continuing her brochure organizing. "I married Pete because I was told to. It's as simple as that."

"That's some crazy shit. Nigga could have almost been your father.

"Pete was worse than my father. He brought my clothes, told me where I was allowed to go without him, which was nowhere, which friends I could have other than his own, which were none. I was just a showpiece in an ivory tower. He never beat me though. He just locked me away. He had his tender side."

"Why didn't you just leave the nigga?"

"And live on what? Pete had all the money. I never got past high school. I never had a job. I wouldn't know where to start-"

"And you wanna travel around the world! On what? I ain't got no fucking money. If I did I would've bailed myself out."

"Pete left me a few dollars."

"It's "gonna take more than a few dollars to do all the shit you talking 'bout doing."

"OK he left me a lot."

"And what's a lot?"

"A few hundred thousand."

Jumm pushed air through his teeth. "I already went through that and I never left New York. You gon' need a lot more than that. Even if you were super thrifty moving to another country, a couple hundred would last maybe three, four years, at the most."

"Ok. Then we could invest it in something quick."

"In what? In drugs? You know how that game works. You were married to Rodriquez long enough."

"Too long," she said. "Pete had some off shore accounts. I know he had millions in those."

"Yeah and?"

"I'm sure he hid the account numbers someplace in the house. Pete never had a very good memory. He wrote everything down and hid it someplace."

"Look Baby, I'm feeling you, I'm feeling your energy, every thing about you, but even if you found Petey's millions I don't know. I mean you don't live with somebody for twenty years and not have some kind of feelings… and you're forgetting, I'm one of the niggaz that kidnapped your husband.

"What? You think I would turn you in?"

"I 'ont know. Bitches are some strange creatures."

"Trust me. I wouldn't have anything to gain."

"I don't trust relationships. I never seen one that didn't fuck up somewhere down the line. And most bitches have a natural tendency to get real nasty when shit ain't going right for them."

"And you think I'm that kind of bitch?"

"Hey. I don't put nothing past nobody." He was thinking about when she unloaded the thirty-eight in the man she thought was her husband.

"What if I confided something to you that I would never tell a single soul in this world. Something worse than you kidnapping my husband."

She wasn't about to confess to Petey's murder was she?. "The only thing worse than kidnapping is murder."

"You don't have anything to worry about then. I'm the one who murdered Pete that night."

"Be serious." He feigned skepticism.

"No I am serious. I'm telling you this because I want you to trust me." She paused and took his hand into hers. Her eyes were watering. She fought back the tears. "After you left I went down to that dark basement and I made sure Petey Rodriquez would never molest another child in his life. Pete was a real piece of shit. He deserved to die a lot sooner than he did."

She confessed everything to him about that night and the nights leading to it and the nights afterwards. About Pete's mother and how she was determined to link her to the murder. Of how the disappearance of Pete's body was driving her crazy.

He listened patiently as her tears and story flowed.

"1 got a little money stashed," he told her to cheer her up. "Maybe we can make something happen.

"Gloria crawled up his body to rest her face in his chest. "You're not going to leave me?"

"We'll see what happens," he said, and pulled her up to him. Right now I need to get at some of this hot Dominican coochie burning up my leg."

"Oh yeah?" She bit at a nipple as she guided him into her. "You like this hot Dominican coochie?" she cooed as she danced above him.

"Do I? Does a bear shit in the woods? Does a river run down stream? Do pigs wallow in the mud..."

"OK OK I get the picture," she chuckled, then asked with a serious face. "So you're saying you like this coochie enough to follow it to Brazil?"

"I wasn't saying all that," Jumm grunted. He was about to nut already.

"What if you had two hot Dominican coochies exactly the same? Would that make you happy?"

"What the fuck you talking 'bout?" he asked, his torso arched to meet her rhythm as she rode him rodeo style. "Ahh shit!" he called out seconds later.

She slid him out quickly, did a reverse cowgirl and drank every baby he spit out until he was ready again.

"If we could bottle this shit we'd be billionaires," he said, her fat ass inches from his face.

"You would put me on the street Daddy?" she asked, her voice smooth and sensual as she released him from her mouth to call back.

"Hell yeah," Jumm quipped. "I'm a pimp by blood. But I wouldn't let yo' shit go for less than a million a pop."

"Ohh Daddy. You're getting me hot," she played along. "That's a lot of money for a little Dominican girl like me."

"That's just the baiting price. After they get a taste I'm doubling the shit. A trick insult me with a penny less I'm laying him out."

"So if there were two of us that would be four million a pop," she stated, going back to work.

What's up with this 'two' shit?" Jumm asked, leaning back and closing his eyes.

Her muffled words hummed past his dick. "You'll see."

* * * * *

Since Great was so good at investigating shit Rachet sent him to Montefiore for the kid, but Great was turning out to be practically worthless. The kid had checked out a couple days earlier and Mister wanna-be detective couldn't even get an address.

"Find the little mutha-fucka and get him too me," Rachet barked into his cell phone. "I don't give a fuck how you do it. Just get it done!" Rachet clicked off on him and dialed Bernstein's office again. It was a good thing he was setting Great up to take the fall, he was thinking as he waited for the switchboard operator to pick up, otherwise he would have pushed his wig back months ago.

"Bernstein and Morgan," the operator answered.

"What? You want I should…" Rachet said away from the phone trying to sound as Jewish as he could, pretending he was talking to some one else. "Get me Bernie, sweetie," he said into the phone, his accent amazingly Semitic.

"Mr. Bernstein is not in sir."

"He's not in or he's not in," Rachet inquired.

"He's not in sir."

"When will he be in? It's very important I speak with him."

"I don't know sir. Let me connect you with his secretary. She might be able to give you the information you need." When she clicked over he clicked off. He had done the Jewish thing with Bernstein's secretary and she had fucked him up when she started speaking Yiddish.

As Rachet stood there trying to figure out what his next move would be, it suddenly dawned on him. "Fucking cameras," he said. "Why the fuck I didn't think about this shit before?"

He slipped on a Kevlar vest and the bullet proof jacket sent to him to wear for the Diablo heist, stuck two guns in his back and stepped into the other room where a team of armed soldiers were sprawled around waiting.

"Let's roll," he said, heading for the exit. Maybe security still had a tape of the garage from that day. If they did, he would know exactly who stole his fucking money. Shit was changing for the better. A crisp Jefferson and the head of Security for the building the garage was located in, suddenly got an excellent memory.

"We review the tapes each day and record over them if nothing out of the ordinary happens." the heavyset ex-cop told him. "It was 9-11, September eleventh and we were glued to Fox trying to figure out what was going on. We didn't notice the girl on the tape until late that night. Just before the midnight shift."

"Do you still have it?" Rachet asked.

"We thought it was strange enough to alert the department," the man said, ignoring his question. "They notified Manhattan Cable but it seems they didn't have a van stolen or missing. Turns out it was stolen though. From Jersey, cloned to look like a Manhattan Cable."

"Do you still have the tape," Rachet asked dramatically, his patience wearing thin.

"Wish I could help you there," Fat man said, lightly tapping on the desk. Rachet slid another Jefferson across. "But I might be able to do you one better," he said, palming the bill and slipping it into his pocket before crossing to a log book and flipping back to entries for that day. "Yeah I thought it was here."

He took a pen, scribbled on a slip of paper and handed it to Rachet. "You didn't get it from me, I don't know you and you were never in my office."

The paper had a license plate number , a name and a Queens's address. Claudia Santiago, 192-50 114th Drive, St. Albans N.Y.

"Feisty little broad, really struggled with those big bags," the security officer said. "Must have been an awful lot of money in them."

"What makes you think it was money?" Rachet asked, anxious to leave now and get to the address.

"You're not the only one interested in those bags." He raised an eyebrow.

"Who else?" Rachet asked. He was ready to shoot the man.

"You wanna know and my baby needs new shoes," he smiled, tapping the desk with a dirty chipped fingernail. Rachet reluctantly placed another Jefferson on the desk.

"A detective from uptown. Wanted it off the record."

"Got a name?. And don't tap another fucking finger," Rachet warned him. Mutha-fucka was trying to tap him out.

"Denareo.. From on the Hill.. As grimy as they come. Whole family is."

Rachet took the glock from his back, shifted the chamber for effect causing the old man to jump back. "I wasn't here either," he said, tapping the man's chest with the barrel. "You don't know me and you never seen me."

Rachet knew Denareo from way back. If he was here the bitch that stole the money bag was probably dead by now and his 30 million long gone. "How long ago was Denareo here," Rachet turned to ask at the door.

"Hell, Couple of weeks back, day after we called it in." he said, sitting on the desk, afraid to reach in his drawer for his heart medication until Rachet was gone.

* * * * *

Rachet and his entourage of rentals were on the Belt Parkway in Queens before he realized the address was on the same block as the house they had gone to meet Jeidar in, Jeidar's boyfriends house. The bitch had set him up. Let him front the money while she ran away with the payload.

"Damn! Fuckin' thirsty bitch!" he shouted, startling his driver. "Jumm told me not to trust that stinking bitch. No wonder she ain't called me no more asking me what happened to her share." He slammed his hand so hard on the dashboard it left a dent. "You fuckin' bitch! When I catch yo' ass you gon' wish to God your mama never dropped you from her womb."

* * * * *

"You're coming back?" Gloria asked as Jumm pulled on the leather jacket. It fit him perfectly. She had watched the way he dressed and picked out a few outfits for him, guessing at the sizes, being right about everything except the Timm's. She had purchased them one size too large.

"Better too large than too small," he assured her. "Now I can put on extra socks when it's cold. Timm's are mostly for show anyway. They don't do shit to keep your feet warm."

Gloria couldn't tell they were too large. In fact they looked perfect on him, he looked great. Gloria was proud of herself.

"You're coming back right?"

"Yeah I got a few loose ends to tie up, but I'll be back."

"You sure she asked, standing and walking over to adjust the collar of his jacket and pull off a price tag they missed.

"You just make sure you be here." He gave her a sexy look.

"Don't make me track you down, because you know I will," she warned.

He smiled then drew her to him and kissed her passionately. When he released her he joked. "1 ain't leaving my bottom hoe for some bum ass pimp to try an get at."

"Well you might need this Daddy," she said, running back to the head of the bed and pushing her hand under the mattress. She came out with a big black plastic 9mm. "Bum ass pimps carry razors."

Jumm could only smile and shake his head. "This thing loaded?" He was already in the motion of popping the clip. Two bullets were missing. That's what you did to save the spring, keep the gun from jamming. Either his little angel had already popped off two or she knew what she was doing.

"1 have extra clips if you need them," she said happily.

"Yeah. Who knows. I might run into a couple of Rachets." He checked the extras. Two bullets short in each of them. He was beginning to think Gloria Rodriquez was a lot more dangerous than a spur of the moment shooting of her husband. Evidently Petey had trained her well.

*   *   *   *   *

Speedy's grandmother had insisted on coming down as soon as she found that China hadn't shown up and Police were trying to take Daquan to BCW because Kisha told them he was a minor. At first they were trying to implicate him as the shooter but he had held on to his story that he didn't know what happen, all he had seen was a flash of light and woke up in the hospital.

Kisha held firm to the story Speedy had given her. She was visiting her best friend. They were watching TV and Trina's cousin, Daquan, was asleep on the sofa when these two men seemed to appear from nowhere. One had a gun. When Trina's cousin woke up they shot him in the head then they turned on her. That's all she could remember. She was so traumatized she couldn't be sure what nationality they were. Eye color-no. They wore ski mask. Don't know-Don't know-Can't remember-

Speedy didn't like the idea of his Grandmother getting involved. That meant Police snooping around, they were in the light now that she had stepped up for Daquan. There was no more hiding in the shadows.

"So what you find out about China?" Daquan asked. He was in Speedy's basement, having been released to his grandmother's custody until BCW could get it all straightened out. He was still pretty fucked up from the explosions even if they were low packed dummy rounds. His head was still throbbing like he had been beaten with a baseball bat, and his equilibrium so fucked up he couldn't stand without tipping over.

"I don't know. She just disappeared." "We can't find your little brother either," Scarecrow added.

"I think Rachet got both of em." Daquan said. "I just got this feeling."

Daquan attempted to stand but the room was tilting so badly Speedy had to catch him or he would have ended up on his face.

"You have to stay in bed Daquan, at least for another couple weeks. You had a really bad concussion. Your brain is still not stable."

"I gotta find Naquan-"

"Me and Scarecrow got that. You just stay in bed like the doctor told you, let Grandma take care of you. We'll take care of everything else."

"You don't know Rachet," Daquan told him. The room was really spinning now and the nausea was climbing from his stomach to his throat. He laid back and closed his eyes. "He ain't like Kountry and them other dudes. He got an army-"

"So do we," Scarecrow said. His voice was coming from a long way a way.

"And he got madd safe houses all over the city." Daquan added. " You might find him but you ain't never gon find Naquan and China. He gon have them killed as soon as you make a move."

"You have a point," Speedy admitted. "So what do you suggest?"

"Your Grandma know all that herb stuff. I know she can fix me up something to get me out of this bed. I'm the one Rachet really wants."

"Ain't nothing gonna help you but rest," Scarecrow said, a thousand miles away now. He had moved to the side Daquan lost his hearing in.

"Shut up Scarecrow and go get Grandma." Speedy said.

"It ain't gon' help," Scarecrow answered dejectedly before leaving the room.

"Right now nothing else is working," Speedy said to himself. "And we don't have much time." Rachet is only going to keep them for so long before they just get in the way and he has to get rid of them. Besides it wouldn't be the first time his grandma had performed a miracle.

Daquan moaned and grabbed his head. "How is Trina doing?" He strained the words past his nausea.

"Why you keep asking about that bitch?" Speedy asked. "She tried to kill you. She almost did. If the gun didn't have blanks she would have…"

"If donkeys had square asses they would shit bricks," Daquan said, repeating one of his mother's favorite sayings.

"Yeah. Whatever. Fuck that bitch! What do you care?"

"I care," Daquan said. "It was all my fault."

"Yeah for giving her the gun in the first place. Good thing I loaded it with blanks or your ass would be in a morgue instead of my Grandma's basement," Speedy was beginning to get a little aggravated by the whole situation.

"I just don't want nothing else to happen to her."

Speedy understood. Daquan didn't want them to kill the bitch. "I don't think she's going to make it anyway. She's still in a coma and they can't stop the bleeding. Plus she's got some kinda rare blood and they can't find a donor."

"What kind," Daquan asked.

"I don't know and I don't care," Speedy answered. "I hope the bitch dies and saves me the trouble."

"Don't do nothin' to her!" It was more a command this time than a request.

"I hope you're not thinking about hooking up with that bitch it she does pull through."

"Hell no! Like my mama say, I only got to get burned once before I realize the stove's hot. I just don't want nuthin to happen to her that's all."

They stayed in silence, each in his own world, until Scarecrow finally returned with Speedy's Grandmother.

*   *   *   *   *

Jumm parked his truck across from the Hamilton Projects in the Bronx instead of driving it into Harlem where it would stand out like a sore thumb, then took a cab across the 138th Street Bridge. All he wanted was to get his stash and get the fuck back to his Baby in Queens. The last thing he needed was to be spotted by a nigga from Rachet's crew so he avoided any routes he even remotely thought one of them might travel in. In fact he had taken the extra long way to get to the Hamilton. The scenic route, Southern Parkway to the Throgs Neck Bridge, Cross Bronx Service roads to 138th. Besides cutting down his chances of being seen it also gave him time to think about this sudden decision he was being forced to make. If he stayed here, even if Rachet didn't kill him the least the nigga would wanna do to him was fuck him in the ass on the regular like he was doing to Great. That was unacceptable. Jumm was like Pitt. He would kill the mutha-fucka before he let him stick his dick in his ass. Actually it would be more like committing suicide cause his chances of killing Rachet were slim to none. Even if he did manage to body Rachet, he would never get out of Harlem alive. He wouldn't even be able to get out of the safe house and that's the only place he would even remotely have a chance to get at him anyway. Other than that Rachet always kept shooters around, and they were loyal to Rachet, not his First lieutenant. Besides, Rachet always kept those killer Rot wielders around him in the safe house, so even that was out of the question.

The more he thought of it the only options he had were not to get caught going to get his stash and bouncing with the Rodriquez chick. Actually he was really feeling her and her whole adventure thing. Plus Brazil wouldn't be that bad. Niggaz said bitches over there were 'craaazy' an they be all over American dick, and if any of them had coochie freto as good as Gloria Rodriquez's it would be like dying and going to heaven. When he really thought about it that was the only reason he had for not just picking up and going with Gloria Rodriquez was that he had vowed since his first dip never to let a bitch whip him and Gloria already had him one nut away from being whipped. He was afraid of taking that chance. If there was whipping be done he would be the one to do it.

The cab driver brought him out of these thoughts as he pulled up to the curb in front of an abandoned building on 128th street.

"Ten-fifty," the driver called back.

Jumm snapped to life, turning in all directions to check the area before handing the driver a twenty then holding a crisp hundred to the Plexiglas divider. "I got this plus the fare back if you wait for ten minutes." The drivers look said it all, he was either going to 'cop' or murder somebody

"Look. It ain't no drugs or guns," Jumm told him, deciding to be honest with him. "I'm going to pick up some money I stashed and I ain't trying to be out here with a lot of dough trying to find no cab."

The driver smirked.

"Tell you what," Jumm said peeling off another hundred from the ten Gloria had given him, "I'll double it."

"The driver shrugged his shoulders. "Ten minutes, no more."

"Shit, I'll probably be out in five," Jumm said, rushing from the backseat.

As Jumm dashed down the stairs leading to a false bricked up wall in the basement he didn't notice J.B. popping out from the hallway of an abandoned building across the street.

Jumm had no idea that the same day he was released J.B. had been released also.

The C.O.'s said something about a time compensation mix up and apologized to J.B. for the mistake but he didn't give a fuck whose mistake it was as long as he was getting out two days early, he was so anxious he was still in the clothes he came over the bridge in. He made only one stop before coming here, which was at his man Jasper's crib to pick up the Ruger. He had gotten here late yesterday but couldn't figure out how to get into the building. The nigga told him about some secret levers but he couldn't get the shits in the right position to open the fucking wall up. He had spent a few hours nervously trying to get in afraid that Jumm might show up and blast his ass while he had his back turned or worse, that Jumm had already been there and there was no money to be gotten.

Something told him to wait and sure enough there he was, about to get his ass bodied. J.B. pushed the Ruger to his side and crossed the street behind the cab. According to Jumm there was well over two hundred G's stashed down there and Rachet wanted him dead anyway. The cabbie looked at him as he eased down the stairs after Jumm, his Ruger already extended ready to unload. The cab peeled off just as the shots rang out.

* * * * *

Denareo was still finding it hard to believe the Rodriquez chick had pulled off the biggest robbery of his decade, millions in cash. When he saw the surveillance tape for the first time he nearly pissed his pants. It was either her or her twin sister Claudia dragging the bags of money from the back of the Manhattan Cable van. It was the second time they had gotten the better of him- twice in two years. It definitely wasn't sitting well on his ego. In fact Denareo wanted not only the money but he wanted to strangle both the bitches. Problem was they were always one step ahead of him. Legally he couldn't charge them with a crime even if he wanted too, except maybe Grand Larceny for the stolen van. No money was reported stolen and officially the Diablo case was being investigated as a turf war.

He had been pulled off the case and placed on desk suspension for leaving the crime scene to an NSA agent who the NSA couldn't or wouldn't verify. In other words, his captain had chewed him out, as far as NSA and NYPD were concerned, the NSA and State Department Agents at the scene were imposters, and only God knows what that phony' Haz-mat team took out of the building! They both knew the most likely things they took out were drugs and money. From what Denareo was hearing on the streets, lots of money. A lot more than the thirty or so mill the Rodriquez twins got. A hell of a lot more than either he or the Captain would ever see in a lifetime.

Denareo sat watching the Domingo house. He had taken a leave of absence instead of being a desk jockey while his family pulled favors to get him re-instated. He divided his time between this house and outside the Everwood complex where the Hernandez sister lived. Both were no shows since the robbery and he doubted they would ever return.

A cleaning woman showed up three times a week for the Santiago sister. She told him Gloria's sister had gone on a short vacation with her children and had paid her in advance to look after the house in her absence. The woman had a strong Island accent and she showed no signs of lying. He had broken into the house afterwards and found no money but he did find travel brochures to Santa Domingo.

They might have made it out of the country but he seriously doubted the money did. Not after 9/11. Not the way they were checking baggage now. No they had stashed the money until the heat blew over then they were coming back to get it. And Denareo was hoping he would be staked out at the right house when they did. They wouldn't pull the switch on him this time.

Denareo lowered the high power binoculars to his lap and dialed a number. The street he was on was a dead end with a small abandoned lot, a cul-de-sac, hidden from view by a thick over growth of weeds and trees. He was hardly noticeable in his dark sedan. It was the quiet end of the street, only one house facing the lot and who ever lived there rarely came out or lifted a shade.

*   *   *   *   *

Serafina answered the phone on the first ring. She was hoping it was Denareo. She hadn't heard a word from him in a week. At least she didn't have to explain the bruises on her body for all those days but she was aching for the rituals Denareo put her through. It was Denareo. The warmth rose in her lower region instantly. "Yes," she answered, wishing for him to command her to touch herself. Do something vulgar and dangerous while Ralph slept inches away from her.

"Where's Ralph?"

"Right here, sleeping."

"Go and get that big dildo. The one with the nasty looking veins on it."

"OK, hold on," she slipped quietly from the bed and went to her hiding place in the closet, got the pink monstrosity and hurried back.

"Got it," she whispered, looking at Ralph sleeping on his side facing her. Ralph started snoring lightly. She kept her eyes on him as she listened to Denareo.

"OK now rub it over your nipples."

She pulled the top of her nightgown down and rubbed them both.

"You like that?" he asked, hearing her tiny moans escape.

"Un Huh."

"Where you want me to put it now?"

"In my pussy."

"And what do you say?"

"Please Master. Please put it in my pussy," she begged.

"OK. But I'm only giving you the head until you show me you deserve more."

She slid it down her body and forced the head in. An ever so soft shudder found it's way to Denareo's ear.

"Does it hurt?"

"Un huh."

"Want more?"

"Yes."

"What are you going to do to show me you deserve more?"

"What ever you want."

"I want you to put the phone close to Ralphs dick then I want you to suck it while you fuck yourself with that big dick."

"I can't. I-"

"What did I tell you about that word can't?"

Serafina hesitantly rose to her knees and faced Ralph.

"I want Ralph to see you fucking yourself with that big shit while you're sucking his dick. When he cums I want you to pull it out and let him watch you fuck yourself in the ass."

*　*　*　*　*

Denareo had his pants down to his knees jerking off to Serafina's slurping and crazy wild woman moans and screams as she beat her pussy for Ralph like Denareo often beat it for her.

Denareo was skeetin' listening to Ralph's excerpts of astonishment at witnessing his wife performing like a sexual maniac for the very first time when an entourage of Rentals eased down the block and stopped in front of Claudia Domingo's house. He dropped his cell phone and picked up the binoculars, his dick still twitching as a dozen men spilled from the four cars.

Who ever they were Denareo knew they meant business. He could tell from the bulges under their clothing they were all packing. Good thing the Domingo chick wasn't home. They were there to put some work in. He watched them surround the house. Two men then got out of the last car and walked to the front door. He recognized one of them, Madd Dogg Rachet. So he was involved in this shit too?

Serafina was cumming loudly on the other end of the phone but Denareo hardly noticed her screams. He couldn't believe it when the front door suddenly opened. He knew no one was in the house, not unless the broad had come while he was jerking off. But he hadn't taken his eyes off the house for more than a second since he had arrived. He zoomed in to see who had opened the door as Rachet and his goon stepped in. It was too dark in the house to even make out a shadow.

Denareo pulled his weapon. Fourteen to one. That was no odds, he decided, He couldn't call for backup. He wasn't on duty. In fact he was no longer, officially, a Grade Two Detective, and he was way out of his habitat. That alone would cause more questions than he cared to explain. He turned the ignition on, reached back for the Mossberg Street Sweeper, resting in his lap, checked the nine-millimeter, turned the ignition on then raised the binoculars. The only way he would become involved was if they left the house with anything resembling bags of money. Then they would think they were in a Rambo movie.

He settled back and waited, with Serafina's hoarse voice coming from the phone on the seat beside him;

"You like this Ralph? You like watching me fuck myself in the ass?"

"I don't know," Ralph said. Denareo could picture Ralph, wide eyed and scratching his head. "Truthfully you have me sorta fucked up right now. When did you become a... Ah-"

"A whore Ralph? A whore and a slut? Whatever I am right now, I'm not that docile bitch Serafina. Right now I'll be anybody you want me to be Ralph. I'll be your slave. I'll do anything you tell me to do. Anything... Anyway you want me to do it."

Denareo laughed. Ralph was finally getting what he wanted from Serafina and now he didn't know what to do with it. Denareo clicked the cell phone shut before he started getting excited again. He knew Serafina was about to break out all her toys and Denareo couldn't afford to listen to that shit. He needed all his attention concentrated on the issue at hand.

Ten minutes later, Denareo sat up straight as Rachet and his goons spilled out of the Santiago house empty handed. Instead of loading back into the cars they moved to a house on the opposite side of the street two lots down. Shit was getting real interesting now. They circled the new house as they had done the previous one while one man went to the door and rang the bell. An old woman answered, he said something to her then forced his way in at gunpoint. The rest must have entered the house from the back or side entrance because the door closed and there was no more activity in the front for the next half hour.

Then exactly twenty-nine minutes and seventeen seconds after they entered the house, Denareo heard three shots go off in the house that sounded like they came from a nine-millimeter handgun. He gripped the Mossberg in one hand and the steering wheel in the other, his foot lightly on the gas as he cruised up the block to stop at the two story Tudor after the Santiago house. He watched the house the shots came from through his rear view mirror.

Denareo wasn't feeling especially heroic when they spilled from the house 40 minutes later and calmly walked in his direction to their cars. He wasn't feeling very sympathetic either for the victims he was sure they had left in the house. He was thinking primarily of the news value and possibilities for promotion and other departmental quirks. One man in the group was covered in blood, like he had taken a bath in it. That's the one Denareo wanted. The other's he didn't give a shit about.

Denareo spun the car around to block the road, rolled out the passenger side door and braced the nine-millimeter on top of the hood of the car. He had who he wanted in his sights and let off three rounds before picking up the Mossberg and yelling out;

"NYPD-Police!" They were already returning gunfire. Denareo ducked behind the car then came up letting the street sweeper go. He didn't care about stopping anybody else, as long as they weren't picking up the body he had just dropped he was good money. The sweeper caught two men trying to pick the bloody man up.

"Leave him!" someone yelled. It must have been a code for kill because one of the men trying to help him stopped and emptied half a clip in his brain with exploding bullets.

Denareo moved to the front of the car and fired off two more rounds from the street sweeper as they loaded into the car, spraying a barrage of bullets back at him then squealing off onto grass lawns to bypass his blockade. He dropped the Mosberg and let off an entire clip after the last car zipped past returning fire. He was pretty sure he hit at least one of them. But he had no intention of putting one in Rachet, though he had a clear shot at him at one time. Rachet was now an Ace in the Hole, as his partner would say.

After he was certain they were long gone, Denareo stood and smashed his phone on the ground before moving to the center of the street displaying his gold shield high above him as he called out to the surrounding houses, "I'm a detective, someone call nine-one-one." He wanted to give Rachet time enough to escape. He walked over and kicked the dead man's gun away. There was nothing left of a face to recognize. He waited for the first response team to arrive before entering the house.

The bodies were in the basement of the neatly kept house. The grandmother, who neighbors described as a quiet thoughtful woman who didn't have an enemy in the world, was found tied to a kitchen chair, gagged and evidently tortured for effect. More than likely to encourage her grandson to talk.

"Two bullets entered here," the Coroner told the lead Detective assigned to the investigation who had been kind enough to let Denareo accompany him on the walk through. "splitting the Occipital and exiting here," she continued. "through the frontal bone between the two orbital. The shots were projected upward. A mercy killing, she most likely died instantly. He on the other hand," she nodded towards the body of the grandson, who was in his early twenties and looked as if he had been awaken from his sleep before his demise, "wasn't so lucky. It took him a while to die and I suspect it was a pretty painful death."

Denareo looked around the room. There was sound equipment everywhere. The kid had a pretty decent studio set up, even a halfway decent sound booth.

A bag of weed and two duchess lay beside a mixing board ready to be smoked. Empty forty bottles were strewn everywhere, some filled with piss, probably because he was too lazy or too high to make it to the bathroom on the next floor, most likely a combination of both.

And then Denareo caught it -a blown up poster sized photo of a thick Dominican chick hanging on a far wall amid posters of Tu Pac, Biggi Smalls, Jay-2, and some rappers he wasn't familiar with. But he was more than familiar with the girl. The inscription at the bottom of the photo read; "To the only nigga I'll ever give my heart to. With all my love, forever, your wifey, Jeidar"

Suddenly it all came together. Jeidar worked for Diablo, she was fucking him and finding out where the money was and how to get it. She must have been fucking Rachet too and let him know Diablo was holding that much money. Rachet hired a team, probably from out of state. His deal with them was probably he kept the money and they kept the drugs. Probably they didn't know about the money only the drugs. More than likely Rachet installed two of his men with their team and they went in the safe. In any case Rachet was wearing a bulletproof coat, the thing that saved his life, now he realized he had planned it that way. He just hadn't expected the shots to break his ribs and puncture a lung. The Rodriquez chick must have been watching him because she knew he was responsible for the kidnapping of her husband. When she realized they had hit Diablo up and left the money unattended in the van, she seized the opportunity and dashed with the cash. Rachet must have finally realized the connections.

If Rachet found either of them it was lights out. Denareo knew Rachet cared more about killing than he cared about money.

* * * * *

CHAPTER 22

IRAQ WAS DEFYING THE mandate for U.N. nuclear inspections and America and Great Britain were gearing up for war. There was no stopping Bush and Blair from moving in the direction of their 'secret' Jewish advisors. Gloria knew what was going on, she could read between the lines. It was just so fucking obvious. She wondered why her twin couldn't see it.

Neither of the two women were particularly political, though her twin had always been the more patriotic of the two.

"You know there was a memo that went out on the internet the day before, warning all Jews who worked in the Towers not to go to work on nine eleven," Gloria stated firmly, not looking away from the television, worried sick about Jumm still not having returned from the previous day. She kept her calm, she didn't want to alarm Claudia by letting her see how truly upset she was.

"You believe that? You're always into some conspiracy theory," Claudia smirked. "You never believed we went to the moon either."

"They didn't!" Gloria said, flipping the channel.

"We went three times and there's ton's of proof."

"Yeah, if you listen to them tell it," Gloria was tired of trying to convince people of the obvious. She let it go and settled on MTV.

"I bet you think your friend is coming back too. It's been twenty-eight hours. He got what he wanted. He's not coming back," Truth was, Claudia anticipated his return probably more than her sister. He was the first dick she had had in a month of Sundays. It wasn't the first time she and Gloria had switched up on a partner without him knowing, and Jumm had fucked

185

her royally. She could live with that for a while, even if he did think he was fucking Gloria when he was fucking her.

"You don't think something has happened to him, do you," she asked with sudden concern.

"I don't know. But he said he would return and I believe him."

"That's your Problem Gloria, you believe all the wrong things. You have to come down from your cloud one day and hang out with the common people."

Gloria smiled, "I believe you wouldn't mind having him around for a while."

Claudia looked away. Gloria was right, she was always right. "So how much longer are we going to wait for him?" She walked to the window and looked out over the parking lot thinking to herself that the black Navigator would pull into a parking spot before she finished counting to 25 in her head. "One-two-three-four- " she counted slowly.

"We're going to be here for at least another two weeks. We can't leave the country without Passports and Visa's." Gloria gathered a few items from her bag and headed for the shower. She stopped at the door and turned back to her twin, "You're worrying about him more than I am," she said.

Claudia pivoted and stared blankly at her.

"Don't worry," Gloria assured her. "He'll be back … I know my man."

*   *   *   *   *

Some bird ass nigga was running around Harlem claiming he slumped the notorious, murderous Jumm, except, according to Speedy, no one had found the body yet.

Daquan had always liked Jumm, he was always under the radar, never had anything bad to say and never bragged or spoke about the things he did. He wasn't really flashy either. He wore a couple' pieces of nice jewelry and drove a Navigator, but other than that, Daquan knew he liked to stack his money. You would never catch Jumm out partying or buying the bar. He had learned a lot from watching how Jumm moved in the world.

"How you feeling," Grandma asked, sitting down a bowl of the special brew she made for him. Actually he was feeling a lot better; the thunder in his head was now replaced with a constant throbbing, but one he could live with. He was even able to stand and walk about the room when he was alone, though his equilibrium was still a little off.

"A little better," he lied.

"Well I warned you not to expect miracles," she said softly, "but a little is better than none." She helped him to prop himself against the headboard, took a seat beside him and began spoon-feeding him the foul smelling brew. He nearly threw up on the first sip, like he did each time she fed it to him.

"You sure you didn't get this stuff from the sewer," he asked after the urge to vomit left.

She smiled and raised another spoon to his lips.

"It's usually the worst things in life that make you better," she said. "Now open up and take it like a man."

He opened, took the sip and forced it down. She was right. It was the same thing Mister E use to tell him.

Daquan waited twenty minutes after the feeding to rise and get dressed, when he was sure she was finished in the kitchen and had made her way to her room on the top floor. He took his switchblade from under his pillow and silently made his way out the side door. Speedy and Scarecrow were out scouting Harlem trying to find a lead on where Rachet was but Daquan knew he was the only one that could find her. He was the one that Rachet really wanted.

*   *   *   *   *

Maybe Rachet didn't have Naquan, Daquan was thinking. Naquan was smart enough to know to go to the safe house in the tunnel. He might have gotten away. If he did that's where he would go.

"Why we gotta live in the subway? " he was remembering Naquan constantly asking as he struggled up the stairs from the 145th street station. "Why can't we live in a house like China?"

"Cause it's safer down here," was always Daquan's answer. It was safer in the underground.

After their mother disappeared, Daquan found out how dangerous it was for two kids with lots of money and no parents to survive on the streets of the surface world. It hadn't taken him long to heed the advice of his mother and seek shelter in the underground. In the short months he attempted to live up top, mostly in an effort to find his mother, he had seen numerous kids his age raped, beaten or murdered in the homeless shelters his mother had warned him about.

Daquan stopped and held on to the railing. He was feeling faint and the world was revolving around him. As he waited for the spinning to stop, his mothers voice and the vision of her tidying his jeans and placing a thick Cuban link with a diamond encrusted piece in the shape of a seven around his neck, became crystal clear in his head.

"I don't care what you do Daquan, you always keep your word. You say you gonna do something you do it, rain sleet or snow. That's what's wrong with niggaz today. They don't know how to keep their word. That's why I got rid of your no good father." She stood back and admired him then tucked the chain in his shirt. "Always keep this tucked in," she warned. "No sense inviting thieves. If they don't see it they don't want it." She paused to look at him again, then added, "We don't need that no good mutha-fucka no way. You my man right?"

Daquan smiled, a slight smile of pride seeping through his serious demeanor.

"Yea. I'm your man now," he said, sticking his chest out. Already he looked older than five. He was as tall as most nine year olds, and as grown as Chi Chi. She often told him he was born with an old man's soul.

"And what a man do Daquan?"

"He take care of his family, an' he protect 'em. He don't let nothing happen to them even if he gotta die to protect them."

"An what else?"

"A man always keep his word. It's all he got in this world an' all he gon' take wit' him to the next one."

"Come here. Give yo' mama a big hug , " she said, dropping to one knee and opening her arms wide, "You so smart."

He didn't feel so smart right now, he didn't have a plan and he was about to put his life in Rachet's hand without a bargaining chip. That's not what his mother would do. She always had a plan. She always planned an escape route.

When the vision evaporated, along with his dizzy spell, he made his way to the surface. He needed to go to the safe house and see if Naquan had made it safely. That would solve all his problems if Naquan was safe. China would have to survive on her own. After all, she had already done her job. Naquan was in school and was doing so well now that even without a mother Daquan knew they would find a way to keep him there. He was their poster child, people from all over the world were interested in Naquan . "Fuck it!" he thought aloud. "If Naquan is safe they just have to kill China. Ain't no sense in every body dying," he rationalized.

"Why you think I just got through telling you about keeping your word Daquan?" his mother's voice scolded him. "Didn't you promise China, as long as she was mother to Naquan you would protect them both?"

"Yea. But-" Daquan mumbled out loud.

"But nothing!" his mother's voice returned. "A man takes care of his family and he protects them even if it kills him in the process. A man's family comes first."

"That's right Daquan," Mister E's voice chimed in. "Always.

* * * * *

Pitt took China to take care of her hygiene whenever she asked and he fed her regular meals. He was surprisingly nice and courteous to her, still he kept her chained to the pipes in between conveniences.

"If Rachet shows up and sees you free, it's gonna cause some problems," he said.

Rachet showed up a day and a half later especially angry and irritated. He took Pitt to an adjoining room and she could hear him chewing him out. She only had one hand cuffed and he was pissed at that among other things. A little of the other she caught was about some kids snooping around asking questions. Seems he had caught one of them and he wanted Pitt to go pay him a visit.

Pitt got his kit and left. Rachet slowly crossed the room, a psychotic grin plastered on his face. It was the look he had just before he killed someone. China had seen that look twice before, two of his girls who had run away and he had forced her to watch what he did to them. She was still having nightmares about that.

She cursed herself for the millionth time for not obeying Daquan, then looked Rachet in the eye and smiled. If she was going to die she promised herself she wouldn't give him the pleasure of one scream. He was leaning over her now, sniffing at her body, his hands caressing her curves, like they use to do. She felt nausea, she wanted to throw up on him, spit in his face, piss in his mouth. But she kept her smile. Finally he pulled away and stared at her hard.

"Goddamm China. In my entire life, I've never seen a bitch as fine as you," His lips approached hers and stopped barely an inch away. His breathing was labored, and she could swear he was trembling.

"If you didn't have that thing, I would fuck the shit out of you," he whispered.

"You can't catch something you already got," she said, wanting to bite his nose off.

" Bitch I ain't got shit!" he said, taking a step back. "I get tested every six months."

"Bullshit Rachet," she said calmly. "So how did I get it if you didn't have it huh? Explain that shit. You were the first and only man I ever slept with before they tested me positive. So you tell me how the fuck I got it."

"Don't give me that bullshit. You's a fucking hoe and you was a fucking hoe when I met you!"

China's eyes suddenly had the coldness of a glacier. "Fuck you Rachet, you slimy piece of shit. "I was a virgin when I met you and you know it. I hadn't even kissed a boy before then."

"You were a horny ass nympho bitch, that's what you were."

"And who brought it out of me Rachet. Who? You did. You slimy bitch. You turned my ass out. You're the mutha-fucka that infected me."

"You finished now?" Rachet asked, fire in his eyes. "Or you want me to cut your fucking tongue out."

"You're fucking lying Rachet and you know it. You got it full blown. I can see it in your skin. The way..."

Rachet smacked her so hard he left his handprint embedded in her skin. China looked back at him, fighting back the tears.

"The way your eyes are all sunk into your skull. You got it mutha-fucka. You ain't fooling no fuckin body." She thought he was going to smack her again, instead he turned her around to face the wall, bent her over and flipped her nightgown up.

"Just like I thought. You might' a got classy but you still a hot, no drawer's wearing, freaky little nympho bitch," he told her, then shoved his smelly dick in her pussy.

He was banging away like a mad dog when China bent to steal a glimpse. Just as she expected, sick nigga wasn't wearing no condom.

* * * * *

Bernstein was purposely avoiding Rachet's calls. He had never left his office let alone New York. He was just flying under the radar until one of two things happened. Either Rachet would kill China, which he not only expected but also hoped he would do. Or China would end up in jail for child abandonment, among other things. He had already spoken to the D.A., a political friend and golf partner, an arrest warrant had already been issued for the mother. The little Black kid had been removed from the apartment, after a week of being home alone, and placed in a group home. Either way it wouldn't be long before Bernstein had his apartment back and the complex rid of the filth. He settled back in his easy chair and read a few pages from the report, slash treatment, slash novel Fred had given him.

* * * * *

John John Wi discovered, after much coaxing, that Gui Song Li was selling her soul to support a tiny baby from a Black Military man who seduced her shortly after he met her. It was her only means of survival and she would rather her family think her dead than face the disgrace of being an unwed mother in China. John John Wi was full of sympathy and promised not to disclose a word of what she told him to anyone.

He lied. And at the first opportunity he contacted Gui Song Li's family in China and brokered a deal with them to kidnap her from her pimp and return her and the child back to her homeland. After her abduction Gui Song Li pleaded with John John Wi. Her family was sure to kill the baby girl and Gui Song would be locked away and tortured for the rest of her life for the shame she brought on her family.

Her Pleas fell on deaf ears. John John Wi returned her and was paid a handsome sum. Her parents, although they didn't embrace her with open arms, were supportive. Though her mother eventually took to the baby girl –somewhat, her father never spoke to Gui Song again and he never even glanced at the 'bastard child'. But even that was a lot more than she ever expected and for a while Gui Song was happy. The child blossomed into the prettiest child in the low lands. Even her mother had to admit how beautiful the child was. Gui Song Li spent her days pampering the child. Her nights were spent lying in bed hating the father of her child or lounging for the excitement she enjoyed being the most sought after whore in the Triad district. Eventually she grew bored and abandoned both the child and her family, found a brothel in the red light district of China, and soon worked her way back to Hong Kong.

Her mother took care of the child until she reached puberty at which time her father, after many years of effort, finally located the father of the child and through much coercion and a couple of hundred thousand U.S. dollars, managed to arrange for a visa, temporary citizenship and for her biological father to meet her at the airport and take her into his family. Of course it took another fifty thousand dollars deposited into the fathers account and the promise of a monthly payment of two thousand dollars before the father agreed to take the girl and arrange for her permanent citizenship. But it was money well spent to be rid of the overly developed bastard child.

*   *   *   *   *

From the very first day she arrived in New York and entered the Jackson' apartment, a five-flight walk up off Lenox avenue, Yuet Ying Jackson stirred only jealously and animosity among the Jackson household.

The stepmother, whom Robert married shortly after returning from his Hong Kong tour of duty, while Yuet Ying was still struggling for her life, held resentment for her husband's illegitimate child even before she met her.

Their daughter, fifteen year old, Jasmine, enjoyed the status of being Harlem's finest until Yuet Ying stepped through the door. From that moment,

Jasmine, knew she was destined to become obsolete. She hated her instantly. No way was she going to share a room with her, even if her room was large and held an extra bed. So after much shouting back and forth, it was determined that Yuet Ying would sleep on the living room sofa.

Yuet Ying didn't understand a single word of what they were shouting, the only English she knew was the phrase she practiced over and over before coming to America, "'Ello. My name Yuet Ying. I berry much 'appy to meet." She could however feel that she was not liked or wanted by the women of the house. Her biological father, though he tried to conceal it, seemed excited to see her.

Yuet Ying had barely reached twelve when her father enrolled her in school, but she had the body of a grown woman, the face of a movie star and the disposition of an Angel, and still she spoke only small phrases of English. Yet her first week, every boy in the school vied for her attention, even the seniors, and the popular basketball players. But when she only ignored them, she was much to shy but mostly because her English was so poor, they too, like every girl in the school began to hate her and call her foul names.

For three years, Yuet Ying devoted every single moment to learning English and doing well in school. She didn't care about being popular like most of the other girls, or having the latest clothing, or what boy was the finest. She didn't even care that Jasmine treated her like cow dung, and constantly did hateful, spiteful things to her. All Yuet Ying cared about was speaking English as well as anyone else and her education. To her it was the only way out of the situation she had been placed in by her grandparents.

One day, just before the end of Jasmine's last year of high school, Yuet Ying, who was now just referred to as China Doll or China, came out of her fifth period class to see a gang of girls beating and stomping some girl in the yard. At first her impulse was to walk in the other direction. She had learned that it was best to mind your business in the streets of Harlem, but something about the girl they were beating drew her near. It was her half sister Jasmine. Yuet Ying went into a fury. Picking up the closest thing, a forty-beer bottle, she began wailing on the girls, screaming, "Get off my sister, get off my sister, you bitch." She had never fought before, never even raised her voice at another human, but she fought like a demon that day, even though she and Jasmine ended up getting their asses kicked pretty badly.

Jasmine didn't thank her for coming to her aid or anything. In fact she didn't speak to Yuet Ying the entire walk home. When they arrived Jasmines mother, seeing how both girls were badly bruised and swollen, immediately assumed the girls had been fighting each other and pulled Jasmine to her side to begin scolding Yuet Ying.

"Putting your hands on my daughter? As soon as Robert returns he's going to have to do something with you. You're not staying in my house putting your hands on my child!"

It was then that Jasmine cut in. "Ma, China just saved my life. If she hadn't jumped in those girls would have stomped me to death or cut me all up. I saw one of them pullout a box cutter right before China smashed her in the head with a bottle."

That night, eating popcorn together in front of the television for the first time, Jasmine and China relived the fight. And after the awards show went off, Jasmine fixed the spare bed in her room and moved all China's things from behind the sofa into a section of the closet she cleared out for her.

Things were about to change in the Jackson household and Mama Jackson was not going to be happy about it at all.

Bernstein closed the pages and called Fred. "Did you read it?" Fred asked without a hello. "I read enough," Bernstein said blandly.

"And what did you think?"

Bernstein could hear the anticipation in his voice. "I don't think it will make a good novel."

"Oh well I'll go ahead with the Gotham deal," Fred said, despondent.

"Wait. I didn't say I wasn't interested," Bernstein hurriedly injected. "I just don't think it would make a great novel."

"Well that pretty much says it all-"

"I think it would make a better screenplay. One of those urban deals. I was thinking Jessica Alba as China and some other top names as supporting cast."

"You're serious?"

"I never play when it comes to money Fred. I'll have some script writers go over it tomorrow, if they agree you and I can sit down with the lawyers and go through the motions."

"I'll have to talk with my daughter first. It's her treatment."

"Just tell her we're going to make a ton of money and we'll put her on the payroll, get her a nice place on Wilshire," he chuckled. Bernstein hung up then picked up the treatment again. It was a good read and he was anxious to get to the Rachet parts.

* * * * *

Daquan was standing on the corner waiting for the light to change when Jumm's Navigator came from nowhere and almost ran the light. Daquan could recognize Jumm's Navi a block away just by the rims. Nobody in Harlem had a Navi with rims like his. For a moment his excitement grew.

Jumm wasn't his best friend but he wasn't exactly an enemy either. Still Rachet probably had everybody in his crew looking for him.

Daquan turned to head back to the subway as the Navigator screeched to a halt half way in the intersection. At least he was happy knowing that Jumm hadn't been killed. The Navi backed up as Daquan took his first couple of steps and a voice called out,

"Yo' kid! Little Man!" Daquan kept walking. He heard the truck door open and slam and then the voice was right on his heels. "Why you in a rush little nigga. You hear me calling you."

Daquan wanted to run but he could hardly keep his balance to walk. He decided to stop.

"I'ont know you Dawg," Daquan said, turning to look at the face belonging to the voice.

"Yea but I know you lil nigga," he said. "And that's all that counts."

Daquan looked back to the truck for Jumm .. It was empty. Then he realized. This must be the dude running around claiming he slumped Jumm. And judging from the look of things, he must have.

"Yea well what you want from me?" Daquan asked.

"Rachet got everybody out looking for yo lil ass. I guess today is my lucky day."

Daquan looked back at the truck. "Look like you had more than one lucky day already."

"You might say that," J.B. smiled. "Get in. Me an' you about to take a little ride."

* * * * *

"You hold the handle like this baby, and you keep your thumb and your finger locked on the blade like this," Daquan's mother was showing him. "If the blade closes on your fingers it'll cut them clean off." She placed the straight razor in his tiny hand and wrapped his fingers around it for the proper grip. "Now when you strike, it's all in the flick of the wrist and you cut them right here." She took his other hand and made him feel behind her knee. "See right there. That's the main vein. You cut him there he'll bleed to death in less than five minutes, especially if you make him chase you."

Daquan gave his mother all his attention. She might not be there all the time to protect him and his brother. He had to learn to do it for himself. He watched carefully then he demonstrated what he had learned.

"God! I don't know how I got such smart kids," she said happily. "You have a photographic memory and your brother isn't even one yet and he's already reading. He's going to be a lawyer one day. God knows you and I are going to need one to keep us out of prison.

"It's true," his mother often bragged to her friends, "He might be only five but all you have to do is show him something once and he's got it and committed it to memory. "

"And what else do you need to practice every day?"

"How to use my right hand. "

"Why is that?"

"So people won't know I'm left handed."

"An what's the advantage of that?"

'If you make them look another way they 'ont never see where the real shit is coming from."

"An what else you learn today?"

"You can't never cheat no honest man, but a greedy man, you can take him for everything he got."

"Good." His mother smiled "Now what do you want for dinner."

"Mister Chows."

"OK, Mister Chows it is," she said, looking at the thick wad of cash she had gotten from today's greedy people who never saw the left hand coming.

The city was all lit up beneath him as he looked out over the river to Brooklyn. Their apartment was huge, they had a day maid, and his mother assured him that every tenant in their building was a millionaire. Chi Chi fit right in. She looked rich, acted rich, and spent money like she was rich. She would hold conversations with their nosey asses, but he was told to never say more than a 'Yes Ma'am or no Ma'am, unless his mother was setting up a jux and then he knew exactly what to say.

"Get your brother," she told him, pulling on a jacket she had just purchased from Bendels. "We're outta here."

*   *   *   *   *

Whatever Rachet said or did with the lil nigga JB didn't expect him to walk out, especially so soon. A street soldier came out behind the lil nigga and whispered to JB that Rachet wanted him to follow the kid. "If you lose him," he warned, "Rachet is gonna lose your ass."

Lil nigga hung out in front of Mister G's for a few minutes, while JB watched him from the back room then he eased off and headed towards Lenox, JB quickly switched hats and jackets with one of the soldiers before trailing, giving the kid a block lead. Lil nigga was walking kinda funny, like he was drunk or something. A couple of times JB thought the lil mutha-fucka was going to fall out before he disappeared down into the 125th station. JB followed at a safe distance.. He didn't have to worry about losing him, the lil nigga was moving at a snails pace.

He took the number 2 to 42nd street then changed to the uptown 9, the Broadway train. He was heading up into Diablo territory. JB had done a lot of dirt up on the Hill and he wasn't too happy at the prospect of trailing the kid through those streets. The kid got off on 96th street, it was the tip of Diablo territory but not the heart of it, JB breathed a sigh of relief, he could deal with 96th. But instead of heading for the exit, the lil' mutha-fucka stumbled to the end of the platform and took the stairs down into the tunnel.

'Damn! What the fuck was this kid up too. JB hurried behind him. When he reached the bottom of the stairs all he could see of the kid was a faint shadow weaving in and out of the darkness. He followed cautiously, trying to stay in the shadows himself as much as possible.

JB had no idea how large and intricate the underground tunnels were. The kid was leading him so far into the maze that there was no way he could find his way back out without the kid. Plus, the further they got into the tunnels the darker it got, and the kid had the only flashlight. It almost seemed like the kid was luring him into a trap. JB unholstered his weapon and pushed the safety off. He would body the little mutha-fucka if he had too. The kid was way ahead of him and JB had to feel his way along the tunnel walls.

At the next turn the kids flashlight disappeared and it was suddenly so dark JB couldn't see his hand when he held it inches from his face. He waited a few, standing perfectly still, turning his head in all directions to see if the kid's light would reappear. An eternity seemed to pass and still nothing. He dug in his pocket for his lighter. He had never been in this kind of darkness before, even as a kid he couldn't remember shit being this dark, and to be honest with himself, it was scaring the holy shit out of him.

JB gripped his pistol tighter as he took the lighter and flicked it. He didn't want to use it for fear of alerting the kid he was being followed but fuck that shit. The kid was playing games. He already knew he was here. When he caught the little mutha-fuck he was going to strangle his little fuckin' ass. The lighter didn't help that much, he still couldn't see more than two feet in front of him or his own two feet below, but at least he could see something. Enough to know there was a dirt wall to his left and if he followed that it was sure to take him someplace. But where? The kid had led him to some foul section of the tunnels. The stench was becoming unbearable. JB held his breath for as long as he could, taking one cautious step after another, pressing on instead of pursuing his better judgment of turning back, which he considered useless at this point. His only hope of ever leaving this shit hole was finding the kid.

He reached what he thought to be the end of the wall and felt his way to make a left turn. On the second step, only the back heel of his shoe made contact with solid ground and he went crashing forward-pushing his gun hand-out to break his fall, he managed not to land face first. He splattered into a muck of slime and his gun popped out. His lighter went out too but he managed to hold on to that shit. When he flicked his lighter again he realized he was knee deep in the source of the awful stench, a cesspool of shit.

"Oh mutha-fucka!" JB exclaimed as he moved the lighter above the surface of the slime searching for his weapon but his gun had already sunk to the bottom of the foul smelling shit. "Mutha-fucka! When I catch yo' lil' ass I'm pushing yo wig back. That's my word to my flag."

He attempted to slide his foot around to feel for it but the shit was all in his sneakers, in his socks, squishing between his toes. "That's my word," he shouted. "When I catch you I'm pushing your wig back.. "Fuck!" JB took a deep breath and shoved his arm up to the shoulder in the muck to feel for his gun. Coming up empty handed for the fifth time he decided all he was doing was drowning himself in shit. He was never going to it and each time he went down he risked tipping over and losing his lighter too. He picked one foot up after another and trudged on.

* * * * *

CHAPTER 23

Silvia Rosenstein was anxious to interview the boy Naquan Jackson. She had first read about him when he was featured on the cover of Newsweek and found his academic achievements absolutely intriguing. She had attempted to interview him on a couple of occasions for her thesis, but the boy and his mother shied away from interviews. After the Newsweek article she read in a tabloid that he had turned down every news organization from CBS to The New York Times to CNN, all the majors, so a little nobody grad student like her didn't stand a chance. He had even turned down very lucrative offers from major film companies. His mother was much too wealthy to be tempted by the attention or the offers. Though paparazzi was constantly trying to photograph the mother and son duo, the only photos they managed to get were of them arriving or leaving the school. The mother seemed very protective of the boy and Silvia Rosenstein didn't believe in the child abandonment charges leveled against the woman. She suspected foul play and had voiced her opinion both to law enforcement and the District Attorney's office. They both assured her they would look into it but Silvia had been around long enough to realize when she was being washed over. Never in a million eons though would she phantom this genius of a child sitting in her chair in a group home.

There was a light knock on the door to her office. She rose and crossed the room to open it, instead of just telling him to come in as she usually would, having the feeling she was on her way to greet a dignitary.

When she opened it, there stood the prodigy child with an attendant, looking like so many of the other boys in the group home that for a second she was embarrassed for herself. What was she expecting, some regal god to be standing at the door? She didn't know what she was expecting but it certainly wasn't this ordinary black kid with the stone face she was extending a manicured hand to.

"Hi. Silvia Rosenstein," she said with a generous smile. "I'll be your counselor." He returned her enthusiasm with a blank look and an ever so minute smirk at the corner of his lips.

Not what she was expecting at all. "Come in. Have a seat. Let's talk a bit," she said in her rosy tone, taking him gently by the hand and guiding him to a small seating area away from her desk. "Would you like a soda and cookies before we talk?" He was ignoring her, instead taking in every little detail of the room like a detective at a crime scene.

Naquan warmed up to Silvia after a while and they had the most delightful conversation. He turned out to be exceedingly well mannered and well informed on current events and he was very charming, even complimenting her on the earrings she wore, naming the designer, how many carats and how many of that design were issued -57, then he told her what she paid for them and the store they were purchased in.

Of course it was hours later, when she was packing to go home before she realized she had misplaced her purse and it wasn't until she had reached home and was relaxing in a bubbly bath that she realized all the information Naquan had given about her earrings was on a certificate of authenticity in her purse and then it fully dawned on her, Naquan Jackson was a thief.

*　　*　　*　　*　　*

There were only two things that JB was afraid of in the entire world. One was his pathological fear of being trapped in confined spaces, the other was an even greater fear of rats and there were packs of rats in the pitch black tunnels. Rats the size of ally cats and a pack of them had been following him for the past half hour or so. JB was at the point that he was beginning to hyperventilate. He couldn't catch his breath and he felt an anxiety attack coming on and he didn't have his inhaler. He had to get the fuck out of this place. If he fell out, he was sure the pack of rats would eat him alive. It was like they were stalking him, waiting for him to die.

He tried to stay close to the walls but often times he would walk head on into another wall when it took a sudden turn, or trip over some debris floating in the sewage. Still he trudged on, following the faint rumblings of the trains in the distance whenever he could hear them. Only problem was they seemed to be coming from every direction. He had to chose one and stick to it. But even that didn't seem possible. The tunnels seemed to be taking him where they wanted him to go.

JB checked the fluid in his lighter, it was less than a quarter filled. He definitely wouldn't get out of the tunnel without light. He held the lighter to his watch, his thumb and fingers were cramped, raw and bleeding from holding it down so long. The watch was useless. The face was smeared with so much shit he couldn't see the dial and if he wiped it on any part of his body he only smeared it with more shit. There wasn't a portion of his body that wasn't covered with the foul smelling gook. It had even found it's way into his mouth, making him so nauseous he kept forcing back the urge to throw up.

"When I find you, you bitch ass little bastard," he said to himself, "I'm gonna peel every inch of your skin off while you're still alive. I don't give a fuck what Rachet says. I'm gonna shit in your fucking mouth and make you eat it, then I'm gonna peel your fucking skin off."

His face almost jumped through his shit soaked shirt when another giant rat advanced on him through the muck behind him. JB jumped and swung his lighter around, the sudden movement extinguished his flame. As he flicked and flicked to regain his light, he felt a sharp sting behind his right knee.

"Oh shit! Oh shit! get the fuck off me," he screamed, swatting frantically at the rat he was certain had latched on to his leg. He must have retreated for another attack JB rationalized, after realizing he was swinging at air. "You wanna play fucking games.. You wanna play fucking games?" JB shouted into the darkness.

As he turned another sharp sting sliced through the fingers holding his leg. The pain was so intense that he dropped the lighter and grabbed for his hand. He couldn't feel his fingers but he could feel blood pouring out. JB was one heartbeat away from going into total shock when the voice of the kid came at him from the darkness.

"What's wrong JB? Can't find your lighter. Scared of the dark. Not a fuckin' killer like you. I know you ain't scared."

"You little mutha-fucka," JB screamed back. "When I catch yo' little bitch ass I'm gonna kill you. You know that shit right?"

"With what?" Daquan called back to him, his voice coming from another direction now. "You ain't got no fucking gun Anyway you gon bleed to death in five minutes if I don't help you, so you better just shut up and listen. You ain't got that much time."

"Fuck you!" JB screamed back, no longer caring how much shit he swallowed while desperately feeling for the lighter. Suddenly there was a flame flickering just inches from his face. "Need a light?" Daquan taunted, JB lunged towards the flame "If you want it you gotta catch me." Then the light went out again.

JB ran right into the wall. Daquan laughed.

"Stupid mutha-fucka." The light came on again, this time a good distance directly in front of him. JB took three steps in the guck and found himself on solid ground again.

"You already wasted two minutes. Half the blood already left your body," Daquan said from the darkness. "But you's a fuckin' idiot anyway. You know what, after I leave you here I'm-a go find yo' mama an make her suck my dick." He flicked the light on and waited for JB to chase him. JB ran a short distance then stopped, clutching his leg. Blood was flowing from it like water from a pressure hose. He was beginning to feel faint. His head was throbbing and the darkness was spinning as he sank to one knee. JB knew he was losing consciousness..

"A'ight. A'ight. Say what you gotta say lil' nigga. I'm listening," JB called out, desperately trying to stop the flow of blood with both hands not even realizing he was missing three fingers from his right hand and its pinky finger was being held on by a thread of flesh

"You tell me where Rachet got China and my brother and I'll stop you from bleeding. If you telling me the truth I'll come back and show you how to get out of here. "

"Naw. You get me out of here first then I'll tell you. " The bright light from Daquan's flashlight was suddenly in his face, momentarily blinding him. "I ain't stupid," Daquan said harshly. "I might as well leave yo' ass here an' go find her myself." He turned the light away from JB and started walking away. JB made an attempt to move but he couldn't. He was too weak.

"Wait!" JB called after him. "How I know you gon come back an' get me?"

Daquan turned back to him. "1 give you my word. All a man really got in this world is his word."

*   *   *   *   *

When a man knows he's dying and you hold the power of his life in your hands, there is nothing he knows that he won't tell you in order to live. The safe house Rachet was holding China and his brother in was a bricked up abandoned building on 127th street off Fifth Avenue with only one way in and one way out.

Turns out JB wasn't new to Rachet's crew. He was a distant cousin and had been an external hit man for Rachet since they were teenagers. He used JB to keep those close to him in check so it was important that no one knew of their connection.

"There's a secret tunnel that connects to the safe house," JB told him, too weak to hold his head up as Daquan tied a tourniquet around his thigh then put a stick in it to hold it tight. "There's another one connected to the chop shop where they cut up the bodies. Then there's one that leads to the cutting house. I know they wouldn't keep 'em there, too many workers. Rachet either got em in the safe house or in the chop shop. If they in the chop shop they probably dead already. Rachet don't keep nobody in the chop shop for more than a week before he feed them to the dogs. It's a rule."

"Hold this," Daquan told him, placing JB's good hand on the tourniquet. Every fifteen minutes you let it loose for like a minute then make it tight again."

"You coming back for me right?"

"If you ain't lying," Daquan said firmly.

"I ain't lying… I swear."

"Then I'll be back for you," Daquan swore, leaving him the flashlight before he rose to leave.

"Oh. Little man," JB called out weakly. " Whatever you do, don't go up on none of them roofs. That's where Rachet keeps the dogs and all they eat is people. They won't even touch no other kind of meat. And they like to kill it they self."

*   *   *   *   *

"We got a few problems," Speedy said. "First we have to get in there past all those mutha-fuckaz."

Speedy Scarecrow and Daquan stood in the shadows of an abandoned building across the street from a team of Rachet's lookouts. They sat on the stoop smoking El's and joking around but Speedy could see they were alert to any thing unusual moving on the block. Down the block and outside 31-11, the building they needed to get into, were some real shooters, who played half way in and half way out the hallway. Speedy knew they were just the advance team. The real artillery was inside and well concealed.

"Then we don't know which place they're holding them in."

*   *   *   *   *

Pitt was coming back from getting China West Indian food when he drove by and noticed the kid Daquan lurking in the hallway with two other kids. What the hell was Little Man doing at 3:15 in the morning casing the safe houses. He knew Rachet hadn't sent him on a mission. Rachet had the entire Manhattan looking for his lil' ass.

Pitt circled to126th street, parked the car and slid one in the chamber before getting out. The kid was crazy to come up here like this. He would have been better off painting a bulls eye on his chest and slinging hot ones at a swat team. At least they would kill him outright. Rachet would keep him alive and torture his lil ass.

*   *   *   *   *

Speedy watched three heads enter the block from Fifth, two chicks who didn't look like they were entirely smoked out yet and one twisted dude. They stopped at the lookout's stoop in an attempt to buy 1 crack. Nobody would serve them.

"Who the fuck told you we sell crack here bitch? Get the fuck off the block!"

"Come on baby. We thirsty. Ain't nobody else out an I know Yall got some shit."

"Get the fuck off the block bitch. I ain't gon tell you again.. Go uptown if you wanna cop, we ain't selling." He raised his t-shirt to show her he was packing. He was basically telling her that even if she was undercover this was not the place she wanted to be.

The crack head nigga was acting more like a bitch than the bitches were.

"We sorry man, we sorry. We leaving."

The smallest one with the big mouth wasn't budging. In fact she was advancing on the one with the gun. "Come on daddy," she cooed. "I got what you want. You got what I need."

"Come on Jackie," the crack head nigga started pleading, tugging at her jacket. "They say get off the block we off the block-"

"Bitch ass. You get off the fuckin' block," she said, slapping his hand away and turning back to the one with the gun. "You don't want no young pussy..? It's the best pussy in the world. Ain't no pussy like this young pussy."

Nigga on the stoop whipped the gun out on her. "Get the fuck off the block bitch! Don't nobody want that shit. You ain't even got no titties yet."

"Yea, and you ain't never been in no, no titty pussy like this one either," she said, grabbing herself.

She was just about to leave when some big black gorilla looking dude stepped from inside the building and called her up to him. He whispered something in her ear and she nodded in the affirmative then disappeared inside with him. She came out alone ten minutes later then her and the other two heads, crossed the street heading straight for the building Speedy was in. Speedy stepped back in the darkness.

As the heads climbed the stairs to the building one of the lookouts called to the trio, "Yo! Yo! Where the fuck you think you going. I told y'all to get the fuck off the block." They stopped. The lookout turned his head abruptly to the dark hallway, listened, then turned back with a grimace. "Go the fuck on. Smoke yo' shit then, but after you done y'all other two mutha-fuckaz get the fuck off the block then shorty gotta come back and finish what she started. Yall lucky this mutha-fucka in here done lost his fuckin mind, otherwise…"

Up close, Daquan noted, the crack head that went in the building with the worker was really pretty. She was about five foot two, maybe three, with golden hair, braided, and cat like grayish blue eyes, and she looked mad young, like a baby.

"It's like walking into a death trap," she said as soon as she was all the way inside. "But I got a bug on one of his lieutenant's. Nigga was so into the way I was deep throating him he didn't even notice when I clipped the shit under his jacket collar." She pulled a receiver from her backpack that looked like a transistor radio, pushed an earplug in her ear and adjusted the controls. She started laughing. "This nigga talking about the shit right now." She took out the plug and passed it to Speedy. He listened for a while, without expression, then passed it back.

"What about the other thing?"

"I slid it under the stairs, they ain't gon never notice it. And if they do…"

"They'll just think its garbage," Scarecrow said.

"What? We having a party," a voice asked from the darkness.

All three of the heads had weapons drawn and pointed in the direction of the voice before Pitt could finish the sentence. They separated slowly, each melting into some crevice of the darkness as Speedy pulled on his night goggles. Scarecrow was already wearing his.

Speedy was real annoyed. He should have never let whoever it was sneak up on them but Vanessa had distracted him. Not good. It meant him and his team were slipping.

"Easy," Pitt said "If I wanted to do something to Yall little niggaz I would have brought a crew."

Speedy asked, "So what the fuck you want Pitt?" He recognized him through the night visions.

"I'll tell you what I don't want. I don't wanna see Yall lil niggaz get yo' shit splattered trying to save China."

"What you care?" Daquan asked from the darkness.

"That you Lil' Man?" Pitt asked.

"Yea."

"I'm here to help, but Y'all lil niggaz got to trust me. We might be able to get China out if Y'all niggaz is as official as I heard Y'all was."

"Why you wanna help?" Daquan asked. "Rachet yo first cousin. China don't mean nothin to you."

"I don't like what he did to her."

"He ain't do nothing to my little brother did he?"

"He ain't even got your little brother. All he got is China and he's doing her dirty. But ain't shit I can do by myself. Shit is like a fortress in there. All steel enforced with madd trap offs. Even Swat couldn't get in that shit without losing a lot of mutha-fuckaz."

Speedy asked. "So how we suppose to get in if you can't do it?"

"I'm-a tell you if you wanna listen," Pitt said, stepping out into the light. "Otherwise all Y'all little niggaz gon' die."

*   *   *   *   *

Shortly after lights out, Naquan slipped from his bed and dressed silently, put his extra blanket and clothes under his covers and waited till the attendant left his post and went over to talk with the attendant in the next dorm. Naquan gave them time to get involved with their conversation then slipped out the dorm and made his way to the corridor.

It took him two hours of hiding, crawling and creeping but he finally made it to a side door that was open and into the dark streets of Brooklyn. His initial plan was to make his way to the safe house in the tunnels, but when he thought about it, Kilo would never let him in without hearing the combination. He always had to take Kilo with him whenever he wanted to leave without Daquan knowing. Anyway China told him Daquan was staying with some girl in the Bronx so he didn't think Daquan ever went back down there. Kilo had probably starved to death by now.

He couldn't go back to the apartment-that would be the first place they looked for him when they found him missing. Anyway old man Bernstein didn't want him there. He would most likely call the Police. He couldn't call Katrina. He had been trying to call her the entire week he was staying in the apartment alone, but he got the same, "This number is no longer in service." She told him she be would be forced to go London suddenly if her mother won the custody battle. That must have been what happened. Not unless she ran away like she said she was going do if her mother won. Still she would have called. Katrina had never missed calling him a day since they met. They were inseparable, in fact they had made plans to run away together if she was forced to move with her mother.

Whatever Naquan was going to do, he knew he wasn't going back to the group home. He had to find Daquan. Daquan had always taken care of him. Together they could find China and Katrina.

Naquan found the nearest subway and headed uptown to the Bronx. He didn't know where Daquan's girl lived in the Bronx or who she was. All he had was a name, Trina, but he knew for a certainty he would find his brother. Everybody in the Bronx knew who Daquan was.

On the train he kept dozing off and he kept hearing Daquan yelling at him; "Wake up Lil' nigga. You know what happens to niggaz who sleep on the train." But Naquan couldn't keep his eyes open and soon he was sleeping like a baby.

*   *   *   *   *

"You ain't so pretty now are you bitch?" Rachet's voice resounded in her head. China didn't have to imagine what she looked like to know she had to look like a beast. Her face was so swollen with blood it felt heavy and lopsided. She could only see the blurred outline of Rachet, her vision had long left from his pounding. He had hit her so hard at one point that he took a whole section of her gums out to send some of her permanent dentures flying across the room.

She didn't see the next blow coming, Rachet hit her so hard in her ribcage she collapsed, the only thing keeping her on her feet were her hands cuffed high over head to a steel pipe.

From all the pain and torture she was enduring China should have lost consciousness long ago but she couldn't go out. Rachet had given her something that he assured her would keep her from losing consciousness and make her feel every iota of pain he inflicted. Something he said the CIA used to interrogate terrorist. "Fuck you Rachet, Go on and kill me. I don't care. I don't have anything left to live for anyway," she managed to gurgle out through the blood gushing from her gums.

"I ain't gon' kill you bitch. That's too good for your stink ass. I'm-a let you live. But when I get through with you I guarantee ain't a mutha-fucka in this world that's gon' want your ugly ass. You gon' be living out of garbage cans for the rest of your life.

"At least I'll still be around. Your worthless ass will be dead by then." The words bubbled out.

Rachet starting laughing his sick psychopathic laugh, then just as abruptly as it started he became deadly serious.

"Bitch you know who I am? I'm a fucking God. I can't die. A bomb could drop right in the middle of this room and I'd be the only one left standing."

"Shit!" China garbled out sarcastically. "That ain't no fucking odds... Put your ass in a room with like a thousand mutha-fuckaz and you're the only one left then I might be impressed. She attempted to spit at him but her tongue was too swollen.

"You got a slick ass mouth. That's why you in the situation you in now. You don't know when to shut the fuck up."

"Eat shit, you dick sucking faggot," China managed to say clearly.

"See…" Rachet was about to backhand her when a static voice came from his two-way. "Base to Chopper One."

"You need to get your stomach pumped," China continued. "I can smell niggaz dick all over your breath."

Rachet gave her a hard look then unclipped the two-way from his hip and shouted into it. "Head Chopper, go ahead base."

"Bulldog has a bag and he doesn't want us to look in it."

"You know how he gets when he's smoking that wet. Let him through."

"You sure. You know don't no bags get through unless we check them."

"Nigga what did I tell you?"

"All right but it's on you."

"Yea right.. Over," Rachet said, still looking at China hard, daring her to say another word. He clipped the two way back on his hip. "Bout fucking time. I thought he went to the Bahamas' to get fucking food, an you better eat every last drop. You gon' need every ounce of energy you can get." He gave her a smile then crossed the room to an adjoining door. When he opened it two massive Rottweiler's stepped in. "You remember Max? Well say hello to his little friend," he imitated Al Pachino from Scareface. "They're a little horny but I'm sure jew won't mind getting out of those chains and on jour knees for a while."

*　*　*　*　*

Pitt came in carrying a giant shopping bag.

"Nigga. I didn't tell you to go shopping," Rachet shouted at him. "I just told you to go get the bitch some West Indian."

Pitt sat the bag down near China and took her food from the top.

"Move that shit," Rachet demanded. The Rottweiler's stood at attention, a low growl directed at Pitt from the tension in their masters voice. "Can't you see I'm about to do some filming?"

Pitt ignored him and the dogs, while searching through the bag.

"What's in that shit anyway," Rachet asked, annoyed that Pitt had violated yet another of his sacred rules. Cousin or no cousin, he was gonna have to get rid of this nigga soon. Pitt continued to ignore him. He came out of the bag with a bottle of iodine and a box of gauze, straightened and began packing China's ruptured gums with gauze.

Rachet was looking at him like he was crazy. When Pitt started treating China's wounds with the iodine, Rachet exploded; "Nigga you lost your goddamn mind? I'm beating the bitch up for a reason and you wanna play doctor."

Pitt continued to ignore him as he whispered something in China's ear.

"What the fuck?" Rachet jerked up from the tripod, nearly knocking it and the digital camera over. The dogs stiffen to attack position. Pitt's hand calmly went to his weapon as he turned to face Rachet. "Nigga, now I know you done lost your goddamn mind," Rachet said, stopping dead in his tracks. "You about to pullout on me? I know you ain't that fucking crazy-"

"Nigga you just getting a little too close for comfort," Pitt warned him. "All I'm doing is trying to keep the bitch alive for you, but you starting to get hostile with the wrong mutha-fucka now. I ain't no bitch, nigga. You can't play me that close."

"Nigga I'll play you anyway I wanna play you," Rachet burst back. He was thinking, now might be as good a time as any to get rid of this stupid mutha -fucka. He was tired of feeling threatened by this bitch-ass nigga.

Rachet gave Pitt the grill face, went back to the tripod and pressed record, figuring he might as-well get Rex and Alexander ripping Pitt apart on film before he let them beat China's asshole and pussy up.

Pitt must have been reading his mind, for no sooner than his finger left the record button than Pitt told him with conviction,

"Go ahead Rachet. Give the command. I bet you I can put three in your head before them bitches reach me." He stared at Rachet hard. "Go ahead. You brave enough to beat up bitches, lets see if you brave enough to give the command." Pitt was staring him down hard. "Go on, let's see if you're really invincible."

Rachet looked down at the massive attack dogs. They were less than ten feet away from Pitt, they were fast and Pitt still had to draw his weapon from the back of his shirt. He seriously doubted if Pitt could get a shot off before the dogs were on him. In fact he was sure of it. He looked back at Pitt, opened his arms up like he was cradling the world, and gave him a generous smile. " I knew since we were kids that one day I was gonna have to kill your stupid ass."

"Yea me too," Pitt said with a grimace, his eyes piercing Rachet's like daggers. "And the funny thing is, I use to think you were a God. Matter of fact I wanted to be just like you. But that was before I saw you make your own brother suck your dick then watched you fuck him in his ass. That's when I realized you weren't no God. You were just a foul ass homo and that it wouldn't be long before you were sucking niggaz dicks and letting them fuck you in your butt hole. You's a fucking bitch!!! I'm a do the same thing to you that I did to Petey, but I promise I won't feed you to the dogs. I got more respect for them. I don't want them to get sick from eating your foul ass."

Rachet still had his sick ass grin plastered across his face. "You been talking a lot of shit since you started fucking with that lawyer bitch," Rachet finally said, "What? You working for the Feds now or something?"

"Nigga stop playing for time, you gon make the command or what?" Pitt smirked, easing the nine from his waistband. Once the dogs saw the weapon pointed at their master they wouldn't wait for an attack command. He would have a split second to pullout, aim and let off three shots. The dogs were that fast. He had seen the trainers demonstrate how fast they were on more than one occasion. They never got their weapons fully drawn before the dogs were at their throats.

* * * * *

Speedy had three teams of ten ready to rollout on command. There was the advance team, mostly drunken women cutting through the block from a late night of partying, they were the most deadly because of their obvious vulnerability. They had gathered a block away pretending to get the last of their drink and jokes on, awaiting the signal to go. Team two, the repelling team, was already in position. Camouflaged in brick faced infantry they were practically invisible perched one story below the roof of an adjoining building. The third team was hidden in the shadows of the buildings on the opposite side of the street.

Speedy and Scarecrow had the most dangerous assignments, confronting the dogs on the roof. There was always a chink in any armor and Pitt had discovered Rachet's months ago. The guards at the security post had to have air to breath,

"How y'all gonna get past the cameras and dogs?" Pitt asked. "There's a hundred of them mean mutha-fuckaz up there and they don't eat nothing but human flesh."

Speedy answered. "I got that, you just get the girl."

If it could be done Speedy and Scarecrow could do it. They were better equipped and probably better trained than the best Swat Team Agents on the East coast. Partly because they spent a ton of money through Speedy's mercenary uncle for the latest technology, and partly because they trained religiously each and every single day. They had stuff that the Police organizations could only sit back and dream about. Stuff that would get them an automatic life bid if they were caught with it.

Speedy checked his watch, Pitt had given them forty minutes and then he was walking out with the girl. Their mission was to inject the odorless nerve gas into the vents and seal the only exit door to the roof. If they failed it meant Pitt and China would be killed. Fifteen minutes had already expired and still Speedy hadn't located the vents.

They had come up on opposite corners of the building, under the radar of the security cameras and motion detectors. They hung just below the roof top, suspended by repelling hooks and ropes. Scarecrow, holding a weapon that looked much like a small rocket launcher, was having difficulty with his repelling rope because the dogs had been attacking the hook so violently it was steadily slipping from the ledge. He looked over to Speedy who seemed to be having the same problem.

Scarecrows hook slipped again, hanging on by the tips now as a massive pit-bull nearly leaped from the roof to knock it completely free. These dogs were not only vicious, they were smart.

Scarecrow signaled to Speedy that he was going down, pointing at his hook.

"No!" Speedy signaled back . "Thirty seconds, thirty seconds."

Scarecrow looked up at the determined pit-bull and dug in. He had scaled this type of brick face freeform countless times before but never with this much weight attached to his body.

Speedy raised the periscope dangerously high, where it would undoubtedly be detected, in an attempt to see all the way to the end. The monitor showed no signs of any vents pumping air. The ventilation system had to be hidden in one of the many vents from the rooftops. That meant they would have to hit each of them. There were two problems with that. They didn't have enough nerve gas for all of them and second, they would have less than five minutes to demobilize the dogs, seal the only door opening, hit every vent they could, then get the hell out of Dodge.

Speedy pulled his gas mask and goggles on, eased the ear muffs down, and signaled Scarecrow to use the flash grenades first, then using his fingers counted down three seconds. On three Scarecrow tossed the first of the flash grenades just over the edge of the roof. Not only would they blind the dogs but they would knock out the infrared of the surveillance cameras.

Just as quickly they were over and onto the rooftop. The dogs, completely blinded, were running into each other but a few, sensing where they were by smell, turned and attacked, while the man-eating packs from the next rooftops were hopping dividers in fast pursuit. Speedy tossed a sonic grenade at the dogs already down as Scarecrow dropped to one knee, shouldering the launcher and hurling flash grenades at each rooftop. The dogs began fighting each other, running into walls some misjudging and leaping off the roof.

After the flash grenades, came more sonic grenades. They were at such an extremely high pitch that only the dogs could hear, they rendered the dog's unconscious if not outright killing them, causing concussions of the brain. Speedy took off right behind the grenades, barely avoiding dogs that were still holding on to consciousness as he dropped the nerve agents into the vents, going on instinct alone as to which to pass up.

There were dead and unconscious dogs everywhere by the time Speedy reached the halfway mark. Scarecrow was at the exit door sealing its seams with an explosive sealant. It took him seconds before he ignited it, the cord sizzled and the door was instantly wielded shut. It would take anyone on the opposite side ten minutes with a blowtorch to get through. He rose and followed Speedy, knocking out any dogs still moving with a dart gun. When they neared the last rooftop, Scarecrow let off two more flash grenades and they were repelling down the Fifth Avenue face of the building.

They were seconds on the ground before automatic gunfire was being exchanged in the middle of the block. Speedy had given the teams the signal to go when he reached the midway mark of the rooftop.

*   *   *   *   *

The soldier blowing Vanessa's back out for the last half-hour jerked out of her and reached for his weapon when he heard the first volley of gunfire but it was too late for him. All the time he was pumping into her Vanessa couldn't wait for the signal so she could split his throat. He grabbed his throat and reached out for her. She sidestepped, catching him in the base of the spine with a roundhouse to instantly paralyze him. It took only seconds for her to retrieve the Uzi from the false bottom of her backpack and assemble it. Seconds after that the lookouts on the stoop were caught in a cross fire. They never had a chance.

*   *   *   *   *

Pitt had injected the antidote into China's arm after whispering in her ear what he was about to do. Before he had taken out the gauze and iodine he had first pulled the pin on the odorless bio agent in the bottom of the bag Speedy had provided him with. Speedy had also injected him with the antidote and showed him how to inject China. Neither of them would be totally immune to the agent, they would suffer some weakness and loss of muscle control but not enough to disable them. Rachet, Speedy assured him, would be out in a matter of minutes if not less. Neither he nor Speedy took in account that Rachet might possibly have the dogs with him. They usually stayed in the safe house under Mister G's. He must have brought them in when he sent him to the store the first time for China. That's why he locked the adjoining rooms door.

The dam dogs dropped before Rachet's stubborn ass did. Maybe he had injected him self with an antidote that worked on this particular nerve agent. He was always fiddling around with stuff that his CIA crack head friend was constantly bringing him for ounces of crack. Maybe it was just sheer determination that kept him standing but he was no longer on his feet after Pitt pumped the three slugs through his forehead. He was slumped in a corner, blood leaking down his face and trailing down the wall where the back of his head rested to form an ever-widening pool of the oil of life. For the first time in years, Pitt actually liked Rachet. He would remember him like that always.

*   *   *   *   *

A maintenance man sweeping the train cars woke Naquan up at the last stop.

"You OK little man?" he shook him. He could see that the kid wasn't homeless by the clothes he wore and how clean he was. Still, he observed by the whiteness of the kid's socks, that some grimy nigga had stolen his shoes. "You ain't sick are you?"

Naquan jerked out of his sleep. He had been having the nightmare again but this was the first time the man with the boot had a gun. He jumped up expecting to be shot. The first thing he saw was the black handle of the man's broom, thinking it to be the man with the boots nightstick.

Naquan slid all the way to the corner in shock.

"I ain't gon' hurt you little man. I just wanna make sure you're OK."

As Naquan came to his senses, he was remembering what Daquan always told him, "You 'on't trust nobody, 'specially on these trains."

'"I'm just trying to help," the man said. His voice didn't seem to go with his body. It was soft and soothing, his body was rough and weathered. His hands and fingers looked like cracked stone and rough sandpaper. He had a three day beard and his eyeballs, blood shot with thick red veins streaking into the retina, looked like they were about to pop out of their sockets. One of them was looking the other way and Naquan couldn't decide which one was looking at him.

"I don't need any help," Naquan practically shouted. "Just leave me alone."

"You look like you need some help," the cleaner said with a concerned look.

"Well I don't," Naquan said, sliding from the seat and squeezing his way past the man. He was on the elevated platform headed for the exit before the man called out.

"Hey where you going? You can't go out there without shoes an' no coat."

Naquan stopped and looked down. He hadn't even noticed that someone had taken his brand new Uptowns. He felt for his Yankee fitted. It was gone too. His chain, the credit cards he had stolen from his counselor. He felt for the money in the fabric bag he had taped between the shoulder blades of his back. At least they hadn't gotten his money. Daquan had shown him that trick a long time ago. At least he had listened to something Daquan taught him.

The man asked, "You see the weather?"

The rain was coming down in sheets. Naquan could hardly see the outline of the buildings through the downpour. He was so disoriented he hadn't even noticed it was raining.

"Where you going anyway. You sure this is your stop?"

"I know where I'm going," Naquan said angrily. "What do you think, I'm stupid?"

"I'm just trying to help," he called out after him as he neared the exit to the turnstiles. "I don't need any help," Naquan said, more to himself than the man behind him.

The subway cleaner went back to sweeping the last car as another train rolled into the station. The rain was coming down so hard it muffled the screeching of the train cars.

Naquan had no idea where he was or where he was going or even where he wanted to go. All he knew was that he was at the White Plains Rd. station. He found a big map on a wall near the turnstiles and studied it. Now he knew where he was but he still couldn't make a decision where to start looking for Daquan and his girlfriend. The Bronx was huge. He was never going to find Daquan or his girlfriend like this. He would have to figure out another way. Where would Daquan look for him?" The only place he could figure out was the safe house in the tunnels. Even if Kilo would let him in he had vowed, once China became his mother, never to return to that black place. But Daquan would probably go there to look for him.

*   *   *   *   *

To Naquin's surprise, Kilo let him in without hearing the combination lock. But once inside Kilo attacked him, jumping into his chest and knocking him to the ground. Naquan was about to let out a horrifying scream when Kilo starting licking him in the face. He was ecstatic to see Naquan. He followed him around the tiny room, running here and there trying to get him to play. Soon Naquan couldn't resist. They were wrestling around the tossing and retrieving and generally tearing up the place until they were both exhausted. Kilo had gotten fat. Daquan had installed a feeder where all Kilo had to do was push the plastic chute and a serving shot from the dispenser to fill his bowl. There was a water dispenser next to it. Enough food and water to last Kilo for a month and it was filled nearly to the top. That meant he had probably just missed Daquan, and Daquan might not come back until he thought it needed to be filled again. Naquan spent two more days and nights with Kilo before deciding to go back to the surface world. There was one other place he hadn't tried and he doubted that Daquan would be back anytime too soon. Daquan might go there looking for him.

He just missed his brother by a hair. Daquan was getting off the downtown train while he was getting on the uptown. Neither saw the other, though something kept telling Naquan to go back. Of course Naquan didn't listen to his inner voice but he did find a corner seat and he didn't nod off once the entire ride to 145th street.

* * * * *

Kilo had never been trained to keep Naquan from entering without hearing the combination lock. Daquan only told Naquan that to keep him from sneaking off. Kilo would never harm a hair on Naquan's body. Daquan was half expecting to see Naquan sitting there as he pulled back the concealing wall and stepped into the safe room. Kilo greeted him with enthusiasm but Naquan wasn't anywhere to be found. He had been there though. Daquan could see signs of his visit all over the room. He had been there and left. He wasn't coming back.

Daquan backed out of the room and made his way through the dark tunnels to the surface world.

"Where would he go now?" Daquan thought aloud. His girlfriend and her father had taken off unexpectedly. No one knew where they had gone. They just vanished in the night. Speedy had learned that from their landlord, who didn't seem overly concerned about their sudden flight.

He wouldn't go back to the apartment, not after Bernstein had him taken away by BCW. He had learned that when the Police came to arrest China in the hospital. She had to have reconstructive surgery and the slime balls were trying to physically arrest her. Shit still had him twisted. Naquan couldn't know China was in the hospital but he might go to Miss Perno's.

As soon as Daquan reached the surface he dialed Miss Perno. "Hello. Ms. Perno here," she answered in a cheerful voice on the first ring.

"Miss Perno, this is Daquan. Have you-"

She cut him off mid sentence, "Oh Daquan. What a pleasant surprise. Haven't seen you since China got rich." He knew the reference to China was meant to be sarcastic but he ignored it. It didn't mean shit to him.

"Yea I know," he said, meaning to sound apologetic. "You seen Naquan?" He really didn't have time or the desire for an extended conversation.

"No I haven't seen him since the day they packed up and left." She was sounding like they left owing her something. Shit Daquan had paid her for the last six months left on the lease and let her keep everything in the apartment China had added, which was a lot. This old bitch was bugging.

* * * * *

When every thing is moving so fast, some times you over look the small details and they come back to haunt you. Pitt should have taken the camera off the tripod before he left with China but he wasn't thinking. His only concern was whether the lil' niggaz had knocked out the security post so he could get China out. Damn! Out of all the shit he had ever done, he would have to get knocked on some bullshit.

"I ain't saying shit till I talk to my lawyer," Pitt said to the detective drilling him with questions. "An' cut the good cop bad cop routine. That shit is old."

"We don't need a confession Mister Edwards," the good cop said, offering him a cigarette. "We already have all the evidence we need for a conviction..."

"Not unless you want to cooperate," the bad cop intervened. "We could probably knock the sentence down to a manslaughter felony instead of pre med..."

"Suck my dick!" Pitt told him with a screw face. "You ain't the DA. You can't offer me shit. Matter fact. You need to stop talking 'cause that's what yo' breath smells like. Like dog shit!"

The Detective rose from the table. "You think you're tough. You're not tough. You're just a useless low life scum ball. I'm about to show you what tough is all about." The good cop stood and restrained him. "Come on, let's go outside for a breather," he coaxed.

"Yea bitch! And brush your tongue while you at it," Pitt grinned. "Bitch ass."

* * * * *

Most of the swelling in China's face had gone down but she had a total of fifty two stitches, a torn retina in her right eye, two broken ribs, a punctured lung and a ruptured spleen. She was a long way from recovery, her doctor's assured her. They were mostly worried about the spleen. It wasn't healing too well. A nurse's aid wheeled in the book cart.

"Good morning Ms. Jackson. How are we feeling today?" She was a bubbly young girl, still attending nursing school, and very conversational. "Let's see," she said, digging in the return section on the bottom shelf. "Your favorite, James Patterson. I had to hide it since you're next to my last stop." She gave China a generous smile, displaying rows of perfectly straight teeth. One of the old newspapers caught China's eye.

"Let me see that paper," China asked as the aide handed her the book.

"Oh those? Those are old, I still have a few of today's left." She reached for a small stack on the top shelf

"No. I want to see that one,"

"Which one," she asked bending back. "This one?"

"No, the one next to it. The one with the cop on the cover."

The headline read; HERO COP'S PARTNER FOUND DEAD. It was that asshole Denareo's face plastered across the entire front of the paper with a small inset of his partner and a notation that read story on page six. She waited until the aide left before turning to page 6.

Hero Detective Romereo Denareo, who brought down a savage murderer in a St. Albans Queens gun battle last week, found his ex partner dead in the basement of his 1.9 million dollar brownstone late last night from an apparent suicide.

Detective Denareo was called to the home of Detective Ralph Santiago by his wife after he locked himself in the basement, to kill himself. When Detective Denareo arrived, Santiago had already shot himself through the mouth with his service revolver. His wife of fifteen years said he was apparently distraught over his gambling addiction and the fact that he had lost all the family savings and the bank was in the process of taking away their 1.9 million dollar home. He reportedly kept telling her that at least if he were dead she would have insurance and pension money to support her and their two kids. His wife suffered from a nervous breakdown and had to be taken to Presbyterian Memorial.

Police also found boxes of evidence stolen from Police evidence rooms and the District Attorney's office, according a source who wishes to remain anonymous. It contained · all the evidence missing from the El Diablo drug cartel case that allowed its recently gangland executed boss to escape 100-year sentences and might over turn dozens of previous cases

"How is my favorite patient," Doctor Guttenberg asked. China jerked up from the paper. She hadn't heard the doctor standing at the side of her bed holding a clipboard to her breast, enter the room.

"I thought you told us you were HIV positive," the doctor said with a look of concern.

"I am," China told her. I was diagnosed five years ago,"

"By who?"

"By a clinic in the Bronx."

"And did that clinic also treat you,"

"Yes."

"And for how long did they treat you?"

"For about two years."

"What made you discontinue the treatment?"

"I don't know," China said, looking away. "Guess I just fell off."

"Humm." The doctor said, giving her a long look as if reprimanding her. "Are you certain this is the address of the clinic that diagnosed and treated you?" She asked, holding the clipboard and pointing to the highlighted address with a silver pen.

"Yes."

"You're absolutely certain?"

"As certain as I am of you standing there."

"Well Ms. Jackson, seems like we have a slight dilemma. There is no record of a clinic ever being located at this location and if there were it was certainly not certified by the Board of Health."

China attempted to sit straight up but it was much too painful.

"And-" the doctor continued, "We've run every test we can run and there is not one single indicator that you have ever even come in contact with the HIV virus. Your immune system is healthy and strong. You do not and never have had HIV or AIDS."

China broke down in tears. The doctor embraced her, pulled her close to comfort her then released her. "I don't know who would play such a nasty trick on you," she said. "But frankly I wish who ever it was to rot in hell."

China knew who it was and he had to be rotting in hell right now. But rotting in hell was too good for him. He should have been kept alive and tortured forever. She wondered how many other girls he had taken to that fake clinic so he could begin the process of breaking them down.

* * * * *

It was the rainy season in Santa Domingo and the air was cold in the mountains where Jeidar was being held like an animal with an iron collar around her neck chained to a metal stake anchored ten feet in the ground. Her neck was thick with calluses and she was as naked as the day she was born, her knees, elbows, hands feet and forearms bore the same thick calluses.

The rain had washed away the food rations they had given her for the day. The red mud like soft clay, causing her to slip and slide down the mountain side until the long rope stopped her descent, nearly choking her to death as she desperately clawed at the slippery substance to get back to flat ground. Sometimes she wanted to let the neck bracelet do its do and end it all . But that would never work. Jeidar was always being watched. If they even so much as imagined she was attempting to kill herself someone would be there to rescue her, then she would be tortured for hours before being placed back in her dog pen.

Every day she was told that she was soon to be released but Jeidar knew they were lies. She was not allowed to speak, only bark or whimper like a dog. She was not allowed to stand up right unless she was placing her forearms on her trainer's chest like a dog would do. She had to eat, shit and piss like a dog. Caked with filth they would only bath her once a week. Her body was full of sores and the itching was so consistently unbearable she would scratch piles of scabs and lay there and examine them to pass the time. Her hair was wild and her teeth had begun to yellow and rot. She was never allowed inside no matter what the weather, blazing hot or frigid cold. The only shelter she had was a small roof built from twigs and covered with tarp.

One of the trainers came out, seeing she was about to choke herself to death, and helped Jeidar back up to flat ground.

"Don't roll around," he warned her. "That's why you keep sliding down the fucking hill."

She barked twice once he placed her under the roof, to say 'thank you,' "If I come back out one more time," he warned, "You go to the big house." The big house was where all the men stayed who loved to torture. "You understand?" She barked once for 'Yes'. Once he left she was tempted to go roll around in the mud again, it was so cool and comforting to her skin, but the thought of torture was a big dissuasion. Instead Jeidar lay there thinking back to how she had been tricked to come to this place voluntarily.

A month after Rachet cheated her out of her share of the money she had been pissed. She knew they had the money. She saw them when they were taking it out, boxes and boxes of it. A hella lot more than the thirty mil they said they were taking, so where was hers?

"That's my word," she remembered telling Rachet. "I don't get my share I'm telling the Diablos who the fuck stole their money and who killed the old man and his sons."

Rachet laughed at her. "You stupid bitch! I don't have the money. For all I know you got the shit, you double crossed my ass."

"I didn't double cross nothing. I don't get my money though…"

"You ain't gon' do nothing bitch… matter fact go tell them fucking

Oyay's. Let them plug yo' ass. I ain't got time to come to Queens and look for your stupid ass."

"You ain't gotta look for me Negro. I'll be right here!" she said angrily, slamming the phone down. That was her second mistake. Her first was getting involved in the first place.

Her and Bamm were really strapped for cash. They had gone out and brought a bunch of shit after the robbery, knowing the money was there. She had maxed out all her credit cards, spent all her savings, even the rent and utilities. Bamm had borrowed money from his grandmother to finish off the studio, turns out it was her mortgage money. They needed funds and quick. So when one of Diablo's lieutenants stepped to her with a 25 thousand dollar offer to mule from here to Santa Domingo and back, she jumped on it. Ten up front and the rest when she returned with a stomach full of cocaine. Jeidar handed over the ten to Bamm and boarded her flight. It would be the last time she ever saw Bamm or the states again.

Three days after the rain stopped Jeidar received her first cooked meat. A big pot of it. It was so delicious she nearly OD'd on it.

"You like," her trainer asked. She nodded, affirmative.

"Would you like more?" he asked. She nodded again.

"It still has a little hair on it but you can eat around that." He left and returned minutes later with another big pot and sat it before her. "Wanna see what you've been eating?" She nodded. When he removed the lid it took an eternity for Jeidar to fully focus on what she was seeing. The flesh was all burnt and toasted but it was definitely the head of her baby sister.

She threw up violently, to the background laughter of the men in the camp, until it seemed her stomach was on the opposite side of her skin.

"Hey, eat up negrito. It's the only food you will be eating from now on. The flesh of your loved ones."

*   *   *   *   *

Amilia watched the girl from a window in the house. She had no pity for her. She had no pity for any rats or traitors. The bitch had not only betrayed her father and caused his death and the death of her two brothers, she had also betrayed the family and nearly caused it's death. The family supported thousands of families, not only in Santa Domingo but also in countries all over the globe. All her Hispanic brothers and sisters were affected by the prosperity of the EI Diablo cartel. She could not allow the stupidity of one reckless whore to jeopardize the lively hood of an entire culture. The vast network of support for her people was the single point that persuaded her to take over her father's position. Well that and the love for her man, and realizing he was right, she always could make the hard decisions. Cold blood ran through her veins when it came to making the hard choices. There was no morality, only what it took to get the job done.

"Gentlemen," she turned and addressed the group of five men standing behind her. "You see before you the consequences of disloyalty, betrayal, deceit and greed. My father once loved this-this, this dog you see groveling before you. He was making preparations to give her the world, but instead she chose to set him up for a few million dollars and take his life in the process. Now she will eat every one of her family members, brothers, sisters, aunts, uncles, cousins, until her family name no longer exist in the world. Until she is the sole survivor."

The men were the new captains and lieutenants she had chosen to replace the old order. They were a new breed, educated thieves who knew the game and had the guts to play it. Most had seen every type of torture imaginable but as one lieutenant blurted out; "I've seen everything but I've never seen anything like this."

"Gentlemen. Consider yourselves in this situation and what I am about to show you, and ask yourselves, would I want to live like this for the rest of my life?"

There was complete silence as the trainer unlocked the padlock from Jeidar's collar, attached a shorter chain to it then led her, on all fours behind him across the yard to the big house. She was whining like a scared puppy all the way.

* * * * *

Amillia suspected the girl immediately. The informer would have to be someone close enough to get the combination. Her father never even let her brothers close enough for the combinations. He didn't trust anyone. So it had to be someone who he would let his guard down with. Someone he was sticking and licking. His secretary. A girl not much brighter than a twenty watt bulb but with the figure of an hourglass.

Amillia had the girl trailed. She had a boyfriend in Queens. Amillia had the boyfriends phone tapped and the rest was history. The plot came together. All that was left was getting the girl to their camp in Santa Domingo. The bitch was so greedy that even that hadn't been a problem.

"Doctor Moreau's island gentlemen. This is where we break them down." Amillia said curtly.

* * * * *

Daquan hadn't seen Kisha since Trina shot them both and he didn't expect to ever see her again. He always wanted to see her but he hadn't been in any condition to look her up and he wasn't sure she wanted to see him anyway. He had sent her messages by Speedy when they were in the same hospital together but she would order him to leave her room at the slightest mention of his name. "She doesn't ever want to see you again," Speedy would return and tell him. "She doesn't even want to hear your name." So Daquan was really surprised when he pushed through the revolving doors of Presbyterian Memorial and saw her sitting in the waiting area going through her purse.

Kisha didn't see Daquan standing over her. He was standing on the side that she had lost all vision and most of her hearing in. She would have never noticed him if he hadn't tapped her on the shoulder. She looked up to see him and all kinds of emotions ran through her. Hate, love, guilt, desire. She didn't know how to react.

"Hi Kish," he said with that sexy smile of his. It wasn't enough to melt her like it usually did. He had lied to her and it had led to her losing her best friend and an eye.

"Why you lie to me Daquan?" she asked looking back down at her purse. A boy of around five started screaming at the top of his lungs when his mother took away some toy he kept tossing across the waiting area . She smacked his hand a couple of times and he started wailing even louder. "Why didn't you tell me and Trina you were only thirteen?"

He shrugged his head. "Y'all never asked me."

"You told Trina you were seventeen."

"I ain't never told Trina that. China told her that shit."

"Yea well you still could have told her the truth.. told me the truth."

"I ain't think it mattered. Y'all liked me and I liked Y'all. Age ain't nothing but a number."

She practically whispered, "Yea until you can go to jail for molesting a child,". It was so low, Daquan barely heard the entire sentence but he got the meaning.

"I ain't no child. I'm a grown ass man. I take care of myself and my family. I'm more of a man than any of them punk ass niggaz you or Trina ever fucked with."

Kisha didn't have to think about it to realize he was 110 percent correct. He was more responsible than any of the men she had relationships with. Still..

"Look Kish," Daquan said. "I know it was all my fault. I should have never fucked with you while Trina was still my girl. That's not something a man does, cheat on his woman with her best friend, but I liked you from the first time Tree introduced you to me.. I ain't never felt nobody the way I'm feeling you. I ain't never stopped thinking about you."

"Yea well stop thinking," Kisha said, rising and brushing her skirt. I'll be sure to give Trina your regards." She walked briskly to the elevator and didn't look back. On the ride up to Trina's room she couldn't deny the fact that her clitoris was swollen from seeing the lil nigga and her panties were wet.

Daquan had a hard on too. Just watching her walk away got him excited and brought back memories. He wanted to follow after her, convince her to come back to him.

"Never chase a woman," Speedy cautioned him. "Let them come to you." But then Daquan could never remember seeing Speedy with a woman unless she was one of the crew, and they were just like the fella's, so what would Speedy know?" He was tempted. Instead he walked to the gift shop and brought the most generous bouquet of flowers they sold then headed for the information desk to ask what room Trina Williams was in.

"Room sixteen 0' seven," the hospital clerk told him.

*   *   *   *   *

China was propped on her bed cutting out newspaper articles when Daquan entered. She seemed especially bright today, like a light bulb was shining inside her face. She was glowing. She put down the scissors and collected the clippings in a neat pile.

"Just like clock work," she smiled. "You're never a minute late."

"You starting to look real good China," Daquan told her, responding to her cheeriness.

"Oh, I was looking bad before?" she jested.

"Uh-uh-uh,'" he stammered. When she first came in she was looking like Quasimodo. "I'm just saying, you looking re-e-e-al good. Like scrumptious."

"So you're saying I look good enough to eat?" She didn't mean to say it, it just slipped out. To her surprised he answered;

"Hell yea. As fine as you are China, I'd eat you any day."

She blushed so hard she could swear she was turning red. "Yea right!" she giggled, reverting her attention back to the clippings. It wasn't hard for anyone to tell she still had the hots for Daquan, especially now that he had grown up so much and was even more handsome than he had ever been.

"I'm serious China," he continued to flirt. "If you wasn't my brothers mother I'd eat you so much there wouldn't be nothing left."

A big smile washed over China's face. Changing the subject before she got wet, she asked; "So did you find Na Na yet?"

Daquan stood next to her gently stroking the hairs from her face. The way he was looking at her did get her wet. Her nipples saluted while blood detoured to her clitoris. He looked at her like that for a long time until she asked again,

"What about NaNa, you find him?"

It was like he was coming out of a trance. "Yea. He over Miss Perno's. I rented your old room for him."

"Miss Perno's," she asked, her mouth wide open. She shifted further up onto the headboard. She was already sitting in a wet spot. "Miss Perno," she repeated. "That old greedy bitch!"

"Yea she is a greedy bitch. I had to pay her mortgage just so she would hold Naquan there till I got there.. Why you call him NaNa anyway? That sound like a girl name."

"I don't know," China shifted again. "I just started calling him that. Why? You don't like it I'll just call him Naquan."

"Nah. It don't matter. I was just wondering." The realization that Kisha was just a stand in for China had hit him like a thunderbolt. He had never really loved Kisha, she just reminded him so much of China. China was who he was really in love with .. who he had always been in love with. Their connection ran a lot deeper than he and Kisha's could ever get.

"It won't work," his thought manifested into sound before he could catch it.

"What won't work," China asked.

Daquan withdrew his hand. "Nothing," he said, turning away in haste. "I gotta go. I forgot I gotta catch up with Speedy and Scarecrow," he lied.

"You coming back tonight," she asked as he opened the door.

"Yea. Ain't nothin' gon' keep me away from you China. Me you and Na, we a family."

It was the second time for the day that China cried her eyes out from happiness.

*   *   *   *   *

To Daquan's surprise, Kisha was waiting for him in the lobby when he came down.

"You wanna go some place and talk," she asked.

They went to a coffee shop around the corner from the hospital. Kisha didn't talk about what was going on between them all through the small lunch they ordered. She talked about Trina and the complications she was having.

"Most likely she'll never walk again," she said sadly. "She crushed the bottom of her spine when she collapsed." Tears found their way into the corner of Daquan's eyes. No matter what had transpired, he still had feelings for Trina. He wasn't in love, but he did love her.

"She need money or anything," Daquan asked, swirling his soup around in the bowl. He hadn't touched it, or the corn beef sandwiches on his plate. Kisha hadn't touched hers either.

"Why do guys always think money will solve everything?"

"It might solve a couple bills," Daquan said, taking a sip then pushing the bowl away.

"Trina does need money for her hospital bills and such, but that won't take care of her heart. She's still so crazy in love with you it's ridiculous."

"I thought Y'all said you didn't want to fuck wit' me cause I'm only thirteen?"

"She doesn't care… I do," Kisha told him, pushing both her plates away. "I'm twenty one Daquan. You're *just* turning fourteen. You do the math," she said angrily.

"You wasn't saying that when we were doing what we do."

"I didn't know then, besides it's not about me and you it's about you and Trina."

"Tree shot you and me in our heads. If she had real bullets we wouldn't be sitting here talking, we'd be dead."

"Who gave her the gun Daquan?"

"Who ever it was I know he didn't mean for her to use it on us."

"You gave her the gun Daquan. And if you hadn't given it to her she wouldn't have shot anybody," her voice rose way above the whisper level. Daquan stood and took some bills from his pocket then placed them on the table.

"I 'ont know what you talking 'bout." He said calmly. "But I ain't stayin' to listen to it." For all Daquan knew Kisha could be wearing a wire. He wasn't taking any chances. "I got a little money saved up. If Tree need some give me a call." He dropped a card, with his cell phone number on it, near the money.

Kisha grabbed him by the shirtsleeve. "You're not going anywhere until we settle this," she demanded.

He pivoted, "You starting to sound like you working for the cops," he said. "Right now I ain't trusting you."

"You think I'm wired?" she asked, giving him a look like she couldn't believe he would suspect her of such a ridiculous thing.

"I 'ont know what your are, but I know I'm out."

"Look Daquan." Her voice softened. "You think I'm wired we could go someplace and I'll show you that I'm not wired."

"Like where?"

"I don't know. You know this area better than I do."

Daquan stood silent for a while and her hand lingered on his arm for a bit too long.

*   *   *   *   *

Amillia was still in Santo Domingo putting the business on track. Thanks to her leadership, The Hill was up and running after the long drought and weight was flowing like floodwater. Abel had E-mailed Ray Ray coded instructions informing him to clear out the rest of Rachet's crew, send the EI Salvadorians home and set the kid up to take over Harlem.

"Give them product and prices that no one can compete with. Make them real visible with all the bling and glamour that goes along with it. I want these kids to be larger than life."

*   *   *   *   *

CHAPTER 24

RAY RAY COULDN'T UNDERSTAND the sudden switch from anonymity to notoriety, but Abel never did anything with out having a means to an end. He wasn't about to second-guess him.

The kid had been MIA for a few weeks after getting shot with the blank pistol. Ray Ray understood he had a lot of street things to clear up. He would give him time before setting things in motion.

Bernstein was still pressing forward with China's eviction from the apartment. He had been a busy boy attempting to fabricate charges against China, doing a lot of underhanded legal finagling to steal the apartment away. Abel wanted him taken down and today was going to be the day. Ray Ray pressed the intercom to the outer office.

"Have the girls arrived yet?"

"Yes sir. They've been waiting for a while."

"Send them in please."

Sonja and Maria Velez were sisters, thirteen and fifteen years old respectfully. They were very pretty, in fact much more attractive than the photo's and video's he had seen in which they were wearing no clothing and quite honestly, with their ample bodies and sexual prowess, didn't look a day under twenty one. That would not play well to the press so Ray Ray had them made over to look as young and innocent as possible.

"Have a seat," Ray Ray smiled to make them feel comfortable. "You sure you want to go through with this," he asked after giving them each a tall glass of cola.

"Hell Yes," the younger one said.

"It could land your mother a minimum of three to five in prison."

"Fuck that bitch," Sonja, the younger one exploded. "She was making me sell pussy since I was nine. Really I wasn't even nine. I was still like eight," she continued. "I wish they would give her life without parole." Her sister remained silent, taking in the elaborate office.

"You know you won't be able to use that kind of language in front of the media," Ray Ray prepped them. "You have to sound as innocent and naïve as possible."

"What's naïve," Marie asked.

"It's like when you're stupid like you," Sonja teased.

"Shut up. I'm not stupid. I just don't know what the word means," she said, looking over at Ray Ray. "You don't know what it means either Sonja. You're not that smart yourself."

"You're cute Mister Carrary," Sonja said, standing and adjusting the long skirt she had been dressed in. "I bet you got a big dick and you know how to fuck too."

Ray Ray didn't bother to correct his name. He was wondering how he was going to pull this off. These girls were way over the top. He doubted if they could be cute and innocent for more than two seconds.

"That fat fucking Bernstein didn't know how to fuck for shit. All he wanted to do was eat my pussy and he couldn't even do that right."

"Shut up Sonja," Maria smirked. "He use to bang Maria out though, with his little ass pink dick. Maria use to like it too," she laughed at her.

"I told you to shut up!" Maria warned, balling her fist.

"You know you use to like it," Sonja pressed on. "You always said he use to hit your G spot every time. I don't know why you trying to front."

It was clear to Ray Ray that the younger one was the more dominate of the two and the most problematic. "Look ladies. If you want the money it's going to have to work like this-" he went on to explain the set up in detail.

* * * * *

Sid Bernstein of Bernstein and Morgan and CEO of Goyim Publishing was arrested for the alleged statutory rape of two underage sisters who are tenants in one of the dozen of tenement complexes he owns in East-Harlem. He was arraigned and released on a one hundred thousand dollar bail. Mr. Bernstein pled not guilty and in a short statement to reporters after his release said; "I have never seen those girls nor their mother in my life. This is an obvious attempt at blackmail."

When asked if he indeed owned the building complex where the girls lived he replied, "No comment." The mother of the girls was arrested and held without bail for child endangerment, forced prostitution and drug possession. In an interview with the girls, thirteen year old Sonja Velez told of how her mother had been forcing her to have oral sex with grown men since she was five in exchange for vials of crack cocaine. She alleges she met Bernstein when she was seven and he would bring her toys and gifts when he came to collect the rent. It was on her ninth birthday, she claims, that her mother ordered her to have sex with him. She says he had been having vaginal sex with her sister for three years before she lost her virginity to him. He treated her well after that, buying her expensive gifts and giving her two and three hundred dollars at a time in exchange for sex after she turned thirteen. The older sister, Maria Velez, was less talkative but assured the press that everything her younger sister said was true.

"Did you read this article," China asked Daquan. "It's about Bernstein."

"Who?" Daquan knew who Bernstein was.

"My landlord, Sid Bernstein.. Actually he's not the landlord he's Chairman of the Tenant Board. The one who's been trying to get me kicked out."

"Oh that asshole," Daquan quirked, walking to the opposite side of the room and flipping open his cell phone. It was Kisha wanting to know if he could meet her in the lobby and give her the money he promised

"Yea I got it right here," he told her, and then turned to China, told her he had to make a run and he might not be back.

Kisha took the packet of money from him, looking at him like he was a stinking corpse. "How much is in here?"

"Ten thousand."

"Hump!.. That's not going to take care of much."

"It's play money." All the bills and stuff been taken care of already. He had Ray Ray pull some strings so her HMO would take care of everything.

"You good," he asked, backing away to leave. Kisha had her hands on her hips, giving him that look that a mother gives a son after the Principle calls and tells her he's been cutting school for half the year.

"Depends," she answered.

"On what?"

"On whether you wanna take me to that hotel again and check my body to see if I'm wearing a wire." Her expression didn't change but Daquan burst out in a quiet laugh.

"Ain't nothing funny Daquan," she said, tapping her foot. "You wanna check this shit again or what?"

Daquan shook his head side to side, grinning from ear to ear. "I think I'm-a take the 'or what'."

"Negro!" Kisha launched into action, attempting to beat him in the head with the packet of money. Daquan covered up, now laughing hysterically. She stomped off to the elevators, stopped midway and turned. "I'm going to drop this off and come right back down. Don't play with me Daquan. You better be here when I get back!"

Daquan was still laughing when the elevator doors closed behind her. "Women!" They 'ont care if you nine, long as you got a big dick and know how to use it," Daquan stood shaking his head long after his laughter subsided.

*   *   *   *   *

CHAPTER 25

MELISA QUIT THE FIRM after the 911 bombing. She could no longer work for the old man suspecting what she suspected. A few weeks after nine eleven she passed the bar exams and officially became an attorney. The old man offered her a very lucrative entry package but she declined, opting instead for a low paying grunt position as an 18B attorney for the city. She did, however keep in touch with the old man. Really he kept in touch with her, calling twice a week religiously to check on how she was doing and to remind her his offer was still standing.

She found it difficult talking to him although she hadn't lost her fondness for him. He had always been like a father to her. Still how could she explain that she believed in the conspiracy theory, that the Jews had planned the World Trade Center attack so they could justify an Islamic war. She had seen the memo, one had been posted in her E-mail box the night before. She just hadn't read it until the night after.

It wasn't exactly what she imagined was sent to the Jewish community that worked there, which was 90 percent of the work force, but a warning never the less.

Please be advised, your services will not be needed on September 11, due to office reconstructions. This will not deduct from your sick day or vacation package and you will be duly compensated with full pay. Enjoy your day off.

She read it that once and when she went back to read it again an hour later it wasn't on her desktop where she had copied it or in her mail box. She ran every retrieval program installed yet there was no trace the E-mail had ever been sent. She had decided then that her instincts were correct, there was definitely some funny business going on.

Still when Pitt called and told her he was in jail being held for first-degree murder, she didn't hesitate to call the old man and ask for a favor. The old man promised her he would have one of his lead criminal attorneys assigned to the case. "Unless they caught him with the gun in his hand he won't do a day." The old man wasn't joking, he was serious. His firm had a lot of pull with the judicial system. He lunched with more judges than the Governor and the mayor combined. Half the DA's office owed their career to him.

"Jose Rivera.. Jose Rivera.." she called as she walked down the corridor in Brooklyn House in search of her client. Six different Jose Rivera's came to the third holding pen gate. "Jose Rivera D.O.B. 6-27-87?"

Two Jose Rivers shouted out; "That's me, I am Jose Rivera 6-27-87."

"Jose Rivera, nineteen hundred East Sixteenth Street?"

Mister wrong Jose disappeared into the crowded cell, leaving a skinny Puerto Rican with a ponytail staring down at her.

"I'm Melisa Estabar. I'll be your court appointed 18B laywer," she said, resting her pad on the gate. "I'll be representing you in this case."

The gate was crowded within seconds as a wave of prisoner's shifted from the back to get a closer look at 'the lady lawyer'. Melisa ignored the stares, the Vaya Mami's, the Vanilla Sweetness-es and being undressed with their eyes. She was not intimidated like most of her Jewish colleagues-who although they would rush with their clients orientation because of all the jeering, nevertheless must have craved the attention judging from the tight clothing and short skirts they flirted around in.

Melisa was much more conservative, almost Islamic in dress, long skirts and flowing tops that didn't reveal too much flesh, if any, or the shape of her body. Even so it was difficult to hide the abundance of junk in her trunk or the genetic goodies the Creator had endowed her with. And it didn't help her job that her features were so flawless she was often approached by agents for modeling assignments.

Mister ponytail didn't do it. He was nowhere near the scene of the robbery, even though there were half a dozen witnesses who positively identified him. Melisa explained to him that because he was a persistent felon the D.A. would be asking for a very high bail. She would fight to have it reduced but he shouldn't have high expectations. In fact, the way his rap sheet read, he should have no expectations at all.

Case after case of persistent felons and 'I didn't do it's', and Melisa was ready to pull all her hair out. All the time her mind was on her man, and what was going on with his proceedings.

After her last court appearance she called Pitt's lawyer. She nearly fainted when he told her the D.A. had a videotape with Pitt actually murdering Rachet in cold blood. They were offering a plea of twenty-five to life versus life without parole.

"Have you seen the tape?" she asked him.

"No. We probably won't see it till we go to trial, but they swear it's conclusive."

"So you're taking it to trial?"

"Well I talked to my client and if his story is true the D.A. is bluffing. They don't have a twenty-five to life, maybe man slaughter two, but we're pushing for self-defense. The most he might get out of this is a weapons possession."

By the time Melisa reached home she was so exhausted she couldn't sleep. Half a bottle of sleeping pills later and she was out like a light. Somewhere in the night she had the strangest dream. She was trying a murder case for some kid and the Mayor was there along with hundreds of cameras and reporters, except the Mayor wasn't the Mayor at all. He was a vicious dog struggling to climb a steep wall. The bricks of the wall were bodies of innocent people who had been murdered by a beast. The Mayor was at the same time a Senator with the body of a snake, the head of a lion and the spirit of the beast who killed. At the bench were seven Judges reflecting light from the cameras like jewels. On opposite sides of the Judges bench sat the Jurors, women on this side, and men on the other. The men showed open contempt while the women drooled over the kid like slobbering fools. The two sides tugged at the boy's body until finally they split him right down the middle. Then thousands of winged spirits emerged from his open wounds and took pieces of his flesh to spread around the world.

When Melisa woke from the dream it was the next morning and she was two hours late for work. Still she took time to jot the dream down in its entirety.

*   *   *   *   *

"You little black bastard," The man screamed after Naquan. "When I catch your little nigga ass I'm going to put my foot in your chest then I'm going to put a bullet in your head."

Naquan dashed in and out of cars but the man was just as fast and agile as he was. Naquan dashed in front of a bus, weaving through on coming traffic, barely escaping being hit. The man was on his tail. He couldn't get away from him. If he could get to a subway he could lose him, but the subway station seemed to keep getting further and further away.

Naquan cut into a block with nothing but abandoned buildings. They weren't tunnels but they were nearly as good. He knew his way in abandoned buildings almost like he knew the tunnels. He dashed into the first one, took the back stairs to the basement, out to the backyard, another basement and the stairs up five flights to the roof. He had lost him. He stopped long enough to catch his breath then eased his head over the edge to see if he could locate him. Good! The man had given up the chase. He took the roof over three more buildings then cautiously made his way down and through the darkened staircase. On the second floor he heard a noise coming from one of the apartment doors. Only a rat, he thought. He went to take the next flight down and the man stepped out of the darkness to block his way. Before he could turn and run the man snatched him by his leather bomber and lifted him into the air. He tried to fight but the man punched him in his chest so hard it took all the wind out of him. He went crashing into the wall before falling to the cold splintered floor. The man stepped in his chest.

"I told you I would catch your nigga ass." He twisted his boot in his chest then pulled out a big gun, pointing it at his head. "You nigga's never learn. Bet this will teach you to never steal from another White man again."

"Please! Don't shoot me please. I promise I'll never steal. I'll never steal from anyone again, I promise."

"You can't promise. You're a kleptomaniac. You can't stop," the man said, the barrel of the gun pressed snugly to Naquan's forehead as sweat poured down his face.

"I can stop. I can stop. Please!" Naquan pleaded. "I swear I will never steal another thing. I swear on my dead mother-"

The man's face shifted into the light. He wasn't grotesque and ugly like he expected. In fact he was quite handsome . Naquan knew he had seen him before but he couldn't quite place the features.

"I know you won't," the man grinned. "There's nothing-to steal where you're going." Then the loudest explosion he had ever heard went off in his head and he was screaming at the top of his lungs.

Ms. Perno shook him awake. He had been having these nightmares since he moved in. Sometimes two and three times in the same night. Ms. Perno had practically moved into his room. She shook him awake and cradled him in her arms, rocking him gently. "It's OK baby, it's OK. It's only a dream you're 'aving. Ms. Perno is ere now to protect you."

Naquan's pajamas were drenched in sweat, his eyes wide in a state of shock. He still hadn't come completely out of the dream. "I swear I will never steal anything again, I swear…"

"I know you won't dear," Ms. Perno consoled him. "I know you won't."

Naquan started screaming at the top of his lungs again. Ms. Perno was at her wits ends. Maybe the boy needed some professional help. She knew she and her other tenants weren't going to be able to take much more of this for much longer. She would call Daquan first thing in the morning. He would have to make new arrangements.

* * * * *

Daquan offered Miss Perno an extra hundred dollars a week to let Naquan stay and look after him.

"That's not enough for an old woman like me to stay up half the night, With all the responsibilities I ave during the daylight. No Sir. It's not enough."

" Two hundred."

Ms. Perno pondered for a moment then shook her head. "No Sir. Not even for two."

"Well I ain't going to three so forget it," Daquan said with finality. "I'll come and pick him up later. That's double the rent. I could rent a whole building down the block for that much.

As Daquan headed angrily to the door, Ms. Perno stopped him.

"How about I meet you halfway? Two fifty extra."

"One fifty," Daquan answered. "Or just start packing up his stuff."

"One fifty? You just offered me two…"

"Yea that was before you got extra greedy. You don't want it don't take it."

Six hundred extra US dollars a month went a long way to adding on to the mansion she was building in Jamaica. She would have been a fool to pass up on such an opportunity. She was usually up on those hours anyway.

"Only because I like you and the boy and ave concern for him," she relented, holding out her weathered hand for the first installation.

* * * * *

The next month went by really fast for Daquan. Ray Ray arranged to have a private instructor teach Daquan to drive, He, Speedy and Scarecrow spent most of their time organizing the blocks they took over from Rachet's crew. They had a little resistance but Speedy's crew of bad bitches resolved any drama without anybody really knowing what or who hit them.

Business was bubbling on the streets and word was if you wanted it the little niggaz had it, from guns to E, it was readily available, the best shit at the best prices.

On the day China was suppose to get out of the hospital, Ray Ray had a brand new, kit-ted out Benz delivered to Daquan along with a city issued drivers license and ID stating he was eighteen years of age. Speedy and

Scarecrow didn't like driving. They went out and brought every one of their crew brand new bikes, there had to be fifty of the fastest, most expensive bikes in Harlem lined up in front of their headquarters on any given day, and two were always not to far away from Daquan wherever he went.

Daquan drove to pick up Naquan from Miss Perno's. Naquan was excited about the car and couldn't believe his brother was actually driving. He took him for a spin to 110th street and back.

"You can teach me how to drive?" Naquan kept asking him.

"Yea. One day," Daquan said.

When they reached back to Ms. Perno's Daquan told him that everything had been straightened out with BCW and that it was finally safe for him to visit China. Naquan was more excited about seeing China than the car.

"When can we go? When can we go?" he bounced up and down on the car seat. He missed China so much, plus he never had those nightmares when he was with her.

"Well you still can't go visit her," Daquan said with a sad face.

"Why not?" Naquan asked, sinking back in the chair.

Daquan looked at him with a stone face, then burst out excitedly, "She ' coming home today, that's why. We going to pick her up. We moving back in the apartment."

"You moving too?. Are you coming to live with us?"

"Yep! I already got me a parking space," he smiled.

"Yes!" Naquan said, balling his fist with the motion like he was snatching something out of the air. "We're going to be like a real family."

"We ain't gon' be like a real family," Daquan pulled Naquan to him and hugged him. "We are a real family."

"So you gon' marry China?"

"Naw. I ain't gon' do that but look." He pulled a small jewelry box from between his thighs and handed it to him. It was the biggest clearest diamond Naquan had ever seen. The ring was exquisite. The settings, everything. Naquan knew a lot about Diamonds. He had a nice little collection himself that he had stolen and stashed away. But nothing like this. He was instantly jealous.

"I'm giving this to China today as a coming home present. How you like it?"

"It's alright." Naquan passed it back to him. "I've seen better."

"Nigga you ain't never seen better than this," Daquan gave him a look. "Maybe in books like the Rob Report or something but I know you ain't never seen nothing like this in person."

"Whatever," Naquan said, his hand already on the doorknob.

"Whatever? Lil' nigga you know how much this shit cost? An I ain't get it from no crack head neither. I could buy ten of these cars with this ring and still have some money to spend.

"Yea you have everything," Naquan said under his breath. "I ain't got nothing."

"What you say Lil' nigga?"

"Nothing."

Daquan turned him around, both hands on his shoulders, and looked him hard in the eye. "I ont never wanna hear you say no dumb shit like that again-"

'If you heard me why did you ask me what I said?' Naquan wanted to ask but he remained silent.

"The shit I'm doing ain't shit compared to the shit you gonna be doing. I ain't smart I just know how to git money, and I can't even do that without breaking the law. How long you think I'm gon' last out here Naquan. Huh? Before somebody either kill me or I end up in prison for the rest of my life? Everything I'm doing I'm doing for you Lil nigga. You the one I always looked up to. You the only one of us that got a future. Me an' Speedy an Scarecrow. We ain't gon' last long in this game. But you-you can be anything you wanna be. You could even be the President if that's what you wanna be. That's how smart you are. This shit ain't nothin' unless you getting it for a reason. And you my reason Lil' nigga. You about to be my daddy. Tell me what to do."

Naquan only tucked his head, "May I go now?"

"Yea get dressed," Daquan said, releasing him. "I'm-a pick you up in two hours so we can go get China. "

Naquan got out and Daquan reached over and closed the door behind him. "Hey you wanna give her this ring?" he asked.

"No!" Naquan said proudly, "I'll get her something on my own. And it will be better than that."

* * * * *

The charges had been dropped on Bernstein but not before he dropped all proceedings against China and convinced the Board to stop the harassment and open all amenities to her and her family, this included the complex pool, Tennis courts, park area, and to include all family members and friends.

It was a hard nut for Bernstein to swallow but after receiving the stack of tapes with him and numerous other underage girls he was paying to have sex with, he had a complete change of venue.

* * * * *

Daquan only wanted a little quickie before heading back to Manhattan to pick up Naquan to get his baby from the hospital, but Kisha's pussy was just too good and a quickie had turned into a marathon with her nuttin' all over the hotel room. Now he had her butt ass on the balcony, bent over the railing looking down at the parking lot and she was showing no signs of exhaustion.

"Oh shit Daquan .. Oh shit!" she moaned. He reached through the railing and massaged both her big ass titties hanging over the other side of the banister. "Pinch my nipples Daquan.. Harder, no harder. Uh Huh, like that." Daquan was nearly wrenching them off. "Oh shit! Oh shit! Oh shit!" Kisha was on her tippy toes gyrating into him. She was cumming again.

Daquan stole another peek at his watch. 2:45. He had less than fifteen minutes to get from the Bronx back to Harlem. He pulled out suddenly.

"Why you do that Daquan?" she asked, sounding like Trina use to sound when he would quit on her. She slithered back to the concrete floor as Daquan wiped his dick on her t-shirt he had slung over his shoulder. "I was just cumming-"

"I'm late," he said, tossing the t-shirt inside. It fell short of the sofa and landed on the carpet. She was going to be pissed when she pulled it on but fuck it, he had decided to dogg her out when she first started talking that thirteen shit, then was practically tearing his clothes off the first time he got her to the hotel to strip search her. "I'll call you later. I gotta pick up my little brother."

"You're full of shit Daquan and you know it."

*   *   *   *   *

When Daquan reached Ms. Perno's he was already 45 minutes late and Naquan wasn't there. Miss Perno told him Naquan had left over an hour ago.

"He told me he was going up to Broadway to buy China a coming home present. I offered to accompany him but he wouldn't have it. He wanted to do this all on his own, he said."

"Thanks," Daquan told her. "If he comes back tell him to sit his ass here an' don't move, in case I miss him."

"Don't worry. He won't be going anyplace this time."

"You know how to drive?" he asked.

"Left hand and right hand," she said with a grin, referring to the steering wheel being on the left of the car in Jamaica. He tossed her the keys,

"Can you move it if the cops come?" He was parked illegally and there was no sense driving the few blocks to Broadway where he knew he would never find a parking spot.

"I'll sit right here till you come back. Matter of fact. If you don't mind I'll sit in the driver's seat just in case."

"Whatever!" Daquan said and made his way on foot up the hill. Behind him two motorcycles roared and popped wheel-es. Daquan stopped long enough to give them the signal not to follow.

*   *   *   *   *

Three blocks down Broadway Daquan caught sight of Naquan sprinting out of a Jewelry store a block away. Sunlight flickered in hues of blues and reds from something he held in his hand. Daquan took off after him. He had run less than a yard before a short man dashed from the store behind him.

"Thief.. Thief " he shouted. "Stop!"

The man raised his arm and pointed at Naquan as he neared the end of the block. Daquan was fast approaching.

"Stop! thief!" he shouted again.

"It was at that point that Daquan realized what the man was holding in his hand... A glock. The Korean braced it with two hands and let off three shots as his wife ran from the store with a cell phone screaming, "Thief, Thief," while talking rapidly into the phone.

Daquan watched his brother stumble to the ground then get back up and attempt to run with a limp, one leg dragging behind him. The Korean braced himself to let off another shot and Daquan was right on him, his razor singing through the air. The man dropped to his knees, clutching his throat for a second, before slumping to the ground where he lay silent with wide eyes. His wife let out a shrieking scream as Daquan sprinted past her.

"Stop him. Stop him. Murderer. Murderer-"

Naquan picked up his gaunt and turned the corner. He was leaking blood.

Daquan no longer heard the shouts and screams from the mob that had gathered behind him. The only voice he heard was his mother's telling him at all cost to protect his brother.

*   *   *   *   *

When the call came over the Police dispatch, Denareo was less than five blocks from the scene. He hit the gas, not throwing the light on the dash. He had to be first on the scene. His instinct told him it was the boy from EI Diablo's.

As he sped past the crime scene a group of spectators were gathered around the victim pointing to the next block. From the expressions on their faces it was gruesome.

At the next block Denareo spun his car side ways in the narrow street more to block blue and whites from having access than civilians. He wanted this collar himself. His new partner pulled along side him to completely block off the street and jumped out of his cruiser right after Denareo placed his flashing light on the dashboard.

"What we got," Denareo asked, joining Sally on the sidewalk.

"Blood trail leading into that alley." He pointed to a building under renovation across the street and half a block down.

"Damn good eye sight," Denareo told him, looking up the block.

"Just logical deduction," Sally half-smiled. "It's the only abandoned building on the block."

Denareo liked Sally from the first day on the job. Not only was he an intelligent cop, he was just as corrupt as Denareo was.

'All right partner," Denareo returned the smile. "Lets go get some bad guys."

His partner sprayed a solution on the blood trail as they hurried along its path. It would dissolve it and leave no clues for the blue and white's. His partner was even more devious than he was.

"Destroying evidence from a crime scene?" Denareo quirked.

"What crime scene," Sally asked as they entered the alley beneath a giant hanging tarp. "It won't be a crime scene until we make it one."

Denareo smiled and shook his head. "You're going to jail."

"Yea to bring in these preps..."

"Dead or alive baby-preferably dead."

"You know it," his partner said, drawing his weapon. "Dead men don't talk."

Denareo really liked this guy. The Police dispatcher told all officers to look out for a diamond necklace. It was valued at over half million dollars. He and his partner had the same thing in mind. If they located it, it would never reach the evidence room.

Daquan left Naquan propped up in a corner where he found him, a plastic covered room on the second floor all the way in the back. He couldn't get a signal there on his cell phone so he made his way towards the roof where he could get a better reception. He had to call Speedy to get some help up here.

Denareo and Sally followed the blood trail around the back of the building to a shed like opening leading to the basement.

"He's lost a lot of blood. He'll never make it to the top floor."

"There's two kids," Denareo warned him. The older one I suspect is pretty dangerous judging from what he left behind."

They moved cautiously through the rooms as they followed the blood. The further they got into the house the more blood they saw covering the floor.

"Twenty bucks says he's in the next room," Sally bet.

"Naw. All bets are off. Too much blood, he's bleeding out."

At the double door entrance to the back room, Denareo went high, Sally went low. As soon as they pushed open the doors, they saw the kid slumped against the wall in a pool of his own blood. Sally searched the room while Denareo stood guard. "Clear" he signaled. "Where's the other one?" Sally whispered.

"Probably went to get help," Denareo answered, staring at the boy slumped in the corner. He was still conscious, clutching the diamond necklace. "Close the door. He'll probably be back in a few. If he intended to leave him to die he would have taken the necklace." Denareo walked over, snapped on surgical gloves, removed the necklace from the boy's hand and placed it in an evidence bag. He removed the gloves and stuffed the evidence bag down his briefs.

"Where's your friend," he asked, studying the boys face. The boy tried to spit blood at him, spraying the cuff of his three hundred dollar trousers and his fifteen hundred dollar Gucci boots. Denareo kicked him in his chest so hard it took him off the wall. He landed on his back looking up at the tall white man.

It was just like in his dreams, the boot in his chest twisting as he lay helpless choking on his own blood. He was dreaming, he tried to convince himself. Soon Miss Perno would shake him awake and rock him in her arms while telling him everything was going to be OK. "It's only a Dream." he expected to hear her say any second now.

What he heard was Denareo taunting him.

"You little black bastard. What makes you think you can steal from White people and get away with it?"

" He wasn't white you asshole," Naquan wanted to say. But he was choking on his own blood.

Denareo kept the pressure on Naquan's chest with his shiny boot. making it difficult for him to breath.

"What? You gon' make sure he bleeds out?" Sally asked from the door.

Denareo applied more pressure. "What do you think?"

Daquan was just returning from talking to Speedy. He was creeping down the hall, nearing the double doors when he heard the voices. He made his way slowly to the doors and peered between a crack where the doors met. He could see the shadow from one Detective just on the other side but he could see Denareo clearly. Both had their weapons drawn. The second officer's weapon kept blocking his view as he kept shifting with nervous energy. They had no intention of leaving Naquan alive and he knew that if they discovered him, he would never leave this place alive himself. Tears streamed down Daquan's face as he watched the life quickly depart from his brother. There was nothing he could do to save him.

Denareo stared at the kid intensely. He looked exactly like someone he knew, someone from the past. Then the realization of who this kid was hit him like a planet had been dropped on him from the sky.

"Mutha-fucka!" he said aloud as the image of two kids standing in the hallway that frigid night eight years ago flashed in his head. Chi Chi's kids," he said low, speaking to himself. "No wonder your brother kept looking at me like he wanted to put something in my ass. He saw me kill your mother." Denareo released the foothold on the boy's chest. "The little bastard wants revenge." Denareo motioned for his partner to toss him the chemical spray bottle. He snatched it out of the air and sprayed the boy's chest to eliminate any signs of his foot print then sprayed the bottom of his boot one at a time before stepping away from the blood spill into a clear area.

The boy's body was limp and Denareo suspected he had already expired. If he hadn't he was close enough that it didn't matter. He signaled his partner as he walked casually to a section of the room he knew couldn't be viewed from the door. Something told him the kid was watching him right now.

"On three' he signaled again. The doors flung open and both Detectives were in the hallway in a flash.

"He's in the building," Denareo whispered. "I can feel him. When we locate him shoot to kill. Remember" he winked, "He's dangerous and armed."

*   *   *   *   *

Ms. Perno watched the two bikes roar past her towards Broadway. They were moving so fast they were almost a blur, but she would have sworn that one of the daredevils was a girl.

Something was going on up the hill. Sirens were coming from everywhere. She started the engine, contemplating whether to take the car for a short spin around the block. She had never driven a car as nice as this. If Daquan complained she could say the Police made her move it.

*   *   *   *   *

241

Police barriers and rows of uniformed officers on both ends of the street now cordoned off the block between Broadway and the West End where Naquan and his brother Daquan had sought safety in. A Swat team took orders from the commanding officer to start a house-to-house search.

"We might have two officer's down," he stated, motioning towards the two Cruisers blocking the street. "They're not responding. The sniper unit stood at the ready, awaiting orders to take their postions on rooftops over looking the street.

"We don't know what building they might be in so we can't send you guys up, but stand at the ready and be ready to go."

*   *   *   *   *

"When you're in a building that doesn't connect, unless you have a helicopter waiting on the roof, always run down instead of up. The closer you are to the ground, the better your options," Speedy often told him. Most people had the tendency to go up, so had Denareo and his partner, now he could hear them making their way back down. Daquan was in the front room an arms length away from the front exit. He peered through the sheet of plastic covering the bay windows, there were cops everywhere. The best thing to do, he decided quickly was to hold his hands high in the air and walk out into the street. If he gave himself up he would just do time. If he stayed here Denareo and his partner would kill him for sure.

He was in the motion of reaching for the knob when his cell phone vibrated on his hip. He flipped it open and tapped on the mouthpiece three times before putting the phone to his ear.

"Count to thirty then run out," Vanessa told him. "Just trust me."

Daquan crouched down near the door and begin counting. He was also counting the steps Denareo would have to take to reach the first floor. They were about even.

*   *   *   *   *

Pitt found out that the prosecution's main witness for the new indictment they were trying to give him was an undercover Police Detective who had been working inside Rachet's organization for the last two years. They would not disclose his identity but when Pitt read the portion of his Grand Jury testimony claiming Pitt cut the penis of his victims off and kept them as souvenir's, Pitt narrowed it down to one of two people-Jumm or Great. They were the only two who had ever witnessed his ritual, and Jumm wasn't the type to cut and tell. That left Great, who he always suspected was an undercover cop or a paid snitch.

Pitt whispered something in his attorney's ear who jotted down the information in his pad. "I'll check into it," the attorney assured him.

* * * * *

The officers lined on the Broadway side heard the engines barreling down on them but most didn't avert their attention away from keeping the crowd at bay. A secondary barrier had formed. A long line of media trucks with reporters and their camera crews, spilling into the streets like an army of ants. They all dispersed when they realized the bikes approaching had to be doing at least a hundred, if not faster, and they seemed out of control. They were headed for a dead on collision with the two Police cruisers.

As everyone braced themselves for the impact, the bikes suddenly reared up on their back wheel, the front wheel grabbing the cruiser's front side to launch the bikes high into the air.

Before anyone could come to their senses, the bikes had touched down and were sliding into a 180-degree turn in the middle of the block. A kid ran from one of the buildings and jumped on the back of the lead bike. They never stopped motion. As soon as he was on they were roaring back towards the same cruisers. At least a hundred weapons were drawn but not one shot was fired. The Commander was in the control van and by the time he was notified the riders had vaulted over the vehicles again and their roar was fast fading.

* * * * *

Helicopters were in the air when the two bikes pulled into the chop-shop garage just over the 145th bridge on the Bronx side. Speedy had sent out a half dozen pair of bikes with an extra rider going in all directions from Broadway. They would never figure out which bike he was on.

Jasmine pulled off her helmet and shouted in jubilation "UUUUH WEEEE! That was the shit! I didn't think we were gonna make it."

"You?" Vanessa turned to Daquan who was still clutching on tight. "You can let go now baby. We safe."

"Where you learn to ride bikes like that?" Daquan asked, still shaking from the experience .

"Man me an Jasmine been riding since we were eleven. All my brothers got bikes and so do hers. That's how we linked up. Them niggaz taught us everything there is to know about bikes."

"They didn't teach us that shit though," Jasmine said still breathing hard.

"Hell Naw! Not hitting at a buck ten. That was some mind altering shit back there."

"Yea some real Evil Kenevil shit…"

"Man, fuck that racist cracker. He can't ride. I'd spin rings around his ass."

Daquan was on the phone with Ray Ray. "I don't know. I know they killed my brother. If they would 'a got him to a hospital he would' a lived,"

"They really don't know who they're looking for right now, but they're going to trace the boy to China. From there you're only a stones throw away." Ray Ray told him. "Lay low for a while and I'll see what I can do about some paperwork."

* * * * *

While all the commotion was going on with the bikes, Detective Denareo turned and pushed his throwaway pistol in his partner's stomach then let off four rounds, changing angles to assure he hit every vital organ. It was a trick he learned in Special Forces. The stomach acted like a noise suppressor, better than a silencer. Sally was dead before he hit the ground.

"Sorry buddy, I really liked you but business is business." He pumped one in his own thigh just as the bikes roared and wined in acceleration. He wiped the gun, tossed it then slid to the floor, purposely bumping his head hard as he went down.

Denareo nearly fucked up big time. The first thing the medics would do was cut his pants off. They would be sure to notice the necklace. He looked around the room for someplace to stash the jewels, then he noticed another necklace hanging on a nail by the front door. It was a Cuban link with a huge bejeweled medallion in the shape of a seven. It must have gotten snagged when the kid ran out.

CHAPTER 26
BRAZIL

TWO YEARS LATER

"LISTEN TO THIS," GLORIA said to her twin, Claudia. "In Brazil five percent of the population owns eighty percent of all the property and land. The twenty percent that is left over is for the most part unproductive and urban, mostly slums." Gloria lowered the booklet, 'Things they don't tell you about Brazil," to her stomach and turned to the reflection of herself. "That's crazy," she said, "That means that with a population of one hundred and sixty three million four hundred and fifty thousand," she laid back and started doing the math in her head and on her fingers. Gloria was always a wiz with math "That's like a little over eighty one thousand people who have effectively stolen what rightfully belongs to over a hundred and fifty million poor people. That's not only greed that's inhumane."

"It's called Capitalism," Claudia said, squinching up her face.

"No it's called genocide," Gloria slammed back. "And it's some evil fucking shit." She pulled on dark shades to shield her hazel eyes from the sun. "No one man should have the right to take it all and leave the masses with nothing."

"Well if you really feel so adamant about it, why don't you donate your portion of the thirty million to the masses?"

"I was seriously thinking about it, " Gloria said with a pinch of sarcasm.

"You're always thinking about something abstract or another." Claudia turned over on her stomach to tan her back. "Unhook me please."

Claudia wore a modest black two-piece bikini but her twin wore what

245

could possibly have been the most miniscule string bikini in Brazil, and believe me you had to really put a lot of effort into having the skimpiest bikini in Brazil.

Gloria reached down for the suntan lotion and a dark erect nipple popped out from one of the tiny triangles barely covering the equally dark areola on her small breast. She didn't bother to tuck it back in. It was only going to pop out again with the slightest movement. When she stood and bent to unhook her twin the other nipple sprang free. Every head in the pool turned in her direction.

"You might as well have left both those in the hotel." Claudia told her.

"Girl! This is Brazil. Nobody wears clothes in Brazil."

"Maybe not. But they don't run around butt-ass naked either." Claudia paused then added, "You might as well just take It all off, it won't matter. And honestly it wouldn't have. The bottom wasn't much larger than the top, and her waxed pussy lips were hanging out on both sides like two golden beef burgers and to top that off both top and bottom matched to perfection her heavily bronzed skin, making her look completely naked anyway.

Claudia sat up suddenly.

"What?" Gloria asked, somewhat startled.

"Come on, get your things," she said with an urgency, searching around to gather her items from the stone squares beneath her. "Don't ask questions, let's just go." She stuffed all her things hastily into her beach towel and walked down the row of pool chairs to stop at a reclining, ghostly white, older gentleman.

Gloria took her time, folding and organizing her things, enjoying all the attention she was getting.

Claudia tapped the balding man lightly on his shoulder. "Excuse me but could I borrow your paper?" Gloria heard her ask.

The man looked up and his face lit up. "Sure," he said, offering it to her. She took it, examined the front page briefly then started folding pages until she stopped and silently read a few lines, a look of terror registering on her face. By the time she reached the man her sister Claudia was off again.

"Come on," Claudia called back to her.

"Hey!" the man called out after Claudia. "I said you could look at it not keep it," he shouted, attempting to rise and give chase. "Gloria pressed him back down. "We'll get it back to you she said in a seductive voice. "What room are you in?"

"Twenty seven forty two," he answered, looking from Gloria to her twin turning into the hotel lobby. Gloria threw the man a kiss while hurrying to catch up. She caught Claudia just as she was stepping into the elevator.

"Girl! Are you losing your screws," Gloria asked with concern. "Stealing peoples newspapers.. What's going on?" Claudia handed her the paper. Gloria's mouth fell open. When she looked back Claudia's face was flooded with tears.

Gloria had no idea Claudia cared for him as much as she was expressing. Tears were welling in her particular eyes as they stepped off the elevator to their suites.

*   *   *   *   *

Sometimes a moment can seem like an hour and this was one of those moments the tall dark man Claudia had learned to love and trust, was feeling. He pulled her to him to comfort her.

"These things happen," he whispered softly below her heaving sobs. "Something's a man has no control over. He just has to let go and trust in Jah."

"I don't believe in God," she grunted between sobs. He's too fucking cruel. Every time I do trust in him he does something to fuck it up!"

"Do you know why some of us go through such extreme hardships and tribulations," he asked.

She nodded in his chest, her tears dripping down his hard chiseled body.

"Because the harder Jah is on you the more rewards he has for you down the road."

She wrapped her arms around him and held him tight. "Why does he have to constantly do things to people I love?"

"To make you stronger, Little Bit. To make you stronger, and to remind you that the only thing certain in life is death." He was remembering how close he had come to death and how Jah had sent two Angels to his rescue. He remembered the conversation he was hearing word for word as he lay there certain he would never come out of the darkness sucking him in.

"I have done all that I am capable of doing Zalahem," a woman's voice loomed above him from the void. It is up to Allah now. There were many bullets but luckily they all missed his vital organs. Still he has lost much blood and his vital signs are weak. My honest professional opinion," she paused. "I think he has less than a thirty percent chance of survival.

"He is strong," Zalahem responded. "And Allah is with him."

"Inshallah," she said. He could feel the contempt in her tone. "By bringing him here, Zalahem, you risk everything. What in a camel's ass made you go back? And worse what would inspire you to bring him here?"

"Look at him Sarah. Look at his features. He is from our tribe. He is Gojam."

"He very well might be," Sarah said. "But he is also Kaffir and you know this place is strictly to treat our own. There are too many things here to risk bringing an outsider, especially a disbeliever."

"It was Allah's will, dear sister. I could not let him die."

Zalahem was the cab driver who dropped him off just before JB emptied his gun in his back. He told him later that something took over his hands and feet and compelled him to return. He said the man who shot him was still inside the building when he helped him to the cab. Zalahem also told him he had wanted to go in and murder the man but he feared from the look of Jumm's condition at the time there was not a second to waste, so he let the man live.

Zalahem would have most certainly killed the man if there were time-he was a brave fighter in his homeland. He was much decorated by their people. After offering that bit of information Sarah said no more about their history.

Jumm had remained in a comma for three days before regaining consciousness. The first words out of his mouth was a request to get word to Gloria at the hotel. He had been praying all through his struggle for recovery that she was still there waiting for him.

Zalahem returned with a message that same day, "She says she would have waited there for an eternity because she was sure you were coming back."

Jumm came out of his vision and held Claudia tight. "I always liked the little nigga," he whispered, "He had character. He was like way ahead of his age."

They had spent six months with Daquan on the Island of Costa Rico. Jumm had run into him on the beach one day and he couldn't believe the little nigga was this far away from Harlem, living it up. Daquan told him everything that happened, the kidnapping, Rachet getting his shit split, everything except what he had just read in the papers.

He Claudia and Gloria had become very close in those six months. Both women took to him instantly, so did Claudia's boys who loved rhyming with him. But Claudia became extra close. She seemed to spend every single free moment with Daquan. When they finally left the Island, Claudia and Daquan embraced for so long Jumm thought they were going to miss their flight. Once they boarded Claudia didn't say another word to anyone until the plane touched down in Brazil. She just kept staring out the window, looking back at the clouds. Jumm and Gloria suspected something else was going on between them but neither ever asked. What was between them was their business.

Gloria took the paper from Jumm's hand then gently guided Claudia's lips to his. They began to kiss passionately. Gloria took the paper into an adjoining room to finish reading the article. Jumm and Claudia would be going at it for a long time. Gloria wasn't quite in the mood to join them. Just the opposite from her sister, when Gloria was feeling sad, sex was absolutely the last thing on her mind. She found a sofa with a serene view overlooking the Brasilia skyline and read the article out loud.

" The international manhunt has ended for the cop killer, razor wielding murderer, who up until now was only known by the name 'Seven', adopted from the necklace in the shape of a seven he left at the scene of the homicide. The necklace, which slain Detective John Sally was still gripping after apparently struggling with his murderer, was stolen nine years ago from a Manhattan jeweler who was found two days after that robbery in the subway tunnels with his throat split in the same manner as Sevens first victim for these crimes.

He was arrested on the island of Costa Rico after a tourist recognized him from the show, America's Most Wanted.

"At first I wasn't sure," the tourist, who requested to remain anonymous, told The Times. "In the photo they showed on the show, he was much younger, but one day near the pool I saw him tucking a switchblade in his pants when he thought no one was looking, and instantly I knew".

He will be extradited back to the United States where the District Attorney says although the passport he was carrying sates that he is a minor he will be tried as an adult. She says she will be seeking the death penalty not a life without parole sentence. "A killer this vicious," she stated, "Does not deserve to be kept alive at the taxpayers expense." When asked what the chances of conviction were, she responded; "With all the evidence and eye witnesses we have it is a ninety-nine point nine percent certainty that he will get the chair before his sixteenth birthday. I will stake my reputation that he will be the youngest criminal on death row to be executed in the state of New York."

* * * * *

TO BE CONTINUED...

SEVEN THIRTY
The continuation of seven

CHAPTER ONE

*   *   *   *   *

"I'M NOT TAKING THE case," Melisa whispered across the visiting room table.

"Why not?" Pitt asked, leaning back in his chair.

Melisa took him all in. He had gotten bigger and more cut since her last visit, which was only a week past. His chiseled body and bad boy attitude always got her wet. Sometimes on a visit she could cum hard just from rubbing her thighs together and looking at him.

"I mean.. What's the problem? The kids got money."

"That is the problem, at least one of them," she answered with a seductive look. She slid forward in her seat to give him access under her skirt. He knew what she was doing but he wasn't taking the bait.

"Explain that one to me," he said with a stern face. He didn't look around to see where the C.O.'s were so that meant she could straighten her hot ass up and sit like a lady. He was more concerned with the kid than her immediate problem.

"How do I explain to the court that a fifteen year old kid who can't read or write can afford a defense team that is sure to run into the hundreds of thousands. They would slay us from the starting gate."

"If you won't do it for the kid, do it for me."

"I'd walk on fire for you baby, you know that, but I'm not even qualified to take on this case."

"You're more than qualified. You told me yourself, the big guy said you were the best to come from under him."

Melisa smiled.

"You know what I mean.. I didn't mean under him under him."

"That's what you say now. You use to think it meant under him under him."

A rare smile from Pitt sent a tingle down below.

"Whatever... Look Liss. If you don't take the case they are going to force him to take a legal aide, then they gon fry his lil ass for sure."

"Do you know how many prestigious firms are soliciting to take his case pro bono?"

"We both know what their interest is and it's not for the kid."

"If they take the case their main objective is to win."

Pitt leaned forward. "You're the only one the kid is going to fuck with. Bottom line. It's either you or lethal injection."

Melisa shook her head. "You can't make me feel guilty."

Pitt gave her look. "Look Liss, you're from the hood just like us. The kid needs somebody like you to tell his story, not some shirt who never even walked through the hood."

"He needs the best defense team he can get, hood or not, and he can't get it from me. I'm not ready. I have less than a dozen bullshit manslaughter cases under my belt, and you're talking murder one, high profile."

The kid is not going to talk to any shirts, I'll tell you that now. But he has a story to tell that will make a hard nigga like me cry, just think about them soft ass jurors."

"Pitt. I've been with the firm a lot longer than I've been a practicing attorney and I've been involved in cases with some pretty hardened criminals, and if it's one thing I've learned, when their lives are on the line they will tell any and every thing to any legal team they think can keep them off death row."

"You don't know this kid," Pitt whispered. "He would rather die than give up a secret to somebody he didn't trust."

Melisa sat back and studied Pitt for a long moment. She knew Pitt like she knew her own soul and with the exception of herself Pitt never showed emotions for anyone or anything, but love for the boy was written all over him.

"I'll go see him," she said. "I'm not promising anything other than that, but I will go see him, She could see the tension in Pitts body relax.

"Thanks," he said, looking around for where the officers were stationed before turning back to her, "How's your poodle?"

Starving. It's been a few weeks since she's had anything in her. Why, you wanna feed her now?"

"Would if I could but this C.O's a real dickhead."

"Well you better put something in this bitch before she goes bananas." She slid forward in her chair until her lower back was resting on the edge of the seat. Pitt rested his chin on the table and put both hands underneath. They stared at each other for a few minutes before Melisa said.

"Oh you big bad criminal, are you molesting my poodle? Trying to shove your entire hand up her throat?"

"All the way up in her belly if I can," Pitt said, his breathing shallow. "Later I got something else to go down her throat."

Melisa let out an involuntary grunt and forced her pelvis forward. "Uhhhh! I hope you've got wipes cause this is about to get real messy."

* * * * *